# PRAISE FOR J[...]

## *Departure*

OCT 1 4 2020

"Joseph Reid delivers a Mach 3, edge-of-your-seat thriller with *Departure*. Strap in tight for a delightfully turbulent ride—Reid grabs you on the first page and doesn't let go."

—Steve Konkoly, *Wall Street Journal* bestselling author of the Ryan Decker series

"*Departure* is the one-hundred-yard dash in book form. Joseph Reid fires the starter's pistol on page one, sending Seth Walker and the reader on a delirious, lung-busting race to solve a mystery that ties together in a satisfying ending loaded with heart."

—Matthew FitzSimmons, *Wall Street Journal* bestselling author

"I fell for Seth Walker in *Takeoff*, the first of the series, and I think I love him more in *Departure*. What I love most is that Seth's brawn, of which there is much to appreciate, is matched by his brain—imagine Clancy's Jack Ryan combined with a young Steve Jobs. The combination makes *Departure* another hold-on-to-your-seat, don't-even-try-to-put-it-down thriller. If you haven't tried Seth Walker, you're missing out."

—Danielle Girard, *USA Today* bestselling author

"*Departure* is sky-high entertainment. With barrel-roll plotting, an eye for detail, and a cast of characters flashing both brains and brawn, Joseph Reid's latest Seth Walker adventure is one hell of a flight. Get on board now!"

—J. Todd Scott, author of the Texas Border series

"*Departure* is a seriously thrilling ride! This action-packed techno-thriller starts with a bang and keeps the momentum going to the final page. Seth Walker is a fantastic hero, and Reid's deft use of dual timelines ratchets up the tension all the way to the explosive conclusion."

—Ellison Cooper, author of *Buried*

## False Horizon

"There are no false steps in *False Horizon*, Joseph Reid's rip-roaring thriller about killer drones, drug dealers, and techno-sleuth Seth Walker set in the mysterious hills of rural West Virginia. Buckle up!"

—Bryan Gruley, author of *Bleak Harbor*

"A deftly crafted and entertaining page-turner of an action-adventure novel."

—*Midwest Book Review*

"What works about Seth's character development in specific, and the novel in general, is how well the author presents backstory and foreshadowing . . . This provides plausibility and trust without diverting from a constant forward motion in the plot. The combination makes for a solid series we can look forward to following for many volumes."

—*New York Journal of Books*

"A very smart, timely, and exciting thriller. Packed with cutting-edge technology, Joseph Reid's *False Horizon* will delight and captivate you from page one."

—Simon Gervais, bestselling author of *Hunt Them Down*

"An exciting final battle, plenty of technical details, quirky characters, and the West Virginia setting all add up to a riveting, fast-moving thriller. Readers will look forward to Seth's further adventures."

*—Publishers Weekly*

"A truly riveting read."

*—K Street Magazine*

# *Takeoff*

"Joseph Reid is a blazing new talent in the action-thriller arena. *Takeoff* does exactly that from page one, and it doesn't land until the end. You'll be breathless!"

—Raymond Benson, bestselling author of the 007 series, *The Black Stiletto*, and *In the Hush of the Night*

"Joseph Reid's novel *Takeoff* is aptly named. This fast-paced novel takes off with a bang, and only gains speed from there. Reid's protagonist, federal air marshal Seth Walker, is much more than a sky cowboy. When not saving lives (or taking them), Walker works on circuit drawings. Those drawings have earned him a number of patents, and might be the key to a new life, that is, if Walker can survive his current travails, as well as past baggage. Assigned to guard sixteen-year-old pop phenom sensation Max Magic, Walker finds himself in the middle of a deadly power struggle. To keep his charge alive, Walker needs to navigate currents most treacherous and distinguish the good guys from the bad guys. Reid writes like a seasoned pro, and yet this is his first novel. I am looking forward to more."

—Alan Russell, bestselling author of *Burning Man*

"*Takeoff* is a blast. From the first explosive scene to the last page, this story pins you to your seat and never lets you go. Seth Walker, the hero of this riveting tale, is a man worthy of many books. It's a good thing he's so well armed with highly unique skills and street smarts and a charming wit, because Seth is on the front lines in a very dangerous world. My money's on this guy in the battles to come."

—James W. Hall, Shamus and Edgar Award–winning author

"Fast paced and adrenaline filled, *Takeoff* is a wild ride that never lets up for a single moment. A thrilling debut by a terrific new storyteller. Joseph Reid is a name to know!"

—Chad Zunker, Kindle bestselling author of *An Equal Justice*

# DEPARTURE

# ALSO BY JOSEPH REID

*False Horizon*

*Takeoff*

# DEPARTURE

## JOSEPH REID

This is a work of fiction. Names, characters, organizations, places, events, and incidents are either products of the author's imagination or are used fictitiously. Any resemblance to actual persons, living or dead, or actual events is purely coincidental.

Text copyright © 2020 by Joseph P. Reid
All rights reserved.

No part of this book may be reproduced, or stored in a retrieval system, or transmitted in any form or by any means, electronic, mechanical, photocopying, recording, or otherwise, without express written permission of the publisher.

Published by Thomas & Mercer, Seattle

www.apub.com

Amazon, the Amazon logo, and Thomas & Mercer are trademarks of Amazon.com, Inc., or its affiliates.

ISBN-13: 9781542041812
ISBN-10: 1542041813

Cover design by Kirk DouPonce, DogEared Design

Printed in the United States of America

# DEPARTURE

# CHAPTER 1

*Thursday, February 23*

More often than you'd think, the troublemakers sit in first class.

Not the upgraders. They're so thankful for a golden ticket to the promised land, they stay on best behavior in hopes of proving they belong in the club full-time. Most of them are business types who simply want to eat their free meal and finish their work.

No, it's the ones who pay full freight. They think that entitles them to be all kinds of demanding. Whether it's some rich-bitch type complaining about the white-wine selection or a slick lawyer with sterling-silver cuff links who wants to talk on his cell through takeoff—something about the extra-wide seats seems to deprive people of their senses.

Watching stuff like that go down, I always feel for the flight attendants. FAA regs force them to handle everything from nausea to a terrorist takeover, while passengers expect them to be attractive, attentive handservants. For their trouble, they pull down maybe twenty bucks an hour, and that's only for "flight time," door-close to door-open.

Despite my sympathy, though, I keep my mouth shut. An air marshal's job is to blend in, not stick out. And while the crazy woman who'd exposed my identity and almost killed me a few months back had ended my run as a rank-and-file air marshal, it was hard to turn the training off. Even in my new, tongue-twisting role as Tactical Law Enforcement Liaison and Principal Investigator, I tried to keep a low profile.

That morning's flight was an exception.

We were a predawn departure from DFW, the plane only about half-full. I felt exhausted, but not from the early hour. The past four days with my godkids in Fort Worth had been fun. Thanks to an unexpected heat wave, I'd spent a bunch of time horsing around in the pool, flipping them over my head, and launching them into the air to have them splash down a moment later. All that action had left my muscles slightly sore, but otherwise my time with them had been invigorating. Seeing five-year-old Rachael assemble some master-level LEGOs, watching nine-year-old Michael hop the curb on his bike . . . it made me realize how fast they were growing up.

What had left me drained was my time with their mom, Shirley. Not because she wasn't nice—exactly the opposite. She was always far more welcoming and trusting than I deserved. She'd opened her home to me years ago; now, she wanted nothing more than to mother me about the dating scene, my new career, my life in Los Angeles. Truth be told, I didn't even mind any of that. If we could have limited our conversation to what was going on in my life, I'd have gladly allowed Shirley to pry into my privacy all she wanted.

No, the past was the problem. And how diligently I needed to avoid discussing it with her. The quiet times, after the kids went to bed each night, were the worst. Shirley would want to sit on the porch and "visit." Those talks invariably turned to Clarence, the kids' father and my old mentor. Her husband.

The dead man between us.

His suicide had left her with a ton of unresolved questions. But while I understood her desire to plow over it, to process things, I had to tread carefully. Clarence had killed himself at work, and I'd been the one who'd found his body. There were . . . details Shirley didn't know that would only make things worse if she did. They turned every conversation into a minefield—every silent smile she gave me, each invitation to go on with what I was saying, would cause my heart to catch in my throat as I hoped that damned mother's intuition of hers hadn't caught on to something. Praying I hadn't let something slip.

It was exhausting.

So, I was looking forward to being home. I hadn't surfed in a week, and while I needed to check in at the office when I arrived, my calculations said I could be on my board before lunch if things broke right.

Because this had been a personal trip, I'd booked my own seats and decided to splurge for some extra legroom in first class. When I saw what we were flying, I knew I'd picked the right day to upgrade. Instead of the 737 you'd usually draw for a short-haul route, we somehow ended up with one of the brand-new 787-9 Dreamliners they normally save for international flights.

The Dreamliner is a double-aisle, wide-body plane—it's so big, it can load passengers through three doors simultaneously if the airport gate is equipped with a multipronged jetbridge (which ours wasn't). In coach, they use a 3-3-3 configuration, but up front, there's just one angled seat on either side of each aisle. I drew 3A, the third window on the left.

Although I'd heard good things, I hadn't flown on a Dreamliner, so I spent the first few minutes after boarding playing with the fold-down seat and examining all the little storage compartments. Even better, the cabin was equipped with the new electronically dimmable windows I'd read about but hadn't seen in action yet.

For the technological marvel that is a jumbo jet—a million-pound slab of steel that can *fly*—the plastic sheets they use as window shades always struck me as a cheap and tacky solution. Those things seem like they might rip at any moment; half of them become twisted in their tracks and get stuck. They don't even block out all the light—the plastic is translucent, especially when the sun shines directly on them. The Dreamliner's designers, though, had taken window shades to a whole new level. Its windows contain a special panel filled with a chemical gel that changes color when exposed to electricity. The more voltage, the darker the gel becomes, all the way to an opaque black. A button below the window lets passengers dim or brighten their own windows, or the flight attendant can control all of them at once from a switch in the galley.

I'm a tinkerer and an inventor in my spare time, so toying with the window gave me a few ideas. I pulled out my pad and mechanical pencil from my carry-on to make some notes. As I did, habit took over, and I found myself scanning the boarding passengers in my peripheral vision. Lots of families with young kids—enough that I figured it must be a school break or something. Other than a couple of muscle-bound guys headed back into coach, I didn't see anyone I'd classify as a potential threat.

The guy across the aisle from me, though, seemed like he was going to be a handful for Amelia, the flight attendant working up front.

He boarded late, carrying the jacket to his navy, chalk-stripe suit over his arm. Tall and broad shouldered with massive hands, he might have been an athlete once. Now, though, his body had atrophied to a thick, doughy frame with a belly roll protruding over his belt. Although the contrast collar of his shirt was unbuttoned, sweat had moistened his forehead and created two dark stains in the pale-blue cloth under his armpits.

Huffing and puffing, the man's first action upon reaching his seat was to check all the nearby overheads for a home for his rollaboard. Although this held up the line behind him, he didn't seem to care in the slightest.

After stowing the bag, he stomped back to row 3 and collapsed into his seat.

Once the backlog of passengers dispersed, Amelia worked her way over. "Can I take that for you, Mr. Abbott?"

The man didn't hand her the jacket so much as he allowed her to remove it from his lap. His only verbal response was, "Jack and Coke."

If Amelia felt offended, it didn't show. She simply swept a lock of her hair back behind her ear and carried the jacket forward, hanging it in the front closet before disappearing into the galley and returning with his drink.

Abbott took an immediate swig, his eyes locked on Amelia.

From the rosy tint of his cheeks, I wondered if Abbott had been held up finishing a round at the terminal bar. Either way, he made short work of the brown liquid; soon the glass contained nothing but rattling cubes.

After Amelia retrieved Abbott's empty glass to prepare for pushback, he reclined and closed his eyes. I figured he'd sleep—a lot of nervous flyers suck down booze to relax themselves into passing out. But when the chime sounded to indicate we'd cleared ten thousand feet, Abbott was awake again. And fidgeting.

Most people requested coffee during the first drink service. I've got a medical condition that keeps me from having caffeine, so I got water. Despite the predawn hour, Abbott stuck with Jack and Coke, belting a second while Amelia prepped food in the galley, then swigging a third with his meal.

He and I both got the southwestern omelet. It was spicy—they'd mixed in jalapeño or something—but I was pretty sure that wasn't what caused the pink to spread from Abbott's cheeks to the rest of his face.

When Amelia came to clear Abbott's tray, he leered up at her and planted his right palm firmly on the side of her hip. Amelia's immediate reaction was to step back across the aisle toward me. Clever move: it made her too far to reach, and Abbott's arm dropped to his side. But as she turned up the aisle, Abbott wound up his arm and spanked her, hard.

Nearly jumping from the impact, Amelia dashed up front, darted through the curtain to the galley, and yanked it closed behind her.

I'd seen enough.

I balled my right hand into a fist and glared across the aisle. I'm not the biggest guy in the world, but I'm not exactly small. Normally between that, my shaved head, and the tattoos running up and down my arms, a good, stern look will put someone in their place.

Not Abbott.

"Mind your own business," he said and went back to his drink. Two more gulps, and it disappeared like the others.

Left with nothing but ice, Abbott began fidgeting again. He tugged at his cuffs, scratched his goatee, wiped his brow. He swirled and rattled the cubes around inside the glass, then loudly slurped up the few remaining drops. Finally, he unclipped his seat belt and rose to his feet. I watched carefully as he went forward, but a moment after he ducked through the curtain, the forward lavatory light switched from green to red, and I heard the door close and lock with an audible clack.

When he didn't reemerge quickly, I turned back to my sketch pad.

Eventually, I noticed the lavatory sign switch color again in my peripheral vision. When Abbott didn't reappear at our row within a few seconds, I glanced up.

The curtain separating the cabin from the galley billowed slightly.

I tucked my pad and pencil into the seat-back pocket and stood. Knowing how the aircraft floor can transmit vibrations, I stepped lightly on my way forward, up on the balls of my feet. Quick glances to either side showed that none of the other passengers were paying any attention. A decent number had reclined and fallen asleep.

Not wanting to change that, I stepped to the bulkhead and ducked through the curtain in one motion.

Amelia stood at the opposite end of the galley, backed against the fuselage. Her eyes were wide, her hand drawn to her mouth. Abbott stood between us, blocking the passage and nearly eclipsing her. He hadn't touched her yet, but his left hand was reaching in her direction.

"Hey. Buddy." I tried to keep the tone friendly. "You don't want to do that."

"Fuck off." Abbott rocked forward on his feet, leaning closer to her.

"I'm serious—come back to your seat. She'll get you some coffee, you can sober up."

He glanced back over his shoulder. "Go fuck yourself."

"Don't make me—"

Before I could finish, Abbott whipped around, leading with the back of his left hand in a clumsy-but-dangerous kind of karate chop.

I leaned back to dodge the swing. As Abbott turned, though, I got a glimpse at what had caused Amelia's distress: his pants were unzipped, his genitals protruding prominently from the open fly.

Abbott's missed swing nearly cost him his balance. With all his weight up on one foot, he teetered, and for a moment I thought he might fall.

But somehow Abbott steadied himself, and a new wave of rage consumed him. He gritted his teeth, nostrils flared. A low noise sounded in his throat. He seized a glass carafe off the shelf to his right and smashed its bottom against the metal edge of the counter.

Then he turned to me.

Although he was drunk and clumsy, Abbott's eyes had a wild look. The broken glass had formed several distinct points with razor-sharp edges between them.

I immediately thought about the Sig Sauer P229 concealed in my waistband but decided the quarters were too cramped. With Amelia standing directly behind Abbott, even if I got off a solid shot, the bullet stood a decent chance of passing through him and hitting her.

He took a step toward me, brandishing the jagged carafe.

As I retreated a step, I nearly tripped over something. My eyes darted to the floor, and I spotted one of those heavy-duty plastic restaurant racks for drinking glasses, standing on end.

Amelia must have set it there while preparing for service.

I scooped the rack up with my left hand, slipping my fingers through the handle hole on one side while bracing the rack against my forearm as a kind of shield.

Abbott jabbed the carafe at me once, then twice.

The second time, I made sure the rack hit the edge of the carafe—I needed to know if it would hold up. Thankfully, the glass scraped the plastic but didn't slice through.

As if realizing that might embolden me, Abbott passed the carafe from one hand to the other, turning it in his grip so it pointed downward. Then, raising it over his head, he charged.

In two quick steps, Abbott managed to gather almost all his mass behind the blow. Even though I braced myself and blocked the carafe with the rack, the force drove me down to one knee.

Thinking he had me, Abbott began smashing the bottle down against the plastic. Shards of glass rained down on me with each impact, and I had to look away to protect my eyes.

That was when I spotted it.

Amelia had been loading dirty trays into one of the rolling carts tucked beneath the galley shelves.

The cart door was still open.

I jabbed my free hand inside and fumbled around until I felt something cold and metallic on one of the trays.

A fork. I've used forks as weapons before.

Clutching it tightly, I jabbed the tines into the back of Abbott's knee as hard as I could.

He simultaneously howled and crumpled on that side.

I sprang to my feet and backhanded the rack against his wrist, dislodging the carafe. My eyes followed it to the floor, where it bounced and rolled out of reach.

Before I could take another breath, a hollow, metallic gonging erupted to my side. Turning, I found Amelia standing over Abbott's head, clutching one of the airplane's stainless-steel coffeepots.

Although dazed, Abbott shook off the impact and tried to turn toward her.

Amelia raised the pot with both hands and brought it down again on the crown of Abbott's head. This time, he slumped to the floor, unconscious.

"Nice shot," I said.

Visibly trembling, she raised the pot so that it dangled from one finger. The dent in its side was unmistakable. "They'll probably fire me for that," she said. Then her mouth turned up in a surprised smile. "But I think it might've been worth it."

I snatched the pot off her finger. Cradling it in my left arm, I wiped the handle with the tail of my untucked T-shirt and then gripped it several times with my own hand.

"There," I said. "Nothing for you to get in trouble for."

◆ ◆ ◆

Abbott woke during our descent.

While he was out, I'd bound his hands behind him with a couple of the zip ties I kept in my carry-on. Now, lying on his side along the galley floor, he struggled against the thick plastic.

"Don't bother," I said. "You'll never bust out of those."

Abbott looked up to find me sitting next to Amelia in the crew jump seats. I had the Sig pointed at his face.

"You'll pay for this," he growled.

"Actually, I'm guessing you will. Assaulting a flight attendant can get you up to a $250,000 fine."

He did a double take.

"That's right," I said, nodding. "Plus jail time. Assault with a deadly weapon—you're looking at life in prison, my friend."

Abbott struggled even harder. "Motherfucker—"

"Hey now." I unbuckled and stepped over him, redraping the napkin over his crotch. "We've got kids on the plane. They don't need to see your junk."

As he realized he was still exposed, the color drained from Abbott's face. "You—you didn't zip me back up?"

I laughed as I slipped back into the shoulder harness. "Not a chance."

Handing Abbott over to police at LAX meant waiting until everyone deplaned, then signing a bunch of paperwork as officers hauled him to his feet and dragged him out. Amelia and I provided statements while technicians photographed the galley and gathered up the coffeepot, remnants of the carafe, and my makeshift shield as evidence.

Although we'd landed on time, the whole exercise put me about twenty minutes behind schedule. Still, surfing felt close enough I could almost smell the ocean.

That was, until I saw my boss, Vince Lavorgna, standing with his arms crossed at the top of the jetbridge.

"Of all goddamn days."

Normally, Lavorgna's words rattle around his hawkish nose a bit before popping out in his Philadelphia accent. Today, they emerged as a growl, straight from his throat.

"I'm sorry, Vince," I said as I reached him at the mouth of the metal tunnel. "The guy was drunk and—"

"What, that?" Lavorgna nodded down the ramp. "We've got bigger problems. C'mon."

Although I hadn't noticed until now, a courtesy cart stood waiting at the edge of the seating area, a blue-shirted TSA agent behind the wheel. Lavorgna stalked over and settled onto the rear seat, his back to the driver. The suspension groaned under the weight of his frame, and the cart leaned precariously, almost comically, to that side.

"What are you waiting for? Let's go!"

As I tossed my bag onto the front seat and turned to sit next to Lavorgna, the driver gunned the engine. The cart lurched forward with a loud electric hum and nearly pitched me off the back.

"What's the big hurry?" I asked, grabbing the armrest and wedging myself down into the seat. Lavorgna had the shoulders of a professional linebacker, which didn't leave much room on the cushioned bench.

"Radio call just came through. Some guy's gone missing at SFO. Loretta found you a ride—we've got a plane holding in Terminal 7 to get you up there ASAP."

Loretta Alcott booked all the flights for marshals working out of Los Angeles.

Terminal 7 was three buildings away, but given how our cart was whizzing down the hall, honking to clear the way, we'd be there in moments. "Who's the guy? Some VIP?"

"Must be," Lavorgna said. "Every agency on the West Coast is being called in."

A glance over my shoulder showed we were rapidly approaching the mouth of Terminal 4. The cart slid to the left, then pulled a hard right to make the swing into the passage connecting the terminals. Thankfully, the TSA driver threw an arm over my bag so it didn't fly off.

"What do we know about the guy? Anything?"

A grim smile twisted up beneath Lavorgna's black beard. "At this point, you have the sum total of all the intelligence I've been given."

As we passed the entrance to Terminal 6, the driver called into a walkie-talkie. When we reached Terminal 7 seconds later, TSA had cleared enough of a path that the cart slowed but didn't stop on its way through the security checkpoint.

"Anything else, sir?" I'd inhabited my new investigative position for six months, but it still felt like we were making things up as we went along.

"This is bound to be high profile, so keep your head down. Don't feel like you need to lead the charge." Lavorgna's eyes bored into me.

I looked back over my shoulder, as if checking the route ahead of us.

"And keep me posted how it's going," he added.

The cart jerked to a sudden stop at Gate 84. Lavorgna hadn't been lying about holding a plane—no one remained waiting to board, and the gate agent manning the jetbridge door looked relieved to see us.

I hopped off and reached for my duffel.

As I did, Lavorgna seized my wrist in one of his giant mitts. "Seth, be careful."

Of all the times Lavorgna's given me advice, this was the one when I really should have listened.

# CHAPTER 2

The flight to San Francisco lasted less than an hour, one of those quick up-and-downs where you start descending the moment you hit cruising altitude.

Shoehorned into a middle seat in the last row, trapped back against the bulkhead, where seats don't recline, I was thankful for my earpiece. I have this condition where, if I'm not listening to something constantly or my adrenaline isn't pumping hard, my brain tends to spiral off into a million different directions at once. To avoid turning into a drooling, incoherent mess, I keep a steady flow of information pumping into my left ear. The good news is, that audio stream also keeps me from being bored—I got to listen to three chapters of a new book about artificial intelligence.

As our descent continued, I craned my neck to try to see out the window. The approach into SFO is pretty dramatic: you zoom in low over the bay, the plane dropping and dropping, the water getting closer and closer. Eventually, the waves below loom so large, you can see the details of their foamy tops, and you picture the landing gear scraping them like the feet of a duck coming in for a landing. Just when you're wishing you'd paid closer attention to the briefing on how to use the life vest under your seat—*boom*—the runway appears at the last possible second.

With the guy in the neighboring seat blocking the view with his head, though, I was left to focus on our touchdown. After a sharp jolt of a landing, the pilot seemed barely to tap his brakes on the runway, harnessing all the residual momentum for a speedy taxi. That was when I realized I hadn't felt us circling, or doing any of the other normal approach gymnastics. Air traffic control had brought us straight in.

While we were still rolling across the tarmac, the lead attendant's voice sounded on the PA. She politely asked everyone to remain seated once the airplane reached the gate. Then, just in case I hadn't made enough friends holding up the flight's takeoff, she added that "a very important passenger" at the back needed to deplane first. I could feel every set of eyes on me as I unclipped, rose, and shuffled my way up the aisle with my carry-on.

Opening the forward door took a minute, but the instant it swung clear, I sprinted up the jetbridge, the soles of my Vans thumping loudly against the metal floor. At the top of the ramp, I hesitated a moment to get my bearings. We'd come into Gate 57, tucked back into a far corner of Terminal 2's Boarding Area D.

Like LAX, SFO's terminals surround a central parking structure. But where LA's buildings are arranged in straight lines, forming three sides of an open rectangle, SFO is roughly circular. That ring is divided into four sections, three numbered domestic terminals and one international, each of which has spoke-like concourses extending from it. SFO alternately calls these spokes "boarding areas" or "piers" (in a nod to the city's famous waterfront) and assigns each a letter. Most people think of the International Terminal's Main Hall—a grand four-story atrium looking out at the 101 freeway—as the "front" of the airport. By that logic, Terminal 2 sits at the very "back," on the opposite side of the circle, where its lone concourse—letter D—points perpendicularly across the runways toward the bay.

Terminal 2 looks way better than it used to. Until recently, SFO's last major face-lift had come back in the 1980s, when exposed concrete and tinted glass were all the rage. While that decor might have looked futuristic then, the thick walls, dim windows, and dark-patterned carpets left parts of SFO feeling like a bunker. The newest makeovers had added sleek white paneling, polished floors, and chrome accents that made the terminal airy and brighter. Out at the tip of the concourse, Boarding Area D is a triangular space featuring a three-story ceiling and angled tiers of high windows that allow natural light to pour in. Lined by trendy restaurants that surround seating in its center, D resembles a high-end food court in the world's most exclusive mall. This early in the day, its cool air still smelled of coffee and sourdough bread.

While I had no idea where to go, heading for the inner ring made the most sense. The TSA agents manning the security checkpoint at the mouth of the pier might know something, or could radio someone to find out.

I'd only taken two quick steps in that direction when a woman's voice called from my left.

"Hey, Seth!"

I recognized her features at once—auburn hair pulled back into a French braid, smattering of freckles across her nose, double strand of pearls around her neck—but I still did a double take. "What the heck are you doing here?"

FBI Special Agent Melissa Cooke raised an eyebrow. "Nice to see you, too."

"No, it is," I said, extending my hand as she opened her arms. We both hesitated a moment before settling on a quick hug. "Good to see you, I mean. I just . . . You're about the last person I expected."

A psychologist by training, Cooke was based in Quantico, Virginia, where she worked in the FBI's Critical Incident Response Group. As nice as it was to see her face again, the fact she'd gotten dragged into this missing-person case made the skin on the back of my neck prickle.

"Did you fly all the way out—"

"I'm teaching down in Palo Alto this week," she said, grinning at my confusion. "Or, at least, I was until this morning. When this broke, they pulled me out of class and brought me here with a police escort. That's when I heard you were flying in."

Her hazel eyes scanned me up and down. Although it might have been my imagination, I could have sworn her gaze lingered on my right forearm. All my tattoos mean something, but Cooke knew the significance of the *SA* inked inside a heart.

"You look a lot better than the last time I saw you," she said.

I grunted. "Low bar."

Cooke and I had worked together twice, most recently a couple of months ago investigating a plane crash in West Virginia. That case had nearly killed both of us, but my body in particular had taken a beating. I'd only really started feeling like myself again a couple of weeks ago.

Before I could ask Cooke any other questions, a slender man in a police uniform stepped from behind her to join us. Two gold bars sparkled on each side of his collar. "Tony Tranh, SFPD."

I introduced myself, and we shook hands. A good head shorter than I am, Tranh was built like a distance runner, with narrow shoulders, a compact torso, and almost all his height in his legs. He sported a graying crew cut, the hair on top gelled to stand straight up. The starched creases in his navy uniform matched his dour expression.

"Sorry to break up your reunion," he said, "but I'm supposed to get you two to the Comm Center. They're waiting." Without another word, Tranh started in the same direction I'd been heading, toward baggage claim. Using long strides, he quickly built a lead that left us scrambling to catch up.

As we fell in behind him, I asked, "Who exactly are 'they'? And what's all the fuss about? My boss hadn't heard much before I left LA."

With a glance back over his shoulder, Tranh said, "Durham will explain."

"Durham?"

"You know," Cooke said. "Former three-star general, just got appointed deputy secretary of Homeland Security. Your boss's boss's boss's boss."

I gave her a curt nod as if I knew exactly who she was talking about.

She smirked at me in return. "You've never heard of him, have you?"

"Why's he so famous?"

"Um, everything he's ever done? He's like a modern-day Patton crossed with some action-movie hero."

"Patton, huh?" I raised an eyebrow. "I had no idea you were a military-history buff."

"My dad was in the army. Durham led a division of tanks through Iraq, then got sent down to Central America to train government forces to fight gangs like the one you ran into. He helped arrest the leader of one of the big drug cartels and lived with a bounty on his head for five years. They say Durham caught someone sneaking in to kill him one night . . . and choked the guy out."

He sounded like a tough customer—I wondered if Lavorgna knew him. What little I'd learned about my boss's undercover background had come from Cooke, but Lavorgna and Durham sounded like a well-matched pair. Hopefully that would be good for the Service.

Cooke elbowed me in the ribs, her smirk broadening. "Did you even know there'd been an election?"

I gritted my teeth and looked ahead as if to check our progress. Although we'd only worked together twice, Cooke had seen firsthand my distaste for anything to do with politics. My former life at Texas Electronics had been filled with the corporate version. When I left the company to ride jets for a living, I'd vowed to leave all that behind.

Tranh cut straight through the clusters of tables and banquettes that filled the center of Boarding Area D. Around us, I could sense the airport on edge: blue-shirted TSA agents dotted the space—some sitting, others milling about—while a K9 unit circled the perimeter. Still, the midmorning crowds of young professionals seemed oblivious, sipping from their cardboard cups while staring into their phones.

When we reached the mouth of the boarding area, the ceiling descended to a single story. Even as we faced steady streams of people entering D for their upcoming flights, Tranh never broke stride. The oncoming crowds parted for him, or his uniform, and we followed him into the concourse hallway, where natural light gave way to fluorescents that rendered it as bright as a hospital.

Given Tranh's silence, I hoped Cooke might spill some details. "You heard anything about this?"

She gave a slight shrug. "All I know is we're looking for a twenty-something engineer."

"Engineer?"

"Electrical," she said, "like you."

"Missing electrical engineers don't rate this kind of attention. Trust me." If I'd disappeared back in my T.E. days, only a handful of people would have even noticed.

"Well, this guy works at Magnet."

I whistled at that. T.E. had been a big company when I worked there, one of the biggest in Texas. Magnet was one of the largest in the *world*, and a Silicon Valley blue-ribbon success story. If Magnet was calling in political favors . . . no wonder SFO was in an uproar.

Originally founded in an attic by three college roommates over summer vacation, Magnet seemed to have more lives than a cat. Its first incarnation, back in the early '90s, had taken the country by storm as a hardware maker: its portable computers were three inches thick and seemed to weigh twenty pounds, but Magnet had foreseen the public's growing desire for laptops. Magnet quickly went public and made its founders rich, but within five years the company had nearly been run into the ground.

Several years later, Magnet reemerged as a service company, promising to help other companies adjust to the new digital reality. That worked for a while, but again, Magnet's leadership didn't seem to have a plan for what came next. Once every corporation had an online presence, the company's stock nose-dived.

Two years ago, just after I'd left engineering, Magnet reinvented itself a third time. After a decade bulking up its coding and engineering talent, the company released a networking app called Field. More professional than Facebook, less formal than LinkedIn, Field generated buzz, especially internationally, as it let you organize and interact with your circle of acquaintances in unique ways, including transferring money back and forth.

Toward the end of last year, Magnet had made a huge splash by returning to its roots. Just in time for the holidays, it released Polaris, a device designed to take another run at the hardware market. It looked like your average smartphone—sleek and sexy—but what made Polaris special was the way it interacted with other devices. There were some not-so-new tricks—trading photos like Apple's AirDrop, or letting someone else hear the music you were listening to, like the old Microsoft Zune. But it also featured new, cutting-edge collaboration capabilities. Leveraging Field, your Polaris could wirelessly trade contact information, meaning no more creating address-book entries for people or messing with invitations and responses. It also had real-time wireless file sharing, so students could share a presentation back and forth, or businesspeople could trade versions of a contract. No more email, no more depositing things in cloud storage for someone else to grab and download—just instantaneous, peer-to-peer connection. It even used inductive charging, meaning you didn't have to plug the phone in to recharge the battery. From what I'd heard, that last part was apparently a good thing, since the device's wireless features tended to chew through power.

Power—the economic and political kind—was something Magnet had accumulated a lot of over the years. With the company's stock price now at an all-time high and its global headquarters still located in Palo Alto, the company could lean on the governor and legislature whenever it needed something. In fact, several former Magnet executives had already made their way to Congress. Magnet, it seemed, was everywhere: in this concourse alone, I saw boxes of Polaris handsets in an electronics store window, while every other retail shop had signs announcing that Polaris payments were accepted.

Still, the back of my brain screamed that something didn't quite make sense. Magnet might be all-powerful, but a missing engineer seemed like an odd reason to burn through hard-earned political favors. One employee was barely enough reason to bang out an email, let alone phone the feds.

Of all people, I ought to know that.

As we drew closer to security and the inner ring, the passageway expanded again. Colorful fishing nets draped from the elevated ceiling, shimmering in light that spilled down from skylights at its peak. On our left, seating for a microbrewery extended out into the hallway, filling the space with a chitchat buzz and the clatter of plates and glasses. The smells changed, too; the air here was scented with the smokiness of bacon and the bitterness of beer.

Recalling my earlier run-in with Abbott, I called out to Tranh, "Are we sure this guy isn't just passed out somewhere?" Talk about crying wolf—if Magnet had spun up all this law enforcement for some lush who'd simply had one too many . . .

"Don't I wish," was all Tranh said.

The security checkpoint separating the concourse from the check-in area was set under another low overhang. Although a couple dozen passengers were being processed through the scanners or reassembling themselves afterward, they were easily outnumbered by the agents overseeing the process. Tranh avoided that whole scene, hugging the wall on our right and steering us through an exit that emptied into the airport's inner ring.

Like Boarding Area D and the concourse that led from it, Terminal 2's check-in area had been completely redecorated. The far wall, which faced out onto the street, was all glass, and while the sun was muted by lingering haze, plenty of natural light poured in, reflecting off the polished floors and white surfaces. And that wasn't all: passengers streamed in from outside, joining those already waiting at the check-in desks or queueing up for security, creating the thickest crowds we'd encountered so far.

Tranh cut through lines for the American Airlines check-in counters and Starbucks, making for the glass wall and then following it to the right. Glancing outside, I saw that the usual collection of double-parked Ubers had jammed things up at the curb, while out in the far lanes, police officers were stationed every dozen yards or so, actively stopping cars, questioning drivers, and peering into back seats. That reduced traffic flow to a crawl.

Ahead of us, the glass wall ended at the entrance to a narrow passageway whose signs promised that Terminal 3 and the International Terminal loomed somewhere in the distance. We appeared to be headed that way until, at the last moment, Tranh ducked into an unmarked alcove on our right. It terminated abruptly at an imposing metal door with a CCTV camera mounted above it. A keypad next to the door read "Safety and Security Services."

Tranh beeped the door open with a card tethered to his shirt pocket, then waved us through. Three quick turns deposited us at another keycard door marked "Communications Center."

The interior of the Comm Center made the bunkerish portions of SFO look well lit. The only illumination inside the windowless room came from televisions lining the far wall. Like our office back in LA, the room was separated into a series of cubes—blue-white light from the monitors reflected off the metal tops of the cubicle walls, giving the impression you were looking over a throbbing, inconsistent maze. Every person in every cube seemed to be talking simultaneously, rendering the tight room an assault on the senses.

"Not here," Tranh said, ushering us to the side. Through another, virtually invisible door, we entered a room that, after the darkened Comm Center, felt uncomfortably bright.

Once my eyes had adjusted, I saw we'd arrived in a more traditional conference space whose windows looked out across the tarmac. Although the oval table occupying the center of the room appeared large enough to sit a dozen, only one person was present: a tall, bald, barrel-chested man in a charcoal suit and metal-rimmed glasses. In case his importance wasn't clear enough, the room had obviously been rearranged to suit him: several of the table's high-backed chairs had been pushed into a far corner, clearing a path for him to pace back and forth before a series of widescreen monitors arranged to face him. He was speaking loudly, apparently projecting for a tabletop speakerphone that sat in front of the monitors. When he saw us, he stopped whatever he'd been saying and announced, "Our celebrity guests are here. Let me mute you a minute."

While Tranh led us around the table, the man looked down his nose at the phone. Eventually he found the "Mute" button and jabbed at it with a thick finger. Once Cooke drew within range, he grabbed her hand and pumped it once, then did the same with mine. As he did so, I couldn't help thinking about the story Cooke had heard, and how large and powerful his hands were.

"Carter Durham." In his Boston accent, the *r*'s in his first name disappeared. "Thank you both for coming."

"I feel like I should salute you, sir," Cooke said.

He waved his big hands in the air. "I gave up all that pomp and circumstance." Still, his eyes twinkled when she said it, and he smiled. Now that we were closer, I could see a day's worth of dark stubble had grown over Durham's square chin.

"And yet you came out of retirement for all of this," she said, gesturing around the room.

Durham chuckled. "I've had jobs with slower first months. Hell, I think Medina Ridge was slower than this."

"Seth and I compared notes on the way in, sir—I'm afraid we're both playing from behind on this one."

The creases around Durham's eyes deepened as his smile turned rueful. "Well, then, you'll fit right in."

He took a deep breath before rattling off the next bit in staccato fashion. "Anah El-Amin was one of five Magnet employees booked on Eastern's 7:55 nonstop to Tel Aviv this morning. He checked in at 5:42, cleared security at 6:08. He met up with his coworkers, but when a weather delay was announced, they separated. When the crew closed the airplane door at 8:30, El-Amin hadn't shown up to board. One of his coworkers contacted their boss. Magnet called Senator Harris. Senator Harris called DHS."

Durham pointed at a spot above and behind us—we followed his thick finger to a large digital clock mounted on the sidewall of the room. Bright-orange numbers screamed 10:13.

"El-Amin's been missing over ninety minutes. Every effort to find him has failed. So now I'm looking for whatever help I can get." When we turned back to face him, Durham had sucked his lower lip in beneath his teeth and crossed his arms, each hand grabbing the opposite elbow. "We've got just over sixty minutes left, and—"

I hated to interrupt, especially after Lavorgna's warning. But the gnawing feeling in my gut had now grown to the point where it was simply too much to overcome. "All due respect, sir, I know Magnet's an important company and all, but it seems like you've turned the airport upside down. How does a missing engineer rate all this attention?"

Durham's eyes locked on me and narrowed. "This fire drill isn't for Magnet, Mr. Walker. It's for the vice president."

# CHAPTER 3

"Wait, what?" I asked.

Durham's lips tightened into a narrow line. "I'm about to read you two into classified information that cannot be shared with anyone without prior authorization. Understand?"

Cooke and I nodded.

"Tony's already heard this. The vice president is currently en route to San Francisco. I've had a team here all week preparing."

"Why—"

Durham shook his head before I could finish. "You don't need to know. This trip is completely off the books. Secret Service is accompanying VPOTUS and acting to secure his arrival. They're siloed, working in parallel with us. The important thing for our purposes is that his plane is scheduled to land at 11:15." He glanced at the giant clock again, which had crept one minute forward. "Which leaves us exactly sixty-one minutes."

"You're thinking El-Amin's planning to attack the vice president?" Cooke asked.

"I'd very much love it if you'd tell me that he's not." Durham's rueful smile returned. "But the timing seems awfully coincidental. Which is why I requested the Bureau's number-one expert on lone-wolf terrorists."

She paid no attention to the compliment. "If this trip is as secret as you're saying . . ."

"How could El-Amin know about it?" Durham shrugged.

Cooke's expression hardened in a way I'd seen several times in our prior cases. Behind her knitted brow, she was turning over variables in her head.

But maybe it didn't need to be that difficult. "Divert him," I said. "Have him land over in Oakland, or down in San Jose. Traffic will suck"—in my experience, it always did in the Bay Area—"but drive him where he needs to go from there."

"Nice idea," Durham said.

Standing next to me, Tranh grunted. "I suggested that, too."

"Unfortunately, VPOTUS has to come *here*. I can't explain why; he just does. And, anyway, even if we rerouted him now, we'd still have a potential threat running around an airport filled with nearly two hundred thousand people and lots of things that can go *boom*."

"Do we have anything to go on?" Cooke asked.

Durham poked at the "Mute" button and reactivated the speakerphone. "I'm back. In sixty seconds or less, let's march our friends through everything we know."

Turning to the table for the first time, I saw that the three monitors were networked to display a series of windows. Some contained images of people communicating by videoconference, while others showed images or information.

"Twenty-six-year-old Anah El-Amin," Durham said, "born to Iraqi parents who fled Saddam's regime during the first Gulf War." A window containing El-Amin's California driver's license expanded to fill half a monitor. It showed the round face of a young man with olive skin, dark eyes, and ears that protruded prominently from the sides of his head. A wispy, black beard compensated somewhat for a weak chin. "Mom was pregnant when they immigrated, so he's an American citizen."

Tranh made a noise in his throat.

"Something to add, Tony?"

"My parents were some of the last people out of Vietnam before Saigon fell. Me and my brothers, we were all born here, all served in the military. Someone flees their country, we offer them a home, and then they turn around and attack us . . ." He shook his head.

Cooke waited a beat before asking, "Where did El-Amin grow up?"

"El Cajon," Durham said. "Suburb of San Diego with one of the largest concentrations of Iraqi immigrants in the country. His résumé says he's fluent in Arabic. He's traveled internationally a total of six times." The driver's license receded, replaced by an enlargement of his passport. "Twice to Mexico while he was in college, then four times since he started work."

"Also Israel?" Cooke asked.

"No," Durham said. "China and Taiwan. This would have been his first trip to the Middle East."

Not surprising for someone with a tech job. Although I'd never been there, Israel was becoming a hub for semiconductor chips. Asia—where I'd spent significant time as an engineer—was still dominant when it came to consumer electronics, though, particularly phones. While Magnet likely had more of its operation stateside than most tech companies, it was no surprise they had Asian offices. Heck, my old company, T.E., had been acquired by a Chinese conglomerate last year—I half wondered if they were going to drop *Texas* from the name and lose the *T*.

A résumé flashed on the screen as Durham continued talking. "He's no dummy—BS in electrical engineering from Caltech, master's from Stanford. Never been in trouble, though. No arrest record, just a couple of parking tickets when he was younger."

This kid was sounding more and more like the kind I used to try to hire for our lab rather than some lone wolf.

"Weapons?" Cooke asked.

"Nothing registered," Durham said. "No car, either. His home address is in San Francisco, but we've gotten the sense he spends most of his time down at Magnet's Redwood City campus. He's officially single; we don't know if there's a girlfriend."

"Or boyfriend," Tranh said. "His address is in the Castro; that's my hood."

"Shia Islam isn't big on homosexuality, Tony," Durham said.

"Depends how you interpret the Quran," Cooke said. "Do we have any sense how devout he is?"

"Pretty strict, according to his boss, a guy named Ajit Singh. But you can ask him yourself."

"How's that?"

"I figured you might want to talk to him—he's holding on the other line." Durham pushed a button on the phone and said, "Mr. Singh?"

When no answer came, Cooke and I traded glances.

Durham pushed the button a second time, again to no effect. "Damn it. Meyers!"

The door opened, and a thin man shuffled in. I couldn't tell whether his navy suit was too small or his shirt was too big, but either way, his cuffs extended far below his jacket sleeves. That, together with hair slicked over to one side and some acne scarring on his cheeks, made him seem extremely young. "Sir?"

"I've lost Singh, the Magnet guy," Durham said.

Meyers stepped in front of the former general and seized a mouse below the monitors. While he was clicking through windows, Durham reached into his jacket and produced an old-fashioned flip phone. "Never have problems with one of these," he said, twirling it between his fingers.

I'd heard about people who still swore by their old phones, but I hadn't seen one of those hunks of metal in a decade. "You don't live out on the bloody edge, I take it?"

"We had plenty of high-tech toys in the army," Durham said, "but I never needed that stuff at home. My late wife got herself onto the Facebook at one point, trading pictures and recipes with her friends. But that's it—none of that Insta-Chat, Snap-Gram, mumbo jumbo for me."

"Here, sir," Meyers said, relinquishing the mouse. "Singh wasn't on the phone; he was waiting on videoconference."

Durham thanked Meyers, who was already scurrying out of the room, then turned to the screen. "Thanks for waiting, Mr. Singh. My investigators are here, and as I suspected, they have questions for you. Melissa Cooke and Seth Walker."

After gesturing to us, Durham retreated, allowing Cooke and me to close ranks in front of the monitor and its camera. On-screen was a fifties-ish man with thin streaks of white dotting his otherwise-black hair. He wore a neon-orange golf shirt that seemed even brighter against his dark complexion. His small, round glasses made him appear to be squinting.

"So, all the stories I've heard are true," Singh said with a bit of a lisp. "It's good to see you again, Mr. Walker."

*Again?* I racked my brain, trying to recall where I might have met him, but I wasn't placing it. Even in my past life as an engineer, I'd never done anything with Magnet.

Cooke looked back and forth between us. "Do you two . . . ?"

"He probably doesn't remember," Singh said, "but I offered him a job once. I was at a start-up called Brilliance then."

*Brilliance.*

A name I hadn't heard in forever. Back when people started messing around with distance learning, they'd developed a forerunner to the kind of videoconference online courses that Khan Academy and others had since perfected. Back in those days, there hadn't been enough bandwidth or processing power to support their needs.

My pulse quickened. I didn't remember Singh, but if he'd recruited me back then, he likely knew all kinds of things about me that Cooke and the others didn't.

Things they didn't need to know.

"We were trying to hire all the best electrical engineers," he said. "I tried to steal Mr. Walker away from Texas Electronics, but he very wisely turned me down. He wasn't interested in leaving his mentor at that time. That decision saved him riding the ship down to the bottom with me."

My ears stopped working at the word *mentor*. Clarence's name wouldn't be far behind. But we didn't need to get into any of that—especially with the clock ticking.

In my peripheral vision, I could feel Cooke's eyes on me. She'd tried several times to interrogate me about my former life, but I'd managed to dodge her questions. The urgency of El-Amin's disappearance had seemed to ensure that it wouldn't come up between us today.

I opened my mouth to say something that would get us back on topic, but my tongue had grown bone dry. I tried to muster some spit, but before I could swallow, Singh continued.

"I was so very sorry to learn of his suicide, Mr. Walker. When I heard, knowing how close you two were, I wasn't surprised you made a career change. Although I don't know that I foresaw law enforcement in your future."

It took everything I had not to look over at Cooke. "Reminiscing is fun," I said, "but we're on a tight schedule here. What can you tell us about Anah El-Amin as an employee?"

"He's very dedicated," Singh said. "We keep statistics on how much time people spend on campus, and Anah is a consistent leader in that metric."

"What's he been working on?" I asked.

"A little bit of everything."

The words came too quickly. Besides, anyone who'd ever done real engineering knew that was the exact opposite of the way things worked: when you got assigned to a project, you went deep, not on to something else. "Can you give us an example?"

Singh shook his head. "Sitting here, I don't have his personnel records in front of me, so I just don't know. I may be able to get you a more specific answer later."

Something told me that update would never come.

"I understand Mr. El-Amin practices Islam," Cooke said. "Can you give us an idea of how devout he is?"

"Anah announced his religious 'awakening,' if you will, at some point in the last twelve months. Since then he has taken prayer breaks each day. Which, of course, Magnet fully supports—we have several interdenominational spaces for worship on campus. I have personally attended social functions with Anah, during which I know he abstained from alcohol."

"When you describe it as an 'awakening,'" Cooke said, "do you know what prompted that?"

"I do not."

"Has Mr. El-Amin articulated any political views related to his decision to practice Islam?" Cooke asked. "Has he made any statements to his coworkers that might have been reported to HR, for example?"

"No," Singh said. "We have fairly strict social-media policies for our employees, and we have a code of conduct that addresses peer-to-peer interactions. Anah has never run afoul of either of those."

Cooke looked to me to see if I had anything else.

"Two more issues, real quick," I said. "First, I assume Magnet owns, or at least controls access to, some of El-Amin's devices—his laptop, his cell phone?"

Singh nodded. "Yes, we provide our engineers with both of those. Employees are certainly welcome to maintain additional devices of their own choosing, but for any device that carries Magnet information, we insist on certain security protocols."

No surprise there—standard operating procedure for a tech company. "I'm guessing we're going to need the MAC address, device ID, and carrier information for those, if we haven't already received them."

"That is no problem," Singh said. "I will have it sent over immediately after this call."

"Great, thanks."

"What was your second issue?" Singh asked.

"Why do you care about this guy?" I asked.

He squinted at me, like I'd asked some kind of trick question. "Why do we care about one of our employees going missing? Our employees are our greatest resource. They, literally, are the reason we exist, and—"

"C'mon," I said. "You've got hundreds of engineers, maybe thousands. He's got a good résumé, but nothing you couldn't find elsewhere. Why the special interest in this guy?"

After several false starts, Singh finally said, "I don't know how exactly to explain the regard we have for each of our employees, but I can tell you, we value them each as individuals. Anah was a part of our community, and so we—"

"You're saying there's nothing special about him? You called a sitting US senator—don't tell me you'd do that for some receptionist or the cleaning crew. Why him?"

Singh shrugged. "I really don't know what else to say, Mr. Walker. Whether it comes from our company's unique history, or the values instilled by our leadership, we value every one of our team members. Anah El-Amin is a fine man and an excellent engineer—we love having him as a member of our community, and we will do anything in our power to help you find him." Then he shook his head. "I obviously don't know what kind of experience you had at T.E., Mr. Walker. But, knowing your colleague's fate, I can only assume it was not a very supportive environment. I am sorry you had to suffer through that."

# CHAPTER 4

*Monday, July 23, Five Years Ago*

Neckties are probably my least favorite thing in the entire world. But, I figured, for the most important meeting of my professional career, why not? If the CEO of Texas Electronics had summoned me for the reason I hoped, he'd be expecting me to wear a suit. Thankfully, I owned one. Just one, although that might need to change.

*God, if I get this promotion, will I have to wear a tie . . . every day?*

I shuddered at the thought but told myself it'd be a small price to pay.

Watching my hands in the mirror as if they were someone else's, I twisted the shiny fabric into a double-Windsor knot—my dad's a single-Windsor kind of guy, that's the navy for you—and slid it up to my collar. Style wasn't the only thing I'd gotten in more plentiful amounts than the old man: I still had all my hair. To save time, I'd cut it earlier this morning, running the clippers over it with the number-one guard to leave a uniform quarter inch all the way around.

Fortunately, I didn't need to worry about time. That was the reason I'd rented an apartment so close to headquarters—I could run home at lunch if I needed something and be back within the hour. That was all I used the little studio for, it seemed: picking stuff up and dropping stuff off. Between the lab and Fort Worth, I barely spent any time at home.

While I wouldn't need to worry much about the clock, one variable I would absolutely need to consider was the heat. In the Dallas summer, I could soak through a shirt walking to and from my car. To be safe, I fished a spare out of the closet and draped my suit jacket over its hanger on my way out the door.

Manny, the gatehouse guy, waved as I pulled my little Honda Civic back onto the Texas Electronics campus. It turned out I didn't even need my badge today—unlike the other fourteen buildings on campus, the main building's doors swung wide open when you approached.

Accustomed to beeping myself in everywhere, I thought it felt a little eerie.

The receptionist made it worse—I didn't know her at all, but she called to me by name as I crossed the threshold and waved me straight back to the boardroom behind her.

Unlike the functional, utilitarian spaces we worked in, the rectangular boardroom had an elevated ceiling and skylights that let the Texas sun shine in. Despite that—or maybe because of it—the AC was on high, leaving the air absolutely frigid. Visually, the room was dominated by the table in the center, a huge slab of white limestone surrounded by high-backed, white-leather chairs. One long wall was covered in sepia-toned photos of the company's early days in the 1960s, while the other displayed memorabilia from Texas's history, including a framed, tattered Texas flag.

In five-plus years with the company, I'd only been invited into this room twice before. My first day, an HR lawyer had met me at the double doors, escorted me to a chair, and watched me sign every page of an inch-high stack of forms. This year, I'd won an award, and they'd called me in during a board meeting to hand me a plaque, although I hadn't had time to sit down before they sent me back out again.

Today, I made sure to take a different seat than before. And I made myself a silent promise that eventually I'd sit in every one of those damn chairs.

Over the course of the next ten minutes, my eyes wandered around the room, starting with the pictures and ending up counting dots in the stone of the table. Still, my heart was thumping hard enough I could hear it, and I knew the goose bumps on my arms weren't from the air-conditioning.

Finally, the double doors opened, and a woman entered.

Over six feet tall even without the heels that clacked along the floor, she took a seat on the opposite side of the table. Like me, she wore a dark suit, although hers included a short skirt that showed off most of her legs. Her black, wavy hair had been pulled into a ponytail behind her, bound by a colorful clip that matched the blouse beneath her jacket.

"You're Amara Brooks, right?" I asked, despite knowing the answer full well. Even at a company as large as T.E., the arrival of a Miss America runner-up was big news. Plus, the barely there Dior dress she'd worn to the company's annual anniversary banquet back in February had turned heads, literally. She'd supposedly grown up in DC and used her pageant money to pay her way through law school. Although she'd started in Legal, she'd quickly been promoted. "Are you still in Compliance?"

Her nostrils flared. "*Head* of Compliance."

I nodded, but her eyes were already on her phone. She scrolled with long, exaggerated flicks of her index finger.

After several more minutes, a tall, well-built man stepped in. His face looked roughly my age, but his starched seersucker suit gave him an older feel. He had a cleft chin, high cheekbones, and blond hair combed just so, but his eyes stood out above all else. Calling them blue was almost an injustice—they were incredibly pale, framed by dark circles around the irises. Although I'd never met Zachary Scott in person, I'd certainly heard his name.

My first thought upon seeing him and Brooks together was that this had better not be a beauty contest: I didn't stand a chance.

Scott stepped over and gave me a warm smile that showed off a mouthful of gleaming teeth. "You're Seth Walker," he said, pumping my hand. "Really a pleasure to finally put a face with the name."

"Thanks. You, too."

Before we could say anything else, a single door at the opposite side of the room opened, and Randolph Rodgers came through it. Our CEO was unmistakable—not only was his picture in the news constantly, but with white hair, a beard, and small glasses, he bore a jarring resemblance to Santa Claus. That was, until he spoke. He had a deep, booming baritone, slathered in Texas twang.

"Glad to see you're all here," he said. "Have a seat."

Scott slid into a chair next to me and across from Brooks, while Rodgers made his way to the head of the table. Once seated, he leaned forward on his elbows, glancing from one side of the table to the other.

"Today is a special occasion," he said. "I simply cannot believe the talent and accomplishments we've managed to gather in this room. What a testament to this wonderful company. You three represent a new generation of leadership for Texas Electronics."

He favored us with a proud smile.

"In case y'all don't know each other"—Rodgers gestured at Scott to my right—"Zachary has been here the longest. Harvard undergrad, Stanford MBA, and what, a three handicap?"

Scott shrugged and grinned. "Maybe a four."

"I've gotten tired of losing to Zachary out on the golf course," Rodgers said, "but he's also a winner with our customers. He's risen up within our sales organization to the point where he's personally managing our three biggest accounts."

Rodgers shifted in his chair and waved a hand at Brooks. "Then there's the lovely and talented Amara Brooks. She joined us from Akin Gump after the University of Pennsylvania and Georgetown Law."

"Don't call me *lovely*, Randolph," she said. "It's an HR violation."

I looked over, expecting to find her wearing some kind of scowl, but she was smiling sweetly at him.

"Even if it's true," she added.

Rodgers clucked several times and shook a finger at her. "That, that right there is the kind of moxie she's brought to our Legal, HR, and Compliance departments. And last, but certainly not least, we have one of the most creative engineers this company has ever employed, Seth Walker."

When Rodgers gestured at me, my eyes dropped to the tabletop.

"Now, the way word travels around here, I suspect y'all have a decent idea about what caused me to call this meeting."

I looked up to find a twinkle in Rodgers's eyes.

"But just so we're all on the same page, let me explain. For twenty-six years, Andrew Alexander has been our vice president of Technology and Products, meaning he's been charged with brainstorming where the market is going and how we're going to beat 'em there. Well, Andy's decided to hang it up and move to Napa with his wife, Eryn. His official end date is September 1, approximately six weeks from today. That means we've got a month and a half to pick the hand that'll be on the tiller around here for the next decade or two, if we do it right. Not surprisingly, whoever that person is will also have an inside track on my job."

Rodgers paused, basking in the looks we gave him. "Not that I'm planning on leaving anytime soon."

That elicited polite chuckles.

"T.E., as you know, is a special place filled with special people. That's why I want to pick Andy's replacement in-house. You three are the finalists." He nodded at each of us. "That's quite an accomplishment; y'all should be proud of yourselves. 'Course, as you can probably imagine, it only gets harder from here.

"As good as T.E. is, we are not without our challenges, and I'm a big believer in killing two birds with one stone whenever possible. So,

I see this little job interview as the chance to solve a few other issues along the way. Zachary, what would you say our biggest problem is in Sales right now?"

"The HighBuy relationship."

"Exactly. We've fucked that account up but good. It's going to take a shitload of handholding, groveling, and wining and dining to get us back in their good graces before they finalize their product lineup for next year. Amara, what's the biggest thing coming up in Compliance?"

"The FCC announced it's considering lowering allowable SAR levels. We've got to respond during the statutory comment period and see if we can drive the process to something we can live with."

SAR stood for Specific Absorption Rate, the amount of radio-frequency energy the body absorbed from wireless devices like cell phones and computers. Ever since the public had gotten spooked that cell phones caused brain cancer, the Federal Communications Commission had worked with governmental health agencies to put limits on the amount of radiation to which users would be exposed.

Rodgers tapped his open palm on the tabletop. "Seth, that leaves your neck of the woods in R & D. What have you heard about Boost?"

Boost was a first-of-its-kind automotive entertainment module. While every car and truck had some kind of stereo system, many had GPS navigation, and some even had on-board DVD players, Boost promised to take all that in a new direction by directly linking your automobile to the internet and adding a voice-controlled interface. Suddenly, instead of having to type in a specific address, you could call out, "What's the closest sushi place?" Rather than listening to the radio or some precollected songs, you could patch into one of the unlimited music streaming services that were being launched.

"It's not our lab," I said, happy to point that out because, while Boost was a great idea, it was also reported to be wildly behind schedule. "But I know from the road maps, it's slotted to release in time for Christmas."

"Which means the design needs to be finalized in six weeks," Rodgers said. "Six. Weeks." He shook his head. "The folks who dug us into a hole are no longer with us, but I don't think I have to tell you Boost is not quite ready for prime time. So, here's where we are: each of you has something to fix in roughly the same amount of time. Fix it. The one who does best gets Andy's job."

Scott cleared his throat. "Sir, what if—"

Rodgers grunted. "Zachary, I know you're not going to ask what happens if you're not successful. Right?"

Scott gave a single shake of his head. "Of course not."

"Of course not," Rodgers said, his mouth spreading into a smile. "'Cause I expect all three of you are smart enough to know that if you fail at this, there's really not much of a future for you here at T.E."

◆ ◆ ◆

I hurried into Clarence Aiken's office without knocking. "Guess what?"

When Clarence didn't immediately look up from behind his computer monitor, I said, "C'mon, guess."

Finally, his round face peeked around the side. As always, his thick glasses made his eyes seem abnormally large. "Andy Alexander?"

"Yes! He's out September 1, so Rodgers is—"

"Did he say what Andy's going to be doing?"

"Something about Napa," I said. "But—"

Clarence smiled what I called his "satisfied smile," the kind of peaceful, happy expression a kid wears when his belly's full of his favorite home-cooked meal. "That's great—he's finally doing it. He's talked for years about moving up there with Eryn and starting some kind of winery."

"That's not the news," I said. "His replacement is. I'm in the running for the job, but it's not just me."

After a long beat, Clarence asked, "Who else is up for it?"

"Amara Brooks from Compliance and Zachary Scott from Sales. Rodgers gave each of us a test we have to complete."

Clarence rocked back in his chair and crossed his arms. "I don't know Brooks. But Zach Scott supposedly has some pretty sharp elbows."

"He didn't seem so bad." Although I hesitated to point it out to Clarence, no one got to director level without being able to assert themselves.

"Well," he said, "you should be proud of yourself, Seth. This is a big opportunity for you."

The way he'd paused, the way he said *for you* made my heart race just a little faster. "For us," I said. "You don't think I'm getting that promotion and leaving you here."

He smiled weakly. "I like it here. This is where I found you. And lots of other people."

"I know. But I need your help if I'm going to pull this off. The task Rodgers gave me is a beast."

"What is it?"

"Boost."

Clarence let out a nervous laugh.

"I'm serious. Rodgers said it's so far behind that they fired the whole team."

His face dropped into a solemn expression. Then his Adam's apple bobbed prominently. "Those poor guys. And their families."

I cocked my head. "Yeah, well. Their mess just got dropped in our laps. And we've got six weeks to fix it."

"Oh my."

◆ ◆ ◆

Two hours later, we'd covered the entire surface of Clarence's desk in reams of paper. Schematics and flow diagrams, progress reports.

Anything and everything we could get our hands on to gauge the status of Boost.

"Now we just need to read it all," I said.

"Do you mind if we take it to the house?" Clarence asked. "I promised Michael I'd read him his story tonight. Plus, I'm sure Shirley has something good cooking."

With rush hour flaring up, the drive to Fort Worth took us a little over an hour, but that allowed me to start plowing through the documents. By the time Clarence pulled his Outback into the driveway outside their little house, I'd read through probably two hundred pages, each of which only made the situation seem worse. I didn't see a bit of functionality that was entirely complete, and some pieces looked barely begun.

Shirley, Clarence's wife, met us as the door between the garage and the house. After giving him a peck on the lips, she put a hand on his slumped shoulder. "What's wrong?"

"Seth signed us up for a dog of a project," he said.

"But we've got six weeks to fix it," I said, trying to sound positive.

"Oh, is that all?" Shirley asked, eyebrows raised. "I'm sure you boys will pull some kind of a rabbit out of your hat—you always do. But you're not going to do it on an empty stomach. C'mon, dinner's almost—"

"Uncle Seth, Uncle Seth!"

"Little man!"

Michael came bounding down the hallway, dodging his parents and flying into the garage. He wrapped his arms and legs around my shin, sitting on my foot. Thankfully, at only four years old, he wasn't that heavy, so I dragged him with me as we headed into the house.

He looked up at me from his perch. "Are you staying for dinner?"

"If your mom is cooking, I sure am," I said.

"Can you read me my story tonight?"

I noticed he was already dressed in his pajamas, which had race cars all over them. Cars were Michael's favorite thing these days.

Clarence looked back over his shoulder. "Hey, I thought I was going to do that."

Michael glanced downward for a moment, then looked up at me again. "Can you babysit soon? You know, so Mommy and Daddy can have a date night?"

"I'd love to, little man. But your dad and I have a big project we've got to work on together."

"Oh."

I felt Michael's grip around my leg loosen. Apparently, even at four, he'd already seen enough product cycles to know what was coming for Clarence. Lots of long hours, lots of missed nights at home.

"I tell you what," I said. "After we're done in a couple of weeks, maybe you can come over to my house for video games. How about that?"

His eyes lit up. "Like a sleepover?"

"Uh . . . sure," I said, wondering what I'd gotten myself into.

"Awesome!"

We'd reached the kitchen, where the air was filled with the scent of something rich and meaty. Rachael, Shirley and Clarence's baby, was already buckled into her high chair in the corner, playing with some toys spread out in front of her.

"You need me to feed her, Shirley?" I asked.

"Would you?" she asked. "That'll let me get everyone else's plates together."

Rachael still had the blue eyes of a newborn, but they lit up when she saw the little jar of blended carrots in my hand. Using the tiny spoon, I shoveled dollops of the orange stuff into her mouth. From the way her legs kicked and her arms waved, the taste of it must have been something else.

Shirley's dinner sure was. A pot roast with onions and carrots that melted in your mouth, along with a spinach salad and silky-smooth mashed potatoes. I didn't even need to ask for the horseradish—she put it right on the table for me, along with the salt and pepper.

Once dinner was over, I moved to Clarence's little office, where I pored over documents until he returned from reading to Michael and joined me. One of Clarence's specialties was his thoroughness: we compiled notes on a whiteboard for hours until we had checklists of things to do and checklists for our checklists. Shirley stopped in on her way to bed, but we kept working until I caught Clarence's eyes closing behind his glasses.

"Go get some sleep," I said. "I'll grab a taxi home."

Midyawn, he said, "Just stay. I can swing you by your place in the morning to grab fresh clothes."

"Thanks," I said.

He stood, pushed up his glasses, and patted my shoulder on his way out of the room. "We'll lick this thing yet."

# CHAPTER 5

*Thursday, February 23*

As Singh's face vanished from the monitor, I looked over to Melissa Cooke. "You believe all that?"

"Yeah, I thought he sounded pretty honest."

I blinked at her several times. Cooke was a trained interrogator—I'd watched her work over suspects for hours. Could she really not see through Singh's act?

"What did you think he was lying about?"

"Uh, everything. Like he doesn't know what El-Amin's been working on . . ."

"He might not. And even if he did, you can't really blame him for wanting to keep the company's R & D secret, can you?"

"All that kumbaya stuff at the end? How they love all their employees?"

"Why does that have to be false?"

I looked up at the ceiling and stifled my response. I'd seen Cooke like this before—sometimes she needed evidence before she could be convinced something was a possibility. It wasn't worth arguing with her, at least not here. But the way Singh had brushed me off about El-Amin's assignments at Magnet still irked me. Fortunately, there was a way around that. I pulled out my phone and typed a quick text to a friend who'd double-check.

"What were those address thingies Singh said he'd give us?" Durham asked.

"A MAC address is a unique identifier assigned to every device," I said. "Every computer, every smartphone. When you're connected to a wireless network, routers use the MAC addresses to keep track of which computer they're talking to. If we know El-Amin's MAC address, then we can track his Wi-Fi connections from router to router."

Given Durham's distaste for tech, I paused until he nodded.

"Phones have a separate device ID number," I said. "The cell carrier uses it as an identifier, just like routers use the MAC address. Have you talked to his cell carrier about using El-Amin's phone as a tracker? What *have* you guys tried?"

"Tony, you want to cover this?" Durham asked.

"Sure," he said. "First, we paged him. Every concourse, multiple times, but no response. We called his cell, but the number rolls right to voice mail—"

"Meaning it's likely turned off," I said. If the phone was powered down, GPS tracking of its SIM card wouldn't work, either.

Tranh nodded. "We've contacted the carrier, but yeah, that's our assumption. My guys and TSA have been patrolling all the terminals. We also conducted a search radiating from El-Amin's departure gate. No sign of him."

"What about video?" Cooke asked.

"We've cued up his run through security," Tranh said, "based on when they screened his ticket, but we haven't run through the rest yet."

I realized the dilemma Tranh was alluding to. With all the talk about facial recognition—now you could unlock your phone by looking at it— people assumed the government tracked you everywhere and could pinpoint you in a matter of seconds. While China was doing that in its cities, it wasn't the case here . . . not yet, at least. Some of the technical hurdles had been overcome—memory was significantly cheaper now, so storing video for longer periods wasn't as unthinkable as it had been even a few years ago. Sensor resolution had gone way up, too, meaning there were cameras that could reliably capture facial information in an everyday setting.

But obstacles remained. First off, facial recognition wasn't as accurate as some people assumed. Although TSA was starting to try to use faces to speed up security and boarding, the results had been mixed. If you couldn't accurately identify someone's face when they were standing still and looking directly at a camera, then following them around using facial—when they were a moving target, with only parts of their face visible—was a giant leap.

And there were even more fundamental problems. Some places—including, ironically, San Francisco—had outlawed facial recognition over privacy concerns. That ban didn't impact the airport, but the simple truth was, not enough high-resolution cameras had been deployed to capture all the images you would need, and even if they had been, insufficient computing power had been dedicated to plowing through all the captured data.

All that meant using security footage to follow someone around was still an iterative process, going camera to camera, roughly in real time. I glanced at the clock. We'd chewed through three of Durham's minutes, but we still had lots of ground to cover.

"You said he cleared security. Can we at least see that to get an idea what El-Amin's carrying?"

"Call up the security footage," Durham said, and quickly the monitors filled with images of El-Amin at the checkpoint. While most were stills, one whole screen contained digital video, a silent movie following El-Amin as he navigated the process. It began at a steep angle, looking down from a camera on the ceiling.

I had to suppress a smile when I saw his outfit: sneakers, cargo pants, and a light fleece jacket over a stretchy, spandex-style shirt. I'd worn similarly practical garb when taking long flights overseas.

In the video, El-Amin looked like he was already overheated: enough sweat dotted his brow that he wiped at it with his sleeve. From above, you could see his black hair was thinning, his movement through security dislodging some of the strands he'd swept across his forehead and plastered down just so.

As El-Amin approached the podium to have his ID checked, the camera angle shifted to one that was head-on. Despite the beard and now-disheveled hair, his full cheeks and small nose combined to give El-Amin a babyish look—from his face alone, I'd have pegged him closer to a teenager than someone pushing thirty. His body screamed middle age, though, as the jacket was draped over slumped shoulders, with the spandex shirt stretched tight across a prominent belly.

I whispered to Cooke, "He look like a hardened killer to you?"

"No." She paused a moment. "But neither did Berkeley."

Hearing that name was a punch to the gut: Berkeley was the woman who'd started all this, who'd taken my covert air-marshal status away, along with the life of my girlfriend at the time. The SA tattoo on my arm sizzled as a million images flashed through my brain.

Cooke had been there that night in Dallas. She'd taken two bullets— bullets Berkeley had meant for me that easily could have added Cooke to my list of ghosts. I bit my tongue and turned back to the screen.

As the video continued playing, I watched it closely. El-Amin's eyes were what struck me most. Despite the hour, there was absolutely no drowsiness in them. No matter his expression, they remained wide and clear, constantly moving, searching as he presented his credentials and stepped to the baggage conveyor.

Still, being awake wasn't a crime the last time I checked.

The scanner at this checkpoint wasn't the typical boxy, gray X-ray machine most people were accustomed to seeing. Instead, the belt led to a sleek white tube shaped something like a jet engine. This CT machine was the latest and greatest in airport security, relying on the same computed tomography doctors use at hospitals. Inside, an X-ray camera spun around, snapping pictures from hundreds of different angles; a computer assembled those into a 3D model you could twist and turn to inspect from every angle.

If El-Amin were surprised or concerned by the new security equipment, he didn't show it. His expression remained unchanged as he hefted his rolling briefcase up and into a plastic bin, then slid it into the mouth of the machine.

International passengers were all subjected to the full-body scanner, so as El-Amin's bag got sucked into the CT, he stepped into the glass booth next to it and raised his arms over his head. He stepped out a moment later after the nearest TSA agent waved him on.

"Where are the images from that?" Cooke asked.

"They don't save them," I said. "At least, they're not supposed to." When the first generation of backscatter X-ray tech had been deployed to look beneath passengers' clothing for contraband, scans had leaked, and the public had grown outraged at the near-photographic quality of the images. That, plus concerns over cancer risk from the extra radiation, had gotten those machines pulled almost immediately. Their replacements, using lower-energy millimeter waves, included all kinds of privacy protections, such as stationing the technician reading the scan in a separate room, only presenting an image of the passenger if there was a concern, and even then, showing a generic body form instead of the passenger's personal picture. The software had also been written to delete the images as soon as the scan was completed. Instances had been uncovered, though, where that feature had been bypassed.

Tranh raised his hands and shook his head. "Don't look at me. Screening is Centurian, not SFPD."

"David?" Durham asked.

On the monitors, a videoconference window popped up showing a man with dark hair pulled back into a tight ponytail and a bright-yellow tie. "David Cisneros, FSD. SFO is an opt-out airport, but I oversee Centurian, and they follow all the relevant regulations."

Cooke shot me a quizzical look.

I leaned over and whispered, "*Opt-out* means they use a private contractor instead of TSA." The distinction was opaque to passengers, as the contractor's employees wore the same blue uniforms and were supposed to follow all the same protocols. About two dozen airports had elected to "opt out" of TSA, but mostly they were smaller, regional fields—SFO was by far the biggest. "Cisneros is the federal security director, so the contractor reports to him."

"The body scanner can't save images," Cisneros said. "But the CT does. We've got scans of El-Amin's bag."

As he was speaking, the third monitor filled with a picture of El-Amin's rolling briefcase. The bag's black fabric walls had been rendered completely transparent, leaving the contents visible in shades of gray.

"May I?" Although I asked, my hand was already on Durham's mouse, sliding the cursor over to that window. Clicking on different icons, I found I could change the colors of items inside the bag to focus on different densities or types of materials. "Grabbing" the bag by holding the mouse button, I could rotate the image 360 degrees by dragging the cursor in any direction.

With three major compartments to search, I started at the back with the system set to look for metal. Two long cylinders corresponding to the bag's collapsible handle immediately jumped out in blue-black, but there were other, similarly colored shapes to investigate. One was a thin, rectangular plate with two small cylinders attached to it. Unsure what that was, I toggled the scan mode, and suddenly you could see that it was a digital picture frame with the border constructed from something organic—wood, maybe? It was wrapped in some kind of bag or jacket.

Toggling back to metal-searching mode, I zoomed in on one of two small zippered pouches. It contained several long metallic cylinders.

"What the—" Durham asked.

"It's a vaping setup," I said. E-cigarettes had grown popular with people El-Amin's age and younger. I'd actually been meaning to take a deeper look into the tech at some point, but hadn't had the chance.

Tranh sighed. "Damn millennials can't even smoke normally."

Cisneros, the FSD, clucked on the conference line. "Our friend was going to be sorely disappointed when he arrived at Ben Gurion."

"What do you mean?" Durham asked. "Why?"

"Israel's banned e-cigarettes. Customs would have seized those on his way in."

There were small bits of metal in the other pouch, so I zoomed in on those next. The metal turned out to be razor blades—the pouch was some kind of shaving kit. More interesting were two rectangular blocks and several smaller circles nearby that glowed orange for organic. By changing modes and zooming in and out, I quickly identified them. "El-Amin thought he was gonna get lucky overseas."

"How's that?" Durham asked.

"He's packing lots of deodorant and a twelve-pack of condoms."

Cooke turned to Durham. "Halal dating doesn't include premarital sex."

The ex-general gave a resigned shrug.

I focused next on the bag's middle compartment. Here, the shapes clearly represented a laptop and a tablet, along with another metal block that looked like a travel battery. I changed modes again to look inside each of them, but there was nothing organic, nothing that resembled hidden explosives, only the typical components you'd expect.

Finally, I moved to the front of the bag. Toggling between modes again, I saw office supplies (pens, markers, business cards), several different kinds of chargers (each fitted with a three-pronged outlet adapter for use overseas), and things El-Amin had jammed in at the last minute, including his wallet, passport, and cell phone.

Overall, the contents of El-Amin's briefcase didn't look a helluva lot different than mine would have back in the day.

"Anything in there worry you?" Cooke asked.

I shook my head. "About the worst he could do with the stuff on him is heat up the lithium-ion batteries in his devices. Start a fire, maybe cause a small explosion. But nothing earth-shattering."

"Or," Cooke said, "he might not be working alone. Someone could have snuck something into the airport and left it for him to pick up once he got through."

"Either way, we're back where we started," Durham said. "It all depends where he is. If he starts a fire near a fuel truck, or a gas line into one of the restaurants . . ."

Cooke, who'd been leaning over the monitor, straightened to her full height. "We need to know more about what he's thinking, what's motivating him. I assume you've got someone digging into his contacts, his online presence?"

"If, by someone, you mean the entire NSA," Durham said, "then, yes. They're currently sifting through every electron El-Amin's ever touched."

"I need to see what they find," she said. "If this is some kind of a suicide mission, he may well have left signs of why he's doing it."

"Like a manifesto or something?" Tranh asked.

"Could be," she said, "although it's not always that overt. If he's been compromised or radicalized by someone else, there'll likely be traces of that, too. And there might be financial activity related to all this."

While I still wasn't sure I believed El-Amin had been converted into a cold-blooded assassin, I knew from past experience that there was nobody better to find out than Cooke. Meticulous to a fault, she also knew how to treat evidence so it would stand up in court.

My eyes kept returning to the clock, though. Our talking had chewed through two more of Durham's minutes—I didn't know that we had time for any more. I also couldn't get past the thought of the crowds we'd seen. "What about evacuation?"

"What about it?" Durham asked.

"We can't just leave all those people—"

Durham crossed his arms. "Mr. Walker, of everyone in here, I'd expect you to know better. Clearing the airport gives El-Amin the best chance of escaping—he picks the right spot, he just walks out with the crowd. Besides, if SFO stops flight operations, you're talking about upending air transportation nationwide, worldwide. So, we do our jobs. We find El-Amin, stop him, and the world spins on, oblivious to our existence. That's the mission."

I sucked a deep breath in through my nose, then released it. Although I didn't say anything, I held eye contact with Durham, imploring him.

From the way he blinked at me, maybe it worked.

"Tony," Durham said after a long moment, "what's the projected evacuation time in the airport's disaster plan?"

Tranh glanced at the ceiling. "Each terminal's self-contained, so we can clear one without affecting the others. Assuming we use emergency exits, funnel people out onto the tarmac, figure we can empty a terminal in about seven minutes."

Durham spun back to me. "There you go. If we haven't solved this with seven minutes to spare . . ."

I swallowed the lump in my throat. That gave us even less time.

My gaze shifted to Cooke, who'd hunched over the computer again. I hesitated to say it, but I wouldn't be much help looking over her shoulder, reviewing signal traffic. "I—"

"You should get out into the terminals," she said. "Follow El-Amin's path."

I nodded, trying to gauge whether she was actually okay with that.

Her green eyes flashed. "Besides, here you'd only be in the way."

I gave her a thankful nod. "Glad I wore sneakers."

"You'll need access," Durham said. "Carla Cavin is the duty manager on shift—are you listening, Carla?"

A deep, raspy woman's voice answered. "Here, sir."

Tranh reached for the table and pressed the telephone's "Mute" button. "We should call someone else in. Cavin's way too young—"

"No time, Tony. This is all hands on deck. I've gone to war trusting my life to kids younger than her." Durham reactivated the microphone. "Carla, you'll be Mr. Walker's guide. Get him where he needs to go, all right?"

"Absolutely, sir."

While I figured I'd reserve judgment about Cavin, Cooke's earlier comment about partners smuggling in weapons or explosives for El-Amin echoed in my mind. "We saw a K9 bomb sniffer in Area D. Can I get one of those?"

"Done." Durham nodded at Tranh, then turned back to face me. His voice grew quiet. "Now, Mr. Walker, I'm grateful you're here, so please don't take this the wrong way. You know the old saying 'Once is an accident, twice is a coincidence, three times is a pattern'?"

I nodded.

He raised a closed fist up by his ear. "Dallas. Austin. Louisville." With each locale, he raised a finger. "I've read all the after-action reports—I know how good you are with that Sig of yours." His eyes flicked down to my hip a moment, before rising to lock onto mine. I suddenly became acutely aware of my pulse pounding in my ears.

"I also know how nasty the Second Guerilla Army can be, so the way you dealt with them earned an awful lot of my respect. But while I appreciate a good shot as much as anyone, this is not the wilds of West Virginia or some rural Texas ranch, you got me? We cannot—and I cannot stress this enough—we *cannot* turn this airport into a shooting gallery. Do you understand?"

"Of course, sir."

"No guns." Durham's eyes widened to the point that bloodshot whites were visible all around the irises. "I mean it."

While I wondered whether El-Amin would be equally obliging about public safety, we had to find him first. Honestly, the thing I cared most about were the glowing orange numbers on the clock. My eyes drifted back to them.

Fifty-six minutes left.

51

# CHAPTER 6

Durham and Tranh gave me a tablet computer linked to their network so they could feed me recorded footage of El-Amin, postsecurity. They also gave me a radio headset. To make room for that, I yanked out my own earpiece—enough adrenaline was pumping through my veins to make my audio feed unnecessary—and stuffed it in my pocket.

When I emerged back out into the terminal, a white golf cart blocked the entrance to the alcove, pointed in the same direction we'd originally traveled with Tranh. Unlike the open carts at LAX, this one had a roof. When I ducked beneath it, I found a compact, curvy woman in a pale-blue pantsuit leaning over from behind the wheel.

"I'm Carla." Her voice matched the one I'd heard back in the conference room, but she looked at least ten years younger than I'd pictured. Her hair was a mass of tight, frizzy black curls that bounced in unison when she talked. She had large, welcoming eyes that seemed to contain a hint of mischief as they scanned me over. "Hop in—I'll get you wherever you need to go."

I'd no sooner slid next to her than she stomped on the pedal. The electric engine responded with a high-pitched yelp even as it pressed me back into the seat cushion. There was so much torque, I half expected us to pop a wheelie.

"Thanks for the ride," I said over the whine of the motor. "I haven't seen many carts here at SFO."

"We don't have many," she said, her eyes fixed on the path ahead. "The police get bikes and Segways, but normally I hoof it everywhere. I average eight miles a shift."

Glancing into the footwell, I saw that Cavin was wearing pastel New Balance sneakers that matched her suit.

"Tranh thinks you're too young to drive or something." I figured I'd better learn whatever the issue between them was as soon as I could.

"That old . . ." Her hair jostled back and forth as she shook her head. "He thinks 'cause I'm twenty-four and a woman that I'm all helpless. But I've been working at this airport since I was sixteen—a lot longer than he's been here. He and a bunch of the police migrated down here from the city three years ago. Thought it'd be easy money."

We'd already cleared the windowless hallway beyond the Comm Center alcove and had begun speeding through Terminal 3. Unlike Terminal 2, the renovations hadn't been completed here; in fact, it looked like they hadn't even been started. We passed a modernized seating area filled with asymmetrical couches and angled, avant-garde LED lighting, but otherwise the concrete columns, dark carpets, and even darker paneling made the route feel foreboding. Even where new features had been installed—Terminal 3 had one of the CLEAR security checkpoints, whose fancy lit-glass facade looked like the entrance to a posh beauty salon—it came across as a tacked-on afterthought.

Terminal 3 belonged to Eastern, El-Amin's airline and the carrier that occupied the most space in the airport, so check-in lines were long. And because security wasn't directly adjacent to the check-in counters, the hallway was filled with travelers walking in both directions. Cavin wove through these crowds like a race-car driver, whipping the wheel back and forth, guiding us from gap to gap with fits and starts of power.

"You drive like this out on the freeway?" I asked. "Maybe that's why Tranh's afraid of you."

Cavin shot me a sly, sideways look. "I'll have you know, I have a *very* healthy relationship with the California Highway Patrol."

When we'd passed the bulk of the arriving passengers, Cavin floored it, the noise from the little engine rising to a crescendo that echoed inside the tight hallway. We gained so much momentum, I wasn't sure we'd have room to stop—up ahead, the passage dead-ended in a two-story atrium built around a set of elevators and escalators.

As we careened toward the burnished steel doors, I winced. Somehow, though, Cavin managed to turn the cart without flipping it, bleeding off speed until we skidded to a sideways stop at the base of the moving staircases.

Before I could react, she grabbed a walkie-talkie off the bench between us and sprang from her seat, circling behind the cart to the escalators. "There's no way to drive up," she said. "We're on foot from here."

Cavin began climbing even as I was hauling myself out of the cart. I took the moving metal stairs two at a time until I caught up. She must not have been kidding about the eight miles—her powerful legs churned pistonlike on the steps.

"That was a pretty nifty stop," I said.

"Go-carts," she said, glancing back over her shoulder. "I used to race my brothers every weekend."

When we reached the top of the escalator, the entrance to International Pier G stood just a few yards away. We crossed that distance quickly to the checkpoint El-Amin had cleared. TSA was waiting for us. One agent had opened a special path through the rope line, allowing us to bypass the waiting passengers, while another agent waved us through the body scanner. They nodded and gave Cavin large smiles as we passed. I thought I heard one even say, "Go, Carla."

Beyond the checkpoint, before a ramp that led down into the concourse proper, skylights draped a curtain of light onto the floor. Cavin dashed into the center of that and paused for me to catch up.

"I may need to bring you on all my trips," I said, drawing up to her. Now that we stood on even ground next to one another, I saw I stood at least a foot taller than Cavin.

"The seas don't always part for you like that?" Despite breathing heavily, Cavin gave me a coy smile. The golden light from above caused her skin to glow even as it cast her dimples in deep relief. As she blinked at me, I noticed she had extremely long lashes.

"The Centurian people like you," I added.

She nodded. "I was one of them for a while—they see me, they see life beyond pat-downs and bag checks. Where we headed next?"

I unlocked the tablet, and the first thing that greeted my eyes was Durham's countdown clock. *Fifty-three minutes.*

I tapped the earpiece to my headset. "Cooke, Durham, are you online? We're at the base of G."

"Here," Durham's voice said in my ear. "Tony tells me your dog friend should be arriving any moment, and we've got the first video clips cued up for you. It's going to be stop-and-start."

The tablet flashed to life, showing the top of El-Amin's head as he collected his bag from the end of the CT conveyor. He set the case down on the floor, extended the collapsible handle, and started away from the checkpoint.

Comparing the image on-screen to the ground beneath our feet, I realized it was roughly the same patch of carpet we were standing upon, minus the reflected sunshine. I craned my neck around and spotted a black-domed camera on the ceiling over my shoulder.

Back on-screen, El-Amin moved to our right, towing the bag behind him. He paused as a group of female flight attendants—China Eastern, judging by their navy dresses and wide red belts—walked by. He watched them go, then resumed his walk, heading off-screen.

I looked up from the tablet and saw an officer in a brown uniform approaching the concourse with a leashed German shepherd. They were still a dozen yards away or more, though, and seemingly in no hurry. "Carla," I said, "can you wait for him while I get started?"

She started to answer, but I didn't wait to hear it. I turned the same way El-Amin had and strode in that direction. At the edge of the checkpoint, a hallway stretched diagonally backward, away from the concourse and the gates. Signs overhead indicated this passage led off to Terminal 3. That made sense—Eastern controlled enough of the airport, it wanted passengers to be able to transfer between international and domestic flights without having to re-clear security. Still, that shouldn't have interested El-Amin, who was only holding an international ticket.

Looking up from the tablet, I spotted a placard on the wall. It bore the Eastern logo.

"The lounge," I said out loud.

The video showed El-Amin from behind, striding past our position toward the same sign. My eyes alternated between the tablet and the view in front of us—in real life, a glass door on the wall slid open as someone exited, while on-screen, El-Amin stepped through it.

That was all I needed. I accelerated to a sprint, dashing through the glass door, then rounding an immediate corner into a brightly lit lobby.

Unlike the dim hallway outside, the floor and walls here were decorated in rich, white marble. Behind a desk of gray stone, a middle-aged man and an elderly woman in identical Eastern blazers sat on chairs tall enough to allow them to peer over the high counter. When they saw me coming, their eyes widened. The man stood as they chimed in unison, "Can we help you, sir?"

I ignored them. My only concern was what the tablet would show next, but the screen had gone dark. "Where to?" I asked into my headset.

"Working on it," Durham said in my ear.

I quickly glanced up and around, scanning the ceiling, checking every corner. No cameras, at least none I could discern. If they didn't have images, I didn't have time to wait. The lobby bent to my left, so I started in that direction.

"Sir, you can't—"

The words came from the elderly woman behind the desk, but I heard Cavin, the dog, and its handler rounding the corner behind me. Assuming they'd explain, I started jogging toward the back.

I'd only taken three or four steps when something struck me hard from behind. The impact pitched me onto the floor face-first. The tablet flew from my hands, clattering against the stone floor. My immediate worry was whether the screen would survive the fall. Then my attention turned to what had taken me down. I tried to scramble back up to my feet but couldn't. Something heavy was pressed down on my back.

As I turned to try and see what—or who—was restraining me, a fat hand slapped down against the side of my head. The blow startled me more than anything else. My cheek met the floor, pressed against the cold stone.

"Don't move, asshole."

# CHAPTER 7

Out the corner of my eye, I could see it was the middle-aged lobby attendant who'd taken me down. His knee was digging into my back, his head hovering over mine as he kept all his weight on me. "We got him for you, Carla."

For a split second, instinct took over, and I thought about a quick maneuver that would dislodge him and put me on top, hand around his throat. As my muscles were tensing to try it, Cavin's voice stopped me.

"It's okay, Fred. He's an air marshal . . ."

"What, *him*?"

Fred's voice dripped with disbelief, but his weight disappeared, and I clambered to my feet.

Once we were on even footing, Fred's expression was suddenly wiped clean. He raised his pudgy hands in front of him. "I am *so* sorry, fella. It's just . . . you look . . . I mean, you don't . . . and they were . . ."

Part of me wondered what he'd reacted to; part of me figured I already knew. While I would have loved to have spent a minute or two enlightening him, I addressed the dog handler instead. "C'mon."

The lobby extended maybe a dozen yards back. At the end of the chamber, through purposefully cut gaps in dark, wooden shelves, an expansive seating area was visible. On our left, escalators led upstairs.

Thankfully, the tablet hadn't suffered any damage, but the screen was still black. "Durham," I said, "if you don't have video, we'll have to clear this whole place."

"The airlines monitor their own lounges," he said. "The video's on a separate server—they're trying to connect us."

"Down here first?" I asked the dog handler.

"Sounds like a plan." The K9 handler's weathered face suggested he was well into his forties, but he stood as tall as I and was solidly built. He had bright-red hair, almost orange, with a bushy mustache to match.

"I'm Seth, by the way."

"Gary. And this here's Bonnie."

I glanced down at the dog, who wasn't paying the slightest attention to me as she sniffed the space ahead of us.

"Let's go."

Airport lounges weren't a luxury I dabbled in anymore, not since I'd left engineering behind. Back then, I'd traveled several times a year to Asia, and lounge access came with the cost of a business-class ticket. In theory, it was wonderful: grabbing a last meal, recharging your devices while you sat in comfort, washing up in a bathroom that was clean and well maintained. Little things to help sand down the rougher edges of long-haul travel.

In my experience, though, the idea of the lounge almost always outpaced the reality. The free food could be as meager as a bowl of stale Chex Mix. Seats were often hard to come by; sometimes outlets worked, sometimes they didn't. And don't get me started on the bathrooms . . .

So, when we stepped into the elongated room, my expectations weren't high. To my surprise, I looked out over the nicest seating area I'd ever seen in one of these places. It had been styled like some kind of upscale library. The left-hand wall was all windows overlooking the tarmac, while the right supported a series of shelves displaying artfully arranged books that I doubted anyone had ever read.

Each chair sat squarely in the middle of its own little cubby, walled off from those on either side. The seats resembled benches, each as wide as two common chairs and covered in the kind of luxurious leather you'd expect to find upholstering a Ferrari. Covered in soft navy fabric, the cubby walls provided each seat with access to a small silver lamp, several charging ports, and a buttressed table large enough to hold a laptop. While marble flooring from the lobby continued across the room in a narrow path, either side was bordered with a lush gray carpet.

Unlike the terminal, which had eye-in-the-sky camera domes dotting the ceilings every few yards, here I saw only a single camera above an employee-access door. Far more common here, though, were blinking wireless router boxes, which gave me an idea. "Did Singh ever send over those MAC addresses? Do we have a trail going on those?"

"He sent them," Durham said, "but IT hasn't built a track yet. They didn't know where to start."

I strode quickly to the end of the hushed space while Gary let Bonnie sniff her way across the floor. Because only about half the luxurious benches were occupied, the crowd here was far different from the young techies we'd seen earlier. About a third were Asian—some families, some men traveling alone. The rest were older white folks dressed fancy, men in blazers, women in dresses or pantsuits. Most paid no attention to the dog, but those who did seemed annoyed by her presence, as if she might relieve herself on the carpet.

When Gary and Bonnie joined me at the end of the seating area, we discovered that the lounge kept going: after a divider came another marble-floored chamber whose only apparent purpose was to host an elaborate coffee station. Three shining silver carafes sat atop a pedestal on a star-shaped table, their ornate lids gleaming like crowns in light cast down from incandescent bulbs suspended from the ceiling. These caffeine kings overlooked an elaborate court spread across the remainder of the table: a small army of ceramic mugs, lined six rows deep with military precision; a stack of rolled cloth napkins, each row turned perpendicular to those directly above and below it; a series of bowls displaying a rainbow of different sweetener packets, as well as honey and, a new one for me, agave syrup. Wooden boxes presented a choice of at least a dozen different teas. Four different milks stood in metal pitchers on a special chilled platform.

I knew people loved their coffee, but this was about the most extravagant display of beverage worship I'd ever seen. I was still trying to wrap my head around it when Cavin's voice got my attention.

"Hard to believe, huh?"

I turned to find she had the elderly woman from the front desk with her.

"I stopped working here when I realized rich folks were just different," Cavin said. "Listen, Ruth here remembers the guy you're looking for."

Ruth stepped forward, wearing a proud smile. "I checked him in. I took care of that whole party."

I unlocked the tablet, pulled up the image of El-Amin's driver's license, and held it out to her. "This guy? You're sure?"

She gave a single definitive nod.

"Can you show us where he went? What he did?"

"My boss told me to stay with them, make sure they had whatever they needed. They started upstairs."

"Then lead the way," I said. "But let's hurry."

The lounge's second floor made the first look like it was designed for steerage class. The escalator delivered us to another elongated room that stretched the length of a football field or two. It had been noticeably partitioned into different spaces, some for sitting quietly, some for socializing. The marble walls and flooring matched the lobby, and all the sitting areas contained the fancy double-width leather chairs we'd seen downstairs, along with high-backed loungers upholstered in a fabric so lush it threatened to swallow anyone who sat down. Lighting was provided by a series of modern chandeliers.

Ruth started toward the far end of the room. While she walked as quickly as she could on her spindly legs, part of me wondered if I should offer to pick her up and carry her.

Along the way, we passed a chrome-accented bar whose counter was formed from translucent stone. Lit from beneath, it made all the drinks seem to glow. After that came a buffet station offering options from cold (sashimi tuna and cocktail shrimp) to hot (steaming bamboo baskets of dim sum dumplings), from light (scotch glasses filled with leafy salads) to heavy (filet mignon finger sandwiches). Despite the many choices, though, the air didn't have any discernible smell. The clientele here looked the same as downstairs, but everywhere you turned, servers seemed to be whizzing by—more of them than passengers, it seemed.

We finally reached a circular chamber that, judging from the stack of leather-bound menus, appeared to be a full-service restaurant. Tables lined the perimeter of the room, while the center was dominated by a massive floral centerpiece atop a stone table. Ruth led us to one table in particular, a six-top with banquette seating against the wall. The table settings featured plates bearing the Eastern Airlines logo and enough glasses and silverware that I wouldn't have known which to use first.

"They started here," Ruth said, "for breakfast. The one you're looking for arrived last. He took out his computer and worked while they ate."

While Gary led Bonnie from table to table, I glanced up. At the center of the dining room, above the flowers, one of the blinking router boxes perched on the ceiling. I got underneath it and saw it bore a small but distinct label.

"Did you see him use his phone by any chance?" I asked, spinning back toward Ruth. "Or just his laptop?"

"I'm pretty sure he used both."

"How crowded was the dining room?"

"Not very," she said. "Most people eat at the buffet."

"General," I said into the headset, "are you there?"

"Go ahead."

"I can jump-start that MAC address track for you. The router box I'm sending you now would have been where El-Amin logged on with his coworkers." I fired off a photo of the router box, then turned back to Ruth. "Did the man we're looking for leave the table at any point? Go off by himself?"

Ruth's face took on a surprised expression. "Yes, actually. He asked where the men's room was."

Before I could repeat the question, she pointed a gnarled finger toward a passage on the far side of the room.

I sprinted over, cutting down the hallway and pushing my way into the men's room. Thankfully, it was small—only two of everything—but a set of cabinets sat beneath the vanity, and a service closet stood off to one side. I quickly tried each, but both were locked.

Gary and Bonnie entered the bathroom just as I was tugging on the final handle.

"Let her give that a shot," he said.

I stepped back, and Bonnie went to work, sniffing along the edges of each door. The canine seemed fraught with energy, circling and pacing the small space as she went. Eventually, after she'd sniffed each one, she looked up at Gary. Her eyes were eager, her tongue hanging from the side of her mouth.

"No hits," he said. With his free hand, he fished into a pocket and produced a knotted cloth that he tossed to Bonnie. She caught it in her mouth, her tail bobbing side to side. He stepped over to her and rubbed her side while whispering to her, then took the cloth back.

"Seth?" Cooke's voice in my ear this time. "Anything there?"

"Nope. Sometimes a bio break is just a bio break." I remembered heading off on my first trip to Asia, wondering when I'd see a normal toilet again. I could imagine El-Amin feeling the same way.

When Gary and I returned to the dining room, I asked Ruth, "What happened next? After El-Amin came back from the bathroom?"

"They sat a few more minutes before going off to the suites," she said.

"Suites? Uh, can you show us?"

Ruth led us back through the buffet area, past the bar and the sitting rooms to the opposite side of the escalator. Here, the lounge appeared to end, but she stepped in front of a tinted-glass panel in the wall. Without warning, it slid to one side, revealing a semidarkened hallway.

She started into the passage, and we followed. Once the glass shifted back into place behind us, the primary lighting came from recessed bulbs near the floor. Our feet sank soundlessly into the thick carpeting with each step. Overhead, pinpoint LEDs in the black ceiling twinkled like stars.

Halfway down the hall, Ruth stopped and manipulated a knob so well camouflaged I hadn't seen it. When the door opened inward, a bright shaft of daylight spilled into the hallway. That helped prepare my eyes for the room we were about to enter.

Cavin stepped in ahead of me, and I heard her whistle. "They never let me up in here. This is *cuh-razy*."

Once I cleared the doorway, I had to agree. It was larger than Durham's conference room, or even Lavorgna's corner office in our LA headquarters. More than anything, it resembled a high-end hotel room: floor-to-ceiling windows on one wall, providing a bay view and equipped with blackout curtains that would descend from the ceiling at the touch of a button. A king-size bed and two steeply angled lounge chairs were stationed on one side of the room for sleeping, while the middle comprised a work area containing an ornate wooden desk, a table, and several fancy chairs. The air felt crisper here, scented with something floral. I wondered if that would affect Bonnie, but she'd already begun sniffing her way around the edge of the room.

On the far side, a door stood ajar. Ruth must have noticed me staring at it. "Full bathroom," she said. "With a shower."

Gary and Bonnie looked like they'd get there soon, so I let my eyes wander around the rest of the main room. In particular, I noticed a glass case by the door—it resembled a refrigerator, but it was filled with plush white towels.

"Cold towels?" I asked.

"Oh no." Ruth shook her head. "That's an oven to keep them warm and toasty."

Cavin shut her eyes and raised her eyebrows.

"Other than wrapping themselves in warm towels," I said, "what did El-Amin and his friends do in here?"

"They seemed to be having a meeting," Ruth said. "They were talking to someone on the phone. Until the weather delay got announced."

"Did you hear what their call was about?"

Her shoulders rose. "It was all . . . computer-y stuff. I didn't really understand."

"Anything at all you remember?"

"Maybe it was about memory, or something? They kept saying *storage* and *capacity*."

I made a mental note to check the memory specs on the Polaris. "How did they hear about the delay?"

"My manager came to tell them in person. They didn't seem very happy."

I wouldn't have been, either. Nothing worse than learning your full-day trip would take even longer.

"But that's when your man spoke for the first time."

I perked up. "What did El-Amin say?"

"He said he was going to buy a few snacks for the airplane, since he'd skipped breakfast. He said he'd meet the others at the gate."

"How did they respond?"

"They told him to keep in touch . . . and they teased him," Ruth said.

"Teased?"

"They said to remember he had the most important job, so he'd better make it to the plane."

"You're absolutely sure about that?"

She nodded. "Oh yes. That bit struck me because, up 'til then, he'd seemed like the youngest, least important one."

"Cooke," I said, tapping the earpiece, "did you hear that?"

"Yes," she said. "I was just about to interrupt you—SFPD's about to execute a warrant on El-Amin's house. We've got a feed from the scene; you should watch."

"Okay." I unlocked the tablet, which opened to shaky video taken by a cell phone or body camera. It showed one of those tall, narrow Victorian-style houses you see standing in long rows in San Francisco, the kind with a single-car garage, a steep staircase at the sidewalk, and slanted bay windows jutting out over them. This particular house, painted blue with white trim, seemed well maintained—better at least than the buildings on either side, which featured peeling paint and dinged-up siding.

The picture shook as whoever was filming climbed the stairs. A fist pounded on the front door with no accompanying noise.

"No sound?" I asked.

"I can talk to the officers over the radio," Tranh said, "but we don't have a separate audio feed."

After a moment, the door opened, and the camera pushed through it. The house's ground floor had been emptied of furniture in favor of a long, wooden picnic table. Several people were scattered around it, working on laptops. Only one of them, a woman with her hair tied in a bun and a pencil shoved through the middle, even bothered looking up at the sight of a pair of police officers moving through.

The image swiveled quickly to the stairs, then bounced again as the cameraperson climbed them. At the top, three doorways were visible, but the camera made for the nearest one. The door swung inward to reveal a room a third the size of the suite in which I stood. Maybe a quarter. The nearest wall had a window facing out to the alley behind the house; beneath that was a plain wooden desk. The three remaining walls were lined with unpainted wooden bunkbeds. The camera zoomed in on one of the lower bunks. Two drawers were mounted below it, along with an empty space next to them that looked large enough for a suitcase. The bed had been made neatly.

"They're saying that's his spot," Tranh said. "El-Amin."

"That's it?" Durham asked. "Magnet said he makes 250K a year."

"That bunk alone probably costs him two grand a month," Tranh said.

"What?" Durham asked. "How are six people living in that tiny little room?"

"It's a hacker house," I said into the headset.

"Wait," Durham said, "El-Amin's a hacker?"

"No," Tranh said. "It's a hacker *house*. One of the ways big tech's been ruining the city."

"How's that?"

"These computer types spend all their time at their offices, but they need a place to live, right? Rent's expensive, and they don't have a ton of cash when they start out, so a lot of them rent rooms or bunks like this."

"I bet there's a half dozen start-up companies being run out of that place," I said.

"They use these places like unregistered hostels; they advertise online, people come and go. With the cash the tech people end up making, rents on these places get higher and higher—before you know it, real people can't afford a real house. We've got neighborhoods that used be full of regular folks with kids and dogs, the whole nine yards. Now we've just got these hollowed-out places, filled with people who won't be there in a year. One of the reasons I moved down here."

"Where's all El-Amin's stuff?" Cooke asked.

After a moment, Tranh responded. "Landlord says it's just the bed and whatever's in the drawers."

"Can you have the officers show us what's inside?"

On-screen, hands reached for the wooden drawers and pulled them open. When the camera peered down inside, one contained a couple of pairs of jeans and a few neatly folded T-shirts, while the other was filled with underwear and socks.

"What is this guy, a monk?" Durham asked. "I brought more than that into the woods for our army FTX weekends in college. What the hell's he doing with the rest of his money?"

"It's more than that," Cooke said. "Look at the walls."

The camera panned again, and where other bunks had pictures, calendars, and other papers tacked up above them, the plaster around El-Amin's bed stood bare.

"That worry you?" Durham asked.

"Lack of attachment's not ideal," she said.

Cavin had sidled up next to me to watch the images on-screen. "Is that where he lives?"

I nodded.

"Can you imagine living there, then coming here?" She waved a hand around the suite.

"We've got an issue."

I'd been so absorbed that it took me a moment to register the voice as Gary the dog handler's. Coming from behind us.

Turning, I realized he and Bonnie had disappeared into the executive suite's bathroom.

I carried the tablet to the doorway and saw the dog sitting, staring intently at the space under the sink, her ears pointed alertly at the ceiling. A cabinet door was open, but the space inside was empty except for some spare rolls of toilet paper. Gary stood by her, holding the slack leash and staring at the same spot.

"What's wrong?" I asked.

"That's her 'hit' signal—she smells explosives."

I double-checked the cabinet, but there was nothing unusual to see. "You sure she's not hitting on cleaning products or . . ."

Gary shot me a look like I'd questioned the faithfulness of his wife. "There was something in there at some point. That's what she smells. Whatever it was, your man must have picked it up, taken it with him."

"Okay," I said, "but El-Amin didn't come in here, so—"

"Oh yes, he did."

I spun around to find Ruth standing behind me.

"Your man stopped in here right before he left."

# CHAPTER 8

*Friday, August 10, Five Years Ago*

After seventeen twenty-hour days in a row, Clarence, my team, and I finally had a prototype of Boost to test.

It wasn't pretty: a shiny metallic container, roughly the size of a shoebox, with a mass of cabling spilling out the back. The installation, too, looked jury-rigged. Our youngest team member—twenty-two-year-old Julian, who'd graduated from Texas A&M in the spring—reluctantly volunteered his tiny hatchback as an automobile test subject after we promised no harm would (probably) come to it. We'd extracted the hatchback's stereo, mounted the Boost prototype on the center console, and plugged the monstrosity's wires in where the stereo had been. For voice input, we duct-taped a microphone to the ceiling of the car.

Julian was adamant that no one else drive—something about his insurance—so that left room for up to two more engineers. I knew I had to go, but I figured Clarence would want to ride along and see how our Frankenstein's monster behaved. When I offered him the front seat, though, he shook his head. After motioning for us to take a step or two away from the rest of the team, he leaned in and whispered, "I'm not up to riding today, if it's okay with you. Rachael was up most of the night, and my stomach's feeling off."

I looked at his face and saw he wasn't kidding: dark rings hung under his eyes, while his normally rosy cheeks had lost their color. I'd seen this look on Clarence's face before. He'd worn it several times in Asia, whenever we'd been forced to go out to exotic dinners or pound booze with the vendors. He'd bailed on enough of those excursions that the higher-ups had eventually stopped sending him over with me. It was the same when review season hit each spring. Clarence hated saying negative things about anyone, meaning you could only tell how he felt about team members by the amount of praise he offered. The lone time we'd had to fire someone, he'd excused himself right before the meeting and run to the restroom. He barely made it back in time, his face as green as if we'd been sailing a storm-tossed ship at sea.

"Gotcha," I said. "I'll ride with Julian. You stay here and track results as we test things out."

He gave me a relieved smile. "Thanks."

Julian got behind the wheel, and I strapped myself into the passenger seat. As he keyed the engine, I switched on Boost and let its operating system boot up. I had a clipboard and a pen for notes, but mostly the plan was for me to maintain voice contact with the team so they could match what we said and did to what Boost was doing as we put it through its paces. For that, I used my cell phone's speaker.

"Team," I said, "is Boost linked to the network?" One of the components inside the metal shoebox was a cellular modem that could connect to the internet like a mobile phone. The system would also connect to our internal T.E. network, transmitting a log of everything it did and experienced to our computers so the team could follow along in real time, then study it later.

"Roger," Clarence's voice came back. "Boost is linked up."

"Let's start out simple," I said. "Take us out to Pappasito's." The Tex-Mex restaurant a half mile from work was a common destination when we had something to celebrate.

Julian dutifully wove the hatchback out through the parking lots and onto T.E. Avenue, the tree-lined street fronting campus that everyone called "The TEA."

"Voice test one," I said, projecting so the folks on the other end of the phone could hear. "Boost, what is nearest Tex-Mex?"

There was a long silence, and Julian stole several quick glances over at me before putting his eyes back on the road. Suddenly, a computerized voice boomed from the car's speakers: "Nearest Tex-Mex, Pappasito's Cantina. Point-four miles."

I let out a huge belly laugh and chucked Julian on the shoulder. "Did you all hear that? Positive for search result."

"Roger, Seth." Clarence's voice sounded through the speaker on my lap. "We heard, positive result for test one: search results."

"Voice test two. Boost," I said, "what are directions to Pappasito's Cantina?"

Again, there was a long pause, followed by a loud response. "Turn left, five hundred feet."

Julian gradually slid over into the left-turn lane. When the light changed, he maneuvered through the intersection onto Wooden Boulevard.

"Pappasito's Cantina in one thousand feet on right," Boost said.

Julian followed the instructions, turning into the strip mall and parking in front of the restaurant.

"Not bad," I said.

"Do we get to eat now?" Julian asked.

"Maybe on the way back. Let's up the difficulty. Give me a destination that's close on 635."

"Movie theater?" Julian said. "Down at Jupiter Road? I met my girlfriend there last week."

I whipped my head around, giving him a piercing look. "You took a date to the movies when we were all killing ourselves on this project?"

Julian's eyes widened. I could see his Adam's apple bob.

I cracked a smile and hit him in the shoulder again. "Just kidding."

He released the breath he was holding and slumped in the seat.

"Okay, guys," I said for those on the phone, "while Julian's heart rate drops back down to normal, we're heading back out again. Voice test three. Boost, what is closest movie theater?"

"Closest theater is Cinemark Hollywood 15."

"Voice test four. Boost: Directions to Cinemark Hollywood 15."

"Turn right on Wooden Boulevard."

I nodded at Julian, who'd pulled himself together enough to pull the car out of its spot and exit back out onto the street. After we'd gone a couple of blocks, the system spoke again. "In two thousand feet, merge right onto 635 South."

Julian followed instructions, and soon we were accelerating up the on-ramp with the hatchback's tiny engine howling in protest. Near the top of the ramp, Boost said, "Merge onto 635 South."

"Voice test five," I said. "Boost, find and play 'Dear Prudence.'" The Beatles were Clarence's favorite, and it was the first song of theirs that popped into my head. "That's for you," I told him over the phone.

Within moments, the speakers sounded with the noise of a jet airplane—the end of "Back in the U.S.S.R."—and the opening guitar licks of "Dear Prudence." Before John Lennon's vocals kicked in, the system interrupted and said, "Continue straight three more miles on 635 South."

"Well," I said, "it can handle two things at once. Let's see what happens if we start throwing lots of stuff at it. Voice test six: Boost, change song to 'Blackbird.'"

Almost immediately, the music stopped, then changed to the Beatles classic.

"Voice test seven: Boost, change destination to AMC Valley View 16."

This new destination would force the navigation to turn us around. If it could handle it.

"Take next exit on right," Boost's voice instructed. Gradually, it navigated Julian all the way through a traffic light and two stop signs to merge back onto 635 North. "Continue straight for nine-point-six miles."

Since it was midday, the highway was relatively empty. Julian pressed the accelerator, and the engine whirred loudly as we veered left toward the faster lanes.

Time for some music that was a little more my style. "Voice test eight: Boost, change song to AC/DC 'Back in Black' and raise volume two notches."

In a moment, Angus Young's guitar riffs were thundering through the car. "This okay?" I asked Julian.

"Can we turn it down a touch?"

*Kids today.* I asked Boost to lower the volume.

But then a funny thing happened. The song got louder.

"Guys," I said, yelling to make sure they could hear me on the phone, "we have our first malfunction. Boost just raised volume instead of lowering it." I repeated the command to lower the volume, but it grew louder still.

"Seth!" Julian yelled. "Turn it down. Please."

But we had no physical controls to do that. When we'd removed the traditional stereo, Boost became the only input into the audio system. I screamed for it to lower itself again, but it rose even louder until I guessed it had maxed out the volume control.

Wondering whether the signals might have gotten reversed, I called for Boost to raise the volume. That had no effect whatsoever.

I glanced over at Julian, who was sweating. His eyes were wide, ticking alertly between the road ahead, the dash, and the rearview mirror. On the steering wheel, his knuckles were white.

"Sorry about the racket," I shouted. "Let's get off the highway. We can weave our way back to the office slowly."

An exit sign loomed ahead: Skillman Street, one exit before Wooden Boulevard.

The blinker started ticking, barely audible over AC/DC. But when I expected Julian to slow, suddenly the seat was pressing against my back. I checked the side mirror, assuming a car behind us or to the side was forcing Julian to accelerate, but the road was completely clear.

"Why—"

"I'm not!"

As I turned to see if I'd heard him correctly, my head got yanked to the left—even more acceleration, like Julian had stomped on the pedal.

"Seth? What's going on?" Clarence's voice competed with the music and the engine's whine.

"You're not doing this?" I shouted.

"No!" Julian yelled back.

The exit for Skillman Street flashed by on our right. So much for taking it slow.

"Uncontrolled acceleration!" I shouted at my lap, hoping Clarence could hear me over the music.

Stunned, I tried to think through the problem. The glitch made no sense. Boost wasn't connected to the car's primary systems—Julian should have been in complete control of our speed.

When I glanced up, a semi was looming directly head of us. And it was going much slower than we were.

"You need to—"

Julian yanked the wheel to the right before I could finish the thought. We missed the bumper of the truck by inches.

"Hit the brakes!"

"I *have* been!" Julian stomped repeatedly in the footwell as if to show me.

Midstomp, as his knee rose, the engine noise suddenly plummeted. I was instantly thrown forward, the seat belt cutting into my waist and chest. The semi flashed past us on the left.

I had no idea how much room we had behind us, but it wouldn't take long for someone to catch up. As I braced myself for impact from behind, the engine roared to life again. Now I was being thrown back into the seat as we rocketed forward.

"Get over!" I yelled. "Either shoulder . . . just get out of traffic!" I started looking both ways, trying to figure out which would be safer. That was when the wipers kicked on. Swishing back and forth, the rubber blades scraping against dry glass.

Annoying, but at least it didn't keep Julian from seeing.

Until wiper fluid shot up and coated the windshield, rendering everything a blurry mess.

I turned to Julian, who was crying at this point. "I don't know . . ."

Glancing around, I found the hazard button in the middle of the dash, between two vents. I punched it with my fist, and thankfully, it worked.

Then I reached across with my right hand and grabbed the wheel.

"We're slowly gonna merge over!" I yelled.

I could see Julian nodding in my peripheral vision as I watched the road ahead of us.

We must have run out of wiper fluid, drained the reservoir dry, as its stream on the windshield slowed, then sputtered and stopped. The wipers were still going—they started to scrape again, but at least we could see.

Things were clear between us and the right shoulder. If we could just get there . . .

I started pulling on the wheel, not turning too fast, easing it over.

"Light on the brakes," I said, and I saw Julian's foot move.

"Nothing," he said.

Keeping my eyes on the road, I fumbled around in the console between our seats until I found the emergency-brake handle.

The trick would be not pulling too fast.

I clicked it up one notch. Waited a second, then another.

We'd shifted one full lane right, so I straightened out. One more to go.

Another click of the emergency brake. You could feel the engine fighting it, making the car bounce back and forth as it sought to break free.

"Couple more," I said. Then I clicked the brake up another notch and continued to edge the wheel over.

We'd made it to the slow lane. Straightened again.

I had no idea how far down the highway we'd traveled, or where we were relative to campus. My only focus was the asphalt in front of us. Only a few more feet and we'd be off the highway.

"We're gonna make it, kid," I said. And with that I started to edge the steering wheel over one last time.

When the whole world suddenly jerked to the left, my only thought was, *I didn't turn the wheel* that *hard.*

That was when everything went black.

◆  ◆  ◆

I had no idea how long I was out.

When I finally came to, I blinked my eyes to try to clear them.

I was looking out the windshield. It had crumpled and spiderwebbed, but I could see green stuff—grass and trees. But they seemed . . . off, somehow.

It took a moment for me to realize we were upside down.

In front of me—protruding from the dash just above the glove compartment, was the remnant of an airbag. It hung limply toward the roof of the car, which was on the ground. Seeing the deflated blob made me realize that my whole body was aching. Not a sharp pain, more of a dull throb.

"Hey," I said. My voice croaked. "Julian?"

I glanced over and saw that his eyes were still closed. His face was bloody, and I wondered if mine was, too. I didn't taste blood. Nothing dripping in my eyes.

I checked the steering wheel, the dash. The microphone was still taped to the roof below me, while the Boost prototype was nowhere to be seen.

I kept looking around, searching for something. Any kind of sign as to what the hell had gone wrong.

Time started to register in my head, and I wondered who'd be the first to arrive. Clarence and our team, or the police.

"Julian?"

I didn't understand why he was still out cold. It seemed like a minute or two had passed since I'd stirred. He should have, too.

I looked over at him again. My vision had cleared even more now, and I realized there was a lot of blood. Like, more than I'd ever seen in my life. All over his face, dripping down onto the ceiling.

My brain questioned why his airbag had left him bleeding while mine hadn't.

My eyes drifted to the steering wheel and I saw that there was no airbag on Julian's side. Only the hard plastic, coated in his blood.

# CHAPTER 9

*Thursday, February 23*

I looked from the sink cabinet to Ruth, then to Cavin, whose face blanched.

"How long was he in here?" I asked Ruth. "Did you see him bring anything out?"

The elderly woman's face fell, and she shrugged her narrow shoulders. "They were all drinking coffee . . . I—I didn't pay much attention. I don't know that anyone did."

I tapped the earpiece. "Did you all hear?"

"El-Amin has explosives," Cooke said. "Yeah, we heard."

Although her voice lacked any trace of told-you-so, it didn't need any. I nodded at Bonnie the dog and asked, "Can she track—"

Gary the handler shook his head. "Doesn't work like that. She's not a plume dog, and even if she was, the scent's gotta be pretty fresh. This guy left here, what"—he looked to Ruth—"a couple hours ago?"

She nodded and glanced at her wrist. "It's ten thirty-one."

The back of my brain reflexively did the math: forty-four minutes until the vice president arrived. Thirty-seven till evacuation. And now we had an entire airport to search for some kind of bomb.

"Our suspect has a rolling briefcase," I told Ruth. "Did he bring that into the bathroom?"

"I . . . I think so."

Although her answer sounded more like a question, we'd need to go with it. "General, can you have them cue up video of El-Amin exiting the lounge?"

"Already on it. And Tony's got a team on the way to process that bathroom."

"C'mon," I said to Gary and Cavin, "we need to get back out there." After explaining that she needed to guard the bathroom until the evidence team arrived, I squeezed Ruth's shoulder. "Thank you. You were a huge help."

Her face brightened, and she nodded.

Once we emerged back into the concourse, I activated the tablet and saw the video feed had returned: a head-on shot showed El-Amin leaving the lounge, towing the rolling bag back toward the checkpoint. I started in that direction at a jog, my eyes darting between the scene ahead of us and the on-screen video feed.

El-Amin passed the spot beneath the skylight where Cavin had paused earlier and descended the ramp into the international concourse, the same direction from which Gary and Bonnie had come. The long, straight hallway stretched into the distance farther than the eye could see. As we proceeded, I saw that the walkway had been constructed a full story above the gates, which were paired together. A balcony overlooked each pair and the common seating area they shared. Other than their numbers, the only thing distinguishing one pair of gates from another was a huge, unique piece of artwork displayed on the wall above its service desk, providing pops of color in the otherwise-bland hallway.

As we followed the video, each snippet of footage showed a similar scene: El-Amin would enter one side of the frame, leisurely cross it, then exit on the far side, where the next camera would pick him up, and the cycle would repeat. He appeared to be in no visible hurry, his path meandering slightly. His fingers gripped the handle of the briefcase loosely, allowing it to drift closer and farther away as he walked. While certain details on his face were pixelated by the cameras, you could tell he was scanning his surroundings side to side, but not in an anxious way. More like he was soaking things in.

El-Amin's pace was so slow, in fact, that it forced us into the odd pattern of dashing several yards forward, then pausing to wait for his video image to catch up to our location. Thankfully, the sunken gates reduced the crowds in the hall, leaving few people to interfere with our progress or get curious about our unusual rate of travel. And those who were making their way up or down the concourse—young, scruffy adults sporting hefty backpacks, foreigners chatting in languages I didn't recognize—didn't seem interested in us in the slightest.

I called to Cooke on my headset.

Durham's voice responded instead. "She and Tony are helping interview the other tenants at El-Amin's house. What's wrong?"

"Watching this, I just keep thinking, he doesn't look like someone carrying around"—realizing I couldn't say the word *bomb* in the middle of an airport terminal, I caught myself—"something unusual."

Durham chuffed. "You ever see video of the 9/11 terrorists? Hell, when I was head of SOUTHCOM, you should have seen the guys from the *maras* we'd run into just sauntering down the street. Well, you know—you dealt with the Second Guerillas. Don't be surprised El-Amin isn't shaking and sweating over this—he probably practiced this run a dozen times."

Durham was right, I had dealt with some tough customers. But that was the problem: so far, El-Amin didn't seem like any of them. And I wasn't sure I bought Durham's point about practice runs. Air marshals drilled constantly for shoot-outs, but from my own experience, that didn't eliminate nerves, not completely. The little pinch in your belly, the flash of sweat across your skin—that never disappeared. How many times could you really practice carrying a bomb around an airport, anyway?

Still, this all kept leading me back to a single question: If El-Amin were really just some lowly engineer, why the hell was he retrieving hidden packages from under the lounge sink? No matter how many times I searched for an innocent explanation, I couldn't muster one.

Logically, there weren't any, unless Bonnie was wrong about the explosives, but Gary seemed to have nailed that shut.

So why then, I wondered, was I tripping over myself to find excuses for El-Amin?

Was it ego? The need to show off, to demonstrate my superior insights and instincts?

The SA tattoo vibrated on my skin in a way that seemed to resonate down to the bone beneath.

That was the mistake I'd made with Berkeley. Thinking I could handle things alone. Believing I was so much smarter than everyone else. Sarah Allen had paid the ultimate price for my arrogance, and now I'd never see her smile or smell her hair or feel her skin again. She wasn't the only one who'd suffered for my sins on that case, but hers was the loss that I couldn't . . . no, wouldn't, forget.

Back on-screen, El-Amin reached a stretch of hallway that included restrooms and two restaurants on one side and a series of stores on the other. After glancing to both sides, El-Amin entered one of the shops, a Hudson News that had far more food, beverages, and souvenirs on display than newspapers or magazines.

Whoever was controlling the video must have pressed "Fast Forward," as El-Amin began ricocheting around inside the store like a pinball. Gary and Cavin peered over my shoulder as our suspect chose one, two, and then three bags of food before moving to the register. Apparently, he had a thing for dark chocolate and beef jerky.

"Dumbass," Cavin said, loud enough for me to hear.

"What do you mean?"

"My first job in the airport was working in one of these places," she said. "Do you know how much they mark that stuff up?"

"Jeez, Carla," I said, "TSA, the lounge, a newsstand? Is there any job in this place you haven't done?"

"Firefighter. I applied, but they said I'm too short." She shook her head. "Anyway, your guy lives in that tiny hole in the city, but he comes here and blows his money on overpriced candy? That doesn't make any sense. It's not like he found out about this trip last night—why not go to the grocery store?"

My cheeks warmed at the memory of buying overpriced snacks before a flight . . . many times. But as I watched El-Amin zip to the register, pay, and then emerge from the store, something about that struck me. "He didn't get a receipt."

"So?" Cavin asked.

I pressed the button on my headset. "General, did you see that, on the video?"

"I saw him walk out."

"You need a receipt to get reimbursed." That was why I'd never been too concerned about paying a little extra back in my engineering days: as long as I got a receipt, it wasn't coming out of my pocket.

"Well, if he was never going back to Magnet . . ."

"Exactly," I said.

I heard a grunt, and Tranh's voice reappeared on the line. "You notice he paid by credit card. Unless it's a corporate card, Visa's gonna have a hard time collecting on that when he's in paradise."

"No one has corporate cards anymore," I said, "not guys at El-Amin's level." I'd been several steps up the food chain, and I'd never been issued a card whose bill the company paid. Those were ancient history, like dinosaurs, company cars, and pension plans. Nowadays companies made you lay out the cash first. If you forgot to ask for reimbursement—or if you completed the forms wrong or forgot a receipt or any other number of excuses—you'd essentially given the company a free loan.

"I don't know that this is a suicide mission, guys," Cooke said. "That's an awful lot of food if you're thinking you've only got a couple of hours left to live."

"Or it's one big last meal," Tranh said.

On the tablet, El-Amin was moving again at a snail's pace. After circling the group tables that clogged the floor outside the newsstand, he skirted around the automatic walkways that began just after them, determined, it seemed, to take as much time as possible.

That allowed me to ask Cooke for an update. "Anything from the roommates?"

"Nothing good," she said. "They said he was barely there, kept to himself. They never saw any friends, or significant others. He treated it like a hotel—come in, sleep, leave again."

"He lived there for months, though, right?"

"Years," she said. "It's been his only address in San Francisco."

El-Amin drew up to the balcony overlooking Gate 98, seemingly to admire the giant mural that overlooked the waiting area. We paused there, too.

"This guy's hardened," Durham said, swallowing the *r* again. "He's been building toward this for a while."

The line went silent, and I pictured Cooke's lips spreading into the grimace she wore when she remained unconvinced. "That's a risk, sure," she said. "But I can't say for certain yet—not until I see more data. For now, from what we've seen, he seems to be a loner."

Durham said, "He's got one partner: whoever smuggled that thing into the bathroom for him. And if he's conspiring with one, there could be more. We could be looking at state-actor involvement. If so, then he's definitely not the only bad guy strolling around the airport."

"We need to interview the family," Cooke said. "They're our best shot at understanding why he's doing this and what his target is. Where do we stand on that?"

"San Diego PD's pulling up at their house now," Tranh said.

# CHAPTER 10

It felt awkward watching El-Amin on one half of the tablet screen while Cooke questioned his family on the other. At least there was audio this time, so I could hear Cooke's questions and their answers.

The interview was being streamed from a small sitting room inside the family's house. The camera pointed across a cocktail table at El-Amin's parents on a sofa. The father, introduced as Hamad, looked to be somewhere in his sixties, with a feathery white beard that stretched down below the neck of his shirt and made his olive complexion seem darker. Age spots the size of coins dotted his bare scalp. Clad in a blue button-down shirt and dark slacks, he had his legs crossed, hands clasped around a knee. Hamad's shoulders rocked, giving him the appearance of nodding. To his left, El-Amin's mother, Zinah, sat motionless, arms at her sides with her shoulders pressed against the back of the couch. Her hair, jet black with hints of gray, fell below the shoulders of her purple dress, and thick-rimmed glasses balanced on her nose.

Two significantly younger women stood behind the parents. Hamad introduced them as Anah's sisters, Sonia and Nadia, but didn't clarify which was which. Although visible only from the waist up, both were dressed more casually: one in a blue UCLA T-shirt with yellow letters had a long ponytail draped over her shoulder, while the other wore a white tank and had a pixie cut accented with blonde highlights.

Cooke started by consoling them all, noting how worried they must be, and assuring them that we were doing everything we could to find Anah. "When did you last hear from him?"

"Several weeks ago," Hamad said. "Perhaps two months. He is very busy."

Zinah gave the camera a proud smile. "He is a good brother and son. He works hard to send money each month to help us."

"What does he pay for, Mrs. El-Amin?"

"The money helps his sisters with their education. And me with my health."

Behind the sofa, the sister in the UCLA T-shirt dropped her chin to her chest.

"Have you been sick?"

"I have chronic kidney disease."

"I'm so sorry to hear that," Cooke said.

Zinah raised her chin. "I am in treatment. I am fighting."

"How much does Anah send you each month?"

"Six thousand dollars."

"Wow, that's generous," Cooke said. "That must not leave him much, living in an expensive city like San Francisco."

Hamad's face grew stern. "Anah is a very important engineer at Magnet. That is why all this has happened—someone will be seeking a ransom for him."

"We're doing our best to figure out if that's the case. You mentioned he's been busy. Has he been under a lot of stress? Has he seemed happy when you've talked with him? Or upset?"

"Of course, he is happy," the father said. "He has a good career. Companies like Magnet ask you to work hard—that is why they pay so well. Anah has a loving family. What more could he need?"

"What do you think, Mrs. El-Amin?" Cooke asked. "Sometimes I've noticed that sons tell their mothers different things than they tell their fathers."

Hamad's eyebrows rose, but the camera focused on Zinah, who beamed. "Anah is growing up. He works hard. He has come back to his faith. We . . ." She put a hand to her chest. "I would prefer if he started a family of his own. But there is still time."

"What do you mean by 'coming back' to his faith?" Cooke asked.

"When Anah was a teenager, in high school and university, he was not so religious. Children rebel." Zinah shot a look over her shoulder at the sister with the blonde highlights. "But in the last year or two, Anah has been saying his prayers, living halal. He is no longer a child; he is growing into a fine man. Like his cousin was."

"His cousin?"

Hamad gestured to his right. Behind the sisters, small Iraqi and American flags had been hung side by side on the wall, flanked by portraits. The picture on Zinah's side showed the first President Bush; the portrait Hamad was gesturing to showed a dark-haired man I didn't recognize. The camera zoomed in momentarily, allowing us to see that the man was wearing military fatigues. A black ribbon was draped diagonally across one of the upper corners of the frame.

"Alaa, my brother's son," Hamad said softly, after the camera had panned back out. "When the Iraq war started, he enlisted in the Marine Corps. He said he would fight for our new country and help free our old one."

"When did he die?" Cooke asked.

"In 2008. In Basra."

"Were he and Anah close?"

"Yes. Alaa was ten years older, so Anah always admired him. Anah was in high school when he was killed."

"Going back, Mrs. El-Amin, you mentioned Anah starting a family. We couldn't help noticing he lives in a well-known gay neighborhood . . ."

Zinah shook her head definitively. "Our son is not homosexual."

"He has no time for romance," Hamad said. "He chose the place to live because it is close to his office."

I'd spent enough time in the Bay Area to know the trip from downtown San Francisco to Redwood City was anything but close or fast. I guessed his commute couldn't have been less than an hour.

Behind the parents, the two sisters traded glances.

"Anah simply has not met the proper woman yet," Zinah said. "With his work, his travel, it is not the correct time. But he is still young—we did not have Anah until I was twenty-eight and Hamad was thirty-two."

"Has he made any new friends or talked about anyone new lately?" Cooke asked.

"No one I recall," Zinah said.

Hamad shook his head. "He is too busy for frivolous things."

Cooke asked a few more questions, including trying to get the sisters to speak up, but they refused. When it appeared that the interview was concluding, Zinah raised a finger.

"I—" Her voice cracked, and she noticeably paused and swallowed before continuing. "I do not know why someone would have done this thing to our son. He is a fine boy."

With that, tears began streaming down her face, and she turned to her husband, who put his arm around her and pulled her close.

"Please find him," Hamad said. "Find our son, and punish whoever has done this."

With that, the feed went dark. All my tablet showed was El-Amin still leaning against the rail over Gate 98.

"Well," Durham said, "I didn't see that coming. The Gold Star family angle."

"Did you get all that, Seth?" Cooke asked.

"Yeah," I said. "He's keeping secrets."

"But not from the sisters, did you notice? They know what's going on—we need to get them alone."

Tranh was saying he'd direct the San Diego police to do just that when El-Amin stirred on my tablet screen. He pulled out his cell phone, manipulated it, then jammed it back into his pocket. Pushing himself away from the balcony railing, he grabbed the rollaboard's handle and started away from Gate 98.

"Walker," Durham said, "the time stamp on the video matches the last appearance of the address thing you asked about."

"His MAC address? So, he took his phone off Wi-Fi right there . . . So much for keeping in touch. Do we have the carrier's data yet?"

"Soon, supposedly."

Cavin, Gary, Bonnie, and I began following El-Amin's path once more. As we passed another pair of gates, Gary gestured forward. "We're coming to the end of International."

I saw what he meant: a dozen yards ahead, the concourse culminated at a final set of four gates.

On-screen, El-Amin showed no sign of stopping—he stalked past the entrance to another airline lounge, then an electronics store. For the first time, he seemed intent on getting somewhere.

Lowering the tablet, I started to jog, and without a word, the others joined in behind me. As the end of the concourse loomed, the hallway widened, making room for a fancy leather-boothed restaurant on the left and an upscale juice bar on the right. The latter filled the air with the shrill whir of blenders and the sickly sweet smell of honeydew melon. At the center of the space, a pair of escalators stretched down to a waiting area that appeared to serve all four gates. A balcony circled the moving stairs, creating a large atrium.

Although the lighting here was dimmer than the rest of the concourse, a harsh glare from outside bled through the tinted windows that lined the far wall, making me squint. Outside them, a small open-air statue garden and patio had been built overlooking the final gates.

Shielding my eyes with my hand, I could see small tables out on the patio, along with silhouetted people admiring the statues and watching the planes move around. These gates served the really big birds, the 747s, the Dreamliners, all of which required extralarge jetbridges.

Back on-screen, El-Amin looked like he was making for the escalators, but at the last moment, he veered right, slowing to take a seat at one of the wooden booths near the juice bar.

"He's stopped on the video," I said into my headset. "Fast-forward—let's see what he does next."

With the booths still several yards away from us, I accelerated my pace to a near-sprint, my Vans slapping the floor as I pulled away from the others.

The clock on the video showed maybe ten minutes of real time elapsing as El-Amin sat at the booth. He checked his phone, then put it away. He fiddled with the briefcase under the table. Finally, he rose from his seat.

I reached the mouth of the booth as El-Amin was walking away from it in the video. For the first time, our paths directly intersected— he crossed the exact spot where I was standing, and for a moment it felt like having a ghost pass through me.

I didn't have time to process that, or to do anything else, before Gary and Cavin caught up. Bonnie seemed excited from the run, panting and sniffing all over the place.

After scouring the floor around our feet, she made for the booth. Tail wagging, her head and shoulders disappeared beneath the table. I half expected her to come back out with crumbs all over her nose from some dropped pastry from the juice bar. But she didn't come back out at all. As I watched her rear end, Bonnie's tail suddenly stopped moving. Her bottom dropped to the floor, her shoulders rose, and she sat erect, ears pointed skyward.

I knelt to one side and peered into the shadows.

There, barely visible, attached to the underside of the table, was a small unmarked box.

# CHAPTER 11

*Saturday, August 11, Five Years Ago*

After the crash, the hospital discharged me faster than I expected. Twenty-four hours of observation—enough time to confirm I wasn't bleeding internally. And for my bruises to really start hurting.

I now had lines painted across my chest and waist, eggplant-purple shadows of the seat belt and shoulder strap. My face looked like I'd taken up mixed martial arts extremely unsuccessfully, while my stiff, creaky movements were better suited to a man of eighty-seven than twenty-seven. But even as every part of me stung and stabbed, I knew how lucky I was. If things had been even the slightest bit different, I'd have been the one unconscious in intensive care instead of Julian.

It should have been me.

It was my team, my project. My people. I should have suffered the consequences of what we were trying to accomplish.

When I was growing up, my father the navy officer reiterated one thing above all else: you had to take care of your people. In his case, it was his enlisteds, the men and women who'd trusted him with their lives on mission after mission, deployment after deployment. And yet I'd managed to put the youngest member of my team in a hospital bed our first time out.

That was why when the doctors said I could go, there was zero doubt where I was headed.

The taxi couldn't pull onto campus—authorized vehicles only—so it dropped me at the gatehouse. Manny looked me up and down with an expression that confirmed I looked as bad as I felt. Thankfully, he took pity and saved me the long, hobbling walk to our lab by radioing a groundskeeper to give me a ride.

Once I reached the building, I still had to get to my second-floor office. Wishing the pain meds worked better, I awkwardly bent to the security panel, beeped myself in, then took the elevator upstairs.

Although my office was only a few doors from the elevator, the walk seemed endless. When I finally reached the door and flipped on the lights, I hung my head at what I saw: someone had delivered a giant cardboard box and deposited it squarely in the middle of my desk. The thing was so big, it left me no workspace, yet lifting and moving it in my condition seemed like a Herculean task.

I hobbled across the room, checked the box's return address, and realized it was Michael's birthday gift, a radio-controlled race car. This was no cheap toy—I'd seen a mock-up of it at the Consumer Electronics Show earlier in the year and knew it would be the perfect surprise for him.

Now it just stood in the way.

I managed to circle the desk and lower myself into my chair, causing all the aches and pains to flare momentarily before dying back down. I promised myself I wouldn't move again until I was completely finished here.

On my computer, I clicked through to the shared network drive where Boost's operations history had been stored. It was a huge file—even though our test had only lasted fifteen, maybe twenty, minutes, the log went on for tens of thousands of lines. As I loaded it onto the larger of my two monitors, the text seemed strangely small and fuzzy. I was going to need to enlarge it to work with it.

I was starting to do that when a soft knock sounded at my door. Clarence stood there, shoulder against the doorframe. "I didn't know they were releasing you. You should have called."

I shook my head and turned back to the monitor. "I figured you were busy with the family after spending last night at the hospital. I grabbed a taxi."

"I heard. Manny called me, worried about you. I really wish you'd have let me drive you." He took two steps into the room and folded his arms across his chest. "And I wish you'd go home and rest instead of coming straight back to work."

"Are you kidding?" I said. "Julian's in a coma, he almost died. We need to—"

"*You* almost died, Seth. You were in that car, too."

"All the more reason to figure this out. We've only got twenty days—"

Clarence took another step forward. "I can work on it. Why don't you let me take you back to your apartment? You can sleep, or do something to relax."

"I can't relax."

The words came out in a nasty little burst. I took a deep breath and tried to soften my tone. "There's too much to do. This is too important, too much riding on it."

Clarence blew some air through his nose like he did when he was frustrated. "It's one thirty," he said. "I'm getting you at four and bringing you to my house. If you won't listen to me, I know you'll listen to Shirley."

The concern on my mentor's face was obvious. And he was right, no one crossed Shirley. "Okay. But give me a couple hours to plow through this. I have to know what happened."

Finding where in the log things went wrong was the easy part. I started at the end and worked my way backward until I found the odd behaviors we'd observed. The songs I'd requested were in there. So were the volume-control commands. As I'd suspected, Boost had somehow gotten its volume signals reversed—when I told it to get quieter, it went louder. That would be simple enough to fix, although I didn't know why it had broken in the first place.

The entertainment problems, though, were the least of my worries. Somehow, the car's fundamental systems—the accelerator, the brakes, even the wipers—had been affected. That simply shouldn't have been possible.

In the old days, cars relied on mechanical controls for everything. When you stepped on the brake pedal, it exerted pressure on a fluid line that caused the brake pad to squeeze against the wheel, and the car would slow down. Nowadays, though, those systems were augmented by electronics. Antilock braking, auto-braking for obstacles . . . all that functionality, together with the transmission, the steering, and any many of the car's other vital systems, were controlled by computers.

Not surprisingly, those computers needed a way to talk to each other—you didn't want the accelerator fighting the brakes—so the car companies linked them together through a network called the CAN bus. Because the CAN bus contained such critical core features, automakers deliberately isolated it from the entertainment system and other systems within the car. When designing Boost, we'd preserved that distinction—Boost had zero connection to the CAN bus.

So, how had Boost affected systems it wasn't connected to?

I scanned the entirety of the Boost operations log and didn't see anything indicating a connection to the CAN bus. Theoretically, there could have been a short circuit, or some other kind of electrical event that let Boost affect the CAN bus, but the odds of that happening seemed astronomical.

What I needed to look at were activity logs from the CAN bus computers, but I didn't have access to those.

I punched a button on my phone that was programmed to speed-dial Clarence's extension.

"Done already?" he asked. "That was fast."

"No, I have a question: Do we have readouts from the computers in Julian's car? Not just Boost, I mean the other systems."

"We never even thought about pulling that data. We were a little busy getting you two to the hospital."

"Where's Julian's car now?" I asked. "Where did they take it after the accident?"

"No idea," Clarence said. "It was totaled, so I'm guessing the police hauled it away."

*Dead end.* I hung up the phone and slammed my fist on the desk, which sent a shock wave through every part of me that was sore, including my head.

There had to be something else, something I was missing.

I went back over Boost's activity logs three more times, until my eyes were screaming in their sockets, before I saw it. It felt like someone was jabbing my brain with something sharp, but there it was, in black and white on the screen. Boost wasn't talking to the CAN bus, but it was repeatedly reaching out to a computer chip I knew nothing about: the V9500.

*What the hell is the V9500?*

A little online research, and suddenly things started to make more sense. The V9500 was a microprocessor, a smart CPU chip that controlled lots of minor systems inside the car. As a safety precaution, the V9500 was wired so it couldn't issue commands over the CAN bus. But it could *listen* to the CAN bus. And if it could listen, that meant it had a connection. If the V9500 chip were malfunctioning, perhaps it had caused the crazy glitches we'd seen.

That prompted another question, though: Why was Boost talking to the V9500 chip at all? I certainly hadn't authorized that—if anyone had asked, I would have told them to keep Boost as far away from the CAN bus as possible.

Fortunately, I knew exactly where to look for the answer: our source code, the computer instructions the team had written that specified exactly what Boost could do and when.

Although we referred to "the code" as if it were a single, monolithic thing, in reality, the source code was composed of thousands of smaller individual computer files, each of which outlined a particular action Boost could take. For Boost to raise the volume on a song, for example, the system would receive a voice command and analyze it using several different source-code files. Once Boost realized the context of the command, it would retrieve—or "call"—the file for raising the volume and follow the instructions inside it.

The Boost source code contained tens of thousands of files. While different engineers from our team had drafted different files, all had to cooperate seamlessly. To make sure we could track down whoever had written a particular file in case it had problems, each one was "signed" by the engineer who'd authored it. In addition, the author of a particular file would insert "comments"—plain-English notes explaining what he or she intended the file to do, why, and how. If I could isolate the source-code file that was talking to the V9500 chip, I could check those comments or, worst case, track down whoever wrote it.

Finding this particular file proved tricky—every time I thought I'd identified the correct one, I'd open it up and find that it cross-referenced something else. Finally, after what seemed like a hundred false starts, I opened a file that didn't call any others. I scanned through the instructions inside the file, and, sure enough, there were references to the V9500. In fact, the file's instructions caused Boost not only to contact the V9500 chip, but also to ask the V9500 to rewrite itself. The rewrite appeared to give the V9500 additional privileges on the CAN bus, including letting the chip issue commands instead of merely listening.

I found myself blinking harder and harder as I scanned my way through the file. This was what had caused all the problems—the V9500 had been able to issue commands to the accelerator, the brakes, the wipers. Every malfunction we'd experienced had come from the V9500 chip.

It got worse.

The V9500 wasn't issuing those commands randomly. It wasn't even creating the commands itself. It was passing them on from Boost's cellular modem.

When we designed Boost, we'd added the modem to allow Boost to talk to the internet and retrieve data from it, but we'd built in security measures and firewalls to prevent someone from hacking in and telling Boost what to do. This single file overcame all those protections. It was what hackers would call an "exploit," or the media would call a "back door": a direct line of access by which someone could remotely control the car.

I skipped to the bottom of the file but found no comments from the engineer who'd authored it. While not completely unprecedented, that was pretty rare. Computer Science 101 taught you to add at least a brief explanatory note for each piece of code. The fact that the author hadn't done so made this file's performance no accident.

It was sabotage.

I scrolled back to the top to see who'd authored the file. More specifically, to learn which member of my team had tried to kill me, and might have already killed poor Julian.

I rechecked the signature five times to ensure my aching eyes weren't playing tricks on me, that my screaming headache wasn't making me see things.

I'd just finished reading the words *Aiken_Clar* for the fifth time when a soft knock came at the door.

"Hey," Clarence said, "it's four o'clock—you ready to go?"

# CHAPTER 12

*Thursday, February 23*

As my eyes fixed on the box beneath the juice-bar booth, everything else receded.

Only a few inches long, maybe an inch tall, it was the approximate size of a paperback novel. In a flash, the many thoughts that had been plaguing me since Lavorgna grabbed me at LAX—questions about El-Amin, memories of Sarah, T.E., and Clarence—all melted away. There was peace in the clarity of it, a serene kind of quiet. For once, I had only a single thought in my head: get rid of that damned thing.

The calm didn't last long. That simple imperative quickly blossomed into a thousand questions. What kind of device was it? How would it be triggered? What was the power source? What sort of explosive? How had El-Amin attached it to the table?

Adrenaline, usually my friend, surged into overload. For a moment, I feared that my brain was about to pull one of its stunts, spiraling off in a million different directions and leaving me incapable of doing almost anything.

Going catatonic with my face a few inches from an explosive device would have been less than ideal.

After the initial rush, though, my mind cleared. I focused on one question: Could the little box be detached from the table?

"Seth? Seth! What the *fuck* are you doing?"

Cooke wasn't usually the swearing type. We've been on the radio in the middle of a live firefight and I think the worst I ever heard from her was a "hell." Her "fuck" cut through the haze.

"I've gotta get rid of this thing, Melissa. We don't know when—"

"Are you insane? You don't know anything about bomb disposal."

"Bombs are just one big circuit. I know more about circuits than anybody else here."

"Tranh's got people on the way," she said. "Specialists. Let them handle it."

"I should—"

"No!" The short, staccato bark in my ear hit like a slap across the face. "*Think*, Seth. El-Amin could have stashed other devices after he planted that one. We need you following his trail, not trying to be a martyr."

The idea of other bombs froze me on the spot.

On the video, El-Amin had left the juice bar and headed back in the direction from which we'd come, toward the security checkpoint and inner ring. Thinking of the crowds we'd seen earlier, my tunnel vision began to dissipate. If he'd gone back out through security, El-Amin could have made for any of the other concourses. Cooke was right—that was the bigger risk.

I squirmed out from under the table to find Cavin and Gary standing over me. Cavin looked pale and ashen, as though she might vomit. So sick, I worried I couldn't leave her here.

"Gary, Tranh's got a team on the way, but someone needs to post up here and keep people away from this thing. Can you and Bonnie handle that while Carla comes with me?"

He nodded, but she merely blinked several times as I climbed to my feet. When I opened the tablet, the countdown clock showed thirty-one minutes.

"Okay," I said into the headset, "we're back on the move. Can you cue up the footage again?"

The video restarted where I'd left it. El-Amin walking back down the concourse hallway toward the security checkpoint where Cavin and I had begun. His pace was faster now, but still not hurried. Nothing an observer would have found unusual.

"We need to make up time," I said. "Let's speed up the video."

El-Amin's movements became herky-jerky as the system started skipping frames. In less than thirty seconds, the cameras had tracked him halfway back to the checkpoint.

I noticed Cavin lagging behind and turned to find her texting on her phone. "Everything okay?"

"Yeah."

When she didn't look up from the tiny screen, Tranh's warning about Cavin's age reverberated in my head, and I questioned the wisdom of choosing her over Gary and Bonnie. "You sure?"

Her dark eyes finally rose. "Sorry. I didn't know I was going to be dealing with . . . things like that back there today. My dad's watching my son, so if there's a chance I'm not coming home from my shift, I kinda need to warn him."

Cavin's words made my chest tighten. I didn't know she had a kid. My godkids were fatherless because of me—the last thing I needed was to create any more orphans. "I . . . I'm sorry. I didn't—"

She shrugged. "S'okay. I told him. Let's go."

When I consulted the video again, El-Amin was drawing close to the security checkpoint. Although I expected him to circle to the right and head toward the exits, he veered left as if returning to the Eastern Airlines lounge. Cavin and I jogged that way, rounding the corner and approaching the sliding door once more.

But that wasn't El-Amin's destination. On the screen he bypassed the lounge, beelining instead to a bank of escalators at the far end of the hall.

"That leads to Terminal 3," Cavin said. "Eastern's domestic departures."

We approached the top of the moving staircases as the back of El-Amin's head dropped off camera. While the escalators weren't crowded, people were riding them in both directions. The regular staircase between the escalators was empty, though, so I hopped onto the metal banister and slid the whole way down. My feet struck the black stone at the bottom with a heavy slap—I looked back up to see Cavin, also using the stairs but taking individual steps as fast as she could.

There was only one way forward here—a bright hallway leading off at an angle to our right. Soon we found ourselves at the start of a long, carpeted straightaway, empty except for waist-high planters evenly spaced down its length. The frosted glass walls on either side were lined with translucent artwork; the sun shining through had warmed the air here noticeably compared to the chilly terminals.

"Show us the next clip," I called into the headset. When video began playing, El-Amin was rolling his suitcase up to the double doors at the far end. I looked at Cavin, and we sprinted the rest of the way.

Bounding through the doors, we arrived in Terminal 3, where the architecture changed yet again. Instead of straight lines and hard right angles, the terminal curved ahead of us. The older construction—formed concrete, tinted windows—remained in place, although the walls had been painted white in a meager effort to brighten things up. The ceiling soared back to two stories, making room for an upper level that seemed unused.

Immediately to our right, another security checkpoint was feeding passengers into the terminal. This was more of a jeans-and-T-shirt crowd: parents with children, couples traveling together, all toting colorful suitcases and backpacks rather than the fleet of anonymous black rollaboards we'd seen earlier. Although another exit to the center ring of the airport loomed on the far side of the scanners, the video showed El-Amin stalking straight past it.

"Where the hell is he going?" I asked out loud.

Cavin shot me a sarcastic look. "You kidding? He's getting away from that thing back there."

"Then why not just leave?" I asked. "Go jump on BART, get miles away?"

Cavin's face said she didn't have any more answers than I did.

"We've seen plenty of exits—he hasn't taken them. He's staying inside for some reason—I just wish I knew what."

We continued to follow his path at a jog, passing gates on our left, stores on our right. After about two hundred yards of curving hallway, we reached a point where the passage broadened at the junction of several paths. I paused next to a railing surrounding escalators that led down to baggage claim. An old-school, wood-and-brass seafood restaurant occupied one corner here, filling the air with the smell of frying oil.

Cavin drew up next to me, her forehead glistening with sweat but barely breathing hard despite all our running. She pointed in each of the different directions using her whole hand. "Left is Boarding Area F," she said. "Fifteen gates spread across two piers down there, plus a food court, another lounge. Right"—she pointed to a set of glass doors—"is the back side of the CLEAR checkpoint we passed in the cart. And forward is Boarding Area E, the new section. Ten gates, but lots of commercial space."

I checked the video—without breaking stride, El-Amin pressed straight ahead.

"E it is."

Crossing into Boarding Area E felt like entering an entirely new airport. As we stepped from gray carpet to patterned epoxy floor, everything brightened. The roof rose dramatically, supported periodically by towering columns, the boring white tiles in the old section replaced by drop-ceiling inserts cutting this way and that at different angles. Light poured down from skylights, windows, and LED strips mounted in the drops, while the wall facing the tarmac had been converted to windows.

The stores and restaurants, too, had been built at odd angles, jutting corners out into the concourse instead of presenting flat fronts.

El-Amin took no notice of the change in decor—he cut a path straight down the center. No meandering like before: no stops at the seating areas, no admiring the murals. He was definitely headed somewhere . . . the only question was where.

I asked Cavin, "What else is up ahead?"

"This section of the concourse dead-ends," she said. "There's one more pier to the left for Gates 60 to 69, but you can't get to Terminal 2 without going back out through security."

"So, there's an exit?"

"Oh yeah," she said. "That very first one we passed in the cart after I picked up you up."

"You mean we're all the way back where we started?"

"Uh-huh. The Comm Center is right outside the exit doors, down that little hallway we drove through."

Trapping himself on a dead-end pier didn't seem to make much sense, unless El-Amin was planning to plant some other device. Unless . . .

"Hey, Melissa," I said into the headset.

There was a long moment of silence before Cooke's voice reappeared. "Sorry, I just got my first data dump from NSA. It's got El-Amin's cell-phone tracks for the last three months, plus his BART card and his Uber account."

"Anything interesting?"

"Don't know yet—most of it's commuting to work and back, but he visited a few addresses in the city that I'll need Tranh's help identifying. What've you got?"

"Have we made sure El-Amin isn't holding a ticket somewhere else?"

"You mean on some other flight?"

"Exactly," I said. "He plants this thing, or things, then jumps on another plane and leaves before they go off."

"I don't think we've checked. I—"

"No," I said, "you're too busy. I know someone who can help. Let me make a call."

When I pulled out my phone, I saw a return text had arrived from Dan Shen, my patent attorney. It directed me to email, where several attachments were waiting. He'd done the research I'd asked for earlier this morning, after I'd spoken to Singh. With no time to look at the files now, I exported them to special software that would convert them to audio for my earpiece. If things ever calmed down, I'd give them a listen. Then I punched in a telephone number I knew by heart.

It took three rings, but she finally picked up. "Loretta Alcott."

"It's me."

"I have a bone to pick with you, mister." Although she was probably the same age as my parents, Loretta reminded me most of my grandmother—in addition to gold-rimmed spectacles and hair sprayed exactly so, Loretta's voice had a distinctive warble to it. "Mr. Lavorgna had me book a seat for you to San Francisco today. I thought you were supposed to be back home for a while."

"Wish I were, believe me. I need a quick favor." I told her we were in crisis mode and explained my concern that our suspect might have booked himself another ticket.

"One second." She put me on speakerphone, and in the background I could hear her long nails click-clacking against the keys as she accessed the airlines' computer systems. "Nope. Only ticket he shows is this morning's flight from SFO to TLV."

"Got it. Thanks, pretty lady. Hey, did that latest box come?" Ever since I'd given Loretta and her husband a subscription to one of those meal services where they sent new food each week, each box's arrival had become a major topic of discussion.

"It did, although I can't pronounce half the darn ingredients. Is it 'whooey-sun' or 'who-sun' sauce?"

"Neither, but you're close," I said, grinning. "Hoisin. It's Chinese." Truth was, I didn't care if Loretta could pronounce the food, so long as she'd eat it. Her husband's cancer had decimated their finances to the point where I'd caught her making a ketchup sandwich from the communal bottle and two stolen slices of bread in the office kitchen one morning. Ever since, I'd done my best to help without running afoul of Loretta's aversion to "taking charity." The boxed recipes were my latest stab at that. "Good luck," I said. "I'll call you as soon as I get home."

"Office romance?" Cavin asked when I clicked off.

Realizing how the conversation must have sounded on my end, I shook my head. "No, she's the mother hen who watches over all of us."

"That's good to hear."

I looked over and found her giving me a sly smile.

Signs for the final pier and the exit gradually grew visible. Meanwhile, on the video, El-Amin strode from camera to camera, a dozen yards ahead of our position. When he finally came to the intersection, he surprised me again by turning left.

"You seeing this, Melissa?" I asked into the headset. "It make any sense to you?"

"Not unless he's planning to install another device somewhere down there."

Next to me, Cavin stopped and grabbed my arm. "You hear that?"

Between talking to Cooke, watching the video, and keeping an eye on where we were going, I hadn't been paying attention to much else. "Hear what?"

"That sound," she said.

I closed my eyes and tried to do nothing but listen. I heard a distant chirping—not like a bird, though. This was electronic.

"What is that?"

Before Cavin could answer, Cooke was in my ear. "Seth, something weird just happened."

Simultaneously, both women said, "It's a fire alarm."

# CHAPTER 13

"Terminal 2!" Cooke shouted in my ear. "Area D, right near where you landed."

I repeated the location to Cavin. "Can't be a coincidence, can it?"

She gave me a hard look, then grabbed my hand and started running, dragging me along for several strides. In seconds, we'd reached the dead end she had just described. Instead of heading down the final pier, we veered out through the security exit while the TSA agent at the door waved us through. Once we'd cleared the doors and entered the inner ring, I recognized the couches from our earlier drive.

After the Comm Center hallway, we reached the American check-in desks and turned up the hallway I'd traveled originally with Cooke and Tranh. This time, we were joined by a pair of police officers who came speeding alongside us on Segways. Although TSA waved us all through the checkpoint exit, as we tried to make our way up the concourse toward Boarding Area D, the crowds became a problem. Earlier they'd been pouring in for flights, now they were flooding out. But unlike before, the policemen's uniforms did nothing to help. Herds of people streamed toward us, their faces etched with panic.

When the leading edge of the crowd reached us, it was like getting smacked by a rogue wave—it physically knocked me backward, and I barely stayed on my feet. The police had it worse, unable to get out of the way and clearly afraid of running over people if they tried. They abandoned the Segways, and we were separated by the on-rushers.

I turned sideways to the crowd, reducing my profile while sliding through the throng. While I advanced past the fishing nets and the brewery, I could tell this was taking way too long. Tranh's comment earlier about seven-minute evacuations stuck in my head—I didn't dare stop to check the time on the tablet, but we had a long way to go. The more seconds that ticked by, the closer the vice president's plane came, and the worse whatever had started this panic would get.

Strobes flashed on the ceiling. The acrid smell of smoke hung on the warm, stale air even as a shrill siren sliced through it. Between that and the sounds of the crowd, the din was almost unbearable. Yet there seemed to be no other choice but to continue fighting for every inch of forward progress.

Amid the chaos, I thought I heard my name. Glancing around, all I could see was the sea of humanity passing me by. But then my eye caught on something—another person moving against the tide. A hand waved, more like fingertips, barely reaching high enough to be seen over the crowd.

Jumping as high as I could, I made out Cavin's hair dancing this way and that. I fought my way through the crowd, traveling perpendicularly to the flow, until I finally reached her, pinned against a water fountain.

Cavin grabbed my hand again and pulled me to her right. After a few difficult steps, I saw what she was after: double doors marked "Authorized Personnel Only." Using a badge like Tranh's, she unlocked it and pulled it open a few inches. She managed to squeeze through, and I followed her, slamming the door behind us.

The door closing locked most of the noise outside. The air in here was cleaner, too, and I inhaled deeply, trying to rid my nose of the smoke stench.

Cooke was talking in my ear, something I hadn't noticed out in the hallway. ". . . on their way. Where are you? Seth, can you hear me?"

"Can now," I said. "We were getting swept away by the crowds so we popped into some service hall."

"Careful," Cooke said. "There's no way to know what El-Amin may have planted, or if he's got some other partner running around. Tranh and Durham are scrambling as many resources as they can to your position—"

While that approach made perfect sense, the timing of all this didn't. Why trigger something now, so far in advance of the vice president's arrival? "We need to keep an eye on the other terminals," I said into the headset.

"You thinking it's too early?"

"Yep," I said. "He may be trying to distract us."

Next to me, Cavin had been sucking down deep breaths of her own. "There's a way around," she said. "Let's go."

We twisted our way through the narrow hall to another set of double doors. She pushed through those, and we emerged into sunshine. I hadn't been outside since the Dallas darkness; even though we'd just escaped the heat of the concourse, the natural warmth on my bare scalp felt invigorating. The air was filled with the whir of jet engines and the odor of exhaust, but it smelled fresh and pure compared to the smoky terminal.

Concrete stairs led down to the tarmac. Cavin quickly began descending them, and I followed suit. At the bottom, she made a hairpin turn to the right. Once I rounded the railing myself, I saw what she was thinking. Twenty-five yards away sat an identical set of stairs leading up to the first of Area D's gates.

I sprinted after Cavin, but she'd built a large enough lead that I didn't catch her until she was unlocking the door at the top of the stairs. We both rushed inside, entering at the mouth of Gate 50's jetbridge.

The sharp, sour smell of sulfur stung my nose first, then my lungs. My eyes began to burn almost immediately.

Two quick turns and we were back in Boarding Area D, on the opposite side from where I'd arrived. The last of the crowds were still fighting to enter the low-ceilinged section of the pier, but from our new angle, it was easy to see why they were running: yellow flames had nearly engulfed one of the restaurants, a chicken place called Clucking Hot.

The TSA agents I'd spotted earlier were consumed with crowd control, trying to calm and evacuate those fleeing the blaze, which left no one to fight it. Plumes of black smoke rose from the restaurant, and already a dense cloud had filled the elevated ceiling overhead, dimming the light and casting everything in a gray pallor.

"Fire crew's supposed to respond within three minutes of an alarm," Cavin said. She coughed heavily.

While I had no idea how much time had elapsed, every second would clearly be critical. Sparks and embers had already jumped to the closest seating area. We had to act now.

I turned to look for an extinguisher or a hose. As I took a breath, my lungs rejected it. My chest started spasming with coughs, and I doubled over.

From that position, I glanced up and spotted a grab-and-go kiosk to our right. Cold drinks gleamed in a refrigerated case by the register. Staying low, I grabbed Cavin's hand and dragged her over to it.

Kneeling next to the case, I yanked off my T-shirt, then wedged the tablet into the waistband of my pants, flat against my back. I grabbed a bottle from inside the case and cracked it open—some kind of bubbly seltzer that foamed up and began to spill out. I tipped it over and poured all its contents over the cotton fabric. Then I wrapped the shirt across my nose and mouth and tied the sleeves in a quick knot behind my head.

Cavin dropped down next to me and stripped off her blazer, revealing a tight, white tank-blouse underneath. Two bottles of seltzer soaked the jacket. She pulled that across her face, and I helped her tie it.

Once it was in place, I backed off and saw that uncertainty had furrowed her brow.

I put my hands on her shoulders, squeezed them, and locked eyes with her. "We're gonna be okay," I said, yelling through my shirt-mask to be heard. "We stick together, got it?"

She gave a resolute nod, and we both climbed to our feet. The smoke had grown even thicker now; I had to squint to see through it. Cavin led me to a wall panel, which opened to reveal a fire extinguisher and hose.

She seized the red cylinder, leaving the coiled hose for me. I grabbed the nozzle—it had pistol-like grip underneath it and a movable bar on the top—and followed her as she started toward Clucking Hot. Several of the banquettes and planters between us and the restaurant were already ablaze, but she sprayed foam from the extinguisher at these, which tamped down the flames.

With Cavin clearing a path, I pulled alongside her, opening the nozzle and letting the water blast into the heart of the flames. The hose's pressure was more than I'd bargained for at first—it knocked me slightly off-balance—but I regained my footing and stepped toward the restaurant.

Keeping the stream focused on the blaze, I started to circle the outside of the structure. As I grew more comfortable with the hose, I began walking the water up and down the walls, trying to soak them thoroughly.

When I got around back, I found an unmarked door. I worried that people might be trapped inside, so I shut the hose and tried the door handle. Scalding hot to the touch, it turned, but the door wouldn't budge. A traditional key-operated lock sat above it.

I banged my fist on the door several times as hard as I could. Although each strike echoed loudly, nothing happened. Maybe there was no one . . . or maybe they'd already succumbed to the smoke.

Durham's "no guns" warning echoed into my head, but I didn't see any way around it. I had the Sig out of its holster in a second, and I put a round straight through the lock.

I turned the handle again, and this time the door gave way when I pulled.

I'd only drawn it open a few inches when something erupted behind it.

# CHAPTER 14

The door struck me square in the face. I saw a bright flash when it hit, and a moment later I tasted blood in my mouth.

It probably saved my life.

Thrown backward by the blast, I landed flat on my shoulder blades and slid several inches across the floor. Tongues of flame leaped out from the doorway; if I'd still been standing there, they'd have roasted me for sure. Instead, they passed over me before bending skyward and reaching for the ceiling.

A moment later the blast receded slightly, allowing me to scramble backward to a squatted crouch. That was when Cavin reappeared, extinguisher extended in front of her. As she sprayed several short bursts of foam through the doorway, the fire retreated inside. For the first time, I could see a few details of the interior: a gray industrial kitchen with appliances lining either side of a narrow aisle. While the flames still filled the upper half of the space, dancing on the counters and across the ceiling, below I could make out shapes on the floor.

*Bodies.*

I flashed Cavin a signal that I wanted to head inside. Her eyes told me I was crazy. But she laid down three short blasts of foam that knocked the flames back.

Staying low, I inched my way across the threshold until I could reach the collar of the first person's shirt. I yanked several times, but the body didn't budge—it was deadweight, and the rubber mats lining the floor for traction didn't want to let go. Finally, rocking back on my heels, I managed to get enough leverage that I moved the body an inch, then another. The flames were still rippling above me, the heat like needles pricking my scalp. Somehow, I managed to drag the body out and away from the door.

As soon I was clear, Cavin stepped in my place, hosing the flames down with another burst from the extinguisher.

I flipped the body over to find it was a heavyset man, maybe in his sixties, with curly hair, glasses that had been knocked askew, and stubble across his face. His shirt looked like part of a uniform, and bore a name patch that said "Rafael" in looping, white script. I wasn't sure if he was breathing, but a quick check of his wrist confirmed he still had a weak pulse.

Not knowing how to help him further, I set him against a nearby column before returning to Cavin's side. Despite her best efforts, the flames seemed to have grown, consuming the walls completely and starting to dominate the ceiling. Her extinguisher was clearly running low, each blast of foam smaller and weaker than the last.

After one final, muted spurt, there was no reason to wait.

As quickly as I could, I dashed through the door in a hunch and made for the second body. This one was lighter, also facedown, and had its feet pointed toward me. Although my back felt like it was roasting, I managed to grab the figure's Air Jordans and pull them out of the kitchen. I dragged them over to the column where I'd left Rafael.

When I looked up, I realized how close a call it had been. The kitchen was completely consumed by fire, and flames had spread up to the restaurant's ceiling, now threatening to reach the elevated roof of the concourse itself. Embers spewed from the flames and cascaded down, undoing all Cavin's progress by igniting smaller secondary blazes.

Given how fast the fire was growing, my brain started spinning as to how we could get Rafael and the other body out of the terminal. I knew I'd need Cavin's help, but when I glanced over at her, she was bent at the waist, hands on her knees. Her shoulders heaved as she breathed in the thick smoke. Even with my jury-rigged mask, my lungs were struggling, too. At this point, I couldn't even see across the terminal to the gates on the opposite side.

Before I could make a move, a security door to our right opened. A peek of blue sky was visible for a moment, and then a line of a dozen firefighters or more streamed in. All wore oxygen rigs in addition to their long coats and helmets. Most hurried to fight the blaze, but a pair carrying what looked like heavy toolboxes broke off and headed for us.

When they reached me, I realized I was still holding the second body's feet. One medic helped me turn the body over—when we did, I had to take a step back and turn away.

The body belonged to a man younger than Rafael. One side had taken the brunt of the fire: half his face, including his scalp, ear, and neck, had all been burned to the point where no hair remained and his skin had liquefied from the heat. It had poured off him, collecting into gobs of what looked like gray Silly Putty.

While I fought to control my gag reflex, the medic removed the T-shirt from my face, stuffed it into my waistband, and replaced it with an oxygen mask connected to a small silver tank he strapped to my shoulder. The tank felt freezing cold against my back, but the mask itself was remarkably light. Instantly, the air smelled fresher, cleaner. In a moment or two, my brain seemed to start clicking faster. I could think more clearly.

I needed info—if this was a bomb, there might be others.

The old guy, Rafael, had been fitted with a mask and was starting to stir. After a moment of sputtering, his eyes blinked open, and he flailed his arms and legs until one of the medics restrained him.

I dropped to my knees at his side. "Rafael, what happened here? What started the fire?" Although my throat was raw, I screamed the questions, not knowing how much the mask would muffle me, or how well he could hear.

"Man . . . ," he said faintly.

"Man? What man?"

Rafael's eyelids drooped, but I couldn't let him fade out without knowing more. I took his face in my palms and turned it until it was mere inches from my own. "What man? What'd he look like?"

He raised one arm toward the nearby body. "Man . . . Manolo . . . my son. How . . ."

I leaned in even closer. "Was there an explosion? Some kind of bomb?"

Rafael's eyelids closed, and his head drooped.

"Rafael? Rafael?"

I could feel him breathing shallowly, but he had fallen unconscious.

I left him with the medics and started toward Cavin, who was now on the floor several yards away, getting fitted with her own mask. I pressed the button on my headset. "Melissa, did you catch any of that?"

Cooke's voice appeared in my ear. "Some. Was this El-Amin?"

"No way to know for sure. How much time's left?"

"Twenty-one minutes. Are you okay? We got the fire crew there as quickly as we could."

I should have known Cooke was behind their arrival—I was lucky to have her watching over me. "I'll survive," I said. My muscles felt heavy, and different patches of skin had a prickly tightness to them that made me guess I'd gotten a little singed. Parts of my face throbbed from the door's impact. Still, the oxygen felt good in my lungs—a shot of much-needed energy after the effort of dragging the bodies out.

"The firemen are reporting they've got things under control . . ."

"I need to get back after El-Amin," I said.

"If you're up to it," Cooke said.

When I reached Cavin, she looked way worse than I felt. Sitting with her legs splayed, she was sucking hard on the oxygen mask. Her white blouse had gotten smeared with streaks of black soot. Ash had snagged in her curls, adding ghostly gray that, together with the fatigue on her face, seemed to have aged her a decade or two. Her gaze remained locked on her feet.

I squatted down next to her and rested a hand on her shoulder. "Carla, I need to get back over to E. You stay—"

Her head perked up, and she blinked at me several times. "No," she said, drawing her legs underneath her.

"You rest. I'll—"

Cavin glared. "No. Screw this guy." Flecks of spittle hit the inside of the plastic mask as she cursed. "He's not gonna fuck with my airport."

As she stood, I took a step toward security.

"That'll take forever with the crowds. This way." She pointed toward the nearest jetbridge.

When we emerged from Area D into the sunshine, it was like stepping into another world. Especially after being buried in that smoky cloud, everything outside was clearer, sharper, brighter. We'd left our masks with the firefighters, but the crisp outdoor air felt more invigorating than pure oxygen.

Metal steps led down from the end of the jetbridge to the tarmac. Cavin went first, and at the bottom, she turned back underneath the overhang of the building. Here, a series of motorized luggage carts had been parked where passengers upstairs couldn't see them.

The door to the cab of the little truck was nothing more than a plastic flap. Cavin raised it and started to climb inside. Still several steps behind her, I stared at the tiny thing, wondering where exactly I'd fit. I looked back at Cavin and found her grinning.

"Only room for one driver," she said. "You're on the back."

This cart had no trailers attached to its hitch, so I was able to step up on that. The roof had metal eyelets mounted on either side—I grabbed one with each hand and held tight.

Good thing I did—Cavin peeled out immediately, tires squealing against the concrete.

If it hadn't been for the part of my brain that kept tracking the time ticking down, the ride across the tarmac might have been enjoyable. The wind whistling over my singed scalp felt like a tonic. I glanced back at Boarding Area D—smoke was still leaking out of the building. Otherwise, though, the rest of the airport seemed to be operating as normal. As we tore across the concrete, planes were rolling in and rolling out. Out on the runway, a midsize jet thundered into the sky.

Although that surprised me a little, I remembered how insistent Durham had been that the airport avoid shutting down. Apparently Tranh hadn't been kidding about each concourse operating independently.

Thankfully, Cavin didn't try any fancy stops with the luggage cart. She drew us up to the base of the jetbridge for Gate 64, and as soon as she cut the engine, she was out of the cab and waiting for me at the bottom of the stairs.

"Just pulling up to Area E," I said into my headset. I hopped off the trailer hitch and joined Cavin, only to find her giving me an odd look as I grabbed the railing to start climbing.

"You know this is San Francisco, right?"

"So what?"

She eyed me up and down. "So, you're gonna get the attention of every straight girl and gay man in that terminal."

I hadn't realized I was still shirtless.

"No shirt, no shoes, no service at SFO," she said with an ash-smudged grin.

Although my T-shirt was soaked and stained, I pulled it on and we climbed the metal steps, unsure what we'd find at the top.

# CHAPTER 15

Although we'd run off to fight the fire from the base of Pier E, Gate 64 stood at the far end of that concourse. That meant when we resumed the footage, El-Amin would be coming toward our position instead of moving away from it.

I pulled the tablet out from against my back. The screen had suffered a spiderwebbing crack, likely when I'd fallen on it. Beneath the shattered glass, though, the LCD was still functional.

"Okay, Melissa," I said into the headset. "Roll it."

Images from a series of cameras sped by. This pier continued the more modern look of Terminal 3: tall perforated-metal columns at each gate supported a ceiling two stories overhead where a zigzag line of skylights cut down the middle like a lightning bolt. El-Amin stepped swiftly through the well-lit passage, stopping before he reached our position at a chic-looking restaurant whose seating extended into the hallway. Its sign read "**Mission Bar & Grill.**"

I looked up and saw the same wood-and-metal sign several yards ahead. "There," I said to Cavin. "C'mon!"

The crowd in this pier was younger and more fashionably dressed than we'd seen before. Disheveled as we were, Cavin and I attracted our share of stares as we hurried to the restaurant.

On the tablet's screen, the place was packed, and El-Amin made for the bar. One empty stool remained, between a heavyset guy testing the seams of a red Harley-Davidson T-shirt and a finely dressed woman with long blue-black hair. Her purse was resting on the stool, but after El-Amin's head bobbed once, she removed it, and he sat.

Cavin and I hurried to the same stool, which now stood empty along with its neighbors. I squatted and checked beneath the counter but found no mysterious box.

When I straightened back to my full height, the bartender was leaning against the counter, waiting. "Help you?"

The young man looked like surfers I see at the beach: twenties, blond, curly hair down to his shoulders, and a complexion that said he spent plenty of time outside. His name tag read "Shane."

I pulled up El-Amin's picture on the tablet and spun it around so Shane could see. "Did you help this guy earlier this morning?"

"Yeah, I remember him."

"Anything special?"

"Dude seemed chill enough," he said. "Mumbled to himself a little, but lots of them do that. Reason I remember him is the way he stood up when I brought his food."

"What do you mean?"

"He'd been sitting there all quiet, sucking on his Bloody Mary, when—"

"Wait," I said, "he was drinking?"

"Yeah. Bloody Mary."

"Virgin?"

"No, man. He asked for Ketel One. But that's not why I remember."

I shook my head, half wondering if the blow from the door of Clucking Hot had done something to my hearing.

"I brought his food over," Shane said. "Put the plate in front of him and turned around for a second. Then I hear this noise—when I turn back, the dude's standing up, staring at the counter like he saw a cockroach or something."

"What'd he do? What'd he say?"

"That's just it—nothing. He sat back down like everything was cool. I asked him if he was all right, and he nodded. He didn't say anything else, but I didn't really wanna ask, you know?"

"Did he seem upset?"

"At that moment, yeah. His face was all twisted up like he was super pissed. But after that, he calmed down."

"And there wasn't anything wrong with his food, right?"

"No, man. He got the breakfast wrap. That's our biggest seller. Bacon, egg, and cheese—all the grease you need to get you on your way."

"You sure?" I asked. "This guy ate bacon?"

"Yup. Dude must have liked it—he cleaned his plate and tipped me twenty-five percent."

"Did he take a receipt?"

"Dunno. I think so, because he paid by credit card."

"Hey, Seth, get a copy of that," Cooke's voice said in my ear. When I repeated her request, Shane made for the register at the far end of the bar.

I turned and looked at Cavin even as I spoke to Cooke through the headset. "Bacon? Really?"

"And alcohol," Cooke said. "Breaking all the rules."

"What the hell was he doing over here, anyway?" Cavin asked. "Wasting time after he planted that . . . that thing over in G?"

"Hey, Seth," Cooke said, "while you were firefighting, El-Amin's financials came in."

"And?"

"He's living in that hacker house because he barely has two nickels to rub together."

"How bad?"

"He's got about 200K in student loans," she said. "That, plus rent and the money he sends home, leaves him living on about a thousand dollars a month."

"In San Francisco."

"Yep," Cooke said. "Pretty tight. Hey, Tranh just walked back in. What's the story on the box at the juice bar?"

"It wasn't a bomb," Tranh said flatly. "The squad brought the box out to the safety area and popped it open. It was a smoker."

"A what?" I asked.

"Smoker. Like one of the grenades we used to use in the marines. Burns chemicals to make a cloud of smoke. Use it for camouflage, or for signaling."

"Or a distraction," Cooke said. "With that and the fire, it seems like we've got at least two of those."

"Hey, Melissa," I said, "can you show us the video of El-Amin standing up suddenly here in the restaurant? I want to see that for myself."

The tablet screen switched to video captured from the middle of the hallway by a camera aimed squarely at El-Amin's back. On fast-forward, he sat there motionless for several seconds until Shane brought his plate. Sure enough, a moment later, El-Amin jumped to his feet and backed a step away from the counter. He paused a beat, then returned to sitting as if nothing had happened.

"I mean," Cooke said, "if I didn't know better, I'd say he was offended by the bacon."

"Then why eat it?" I asked. "And why tip so heavy?"

"Exactly. I wonder if he's suffering some kind of episode," Cooke said. "Some . . . crisis of faith. A little breakdown as he violates his own rules."

On the video, El-Amin sat for a few more moments. As I watched, Cooke's words seemed to echo in my brain. I'd faced my own dark times back at T.E. Particularly at the end, I'd been desperate to escape, to go anywhere and do anything else. Like being locked in a cage that was shrinking around me—the pressure mounted until it grew unbearable. Until I would have done anything to claw my way out.

I'd escaped, barely. But if I hadn't fled, if I hadn't gotten away when I did, who knew what would have happened. What I would have done.

I had no idea what was eating at El-Amin. Like Cooke said, we needed to figure that out, and quick. But watching him there, realizing that no matter how relaxed he looked on the outside, inside he was wound like a coiled spring . . . well, let's just say I could relate.

After paying, El-Amin rose, collected his rollaboard, and stormed out of the restaurant.

"Not much help," I said.

"Hey, Cooke." It was Tranh's voice. "These addresses you circled?"

"The places El-Amin frequented."

"They're nightclubs," he said. "In the Tenderloin."

"What's the Tenderloin?" I asked.

Cavin nodded knowingly. In my ear, Tranh said, "It's a neighborhood. Downtown, near Nob Hill. Historic, but it's always been a little shady."

"Do you know any of these clubs?" Cooke asked.

"A couple," Tranh said. "Aunt Charlie's is pretty famous. But I sent the rest of the names to Vice. Far as I know, they're all gay clubs. A couple are pretty hard-core."

Durham's distinctive voice returned. "Where are we? Progress?"

"We're still tracking," I said. "Can you play the video?"

The hallway cameras picked up El-Amin as he left Mission Bar & Grill. He started back the way he'd come, toward the main part of the terminal. He made it only a few yards, though, before turning into the men's room.

"There're no cameras in there," I said, "so fast-forward until he comes out."

Images of the doorway started flashing by faster and faster on the tablet. Every man who came out, I examined for the receding hair, wispy beard, cargo pants, and light jacket. When the clock in the corner of the screen suggested that we'd seen fifteen minutes of tape, though, I worried we'd missed something. "Anybody think he's taking an awfully long time in there?"

The images kept cycling, and after another ten minutes of video had elapsed, I'd seen enough. "We must have missed him. Let's go back and do it again."

Whoever was controlling the video rewound all the way to the point where El-Amin entered the restroom. The twenty-five minutes of footage played again, slightly slower; we even went five minutes longer this time. But I still didn't see El-Amin among those leaving. "Am I missing something? Did anybody see him?"

The voices in my ear indicated their agreement.

"Okay," I said, "one more time. Freeze it whenever anyone exits the doorway."

After a quick rewind, the video jerked forward in fits and starts through the footage. With Cavin looking over my shoulder, I concentrated on the face of each man who left. We'd gone through ten, maybe twelve, when something caught my eye.

"That one, right there!"

The video froze on the image of a man wearing a black San Francisco Giants baseball cap with a well-worn brim. Dressed in a white T-shirt and jeans, he was clean-shaven. A navy duffel was slung over his shoulder.

But the ears . . . the ears were unmistakable.

"That's him—it's got to be," I said.

"Agent Cooke, am I correct in guessing that this costume change is not particularly good news when it comes to the intentions of our subject?" Durham asked.

"Probably not," she said. "But with the evidence we've got, I have a theory on what he might be after."

"And that is?"

"So far," Cooke said, "everything we've seen suggests El-Amin's living some kind of secretive, double life. Given his parents' reactions, where he lives, the places he frequents, El-Amin may be homosexual. We know his religion, like many, isn't accepting of that orientation, and it sounds like his parents likely aren't, either. If he's actively repressing that side of himself, if he's angry about it, he may be lashing out. Either at others, or by proxy, at himself for having those desires and feelings."

"O-kay," Durham said, drawing out the word in a way that sounded unconvinced.

"Don't you see?" Cooke asked.

"See what?"

"The vice president has a bit of . . . history on that issue, don't you think?"

Despite Cooke's dig earlier, I actually *did* know there'd been an election. While I personally tried to stay removed from politics, that didn't mean my friends felt the same. Ever since leaving the tech industry, I'd been patenting inventions, and my patent attorney, Dan Shen, and his partner, Brian, had become good friends. They paid close attention to the political landscape, and as the election had drawn closer back in November, they'd invited me to an event or two. I'd always politely declined, but I knew from comments they'd made that they were not big fans of this particular VP. He came from someplace in the Midwest—I couldn't remember which state, Missouri?—but he'd apparently been one of the original congressional sponsors of "Don't Ask, Don't Tell." Shen had served a big chunk of his time in the army with that rule in place and had strong opinions about the politicians who'd instituted it. Especially ones who hadn't served in the military themselves.

So, yeah, Cooke had a point about the vice president's "history."

"All due respect, Agent Cooke," Durham said, "I think you're off-track on this one. Tony, get a team to search that bathroom. He could have left God-knows-what in there."

"Sir, all the evidence consistently points—"

"Agent Cooke, you don't have all the evidence." Durham's voice boomed in a way I hadn't heard before. "If you knew what I knew, you'd see this is likely a little more geopolitical than you're thinking. What I need you to do is give me your best estimate of what he's planning to do and how."

"I understand the mission, sir," Cooke said, "and the need for secrecy. But I can't do my job if you won't give me all the facts. If you're saying there's something we haven't been told . . ."

A long silence followed. On the tablet, cameras showed El-Amin's baseball cap reaching the connector between concourses. He turned right, as if to head back toward the International terminal, where all this had begun. Cavin and I were rounding the same corner when Durham spoke again.

"Fine," he said, "clear the line so it's only Walker and the control room." He gave it a moment, then continued. "While I wish it weren't the case, we think this is about nuclear weapons."

# CHAPTER 16

*Saturday, August 11, Five Years Ago*

At Clarence's house, I actually felt thankful for my injuries. Whenever he or Shirley studied my face and asked what was wrong, I could blame the pain without revealing what was eating at me.

In truth, though, as much as my body hurt, I couldn't stop thinking about what I'd seen at the office.

And every time I did, I reflexively glanced at Clarence. Scanning him for any sign of guilt, as if I could peer into his intentions by analyzing the way he chewed his meat loaf or sipped his iced tea.

How did the kindest man you knew—the one who'd treated you like a brother, or a son—come to want to kill you?

After dinner, Michael begged me to read him a story, and Rachael started screaming, needing to be changed. That provided the opening I needed: citing the headache, I thanked Shirley for the meal, politely declined their offer to stay over, and called a taxi to bring me home.

The sun was already down when I trudged up the cement steps to my little studio. The metal railings vibrated with each of my footfalls, and my brain felt like it was resonating with them. I left the lights off when I got inside—fortunately, the red numbers on my digital clock said it was time for another round of medicine.

After washing the pills down, I flopped onto my mattress. The fog that had filled my head through the afternoon finally started to recede, and I stared at the ceiling, trying to understand what had happened.

I'd first met Clarence when I was twenty-two, interviewing for a job as I was finishing college. My brain condition had prevented me from doing ROTC like my father, much to his chagrin. That, in turn, had become a double whammy—not only did I have tuition bills he'd never anticipated, but I wasn't guaranteed a job at the end of school, either. While my parents tried to help, I passed on places like Caltech and MIT and moved myself to Indiana, where I set up residency and applied to Purdue. I hurried through my engineering major to graduate in three years instead of four, but when the week of on-campus job recruiting arrived, I was feeling the pressure. I remember throwing up before attending my first interview, still tasting the sting of the bile in my mouth while trying to answer the guy's questions.

T.E.'s interviews fell on the second day, and . . . well . . . it was T.E. Who wouldn't want to work there? I showed up five minutes before my assigned time slot to find nearly every senior in my program already waiting for their later interviews, studying everything from differential equations to T.E.'s worldwide locations.

I didn't bother throwing up this time. I was so outmatched, I figured there was no need to get sick over it.

When the door to the interview room opened, though, the interviewer wasn't some slick-suited HR guy. He was pudgy, with thick glasses and a genuine smile. Although he wore a blue button-down and khakis, he'd pulled a white T-shirt on over the dress shirt that had the words *All You Need* written at the top, followed by a series of equations:

$$y = 1/x$$
$$x^2 + y^2 = 9$$
$$y = |-2x|$$
$$x = -3|\sin y|$$

After he closed the door, I nodded at his shirt. "My dad's a big record guy. He loves 'Please, Please Me.'"

Clarence stopped where he was, hand still on the knob. "You get it? My shirt?"

"Yeah. You're a Beatles fan."

He nodded at one wall of the room, which held a blank whiteboard. "Show me."

I uncapped a marker and drew four sets of axes. Then I filled in the graphs of the equations from his shirt:

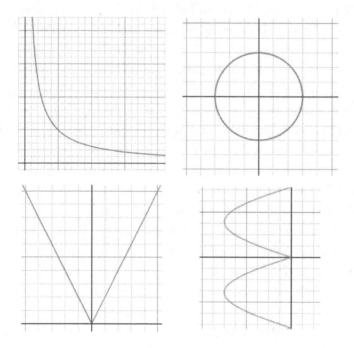

I turned around to find him nodding and smiling. "Have you seen this before?" He snatched the marker from my hand and scrawled out an equation that would change my life.

My fifteen-minute interview ended up lasting ninety-three minutes. When we finally emerged from the interview room, Clarence was stunned to find that all the other candidates had stormed off.

That was how our relationship started. When he called to offer me a job, my only question was whether I got to work directly with him. He said yes, and I accepted on the spot.

When I moved to Dallas, I didn't have a car. I flew down from Indianapolis and was surprised to find Clarence waiting to pick me up at the airport—along with his wife, who was eight and a half months pregnant. He hadn't wanted to leave her alone in that condition, so he brought her along. He made it clear from the start that their door was always open—always a hot meal waiting, or a comfortable chair.

Being loved by Clarence was so easy, so simple.

Eventually, I found out it was loving him back that wasn't.

I got the first inkling when we returned from our initial trip to Asia together. I'd gotten called to a meeting with Clarence's boss, a guy named Hendricks. I figured it was some kind of team debriefing session, but when I arrived, it was only him and me. And all the questions concerned Clarence's performance—how he'd behaved in front of the client, whether he'd taken them out drinking and shown the proper level of obsequiousness. From then on, Hendricks or someone else would grill me about Clarence about once per quarter. How hard he worked. His "dedication." Whether he could "step up."

Those guys never wanted to hear about the good stuff Clarence did. The way he supported our lab team. How he encouraged people's creativity.

But as much as I wanted to defend Clarence, he didn't make it easy. Customers and clients in Asia loved to go out eating and drinking, but Clarence was horrible at both. He couldn't see a fish with its head on without gagging; he'd try to sip his way through a single beer while everyone else was pounding shots of baijiu or sake. At home in Dallas, he'd skip social events with the bosses to go home and help Shirley with the kids. It wasn't something you could overtly criticize. Who could tell him, *You need to skip out on your family?* But after a while, the pattern became so noticeable, no one had to say anything.

Finally, the company restructured things, combining a bunch of little labs into three bigger ones. That created an opening at the top of our new lab for a supervisor. When they called me in to discuss it, I figured they'd ask who I thought should get the job. But they offered it to me on the spot. Twenty-five thousand extra dollars a year, a new title . . . I didn't think to ask about Clarence until after I'd accepted. I mean, I'd assumed he'd be installed above me, overseeing all three labs. When they'd told me I'd be *his* boss, my heart sank.

I trudged back to the lab, nervous how he'd take it. I inched into his office and stared at the floor as I told him. He didn't say anything, and my heart caught in my throat for a moment. But when I looked up, he was . . . beaming. He popped out of his chair, came over, and wrapped me in a huge hug. From then on, there'd never been any issue, no jealousy, no bitterness.

Until now.

I lay there a long time in the darkness, wondering what had changed. What possibly could have snapped inside him.

I fell asleep still wondering.

◆　◆　◆

The next morning, I woke early. Hours before the alarm was set to chime.

An idea had crept into my brain overnight—what if Clarence *hadn't* written the exploit? What if the file signature was some kind of setup?

Author signatures weren't definitive. You could sign a source-code file as anyone, and the fact one engineer signed the file didn't preclude others from modifying it. We all worked on each other's code constantly. Now, a strict procedure existed to control all that—an engineer typically left notes inside the file whenever they altered one, and they were supposed to create a new version, logging the new filename in a separate tracking document. But all that was based on an honor system; the mere fact the exploit file was signed with Clarence's name didn't prove he'd written it.

It did, however, mean he'd be the first one blamed when someone else got around to investigating the incident, like I had. And that left precious little time to get to the bottom of who'd really written the file.

Besides, I needed to know if it was Clarence.

For my own sake, I had to.

Our source code was so sensitive, so confidential, we maintained it inside a single windowless room in the bowels of our laboratory building. The repository room contained several terminals, allowing multiple people to work side by side, but the door was locked with a keypad, and only certain people's badges would open the door. For this reason, my first step would be to check the records of who exactly had buzzed in and out in the days preceding the crash.

I dressed in a hurry despite stiffness that had set in overnight. Although Manny's shift started before sunrise, I reached campus before he assumed his post at the guardhouse. I made straight for the security office, where a woman named Mary was stationed at the front desk. After a little bit of work proving who I was, which room I cared about, and what exactly I needed to know, she escorted me into a back portion of the office where a desktop computer was linked to the security database.

After pecking away at the keys for several minutes, Mary said, "Here you go."

She turned the monitor toward me and revealed a spreadsheet displaying dates, times, and badge-holders for all the entries to the source-code room. As I scanned down the list, though, all the names were ones

I recognized, members of our team. Clarence's name was listed more frequently than anyone else's.

"What about video?" I asked. There were cameras mounted inside the source-code room, as well as in the hallway leading to it.

Mary raised an eyebrow. "How far back you wanna go?"

"How far back do we keep?"

"That's the thing," she said. "We've got three days' worth."

"That's all?"

She smiled like I wasn't the first one to ask that question. "I don't know if you know about this kind of thing, but video files are really big."

While I grunted at Mary's suggestion that I needed a lesson in video compression, I knew she was correct. Three days didn't seem like much, but video for the entire campus over that period would easily be measured in terabytes. "I'll take whatever you've got."

She clicked some keys. "Oh, you're in luck."

"How's that?"

"The erasure happens at seven thirty." Mary pointed at an old-school clock on the wall. It showed six fifty-six. "That means I can give you four days' worth."

◆ ◆ ◆

Mary set me up in a spare interior room containing only a computer mounted on a narrow desk and a metal folding chair. Video for each day was divided into eight three-hour files, so I started with the most recent one and began working my way backward. Luckily, with the time stamps from the door-entry spreadsheet, I could fast-forward to the moments I cared about.

I found it in the final three-hour file, the one due for erasure in twenty-four minutes.

Mary's spreadsheet showed a door entry by Clarence at 3:55 a.m., four nights ago. In preparation for the Boost test, Clarence had been working ridiculous hours—we all had—but there was no way he'd have been coding at 4:00 a.m. The man didn't function on less than six hours of sleep.

When I fast-forwarded to that time stamp, the video showed a person entering the code room and sitting at one of the computer terminals inside. But the person looked nothing like Clarence—to the extent you could see what they looked like at all. Taller and slimmer than Clarence, the person wore loose black pants and a black sweatshirt with the hood pulled over their head. As if that weren't disguise enough, the intruder also wore dark glasses and a surgical mask, plus gloves, making fingerprints a nonissue.

In all, I watched the footage of the Clarence impersonator four times. Doing so wasn't particularly difficult: the person only spent a total of ninety-six seconds inside the lab, typing away at the terminal before standing up and stalking back out. The short window of time meant the coding of the exploit file had been done in advance. It also meant the person had some understanding of our systems and how and where to load the file so it would be installed with all the others.

All that suggested an inside job, and the impostor's efforts to cover their tracks all but confirmed it. Our security badges contained state-of-the-art RFID chips—to spoof one, you'd not only need materials and technical know-how, but also insight into the kinds of information HR encoded on our cards and how the information was formatted. Several stolen badges might allow you to reverse engineer that, but it still wouldn't tell you the location of our security cameras, or the frequency of the video scrubbing. The longer the rogue exploit file sat around in our database, the greater the chance one of my engineers or I would discover it. Which meant that the impostor was incentivized to download it as close to the time of the test as possible. But the impostor had also known to balance that against the time when the video evidence would be deleted, leaving the spoofed card entries as the only record of who'd come and gone.

*Come and gone . . .*

The longer I considered it, the more I realized I needed to look at additional video from elsewhere around campus. To try to catch another glimpse of the impostor, either before they disguised themselves, or as they'd entered and exited the building. That might be my best chance of determining who the masked figure was.

But when I glanced down to the corner of the computer screen, the clock said 7:27 a.m.

I bolted out of the folding chair, tossing it backward onto the hard floor with a loud clang. Dashing out to the main portion of the office, I shouted Mary's name, only to find her back at the front desk, helping someone else.

"Hang on—"

"No," I said, grabbing her elbow and turning her to face me. "I need you to stop the seven-thirty video scrub."

"What? Why—"

"No time to explain—please, just do it."

Mary looked back and forth between me and the guy on the other side of the counter. Finally, she gave him an apologetic shrug and ran back with me to the little office.

When we crossed the threshold, Mary slid in front of the computer, seized the mouse, and started clicking through menus.

I glanced down at the clock in the corner again.

7:28 a.m.

Mary kept pulling down tabs from the video software's list of menu items, then releasing them without selecting anything. "I don't know . . . where are you . . ."

Standing behind her, I bounced on the balls of my feet and fidgeted with my fingers. When the clock switched to 7:29 a.m., an electric charge spread across my skin. "One minute left, Mary. *Please*—"

"Please be quiet," she said.

She slid the cursor back to the upper left and began clicking through several of the pulldowns she'd already seen. At several points, she scrolled down to submenus. One time, she went four layers deep into the options.

My heart seemed to stop beating as my brain tried to tally the seconds that had passed and how many remained.

"There you are," Mary said. She clicked an option that opened up a dialog box full of choices on the screen.

I checked the clock again, wincing ahead of the imminent changeover.

"Here, it's right here," she said.

I heard a click and the twenty-nine changed to thirty.

When Mary didn't say anything, I asked, "Did we make it? Are the files still there?" Not wanting to look, I glanced up at the ceiling.

"No," she said, "I'm sorry. Those other files are gone."

# CHAPTER 17

*Thursday, February 23*

"Excuse me?" Cooke said. "Did you say nuclear weapons?"

"Yes," Durham said, "the reason the vice president is coming here involves nuclear weapons. You may have heard the Iranians are slightly eager to develop those?"

"Sure," she said.

"Well, the last administration began nonproliferation talks with the Iranians several months ago, and we're planning to continue them. This is the first sit-down since the inauguration, so the White House thought it was important to send someone significant."

"Even if El-Amin knew about these talks," Cooke said, "and I don't see how he could—"

"We don't know what contacts he's maintained through his parents," Durham said. "He could have access to all kinds of intel coming from over there. And we already know he's not working alone."

"But even if that's right, why would El-Amin want to get in the way of the talks? He's Shia. Iran is ninety percent Shia. They should be on the same side."

"Right," Durham said. "But if El-Amin still harbors the family grudge against the Baathists and others in Iraq, who better to trust to settle it than the Shias next door in Iran? How better to do it than with the deadliest technology known on earth? And, if you're wondering about Iran's side of it, think about the hard-liners. The mullahs are currently on the outside looking in. If they ever want to get back to calling the shots, they can't let these talks succeed. If they can scuttle them in some way that they can turn around and blame America for? So much the better."

"You saw his parents," Cooke said. "That portrait of his cousin. Do you really think El-Amin's out plotting to betray America like that?"

"Loyalty's funny, Agent Cooke. People hold all different kinds of allegiances these days. Maybe El-Amin hates the cousin. Maybe he feels like he'll never live up to the memory of the dead war hero. Maybe he's being manipulated, used as a stooge. I have no idea. All I know is, El-Amin comes from a faith and a family that's extremely interested in the outcome of the region. He's here, he's acting suspiciously. And, most of all"—Durham's voice rose to a crescendo—"if someone wanted to interfere with our efforts to keep nukes out of the Iranians' hands, attacking today's get-together would absolutely be the easiest way to do it."

I doubted whether El-Amin could have planned this all out himself. Something about this whole thing had seemed wrong from the start— there was some other angle I wasn't seeing. "Where are we on time?"

"Fifteen minutes," Durham said.

"We need to go faster," I said. "Faster on the video, faster running."

On my screen, El-Amin's Giants cap had maneuvered through the crowds all the way back to the junction where Terminal 3's clashing architectural styles met. Instead of continuing onward, however, he ducked into Compass Books, which stood at one corner of the intersection.

"Bookstore," I murmured. "Why the hell's he going in there?"

Durham's voice thundered in my ear. "He may've planted something. Get in there and search."

I rushed inside with Cavin on my hip. Promotional tables surrounded a central register, while stacks of shelves lined the walls. On the video, El-Amin didn't make for the bestsellers or the mysteries or the romances. Instead, he headed straight for the far corner of the store, where a sign above the stacks said simply, "TRAVEL."

I started scouring the shelves, one by one, looking for anything strange, anything he might have planted or a sign that he'd picked something up. Most of the book spines said they were about Asia—China, Japan, Korea, Taiwan. Some Europe, South America. Nothing at all about the Middle East.

On the video, El-Amin didn't budge from this spot. That meant whatever he'd done—or whatever he was after—had to be right here.

"What are we looking for?" Cavin asked.

"No idea," I said. "Anything out of the ordinary."

We both scoured the rows, then switched positions and checked the other's work. As at the Mission Bar & Grill, though, we found nothing.

When I reported that, Durham wasn't pleased. "Tony, get a goddamn K9 unit to that store. ASAP!"

In the footage on my tablet, though, El-Amin was already back on the move. He emerged from the store, and we did the same. While walking, El-Amin dug into his pocket, pulled out his cell phone, checked it, then replaced it as he turned the corner and entered the older-looking section of the airport.

"Hey," I said, "I thought there were no more MAC address hits for El-Amin's cell phone."

"That's what IT told us," Durham said.

"Okay, then he must be using the cell network and staying off Wi-Fi," I said. "We need that carrier data."

On my tablet, El-Amin turned to our right, toward a section of terminal we hadn't explored yet.

"Remind me what's down here?" I asked Cavin.

"Gates, mostly," she said. "Some restaurants, a lounge, couple of stores."

"Okay, let's get moving." We started jogging, but after a few steps, I had a thought. "Hey, Durham?"

"Yeah?"

"The, uh . . . special guests you said are visiting. They're not coming here to the terminal, are they?"

Durham grunted. "We're not that stupid."

That was a slight relief. "So, where's the meeting? In the city?"

"No, the more places these people go, the greater chance they might get seen. The talks will be held out at the coast guard station."

I pictured the SFO airfield layout in my mind. The runways cross perpendicularly, like an X. Two of the four arms stick out into the bay; the main airport is wedged on the opposite side, between the two landlocked arms. But on the north end of the field is a tiny scrap of spare land, hemmed in by the bay on one side and the runways on the other. That's where the coast guard station was located, along with some cargo hangars.

And the FBO.

I stopped cold in my tracks. "What about the fixed base operator?"

Like rest stops for private planes, FBOs offer private pilots and their passengers certain services—jet-fuel refills, restrooms, coffee, maybe a shower. In general, they are no-frills facilities. But they also don't have the same level of security that commercial airports use. I knew firsthand how easy it was to use private aviation to hop around without being noticed—it had helped me keep a girl alive last year when the Second Guerilla Army was trying to kill her. If you wanted to attack the coast guard station, the FBO would be a much easier base to start from than trying to dodge the cops and TSA around the main terminals.

"The FBO's the closest building out there," Durham said. "But the Secret Service aren't dummies. They'll have men stationed inside the FBO, and they'll be watching that building like a hawk. Same thing with the cargo carriers. They liked the coast guard building because it's so isolated."

I turned Durham's words over in my brain. Secret Service had evaluated the layout the same way I had. Maybe that was the key. For the first time, El-Amin's moves were starting to make some sense. "Carla, what's out at the end of these piers? What do they look out at?"

"Runways," she said. "Bay in the distance. Same things they all look at."

"Which pier points toward the coast guard station the most directly?"

"Probably this one."

"That's what I was afraid you were going to say."

"What are you thinking, Seth?" Cooke's voice, steady as always. A welcome change from Durham's.

"I think this is like that hillside in West Virginia. Remember?"

In our last case, Cooke and I had been forced to navigate some treacherous terrain. At night, in misty rain.

"I'll never forget it," she said. "But what does that have to do with anything?"

"We knew that climb would be hard when we started. The whole reason we went that way was because we worried the main path was booby-trapped."

"So?"

"Here, the FBO and cargo hangars are like the main path—Secret Service has them booby-trapped, and they're waiting to ambush anyone who comes that way. El-Amin, and whoever he's working with, they know those places will be well guarded. The safer play is to go the hard way—the path no one expects you to take. The security here makes it seem crazy to use this terminal as a base. But if you wanted to target the coast guard building from here, the place you'd go is exactly where El-Amin is headed on the video."

"What's the distance between the end of the terminal and the coast guard station?" Durham asked.

"As the crow flies," Tranh said, "seven, maybe eight hundred yards."

"Well within sniper distance," Durham said.

"And if we were all distracted," I said, "like thinking there was a fire in the international concourse, or fighting an actual one in Boarding Area D . . ."

"Tony," Durham said, "roll units to the end of that pier Walker's in. If El-Amin's holed up somewhere, we need to flush him out. We've got about twelve minutes to do it."

# CHAPTER 18

A long hallway stretched between the terminal junction we'd just left and Boarding Area F at the end of the pier. Although El-Amin rode one of the people movers in the security video, the moving walkways were too packed with passengers now to be of any help to us. Instead, Cavin and I sprinted down the middle of the passage, dodging the occasional dawdler and weaving around the Plexiglass cases that had been stationed throughout the hallway to display an art exhibition.

The hall emptied into a wide rotunda-like room with curved walls and a ring of skylights overhead. Models of old-fashioned biplanes were hung from the ceiling, chasing each other in perpetual dogfights. Two corridors on opposite sides of the rotunda led to separate sets of gates.

On the tablet, El-Amin didn't move toward either corridor right away. Instead, he hugged the wall to our right, which was lined with shops. After passing a hat boutique, a small newsstand, and another electronics store, he stopped outside the final place, a lingerie shop called State of Lace.

Cavin and I paused in the same spot where he'd stood, watching him on-screen as he gazed at the plate-glass windows. Inside, a trio of tall, headless mannequins modeled elaborate corsets, garters, and stockings, each in a different color.

I glanced down at Cavin and found her grinning wickedly. "Not the kind of thing you find at every airport terminal," she said. "But I guess if you've been on the road awhile . . ."

"Anybody else think this is weird?" I asked into the headset. "The gay Muslim who eats pork, drinks alcohol, and scopes out women's lingerie?"

"Cross-dresser?" Cooke asked.

"Doesn't help with the bacon or the booze."

The clock at the bottom of the tablet screen showed El-Amin standing there for a good minute and a half. While waiting, he checked his cell phone again.

"Seems almost like he's killing time," Cooke said. "Waiting for something."

"Where are we with the carrier on his device ID?" I asked. If El-Amin had left the phone on, the cell towers would be able to triangulate his position and lead us right to him, even if he were hiding.

"They just got back to us," Cooke said. "It doesn't match the device he's holding."

"Wait, what?" I asked.

"I said, the numbers don't match. The phone Magnet issued him wasn't connected to any of the airport cell towers when this video was taken."

Cooke's words sent my brain racing. There was a ton of commercial software available that would let you hide or spoof your MAC address because people logging on to the internet in public places worried about having their Wi-Fi sessions spied upon. Device IDs, though, were a different animal. Although they served an analogous purpose, the only time your phone ever used that ID was to talk to a cell tower. Because call privacy was sacrosanct, the telephone carriers had thrown a ton of money and brainpower at securing their cell networks. Hacking a cell tower was a different order of magnitude of difficulty than breaking into a cheap router at the local coffeehouse. But all that security left users little reason to cloak their device IDs.

Even if you could disguise your device ID, I could think of about ten technical problems that doing so would cause right off the bat. That didn't mean El-Amin hadn't found a way, of course—it merely meant it was unlikely. Especially when there was a much simpler explanation.

"So, he's using a different cell phone than before," I said. "But he only had one handset when he cleared security. I wonder when he picked up the replacement."

"Maybe in the men's room, when he changed clothes?" Cooke said.

"We'll need to pull—"

"The call records from the new phone," Cooke said. "Already on it. We're working on tying the new device ID to a phone number. There are only four main cellular carriers in California, and we've contacted them all."

While I didn't voice it, the question was whether any of them would respond in the few minutes we had remaining.

On the video, El-Amin finally broke away from the lingerie store. Once he started walking, he made for the entrance that led to Gates 80 through 90.

"One last jog," I said to Cavin.

Her eyebrows rose skeptically, but we began running once again.

I kept alternating my gaze between the tablet screen and the hallway ahead of us in case ElAmin stopped somewhere else. But he bypassed a wine store, a chocolatier, and, somewhat ironically, a San Francisco Giants–themed restaurant. None of the art, not even a science display from the Exploratorium, caught his attention. Instead, he continued on a beeline for the end of the pier, taking moving walkways whenever he could.

We followed his path as quickly as possible given the crowds, which were as thick here as they'd been back in the rotunda.

"Hey, Walker," Cavin said.

"Yeah?"

"One thing you haven't told me . . ."

My stomach tensed, worried which piece of top-secret information she was wondering about.

"What exactly do we do when we find this guy?"

I glanced down to find a look of genuine concern etched on her face.

"I mean, do you just . . . tackle him? What am *I* supposed to do?"

I fought off the chuckle her perfectly reasonable question inspired. Truth was, every time I'd ever done this, the bad guy hadn't left me a whole lot of options. We'd need to see if El-Amin would be different.

I didn't think that would sound very comforting.

"Play it by ear," was all I said.

Cavin gave me a knowing nod, as if that were exactly the answer she'd expected. Then, before she could ask anything else, Gate 90 loomed ahead of us. Unlike the other terminals we'd explored, this one had no fancy seating, nothing to help passengers pass the time. Just a few old-fashioned plastic-and-chrome benches beneath a final bank of windows.

Realizing how close we were to the end . . . of the terminal, of our time . . . I accelerated to a dead-sprint, only checking the tablet when I reached the end of the pier.

Durham's comment about snipers had me imagining El-Amin climbing to the roof or seeking some other secluded spot. But on-screen, he didn't sneak outside, jimmy an access door, or anything else.

When he reached the end of the hallway, he simply stood there.

Gazing out the windows. Serenely.

"C'mon, c'mon," I said into the headset. "We need to see where he sets up." Raising my eyes for a moment, I got a good look across the runways. In the near distance I could make out the coast guard building. White '70s-era construction—a boxy, nondescript rectangle near the horizon.

It seemed forever away and eminently reachable, all at once.

Back on the tablet, El-Amin still hadn't budged. We sped through five solid minutes of footage, his only movement an occasional check of his phone. Like Cooke said, maybe waiting for a signal. Or—I hadn't seen a watch—perhaps he was using it as a clock. Waiting for some precise moment.

Finally, he took a step to the side.

*Here we go,* I thought, *now we'll see where you went.*

El-Amin spun a 180, putting his back to the windows and walking again, following his own footsteps back the way he'd come.

"I don't believe this guy," I said. "Where the hell is he going now?"

On-screen, he'd already reached the Exploratorium exhibit.

"He didn't drop something, did he?" I asked. "Or plant it? I didn't see him move a muscle."

"Play it again," Durham said. "Frame by frame if you have to."

"We don't have time."

"Seth," Cooke said, "we got a hit from one of the carriers. That new phone, it's on the T-Mobile network."

"Is it still functioning?"

"No, it's gone quiet," she said. "But they're pulling texts and messages. We should have those in a minute. And a track of where he went."

"We don't need to wait for the tracking," I said. "Cue up the video feed." I turned to Cavin and looked her squarely in the eye. "Time's getting tight."

"So, let's go." One corner of her mouth turned up in a smirk. "*I'm not tired yet.*"

"It's not that," I said. "Somebody's got to search around here and make sure he didn't plant something."

Cavin's eyelids pulled back slightly, and she started to stammer.

"You can do it," I said. "You know this airport better than anybody, remember?"

She swallowed deeply, but still didn't seem convinced.

"If anyone can spot something out of place here, it's you. Don't be stupid like me—you find something, you call for help, okay?"

Finally, she nodded.

I took one step back in the direction from which we'd come. "You got this."

"Go," she snapped. "Get out of here."

I gave her what I hoped wouldn't be a final smile, then sped back toward the concourse.

"Okay, I'm moving."

Cooke's voice sounded in my ear. "El-Amin's new phone is a pre-paid disposable. Bought with cash in Oakland last week. Three others were purchased in the same transaction."

"Have the carrier and IT scour the airport for those device IDs," I said. "If we can find those other phones . . ."

"Working on it," she said.

The video showed El-Amin halfway back to the rotunda now, but I was catching up. I was passing the baseball restaurant again when Cooke screamed in my ear, "Got it! Two of the other burners went live at different points."

"Where?"

"They just gave me coordinates and times. Some were earlier this morning, but one lines up with the time stamp of what you're watching. Tony, where's this one?"

The seconds ticked by way too slowly. I'd made it another ten yards down the hall by the time someone spoke again. Tranh, this time. "Restrooms. Near the bookstore."

"There's no movement on the signal, Seth," Cooke said. "The phone flashed on for a minute, then disappeared again."

"Clever," I said. "No cameras in the bathroom. Take a phone in there, no one sees you texting."

"I've got the security feed from the lav doorway," Tranh said. "We'll check faces of everyone who went in and out."

My screen still showed El-Amin, entering the rotunda now. Although he'd been keeping up a pretty good pace, now he slowed. His head turned to the left, and eventually he stopped.

Outside the lingerie store again.

El-Amin's head swiveled, glancing ahead to the entrance to the long hallway, then back again. After a long moment, he ducked into the store.

"Oh, Christ," I said.

In my ear, I could hear Cooke and Tranh talking about facial scans. They'd identified forty-eight men coming or going from the lavatory near the bookstore. Kicking myself for leaving Cavin behind, I dashed into State of Lace.

It only took a step or two on the way to the counter to realize there were women shopping in the store. My cheeks burning, I dropped my eyes to the floor and made for the register as quickly as I could.

Although the clerk looked barely old enough to drive, the purple satin straps protruding from her white tube top suggested she'd taken advantage of her employee discount. Her name tag, in handwritten bubble letters, read "Rasheeda."

"Hey," she said, drawing out the syllable. "Help you?"

I held up my ID so it flipped open.

She straightened her posture, and the smile disappeared.

"I'm looking for this guy," I said, showing her El-Amin's license photo. "He came in a little while ago. You remember?"

She leaned forward and squinted at the screen. "He looked different."

"Maybe without the beard?"

"Oh. Yeah."

"Listen, I'm in a huge hurry. Did he do anything suspicious?"

"Not really," she said. "Seemed like he knew exactly what he wanted."

"What's that?"

"He bought this pretty little white teddy . . ." She glanced toward the back of the store, as if searching for the right rack.

"I don't need to see it," I said, my forehead feeling hot now, too. "Just . . . tell me what size and how'd he pay?"

"Extra small. With a credit card."

"Thanks!" I ran out of the store, relieved to get back to chasing our fugitive.

Melissa's voice sounded in my ear. "Hey, Seth, the records from the cell carrier came through."

"And?"

"El-Amin's phone got a single text from one of the other disposables. I forwarded it to you."

My phone buzzed in my pocket as I was reaching for it. When I pulled it out, the screen lit up with only three characters.

G95.

# CHAPTER 19

"How much time?"

I was sprinting. The sound of my pulse was so loud in my ears that I shouted the question into the headset.

"Three minutes," Cooke said. "Gate 95, that's—"

"International," I said. "Right near his original gate."

"What's there now?" Durham asked.

"Eastern 1755 arrived from Guadalajara about a half hour ago," Tranh said. "That plane becomes Eastern 1862 to Tokyo."

"Departure time?" I asked.

"That's the thing . . . not for thirty-five minutes, at least."

Durham ordered Tranh and Cisneros to get their people into International G. "Where are you, Walker?"

"Just left F." I'd nearly reached the end of the long hallway, and now I was having to decelerate to make the turn at the seafood restaurant. The aftereffects of the smoke were still dogging my lungs. I felt as if I'd run a marathon through one of LA's nasty brushfires. "Any luck on . . . whoever's using that other phone?"

"We've run everyone who went into the men's room through the facial databases," Tranh said. "Nothing."

"Seth," Cooke said, "what did El-Amin buy at that store? I didn't get to listen."

"A white . . . thing," I said. "Extra small."

"So, it wasn't for him, then?"

"We didn't have time for a runway show."

She snorted. "There's no way he could squeeze into an extra small. That means it's for someone else. Tony, pull that bathroom footage back up."

The earpiece fell silent. While the back of my brain wondered what they were working on, my main focus was getting to Gate 95. I'd rounded the corner and could see the double doors leading to the glass hallway and International G up ahead.

The gates and passengers flying by in my peripheral vision reminded me of the last time I'd chased a suspect through a terminal. But Berkeley was the last thing I needed to be thinking about now. I tried my best to push those thoughts to the side, to tell the SA tattoo sizzling on my arm to shut the hell up.

Thankfully, Cooke's voice reappeared. "That's it!"

"What?" Tranh asked.

"See the ribbon? In this woman's hair?"

"Okay . . . ," he said.

I couldn't see what they were looking at, but Tranh sounded incredulous.

"Don't you remember?" Cooke asked. "Pull up the Mission Grill footage." After a pause, she said, "See, it matches. Seth, El-Amin sat next to a woman at the counter. She went into the restroom right before the text was sent to him, then came out afterward. Asian, long hair. Wearing a dark jacket and skirt."

"Got it," I said, recalling the woman who'd made room for El-Amin to sit on the adjacent barstool. The blue-black sheen of her hair. "Almost to International."

I'd cleared the glass hallway connecting the two terminals and reached the stairs Cavin and I had descended earlier. Thankfully, the "up" escalators were empty this time. Given my smoke-damaged lungs, I wasn't sure if I could handle regular stairs.

I took the escalator steps two at a time. As I did, though, my brain reflexively flashed back to Dallas. Chasing Berkeley, I'd scrambled up a set of escalator stairs exactly like these. For a moment, all the daylight in the stairwell faded away; daytime reverted to night, and I was back at DFW.

I'd barely missed her at the top of the escalator. If I'd only been a hair faster . . .

Couldn't repeat that mistake today.

I shook off the vision and focused on the stairs in front of me. My lungs were actively fighting me now—itching, hurting, desperate to cough. I managed to overrule them, for the moment. Oxygen debt burned in my thighs and calves.

When my eyes cleared the top of the escalator, I launched myself upward, landing on solid ground. In three strides, I passed the Eastern Airlines lounge. I gave into a series of racking coughs as the ramp down to the concourse came into sight.

"Do we have . . . eyes on 95?" I asked, clearing my throat. "What's going on?"

"Nothing unusual," Tranh said. "No sign of El-Amin."

Durham's voice cut in. "We're two minutes out from evacuation time. I need to make a call—are we clearing the terminal or not?"

"Sir, if you evacuate now," Cooke said, "odds are, we lose everyone. El-Amin, the woman. Let's keep going."

Tranh grunted, his meaning unclear.

"Almost . . . there," I managed to cough out.

"All right, Walker. Let's see what you find."

I'd just passed the escalator for Gates 92 and 94, the first pair on the right. Directly ahead lay the first pod of restaurants and stores. Remembering the lopsided numbering from earlier, I saw 95 paired with 97, up on the left, closer to the end of the pier than to me.

My lungs, the muscles between my ribs, all screamed at the distance I had left to run.

To block that out, I tried to focus on the passengers ahead. Until now, I'd been ignoring people I passed, their faces blending into a two-dimensional blur. Maybe I could pick El-Amin out from the crowd. Or the Asian woman Cooke had identified.

As I started watching faces, I became suddenly aware of how many people were watching me back. Virtually everyone in my path turned as my footsteps approached. Their expressions when they saw me were an odd mix of horror and curiosity.

I must have looked like hell, an arson victim with his ass on fire.

I didn't see either of the people I cared about in the crowd. Nearly all the passengers here were Asian, so I gave up looking for Cooke's mystery woman. I'd never seen her face, after all—I couldn't even be sure I'd recognize her if she bumped into me.

El-Amin was the key.

I'd spent enough time with his picture that his appearance was baked into my memory. Even if he'd changed clothes again or tried some minor disguise, I was confident I'd spot him.

At the end of the first set of moving walkways, I'd reached Gates 98 and 93. Gate 95 was visible ahead, after yet another grouping of shops and eateries.

I slowed my pace slightly in hopes of catching El-Amin's familiar face. The duty-free shop on the left, the massage center on the right, the tables in between. A sushi place on the left, a candy store on the right. A grab-and-go market. Another bookstore.

Nothing.

No sign of the black baseball cap or the receding hairline.

No one with El-Amin's complexion.

At the next set of moving walkways, I stayed left, racing past a men's bathroom and a series of anonymous access doors. Up ahead were the juice bar and outdoor patio. Finally, I reached the escalator down to Gates 95 and 97.

My Vans made plunking noises as they struck the metal treads at speed. When I reached the bottom, I paused a moment to draw a deep breath and call "Here" into my headset.

With that, my lungs took the opportunity to force me into a series of violent, smoke-flavored coughs.

On my left, the back wall of the waiting area formed a small, sheltered hallway beneath the curved balcony of the concourse above. My eyes scanned it quickly, both for El-Amin and a water fountain, in hopes a quick sip could get my coughing under control. I found neither. Instead, a series of metal booths lined the wall, remnants of pay phones whose handsets had been removed long ago. Passengers were using these booths as private seating, but when a quick check confirmed none was El-Amin, I circled back out to the main waiting area.

The jetbridge doors stood in the far corner of the room, next to a desk occupied by a lone female gate agent. Dressed in All Nippon's light-gray jacket and bright-blue scarf, she was hunched over her computer, not paying attention to any of the passengers seated in the rows of benches before her. I strode up and down the rows of seats, taking my time, checking every face. Some brave souls glanced up at me, but most wedged their noses down into whatever they were reading, focusing on their phones, or staring at their shoes.

It didn't matter—El-Amin wasn't among them.

"All clear down here," I said after finishing my inspection of the final row. "I'm going to ask the gate agent, then head back up and check the bathrooms—"

At that moment, a noise interrupted me. It sounded like a low-pitched grunting. At first, I mistook it for Tranh in my earpiece. But a second noise that sounded immediately after made more of a clatter.

Realizing it came from above me and to my right, I looked up. That was when the first shots rang out.

# CHAPTER 20

*Monday, August 13, Five Years Ago*

Three days after the crash, my body continued to heal—my bruises had turned yellowish-green, plus the stiffness was subsiding—but my mood had grown considerably worse.

Having lost the chance to search for any additional video traces of the masked impostor when the security camera files automatically erased, I'd been forced to look elsewhere for clues to the person's identity. The impostor's exploit file seemed a logical place to start. After all, the person must have had some kind of a technical background even to come up with the idea; creating, polishing, and debugging a finished program would have taken some pretty deft coding skill.

When I thought about who might have wanted to sabotage Boost—or Clarence, or me—there weren't many candidates with the requisite résumé. The original Boost team might have been able to do it, and they likely bore a grudge after getting fired, but the chances they could have gotten someone on campus and into our lab were pretty slim. I had to think security would have been warned to watch for them, plus their badges and other credentials would have been turned off. That meant I had to consider that an engineer from my new team might have been behind the exploit. Someone tight with one of the team members who'd been fired, maybe? There were probably also other technical folks inside

T.E. who wanted Boost to fail. Zachary Scott for one, although he'd seemed reasonably nice at the meeting with Rodgers. Besides, I didn't know that his BS in computer science was enough to pull off this kind of hacking—Scott was a salesman more than anything else.

With all that in mind, I returned to the exploit file itself. Source code is written in computer language, but there are still plenty of stylistic choices when you write a program. Habits, tics, preferences—they all influence the command structure you use and how you lay out the steps the program will follow. After reading tens of thousands of lines of code from my own engineers, I could generally distinguish one person's work from another's. In poring over the work of the original Boost team, I'd seen enough of their code that I thought I could identify it.

But when I examined the hostile code again, I didn't see any hallmarks I recognized. Clarence certainly hadn't written it—his code reminded me of the way my eleventh-grade English teacher described Ernest Hemingway: minimalist. Clarence's programs were extraordinarily pristine and precise, without even a single command or line more than he absolutely needed. This exploit file . . . wasn't that. I understood the code, but the lines were much more regimented, the structures far more repetitive, than I was accustomed to seeing. The file was probably 20 percent longer than I would have expected from someone junior on my team, given the shortcuts we'd all learned in school and become accustomed to using at T.E. It wasn't that the exploit code was badly written—it had certainly been brutally effective—it just seemed . . . off. Like a really old book that sounded stilted and wordy, or text written by someone who had learned English as a second language.

I went through the exploit file over and over until my eyes ached and the glowing characters felt etched onto my retinas. But it got me nowhere. If anything, I was more confused than before—had someone bought the exploit file somewhere on the dark web? Could this have been the act of an outside competitor determined to keep Boost from reaching the market?

With virtually nothing else to go on, I decided to focus on Zachary Scott as the suspect with the best combination of motive and know-how. I trailed him home one night—his car, a bright-red BMW z4, was easy to follow—but he didn't head off to some secret rendezvous or meet any shady characters. He simply made straight for his apartment building in Uptown, and twenty minutes later, a food-delivery guy pulled up and carried dinner inside.

A complete waste of time.

And that wasn't something I could afford, since I was conducting my private investigation on top of the rest of my work. Clarence, the team, and I still had to get Boost back on track, and that challenge had only increased, with our team down a man. While half of the team was constructing additional firewalls and override precautions and the rest were working to finalize the user interface, I found myself in my office, door closed, going over the mystery time and again.

I'd watched the lone snippet of masked-intruder video so many times, it felt like I'd memorized every frame. When I played the sequence back now, my knowledge about digital video compression started kicking in: instead of watching the action, my brain focused on how the images were being processed.

What we call "video" is a series of still pictures that, when flashed by your eye quickly enough, trick your brain into thinking they show smooth motion. That idea is the basis of everything from movie pro-jectors to animated cartoons—most people understand that. The trick comes when you're trying to save all those pictures electronically. The movies we're used to seeing in the theater show your eyes twenty-four frames every second—at that rate, a two-hour movie contains 172,800 still pictures. That's a lot of digital memory.

So, engineers have created tricks to save space. In certain film sequences, not much changes frame to frame. During close-ups of dia-logue, for example, a person's mouth might be moving, but everything else around them might remain exactly the same. Even action scenes don't always involve a lot of changes: a car or airplane might streak across background scenery, for example. In those cases, we don't have to save the entire picture over and over. Instead, in effect, we save a single frame and tell the computer, *Reshow the same picture again, with this one thing changed.*

As I watched the security video, I naturally started tracking which details stayed constant versus which were changing and then thought about how those changes were encoded. When entering the room, the masked impersonator took several steps directly away from the camera—in those, the scenery on either side of the figure was fixed. As I focused in, I noticed portions of the impersonator's body—the back, the head—weren't changing appearance so much as moving from one point to another. That meant the computer was likely using motion vectors to keep the images intact while incrementally shifting them upward from frame to frame.

Gradually, my eyes narrowed in on the parts of the figure that *were* moving. The legs, the feet.

*The feet.*

Something about the figure's right foot caught my eye. I rewound the snippet of video several times, watching the figure take the same step again and again.

The shading was odd at the figure's heel. The back of the heel should have been a flat or mostly flat surface, but something didn't look quite right. With dark patches on either side, it looked almost like the figure's foot was deformed. But there wasn't enough detail to tell whether that extra shading was from some odd pattern on the figure's shoe, a shadow from something else in the room, or some other cause entirely.

I let the video continue forward several seconds. The figure rounded the corner of the table inside the code room, then sat down at a terminal.

I rewound and watched that same sequence again, focusing on the figure's feet.

Then again. And again.

Finally, I saw it. When the figure turned at the corner of the table and stepped toward the chair, you got a quick glimpse of the foot in profile, rather than from the back. The shoe had a pointed toe, and a patch of light was visible between that and the heel.

I bolted up straight in my chair, then leaned so close to the monitor I could almost see the individual pixels. I reran that sequence over and over again, maybe twenty times, and every time I became a little more convinced.

It was a high-heeled shoe.

The masked figure was a *woman*.

I leaned back in my chair and rubbed my open palm against the bristly hair behind my ear.

A woman saboteur changed everything.

I'd been assuming the intruder was a man because, well, that's the way engineering was. Our lab—indeed, almost the entire products division of the company—contained only men. That wasn't by choice . . . at least, not completely. While some T.E. engineers were perpetually awkward around women, and others likely enjoyed the fraternity-house/locker-room atmosphere, some of us would have preferred a more diverse workplace. But in some ways, it was a chicken-and-egg problem—so few women went to engineering school, it was hard to find women to hire, yet because there were so few women on the tech side of our company, women felt disinclined to join T.E.

The dearth of women led me to the obvious conclusion—the only woman in the company who had a good reason to want Boost to fail: Amara Brooks.

*Brooks.*

I recalled her sitting across the table from me. The scowl etched on her face, except when laughing at Rodgers's jokes.

She wasn't technical, not that I knew of. If she'd learned coding on the side, though, or gotten the exploit from someone else—someone foreign—that might explain the weird coding style. And once you set the technical aspect to the side, Brooks had all the other tools necessary to pull off the scheme. Having worked in HR, she surely knew all about our security badges—and probably would have had no trouble getting ahold of spares or recoding existing cards. From her time in Legal, she'd know T.E.'s security policies intimately, including the video-scrubbing timeline.

*Amara Brooks.*

The clock on my computer said it was a few minutes past two in the afternoon. That gave me several hours to do some research before she'd leave for the night.

◆　◆　◆

I knew something was up when Brooks turned the wrong way out of the T.E. parking lot.

About 4:00 p.m., I moved my little Honda over to the lot outside her building on the opposite side of campus. Thankfully, I managed to score a parking space in the shade—not knowing how long I'd need to wait, I hadn't wanted to roast in the summer sun for hours. Backed into the spot, windows down, the temperature was tolerable even without much of a breeze, and I could keep an eye on the door while working on my laptop.

Good thing I did, since Brooks didn't emerge for another four hours. The lot was virtually empty by then, though the darkness helped conceal me, as did a thin layer of yellow pollen that had coated my windshield.

Wearing tall heels and a short pleated skirt, Brooks couldn't have hidden in a crowd. Her hair was down, feathered into thick waves that hung over her red blazer, and she carried both a small purse and a large leather tote. She made for one of the only vehicles left, a black Range Rover in the front row, tossed the bags in the back, then climbed behind the wheel. I let her start for the exit before keying my ignition and sliding out a short distance behind her.

The T.E. employee directory said Brooks lived in Frisco, one of the fancy suburbs that had sprung up north of Dallas, so I expected she'd turn left on T.E. Avenue and catch 75 North. When she cleared the gatehouse, however, her right blinker flashed, sending her in the opposite direction.

Brooks drove fast: she sailed down T.E. Avenue at least ten miles over the limit, and once she steered up onto 75 South, she really hit the gas. Enough traffic had cleared that she was able to weave down the highway, passing car after car. Sticking with her as she zigged and zagged from lane to lane was tricky, but as the pursuit wore on, I grew bolder, certain that darkness would keep her from recognizing me as I followed.

When we turned onto the Woodall Rodgers Freeway, downtown Dallas's skyline glittered ahead, and I guessed that was our destination. Brooks's blinker confirmed it when she exited at North St. Paul Street. After crossing back over the highway, she steered through the stone-and-steel skyscrapers before finally slowing at an entrance on North Akard. The sign said this was the Freemont Hotel. Although I'd never stayed here, I'd heard the name.

The Freemont's driveway was cut into the side of the building like a tunnel, shielding it from the sidewalk and the elements. Once you pulled in off the street, the driveway curved around to a valet stand at the far end. The entire wall facing the driveway was glass, revealing a warmly lit, wood-paneled lobby inside.

Brooks pulled her SUV all the way up to the stand, where an attendant was hovering on the curb. I hung back at the mouth of the driveway, my Honda's trunk still poking out into the street, until she dropped her keys into the guy's palm and started inside. Once she rounded the front bumper, I gunned the Honda forward, stopping inches short of the Rover's rear end.

While the attendant took down my particulars, I kept my eye on Brooks inside at the front desk. She spent only seconds there, then made for the elevators behind registration. As soon as the valet finished with me, I dashed inside and headed straight for the elevator bay, arriving in time to see one set of doors sliding shut.

The floor indicator above those doors rose gradually to fourteen before stopping. I hopped onto a neighboring car and pushed the "14" button, noting it was the uppermost floor, the hotel having skipped "13" entirely.

My muscles grew increasingly twitchy as the elevator beeped its way upward. When we reached fourteen, though, the doors didn't open. Instead, a second set of doors at the rear of the car parted.

I backpedaled into the hallway and glanced quickly to both sides. Although Brooks was nowhere to be seen, a loud clunk at one end sounded like a room door closing. I started in that direction, tiptoeing until I realized the thick carpet would mask the sound of my footsteps.

For some reason, room doors were only disposed on one side of the hallway here. But even halving the number of rooms didn't help—when I reached the end of the passage, it was impossible to tell which of the final pair of doors was the one I'd heard shut. I checked the peepholes for signs of light or movement inside, but they appeared identically dim.

That left me standing there, pondering my next move.

Brooks had received a key way too quickly to have checked in. She hadn't presented a credit card or even dug into her purse at the front desk. That suggested she was joining someone.

Could it be whoever had helped her sabotage Boost?

While that possibility seemed too good to pass up, it left me wondering how I could figure out who was inside with her. I could try to wait and see who eventually emerged from the room, but there was no telling when that would happen—the leather tote Brooks had been carrying was large enough to be an overnight bag. I doubted I could loiter in the hallway for long without provoking hotel security.

Was there a way to see inside the room? I thought about the skyscrapers on the surrounding blocks, but I had no clue whether any were hotels, and anyway, obtaining a room that looked out in exactly the right direction seemed impossible. I didn't even know what the side of the Freemont building looked like, let alone how you'd pick out which room was which.

If it was a matter of staking things out, doing so in the lobby seemed a safer bet—security still might hassle me, but I could come up with some story about who I was waiting for and why. With my brain still spinning on that, I returned to the elevators and stepped back into the same car that had delivered me upstairs. After I pressed "L," my eyes were drawn to a small screen above the floor selector. It was showing a series of videos about the hotel's amenities on a nonstop loop. I'd only half noticed it on the ride up, but now I watched as slow-motion close-ups of a butter-topped filet mignon at the hotel restaurant faded into aerial shots of the rooftop pool and its surrounding outdoor deck.

The picture tickled my brain, and I suddenly remembered how I'd heard about the Freemont. Back in the spring, the hotel had run ads about its recent renovation. They'd redone the pool area and were encouraging Dallas residents to book staycations and see the new layout.

As the elevator's video continued, the perspective switched to shots taken from the pool deck, which consisted of two separate tiers. The lower tier featured a thatch-roofed bar and lounge chairs around a large rectangular pool. One story above, the upper tier had a smaller infinity pool that spilled down a glass wall into the larger pool like a waterfall. While those on the lower deck could see into the upper pool, they couldn't use it—only a small row of cabana-like rooms had access. Each of these special rooms had its own deck space and hot tub separated from its neighbors' by high hedges.

Suddenly the fourteenth floor's odd room layout made sense: the doors were situated on one side of the hall because they were the special cabana rooms. It also explained why the rear door of the elevator was the one that opened.

When I reached the lobby, I circled to the front desk and asked about one of the cabana rooms. They were sold out, and it was just as well—at $4,000 a night, they were way outside my price range. While the back of my brain wondered who was footing the bill for Brooks's cabana, I settled for a regular room on the twelfth floor that "only" cost $500. It came with access to the main pool, so I'd have to hope it would be enough for me to get a glimpse of Brooks's companion.

By the time I got back upstairs, it was past nine thirty. The front-desk clerk had warned me that the pool closed at ten, so I followed the smell of chlorine and small signs through a twist of hallways until I reached a set of glass doors.

Stepping onto the deck felt otherworldly. In contrast to the hotel's air-conditioning, the warmth outside felt jarring but not oppressive, thanks to a strong breeze that blew into my face. Directed to my nose by the breeze, the chlorine scent smelled stronger here, but also clean and reassuring. The doors must have been well tinted, as the bright light from the interior hallway barely seemed to pierce the darkness once they closed behind me. It was late enough that the windows in the surrounding skyscrapers had blackened, leaving tall shadows outlined by white LEDs.

The bar I'd seen in the video stood to my left, the same direction as the rooms I needed to check for Brooks. The only other person in sight was the bartender, who was already locking up bottles for closing time. As soon as his back was turned, I darted to the right and ducked into the men's bathroom on that side. I hid inside one of the stalls until my phone showed 10:30 p.m.

When I opened the bathroom door and crept back out, the bartender was gone, but nothing else had changed. Most of the illumination now came from blue bulbs built into the walls of the pool. Looking around, I didn't spot any security cameras, but assuming there must be some kind of surveillance, I stayed tucked against the wall as I worked my way back to the bar. Climbing onto its back counter, I found space to stand between the various cages holding the liquor bottles. That put my head against the arch of thatched roof.

Thankfully, the roof was made from real, woven thatch—I managed to wriggle my fingers between the fibers and create a narrow slit to peer through.

The cabanas' private decks stood less than ten yards away, and I had a perfect angle to watch the two I cared about. There was nothing to see, though. Light was visible around the curtains of the room at the end, while the one next door remained completely dark, as if the room were empty or its inhabitants asleep.

All I could do was wait.

◆　◆　◆

By twelve thirty, I'd run out of tricks to keep myself awake. My earpiece was still pumping an audiobook on Descartes's creation of analytical geometry, but I'd missed enough sleep over the past few weeks that my eyelids started drooping. I worried that falling asleep here would mean literally falling—off the bar, likely cracking my head on the way down. It was all I could do to catch myself each time I started nodding off.

I slapped myself on the cheek a few times, but my body seemed determined not to listen. I was weighing whether to catch a quick nap on one of the lounge chairs or give up completely when the gurgling started.

The noise was loud and obvious: an odd mix of bubbling and hissing. I couldn't be imagining it. Unless I was already asleep and dreaming . . .

As I peered through the thatch roof, a deck curtain started to open.

It was the room on the end, the one that had stayed lit inside. The curtain retracted steadily, as if being driven by a motor. First, a shaft of yellow light appeared. Then the foot of a bed. More of the bed was revealed, its covers askew. Finally, the curtain stopped two-thirds of the way across the glass wall.

I craned my neck, straining to see beyond the mattress and who might be occupying the room.

A moment later, Amara Brooks stepped out from behind the curtain.

Her fancy hairdo had disappeared—her dark hair was now slicked back straight, hanging wet and heavy. Her outfit, too, was gone, replaced by a fluffy towel wrapped snugly around her. Without her heels, she seemed strangely petite.

She opened the sliding glass door and started in my direction. My first thought was that she was going for the upper-tier infinity pool— my heart pounded as I wondered whether my hiding spot would hold up if she swam close enough.

A few steps outside the room, though, she stopped abruptly. A light switched on at her feet, a strange, soft shimmer, and that's when I remembered the Jacuzzi. That explained the gurgling noise—I'd forgotten each cabana had its own private hot tub.

After seeming to bask in the light for a minute, Brooks dropped her towel to the deck.

In case her sudden appearance hadn't completely shocked my sleepiness away, the sight of her naked finished the job. My whole face flushed, and I froze. My brain said I should look away, but my head and eyes weren't capable of doing so. For a moment, I wasn't even breathing—the only thing functioning was my heart, which thundered in my chest.

Brooks stepped down into the tub, disappearing completely for a moment before her head reappeared. Gazing skyward, she ran her palms back past her ears, slicking her hair behind her once again before settling with her back to me in the tub.

My eyes rose to the sliding glass door, where another figure was silhouetted.

A man.

He stepped out onto the deck in a towel and with another draped over his head like a hood. While he was fair skinned and reasonably built, I caught no obvious signs to his identity. The hood-towel completely obscured his face.

The man wasted no time joining Brooks in the hot tub. As he descended into the water, she moved to meet him. She yanked the towel from his head and tossed it to the side, but her head eclipsed his face as they kissed. Soon, the man retreated to the far side of the tub, but Brooks followed him, blocking my view of his face as she climbed onto his lap.

Despite my embarrassment, I continued to watch for any glimpse I could get of the man's identity. I had a moment's hope when they spun together, but the man's face was buried between her breasts, and Brooks's arm blocked even his profile. Soon, the back of his head faced me, showing nothing but water-darkened hair.

The two lovers continued at each other for a while, but I never did get a look at the man's face. Finally, Brooks rose from the tub, retrieved her towel, and retreated into the room. The man followed suit, but all I managed to see was his naked back and buttocks as he scampered after her.

The door and curtain slid closed, killing any hope I had left. I stayed another half hour in case they reemerged, but they never did, and eventually the lights behind the curtain flicked off.

I grabbed a couple of hours of sleep in the room I'd paid way too much for, then grudgingly forced myself from the bed when the alarm sounded at quarter to five. I figured if I set up in the lobby early enough, I could get a look at Brooks's companion when the pair came downstairs.

I found a couch outside the entrance to the hotel restaurant that faced the front desk and the lobby's revolving door, but away from the elevator bank. Over the next few hours, I pretended to read every section of the *New York Times* and *Dallas Morning News*, but the only people who came or went were an elderly couple checking out, a trio of businesswomen meeting for breakfast, and a half dozen Asian men who left in cabs.

Finally, at 7:45 a.m., Brooks appeared alone, clad in yoga pants and a zip-up hoodie. The leather tote made her easy to spot as she rounded the corner from the elevator. She didn't revisit the front desk or hit the restaurant, though. Instead, she beelined for the valet stand, where they had her Range Rover waiting.

Fearing I wouldn't recognize the man unless he was with her, I rose from the couch and headed back to the elevators as Brooks pulled away. I rode up to the fourteenth floor, but when I entered the hallway, a maid's cart stood at the end of the hall.

I jogged over and saw that the final room door was ajar—inside, a maid was stripping the sheets from the bed. Seeing me, she smiled and shook her head. "They left."

I blinked at her.

"They checked out," she said. With her index finger, she pointed down at the floor.

My stomach dropped. What she was saying was impossible.

I sprinted back to the elevator and rode it down, recounting everything I'd seen since I hit the lobby at five. I'd been on the lookout for single men in case Brooks and he had separated, but no one like that had passed through the lobby. There was no way I'd missed him . . . Had he left even earlier than I'd come down?

I checked the floor options on the selector panel. Sure enough, everything other than the guest rooms and the pool—the gym, the restaurant—was located off the first floor. The mystery man should have had to pass me.

A bell chimed, and the elevator doors parted. I strode from the car still thinking it through, trying to see what I had missed. I got to the mouth of the elevator bay and looked out toward the valet stand and the couch where I'd been sitting.

How the hell had he gotten away?

I ended up turning around, and as I did, I spotted a narrow hallway on the opposite side of the elevator bay that I hadn't noticed before. I started that way slowly, then accelerated.

I reached the mouth of the passage thinking—hoping—it led to a set of restrooms or maybe a hotel office. But when I turned into it, I saw the passage continued several dozen yards to another corner. I jogged to the end, then turned to find it continued again, even farther this time.

At each corner, the floor sloped downward—I was descending, and after several twists and turns, I guessed I was underneath North Akard or Ross Avenue, the streets bounding the block the Freemont occupied.

After another long straightaway, I found myself at an intersection of three hallways leading in different directions. There was even a Dunkin' Donuts where they met. I'd never heard of a tunnel network below Dallas—Houston had one to avoid the heat—but if the mystery man had left this way, I'd never find him. There were too many options.

I'd missed my chance.

# CHAPTER 21

*Thursday, February 23*

Some folks describe the sound of gunfire as firecrackers popping. I've never thought that was quite right.

Too much *crack* in a firecracker. Too high pitched, too hollow.

Bullets have mass. That adds depth to the sound, at least to my ears.

Either way, the crowds of passengers around me had no doubt about what was making noise on the balcony above Gate 95. Most rose instantly and sought to run. But as they did, a realization rapidly spread among them: the waiting area was essentially a four-walled, open-topped box. Whoever was firing from above not only held the high ground, but also was blocking the only exit.

That was when panic really set in.

Only a few screamed, but nearly everyone rushed the escalator. Not to ride it up and face the incoming fire, but to take cover under it from the balcony above.

The waiting room sat close to two hundred people, and virtually all those seats had been filled. There simply wasn't enough room for that many bodies in the narrow passage between the escalator and the rear wall. That led to a massive crush of people trying to press into a space that was already hopelessly full.

"Walker," Durham's voice said in my ear, "you need to get upstairs. Now!"

"Trying," I said, attempting to push my way through the fearful mass, but no one would let me pass—to them, I was another terrified bystander, hoping to save myself at their expense. I considered pulling my badge or drawing the Sig, but I worried it would make things even worse.

Instead, I retreated from the crowd and circled around the side of the escalator. While lots of people had taken shelter beneath the moving staircase, the crowd wasn't nearly as dense along its side rail. Particularly toward the back, where the handrail rose above eye level, there were gaps I managed to squeeze through.

Giving myself some room and a couple of deep breaths, I took a quick running start toward the escalator and jumped as high as I could.

When both my hands touched the top of the rubber handrail, I thought I had it made. But while my right hand caught the lower end of the moving banister fine, my left slid off.

That left me dangling by one arm. I'm not crazy about heights, so as the railing carried me up and away, I didn't dare look down.

With the odd upward angle, it took three tries, but I finally got my left hand up onto the railing. Once I had a solid grip, I was able to pull myself up and over.

Once both feet were solidly on the metal treads, I crouched like a sprinter and drew the Sig. My heart was pounding in my ribs. I was already three-quarters of the way up, and short bursts of gunfire continued to ring out above.

"Walker, report," Durham shouted in my ear. "What the hell—"

"About to find out," I whispered.

As the escalator carried me steadily upward, I tried to get a peek at what I was facing, but a three-foot-high wall separating the escalator from the concourse blocked my view. Once I reached the top, I used

that half wall for cover. Poking my head up, I finally saw what was causing the commotion.

The hallway was bisected by moving walkways. Beyond those, to
my right, three cops had their guns drawn. Positioned behind the columns and corners of the entrance to Gate 100, they were pointing and
shouting across the moving walkway to my left.

There, a half dozen clustered figures were moving slowly as a group
along the wall toward the end of the pier. Four of the six were big,
bulky men, dressed in gray coveralls, thick helmets, and gas masks. All
carried semiautomatic weapons. The way the oversize jumpsuits were
stretched across their shoulders and chests, I guessed they were wearing
some kind of body armor—vests, if not more. Arranged in a semiwedge
formation, the two men on the sides faced up and down the concourse,
guarding their flanks, while the two gunmen in front engaged the police
across the way. They weren't firing indiscriminately; each time an officer
poked his head out, one of the gunmen would let off a short burst in
that direction. Enough to force the cop to seek cover, but nothing more.

While the police likely couldn't see the two people the big guys were
shielding in their wedge, I had a better angle. One was a petite woman
in a dark suit with long, straight, blue-black hair down to her midback.
Big sunglasses and a paper surgical mask hid her face. Unlike the others,
she didn't have a gun; her hands were clutched around the arm of the
final person, pulling him along with her.

Anah El-Amin.

At least, I figured it was him. The figure had a pillowcase or something similar draped over his head, and his hands were bound in front of
him. But the white T-shirt and jeans matched what El-Amin had been
wearing. Same with the paunch under his shirt and his complexion.

"I've got eyes on the shooters," I said into the headset. "Four masked
men plus the Asian woman. El-Amin looks like he's their prisoner."

"Prisoner?" Durham sounded shocked.

"What about civilians?" Cooke asked.

My eyes swept the entire hallway. Thankfully, it looked mostly deserted. "None in the current field of fire. But that's gonna change if these guys keep moving."

Playing it out in my mind, there were only two ways out for the group of gunmen. They'd nearly reached the waiting area at the end of the concourse—they could descend to that and try to escape through one of the four gates down there. Or they could remain on this level, but since it dead-ended, they'd have to fight all the way back to the security checkpoint in order to escape.

The first option seemed a hell of a lot better.

"From what I saw at 95," I said, "if these guys make it downstairs, it'll be like shooting fish in a barrel."

"Not just that," Cooke said. "It's hundreds of potential hostages."

"So we take them down where they are," Durham said, "right here, right now. Do you have a clean shot?"

I grunted. "Now I'm allowed to shoot people?"

"This is no time—"

"Let me see what I can do."

I stopped paying attention to the orders Durham was barking at Tranh and focused on the hall. Preoccupied with the cops, none of the gunmen had seen me yet. I crossed over from the short wall I'd been using as cover to a column on the opposite side of the entrance to 95 and 97.

Leaning into the hallway, I was able to draw a bead on the bulky guys. But from what I'd seen so far, the police bullets hadn't had any effect against their body armor.

Instead of head shots or center mass, I needed a different kind of target.

All the gunmen were right-handed shooters. Eyeing down the Sig's sights, I aimed for the right shoulder of the nearer of the two gunmen in front of the formation. The way they were sidestepping down the hallway created plenty of pauses—at the next one, I squeezed off a single round.

The bullet struck exactly where I wanted. Not the front of the gunman's shoulder, which might have been armor protected, but the side.

The guy's arm fell limp when the bullet hit. I was guessing it had shattered the humerus and maybe the rest of the joint. Even as he howled in pain, his gun clattered loudly to the floor.

The gunman closest to me, the one guarding their near flank, wasn't pleased by this turn of events and fired off a long stream of shots in my direction. While I took cover around the column, his bullets walked up the stone wall with heavy thuds, kicking up a cloud of dust that made the air taste chalky.

As soon as he paused, I popped back out again, this time down on one knee. I let off three shots, all aimed at his legs.

At least one of these scored: his left knee erupted in a cloud of red. He crumpled to that side, twisting as he fell and dropping the gun. He ended up facing the moving walkways as he clutched his leg and writhed on the floor.

The guy I'd shot in the shoulder had managed to retrieve his weapon with his off hand. He'd stayed with the group despite the injury, and they'd now advanced another ten yards or so toward the end of the concourse without their downed comrade.

Were they really planning to descend to the waiting area?

Deprived of a significant portion of their firepower, they now faced an increased barrage from the police across the hall. The cops had also advanced and were able to keep at least one gun on the group.

If I was going to move, now was the time.

Ducking into a low crouch, I stuck one foot out around the column. When no gunfire came, I sprinted forward.

The railing of the moving walkways gave me a little cover as I advanced. I was planning to pop up a few yards short of the end and hit as many of the gunmen as I could from the side. I was maybe three strides short of where I wanted to be, still sprinting, when something moved in my peripheral vision, low and to my right.

The gunman on the floor. All the writhing must have enabled him to retrieve his gun—I saw his body roll and the muzzle start to swing up and over.

I raised the Sig, hoping I could hit his side before the body armor faced me, but the gunman was too quick. He started firing even before the muzzle had made it all the way around.

A line of bullets tracked across the ceiling, down onto the wall, headed directly for me.

# CHAPTER 22

I did the only thing I could think of and dropped to my right hip.

My momentum carried me forward, allowing me to slide across the slick epoxy floor. As I slid, I let off a string of shots, starting at the gunman's head and tracing down the center of his body.

His helmet and vest stopped several of my bullets, but a couple got through.

One hit the masked man's throat, sending a plume of blood into the air. Two more struck his midsection, doubling him over. While his finger stayed clamped on the trigger and bullets continued to spray from his automatic, the impacts of my shots sent his careening away from me.

My slide left me short of the end of the moving walkway. As soon as I was sure my shots had finished the gunman on the ground, I rolled to the base of the railing for the little cover it would provide.

With my feet pointed toward the group, I needed to reorient. I swung my body around on the floor, waiting to be hit, but nothing came. When my head was finally pointed downrange, I saw why: for some reason, the group hadn't descended to the gates but instead had stopped in the open to engage the cops. One of the gunmen turned around and seemed to be arguing with the Asian woman. She struck El-Amin, slapping him across the back of the head.

The two sides appeared locked in a standoff. While the police had superior cover, thanks to the pillars and walls by Gate 102, the gunmen's automatics and body armor neutralized that advantage. Neither side appeared ready to budge.

Out past the group, I noticed something moving. In the seating areas around the juice bar, people were huddled behind chairs and under tables. They'd been safe from the cross fire until now, but if the gunmen shifted their orientation, or if I started shooting from my angle, they were in prime position to catch a slug.

"I have one down but alive, another winged," I said into the headset. I'd nearly emptied my primary magazine, so I grabbed a spare from my belt and changed it out as I spoke. "They're almost to the end of the concourse, but there are civilians trapped by the juice bar—"

"Walker, SWAT's infiltrated the lounge downstairs," Durham said. "Herd the group down there—let's end this. Now."

Driving the gunmen to where they should want to go seemed easy, in theory. I figured if I popped up and surprised them, it might be enough to drive them to the escalators. I took two quick breaths, gathered myself, and came up firing high to avoid the civilians.

But the space was vacant—I missed completely. The group had moved, but not downstairs.

They were entering the juice bar.

"They're going the wrong way," I called into the headset.

Although trapping themselves at the dead end was a dumb move in the long run, their decision to avoid the escalator had taken SWAT out of the picture. Or so I thought.

"Pin 'em there at the bar," Durham called. "SWAT will ascend in the elevator and outflank."

On the opposite side of the hall stood a single elevator door. Looking at the angles, I saw what Durham meant—if El-Amin's abductors stationed themselves at the juice bar and continued to face the cops and me, SWAT would have an opening to hit them from the side.

The problem was, the group seemed to sense its vulnerability. And the only card it had left to play.

While two gunmen returned fire, the third one—the one I'd shot in the shoulder—started pulling terrified passengers off the floor and lining them up perpendicular to our position.

"They're using the civilians!" I yelled. "Making a human shield."

The police officers saw what I saw and had no choice but to cease fire.

"This is ridiculous," Durham said. "They're cornered. Why would they—"

Cooke had been remarkably quiet—so much so, I'd wondered if she was working on something else. But now her voice reappeared. "Seth, what about the—"

"The patio," I said under my breath.

While the line of passengers obstructed our view, the glare from outdoors shone on the ceiling tiles above their heads. From the way the light suddenly changed, I could tell the patio door was sliding open.

"They're headed outside!"

As soon as I realized this, I took off in a sprint. This whole time, we'd been banking on the idea that this upper level was a dead end, a trap, and the only way out was downstairs. Safe assumption, since the outdoor patio was ringed by a ten-foot-high Plexiglass wall, and it was a sheer, forty-foot drop from there to the concrete tarmac below.

But now I realized there was something the architects hadn't accounted for. I wasn't completely sure that was what El-Amin's captors had in mind, but if my hunch was right, I needed to get outside. ASAP.

When I reached the human shield, the passengers allowed me to squeeze through. Although the sliding door was still several strides away, I finally got a clear glimpse outside.

The group had its back to me. The Asian woman had pulled the hood off El-Amin's head. His black cap was gone, and the wind tousled both his hair and hers.

*Three more steps,* I thought.

One of the gunmen stepped to the Plexiglass wall facing the tarmac. Bracing himself, he walked a tight line of bullets up the clear surface. The panel must have been bullet-resistant acrylic, as it didn't shatter under fire. Instead, at that range, each shot left a hole and a spider-webbed crack behind.

*Two more steps.*

A second gunman raised a heavy boot and launched a powerful kick against the acrylic plate. The bullet holes and intervening cracks acted like perforation—his kick split the panel nearly in two.

*One more step.*

A second kick by the gunman finished the job. The two halves of the acrylic panel separated and dropped away from the metal framing, leaving a three-foot-wide hole in the wall.

My foot hit the patio door's pressure pad on the floor, causing the sliding door to open. With the Sig up and ready, I rushed through it, yelling, "Freeze!"

Two things happened simultaneously.

To my right, one of the three remaining masked gunmen—the one I'd shot earlier—turned and began raising his automatic at me.

Past him, the Asian woman grabbed El-Amin's shirt with both hands. His eyes, which had been squinting against the sun, widened with confusion.

They grew even wider when she pushed him through the hole in the wall.

# CHAPTER 23

While the back of my brain tried to process what had happened to El-Amin—calculating how long it would take for him to fall to earth, the force with which he'd hit the concrete—the wounded gunman posed a more pressing problem.

Thankfully, my training took over.

I squeezed off two shots at him, aiming at his waist to account for the armor. At that range, the .357 slugs knocked him backward and sent his gun hand flailing.

That left the other two gunmen to my left, partially turned toward the glass wall. Although one started to raise his weapon to stop me, I didn't give him the chance.

A jab step to my right lined us up so that his companion stood directly between us. Then I closed the distance to the nearer gunman, firing as I went. One shot struck his lower side, likely piercing his kidney, while the next entered below his ribs.

I glanced at the Asian woman to confirm she wasn't armed, but all I saw was a flash of blue-black hair disappearing through the hole in the Plexiglass barrier.

When I turned back to the final gunman, he followed suit, taking two running steps and leaping through the gap. I fired once after him, but the shot missed high as gravity yanked him out of sight.

I scrambled to the opening in the wall and found that my concern had been realized: instead of falling all the way down to the concrete, the Asian woman had instead thought to push El-Amin onto the top of Gate 101's jetbridge. While still a fifteen-foot drop, it was survivable—now she and the final gunman had joined their captive and were racing away from the terminal along the roof of the metal tube.

Standing at the gap in the glass wall, wind whipping at my face with nothing between me and the sheer drop, my vertigo kicked in. The narrow jetbridge below me seemed to grow even thinner, while the concrete began to dance below it. As my knees liquefied, I grabbed the metal framing on either side for support.

To overcome the disorientation, I forced my gaze from the ground, telling myself to watch the fleeing trio. It was a good thing I did, since the gunman was turning to take a shot at me.

When I saw his muzzle rising, I instinctively dived down and to the side, landing flat on the patio's tile floor. Getting shot at was actually a relief—hitting the tile snapped the vertigo away and allowed me to focus. Bullets sprayed through the opening in the glass, striking the terminal wall behind me, followed by another fusillade that pocked holes in the remaining acrylic panels.

Once the barrage halted, I forced myself to my feet. Before the vertigo could flare again, I took a running start and launched myself at the opening.

My eyes automatically squeezed shut as I cleared the hole in the wall. After a moment of weightlessness, I could feel gravity grab hold. The wind shifted from blowing directly into my face to up and over my shirt.

The drop seemed to take forever. Long enough that my eyes flicked open, and my brain had time to calculate how fast I was falling, and whether I'd hit the jetbridge or the tarmac beneath. Enough time to realize that, no matter how much I cycled my arms and legs, it wouldn't change my direction in the slightest.

Finally, my soles struck metal with a hollow thump. I rolled forward to bleed off some of the force, allowing the momentum to put me back up on my feet so I could start running with the Sig out and ready.

Ahead, I saw that the jetbridge had been lined up to service a giant Lufthansa A380. After a long straightaway, the jetbridge forked into a trio of smaller tubes that bent to my left and connected to each of the airplane's three doors, two on the main deck and one up above. Dragging El-Amin with her, the Asian woman had gotten halfway along the first-class tube, which ended closest to the airplane's nose. The gunman was following her but had fallen behind and was only now reaching the fork.

"They're on one of the jetbridges!" I called into the mike as I ran, unsure whether Cooke and the others could hear me over the engine noise and the whipping wind.

I dropped to one knee and lined up the gunman. Leading him slightly, I ripped off three shots at his waist and hip. At least one of those hit—he stumbled and fell forward. When he landed on the metal roof, his momentum proved too much—arms flailing, he slid over the side headfirst. From the awkward angle of his neck, I could tell he was dead.

Panning the Sig's muzzle forward, I tried to target the woman, but she'd drawn El-Amin closer to her body as they approached the end of the tube, taking away a clear shot.

I took off after them in a sprint. My sooty lungs were unhappy about the exertion, but slightly less so than last time. Thankfully, she still hadn't shown a gun yet, so I didn't need to worry about dodging anything. The only time I slowed was to make the turn at the fork—otherwise, I ran all out.

At the end of the jetbridge, the woman forced El-Amin onto a service ladder. The rungs ended at a small platform, which in turn connected to metal stairs that descended to the tarmac. Fortunately, both the ladder and stairs were narrow, one-person affairs. Controlling El-Amin and getting herself down slowed the woman significantly—I'd drawn to within a couple of yards of the ladder when they reached the platform.

I scrambled down the first couple of ladder rungs, but as the Asian woman rushed them down the stairs, I skipped the rest. My Vans hit the metal grate with a clang as I dropped to the platform.

Below me, the Asian woman and El-Amin reached the bottom of the stairs and turned back underneath the jetbridge. The staircase railing felt too flimsy to support my weight, but a metal half-pipe slide had been installed next to it for gate-checked baggage. I hopped the railing, landing flat on my ass on the slide. It wobbled at first but steadied as I cascaded down.

Looking ahead, I could see what the Asian woman was thinking— a baggage cart like the one Cavin and I had ridden earlier was parked several yards away, pointed toward the runways. She was beelining for the cab door, dragging El-Amin by the hand behind her. Although I tried to line up a shot with my Sig, El-Amin was in the way again.

I hit the ground running at the bottom of the slide. Instead of chasing directly after them, though, I took an arcing path to get an angle on the nose of the cart.

When the Asian woman reached the cab door, she pushed El-Amin inside ahead of her. Although it looked like an extremely cramped fit, she squeezed in after him.

The cart was five yards away, maybe ten, and I now had a clear angle on both tires on this side. I recounted my shots—I'd fired nine of the twelve rounds in this magazine, which left me three more shots.

Setting my feet and staring down the sights, I put two bullets into the front tire of the cart as its engine roared to life, then I lined up a rear wheel for my last shot.

And that was when my lungs betrayed me.

They'd burned on and off since the smoke I'd inhaled earlier. When I exhaled before the first pair of shots, they'd itched, but I'd managed to overcome it. On the next breath, though, as I was letting the last of the air go and starting to squeeze the trigger, they erupted in a huge, uncontrollable cough.

My final shot went wildly off course, ricocheting off the metal side-wall of the cart.

Inside the cab, the Asian woman was at the controls. The cart kicked into gear and lurched forward a few feet. With the flat tire in front, its first move was a sharp veer to the left, which pointed the nose in my general direction.

As she gently reapplied the gas, the cart wobbled forward, and you could see her figuring out how to correct for the imbalance.

Then she gunned it straight at me.

# CHAPTER 24

Hauling two fully loaded baggage trailers, the little white cart easily weighed several thousand pounds. And while that meant it needed several moments to reach full speed, my brain knew the math on how much momentum it would have once it got there, and how much force it would pack when it hit me.

With the cart leaning left because of the flat tire, my best chance to dodge it was the opposite way, to its right. I juked in that direction as fast as I could.

To maneuver around jets, the cart had been designed to pull an extremely tight turn. Through the windshield, I could see the Asian woman cranking the steering wheel back toward me.

As the distance closed, I took one last step, then threw myself as far to the side as I could.

The front bumper missed me by a foot.

I landed hard, my shoulder and side bearing the brunt of the fall. While I rolled to soften the blow, concrete scraped through my T-shirt, taking layers of skin with it. When I finally stopped and looked up, the cart had pulled a 180 and was speeding away toward the runways.

I immediately gave chase on foot. Despite the fire in my lungs, the soreness in my side, and even the sting of my new road rash, I ran as fast as I ever had.

Still, the back of the final baggage trailer continued to shrink ahead of me.

I pumped my arms harder. My brain screamed at my legs to go faster.

No matter what I did, though, I was no match for the speedy little engine—I kept falling farther and farther behind. I imagined El-Amin captive in the cab, the fear and confusion he must be feeling, but there was nothing I could do.

I would have screamed if I'd had even the slightest bit of breath left, but I wound up bent over, hands on knees. My heart fluttered while my lungs began a brutal series of hacks, each of which seemed to shred my lungs inside my chest. Between coughs, I sucked down what oxygen I could get in deep, gulping breaths. A trickle of smoky bile crept up my throat, but I forced it back down with a hard swallow.

Rising back to my full height, I raised my arms over my head, trying to make the air come easier, as I gasped into my mike. "Lost . . . them. White . . . cart."

"Say again, Walker," Durham said. "We couldn't make that out."

I knew I needed to speak, to get Durham and Cooke as much information as I could. But when I tried to push the words out, there simply wasn't anything behind them.

Watching the cart disappear only made things worse—as I tried to focus, the horizon seemed to lurch to one side, then the other. I spun back toward the terminal building, hoping that locking my eyes onto something solid would rebalance me. But even that slight spin left me tipsy. And when something whizzed by my blind side, the blast of air from it nearly knocked me off my feet.

"Walker, hop on!"

Still bent over, I turned and saw Cavin, her head upside down and poking out the door of what looked like the same blue luggage cart we'd used before.

"C'mon!" she said, waving at me frantically. "We can still catch them."

That didn't make sense until I straightened up and saw that this cart wasn't burdened by luggage trailers. While my brain struggled to figure whether the difference in weight might translate to a large enough gain in speed, I forced one foot in front of the other until I was behind the little vehicle. Through sheer muscle memory, I also managed to switch out the empty mag in the Sig for my final spare.

Before climbing up on the hitch, I blinked several times and shook my head to clear the cobwebs. With the Sig in my right hand, I grabbed one of the cart's tie-downs with my left. Two taps on the metal roof with the butt of the gun, and Cavin gunned it.

Given my light-headedness, I didn't feel sure-footed on the hitch, and I worried about my grip giving way, but the air rushing by as we sped along seemed to help clear my head. If nothing else, it forced more oxygen down into my lungs.

Breathing got easier, and with that, thinking did, too.

From my slightly elevated vantage point, I had a good view of our surroundings. On our left, the tarmac ended abruptly at a concrete barrier separating the airport from a complex of buildings that belonged to the airlines and cargo carriers. Following this barrier, we were tracing the western edge of the apron, the broad swath of concrete tarmac that surrounded the entire airport but was separated from the runways by oblong islands of grass. While taxiways cut through the islands at various points, the white cart was steaming straight for the westernmost taxiway, the one that led to the ends of Runways 10L and 10R, the left-hand foot of the X.

To our right, back across the apron, I could see Boarding Area F while, beyond it, tendrils of black smoke continued to rise from E. The runways continued to operate, though: even farther out, a Southwest 737 and an Eva 777 were on final approach, descending in unison toward touchdown at the far ends of 10L and R.

Now that I could focus better, I saw that we were, in fact, moving faster than the other cart. A lot faster. As quickly as it had shrunk away from me before, now it grew steadily closer and larger as we rapidly chewed up the distance between us. Better yet, reinforcements were coming: a line of police and emergency vehicles, their flashers spinning, were speeding from the opposite side of the airport, tracing the line of grassy islands to intercept us at the final taxiway. Based on their pace, it looked like they'd beat both of us there—if they blocked access to the runways, the Asian woman's cart would be trapped.

She must have sensed that, too.

Without warning, the white cart cut sharply left. A narrow gap had been provided in the concrete barricade so vehicles could enter and exit the building complex. The Asian woman took full advantage, plowing through it at full speed.

As soon as the white cart made its move, Cavin responded. She angled our cart for the opening, and by making a less aggressive turn, she also kept our speed up. That reduced the distance between us even more.

Before we entered the complex, I gave a quick glance back over my shoulder. Most of the police cars were turning to follow us into the maze, while a couple maintained their current course. I had to hope they'd block whatever exits the Asian woman might try to use on the far side.

After passing the concrete barrier, our out-of-place vehicles were the only reminder of the airport we'd left behind. The roads here were marked like city streets, complete with traffic signs and crosswalks, while the two- and three-story buildings blocked any view of the terminals.

Close ahead, the white cart drifted onto the left side of the two-lane road, then cut back across, turning into the parking lot of the first warehouse on our right. The luggage trailers bounced loudly as they hit the angled driveway, threatening to tip over.

Cavin was doing a good job of following closely while allowing the trailers a wide berth. Still, we couldn't keep this up forever. Although I hadn't noticed it before, there was a window along the back wall of the cab of our cart. I rapped on it with the muzzle of the Sig.

It slid open, and Cavin called from inside. "Yeah?"

"Pull up on their left," I said. "I can take out the rear tire. Or maybe nail the driver."

Cavin didn't have the chance to take me up on the idea. No sooner had I spoken than the white cart curved right to follow the parking lot around the building. We followed, and once we'd rounded the corner, a more pressing problem loomed ahead: a couple dozen yards in front of the white cart, a group of workers was exiting the warehouse. Dressed nicely in slacks and skirts, maybe a dozen people were crossing the parking lot. Likely headed out for the lunch hour, most had their eyes on their phones—none seemed to sense the danger bearing down on them.

I shouted and waved my free hand wildly, trying to get their attention. From inside the cab, Cavin yelled, "There's no horn!"

Behind us, the police cars still hadn't turned the corner yet. While they'd activated their sirens, the wailing sounded far, far away.

With seemingly no other choice, I pointed the Sig at the ground and fired one off.

That got the pedestrians' attention.

Most looked up in surprise, only to have their expressions immediately turn to horror when they spotted the white cart. Everyone seemed to recognize the danger at once—the crowd split into two groups that clambered toward opposite sides of the lot. I could see individuals pushing and pulling each other, trying to get everyone to safety.

A second later, the white cart barreled through the walkway where the workers had stood.

After another curve, we reached a relatively long straightaway. Here, Cavin slid our blue cart to the left, looking for a passing lane. Before she could complete the maneuver, though, the white cart veered to the side, blocking her path.

Cavin wasn't done.

She eased our cart back to the right, getting the white cart to follow. Then, as soon as the white cart had shifted its momentum in that direction, Cavin zipped back left. She cut around the back corner of the rear trailer and gunned the engine, which howled in response.

The burst of speed nearly threw me off the back, but I tightened my grip on the eyelet. The nose of our cart had drawn up as far as the front edge of the forward luggage trailer. Although it didn't waver as much as the one behind it, it still lurched back and forth, alternately coming within a couple of feet of our cart. When it came closest to us, I saw dozens of suitcases inside, restrained only by a web of black safety mesh fastened across the trailer's open sidewall. When it swerved farthest away, I caught what I was looking for: the white cart's left rear tire. The one I'd missed earlier.

Leaning right, I extended my arm to that side, trying to line up a decent shot. Each time I did, though, the luggage trailer would whipsaw toward us, threatening to crush my arm and forcing me to withdraw.

After the third near miss, the white cart pulled even farther away, and I saw my chance. I lined the Sig up on the tire and squeezed the trigger.

As I fired, both carts hit a bump—some kind of a drainage channel cut across the lot. The bounce threw my aim off, and I missed high.

I started leveling the Sig for another shot, but this time, the Asian woman was ready—she jerked the wheel left, and the white cart cut across our path.

As the fully loaded trailers careened toward us, time dilated. We were about to be crushed between the luggage trailers on our right and the line of parked cars on our left.

Cavin's driving saved us again.

She slammed on the brakes, letting the white cart and its trailers zoom past us.

The sudden deceleration threw me into the rear wall of the cab. My head whipped forward, and my chin smacked the roof so hard, my teeth collided, and I saw stars. My chest banged the cart, too, knocking what little air was in my lungs back out. But the worst part, even as I was scrambling to recover my breath, was that it nearly cost me my balance. As I pitched forward, one of my feet slid off the hitch, shifting my full weight suddenly to my right foot and left hand. I felt my fingers slip on the eyelet, leaving only the last knuckle of each finger curled around the metal.

Somehow, I managed to yank myself back up. Once I did, I saw how good it was that Cavin had dodged the white cart.

The Asian woman must have expected the impact with us to blunt their sideways momentum—without our cart to break the swerve, the white cart slid to within a yard of the parked cars before clumsily jerking back to the right. That wasn't enough to stop the trailers, though. They whipped sideways, the rear one colliding with a parked SUV with a thunderous crash of metal and glass. A moment later, the car's alarm began squealing, and an ear-piercing screech cut the air as the trailer scraped across the SUV and several cars after it.

This friction against the trailer was clearly a drag on the white cart—its rear tires began smoking as it struggled to break free. Cavin smartly pulled us around our quarry, blocking the white cart's path.

I stepped off the hitch and leveled the Sig at the white cart's windshield. Glare from the glass kept me from seeing through it, so I sidestepped to ensure I was targeting the Asian woman rather than El-Amin. Once I could finally see inside the cab, though, something looked different than before.

I realized that the white cart's rear window was ajar at the same time it became apparent why the Asian woman had opened it: from there she could reach the latch on the trailer hitch.

I started to scream to Cavin, but the little white cart beat the sound from my mouth. As soon as the resistance from the trailers was removed, all the torque from the tires took over: the white cart leaped forward, ramming directly into the driver's side of our cart at full speed.

# CHAPTER 25

"Carla!"

I stepped toward our cart, squeezing off two shots as I moved. Although they struck the white cart's side window, breaking the glass, they didn't stop the Asian woman from plowing ahead. After the white cart shoved our cart a few feet, she reversed, then rammed forward again, striking the rear end of our cart and spinning it around.

Despite its now-crumpled nose and flat front tire, the white cart started motoring away, grinding slowly at first, then gradually accelerating.

My immediate concern was Cavin. With the driver's-side door completely crumpled inward, I sprinted to the other side and yanked the door open. She was collapsed, facedown, over the steering wheel.

"No, no, no . . . ," I said.

Before I could even think through how to check her for injuries, she stirred, turning her head to my side of the cart. In a soft, determined voice, she said, "That bitch is gonna pay . . ." Although her face betrayed her pain, she shifted in the seat as if she wanted to climb out.

"Are you sure you should . . ." I moved a hand toward her arm, but she backhanded it away.

"I got this," she said, hauling herself from the cab. Although her head hung low and she limped heavily, her movements displayed a slow, steady determination.

After two or three halting steps together, we looked at the white cart hobbling away and then at each other. I checked for any of the vehicles that had followed us into the lot, but they all seemed to have disappeared. Helping the pedestrians, maybe?

Remembering the headset, I tapped the button at my ear. "Cooke? Durham?" The line had been silent for a while, or at least I hadn't heard anything, and now I wondered if it was functioning. "Anybody?"

When I glanced down at Cavin, she raised her eyebrows.

Then a siren whooped behind us.

We both turned to find a bright-yellow fire truck rounding the previous corner and barreling for us at top speed. The rig rumbled to a stop a few feet away, and the passenger door opened. General Durham's face poked out. "You two need a lift?"

I helped Carla up into the rig, then climbed up behind her. Durham had the driver resume moving immediately, even before we'd gotten settled. Carla fell into a seat, while I stood next to Durham, bracing myself against the rear wall of the cab.

"Not quite the Abrams I used to roll around in," he said, "but with the yellow and the sirens, it does make a statement." He turned forward to gaze out the windshield. Quietly, he said, "You were right."

"How's that, sir?"

"This wasn't ever about the vice president. It's about whatever work that kid was doing."

I grunted. "Let's just nail these two—then we can worry about the why."

Durham looked back at me and gave a firm nod. "Road's blocked ahead. Hopefully that'll do it."

Through the windshield, I could see we were approaching a fork where the road split to encircle a building that had been built at an angle to all the others. The white cart was rolling, as best it could, toward the right-hand path. That led back in the direction of the runways.

"Who's waiting for them?" I asked.

"Some of Tranh's guys," Durham said. "Should be police cars at both exits."

Compared to the little engine in the cart, you could feel the power of the fire engine's diesel through the floor. In seconds we'd reached the fork; then a moment later I saw a police car ahead, its flashers spinning. But it wasn't blocking anything. It wasn't even stationary—it was peeling out, turning its back toward us in order to speed in the same direction we were headed.

It didn't take long to figure out what had happened—this entrance to the tarmac was guarded in part by two gates that looked like toll booths. While the police cruiser had blocked the area to the side of the little structures to prevent the white cart from circling around them, the white cart had smashed through one of the wooden gate arms. It was now back out on the cement apron. Instead of swinging left toward the taxiway, though, the white cart was barreling straight ahead, rolling parallel to the runways and the islands bordering them.

And one other thing had changed: the green-and-white Eva 777 had taxied far enough in that it stood directly in the white cart's path.

Boeing's Triple Seven is not a small airplane. A successor to the 747, it manages to carry the same 400 passengers on two engines instead of four. It's nearly 250 feet long, with a tail that rises over 60 feet in the air.

The looming obstacle didn't seem to slow the white cart down in the slightest, however. It steamed straight ahead, almost daring us to follow.

Our advantage was speed. With the flat tire hampering the white cart's mobility, both we and the police car gained rapidly on it. Halfway to the jet, we'd already made up most of the gap between us. But it wasn't clear we'd catch and pass the cart before we all reached the 777.

Durham produced a walkie-talkie and barked into it. "Use the plane as a backstop. Have the cruiser go left, we'll cut right. Whichever way the cart ends up turning, we'll have 'em covered."

Slowly, our truck began to veer off the straight course the cart was following. A glance out the side window by Cavin showed the police car going left, increasing the gap between us. A little at first, then more.

We'd almost reached the jumbo jet now. It was close enough that you could make out faces pressed against the Plexiglass windows. Behind the jet, waves of hot exhaust blurred the landscape in the distance.

Still, the cart showed no signs of changing course.

Durham ordered our driver and the police cruiser to flank even wider to the sides. We'd separated enough, I wondered if the white cart could pull a tight 180 and zip back between us.

Although we'd nearly pulled even with the back end of the white cart, the plane loomed so large, most of it was above our windshield.

"They gonna ram it?" Durham posed the question quietly, almost under his breath. Then he shouted into the walkie-talkie. "Tell ATC to get that plane moving!"

A moment later, the 777 started rolling faster. But the cart adjusted its course to match. And it accelerated.

We all were a matter of yards from the tip of the 777's wing.

"Steady," Durham said.

"Sir, we need to—" the driver said.

"Steady."

As we remained on course, the wing loomed larger and larger. The cart, to our left, kept going.

"Sir, we can't—"

"Goddamnit!" Durham yelled. "Turn!"

The fire truck veered sharply right—so steeply, I wondered if we could make the turn at all. The entire cab of the truck tilted, threatening to flop us over. As the floor pitched to nearly forty-five degrees, I leaned all my weight against the opposite wall, trying to add any force I could to fight the lean.

After seconds that seemed like minutes perched on one side, the fire truck finally straightened out and settled back onto all its wheels.

The cab bounced violently, the suspension groaned, but somehow we made it through.

As soon as we were stable, I dashed to the opposite side of the cab and pressed my face against the side window.

Like us, the police cruiser had swerved away at the last moment, albeit in the opposite direction. But the white cart had continued on. I reached the window in time to see the little cart scoot beneath the belly of the airplane with only inches of clearance. And, once it reached the far side, it kept going. Before we could resume pursuit, it had streaked almost halfway across the field.

With Durham yelling encouragement, our truck pulled a three-quarter turn and sped after the cart. The police cruiser fell in beside us. In the distance ahead, the white cart turned onto one of the taxiways that crossed the runways.

Out at the far end of the field, two more planes were on approach for a synchronized landing. This pair looked smaller than the 777, probably 737s. Pointed almost exactly toward us, their speed was hard to gauge against the cart's. But the cart never slowed down—it barreled across the first runway with absolutely no regard for the oncoming jets.

We accelerated toward the taxiway, turning into it as the cart was beginning to cross the second runway. Watching only what lay ahead of us, Durham and I were unprepared for our driver to slam on the brakes. We both pitched forward, him colliding with the back of the driver's seat, me careening into a Plexiglass shield behind the passenger's.

Durham scrambled to his feet first and growled. "What are you doing?"

Before the driver could answer, the closer of the two airplanes—an Eastern 737—touched down to our right. A split second later, it whizzed in front of us, its nose not yet completely down.

"That's why, sir," the driver said.

Durham's voice softened. "Get on with air-traffic control, and get us across these runways."

We eventually received clearance to cross, but by then the white cart had disappeared. This side of the field was devoted to private aviation, including the FBO building and a broad patch of concrete where private planes could park and tie down.

The tie-down area was packed with a mix of prop planes and private jets, so it took us a minute to spot the white cart, off by itself in a corner. We approached it quickly, our fire truck on one side, the police car on the other. I had a bad feeling about what we'd find, but the moment the fire truck's wheels stopped, I was out the side door with the Sig drawn. I took a sharp angle to get a look inside the cab.

When I got there, a lump formed in my stomach.

It was empty.

I started back for the fire truck as Durham emerged from it. When his eyes found mine, I shook my head.

"Cooke called," he said. "They watched the Asian woman and El-Amin pile into a private plane while we were crossing."

"Which one?" I glanced around—almost every spot was filled.

"That one," Durham said, pointing a thick finger at the far southeastern corner of the field. At the start of Runway 1L, a private jet—a small one, maybe a twelve-seater—was completing its final turn. With a pointy nose and narrow profile, it looked like a shiny silver pencil with wings compared to all the commercial jetliners.

Straightening onto the strip of asphalt, it tore down the runway until, about a third of the way along, its nose popped up into the air, followed shortly by the rest of it.

As the knot in my gut cinched tighter, the plane soared steeply upward before banking out over the bay and turning south. With my hand shielding my eyes from the sun, I had no choice but to watch it go.

# CHAPTER 26

*Monday, August 20, Five Years Ago*

"I thought it'd be good for us to sit down again and talk about how things have been going."

Zachary Scott, Amara Brooks, and I were seated in the boardroom while Randolph Rodgers addressed us again from the head of the limestone table.

"I mean, I know y'all didn't start with much time, but we've only got two weeks left until one of you gets the biggest promotion of your life. Two weeks! How come y'all don't seem excited?" His eyes flashed, and he gave us a broad, beaming smile. "Maybe a little tired? Well, let's get a move on then, so y'all can get back to leading your troops. Amara, ladies first, as they say. Where do we stand on the SAR reduction?"

Brooks, seated opposite me as before, launched into a lengthy status report. I couldn't help but notice the way she held eye contact with Rodgers, how she'd built little jokes and other reasons to smile into her remarks. But I barely listened to the words she was saying.

Over the past week, I'd shadowed her whenever I could get away from the lab. She'd traveled to DC briefly, while her Range Rover sat in the same T.E. parking spot for several days, collecting layers of pollen. Even after she'd returned to Dallas, though, she hadn't visited the mystery man or the Freemont hotel—all her trips had been strictly local, between her house and the office.

When Brooks finished, Rodgers thanked her, then glanced down the table at Scott. "Zach, how's HighBuy?"

In a dark jacket and neatly pressed shirt with the collar open, Scott looked as dapper and put-together as Brooks. "I've been working their reps pretty hard."

Rodgers grunted. "I've seen the bills. Lots of high-end hotels, fancy meals, and booze."

For the first time, I saw something on Scott's face other than complete confidence. "You said it'd take plenty of wining and dining . . ."

Rodgers chuckled. "I did. And it's true. I just hope you're enjoying your relatively unbridled access to the expense account."

Now Scott grinned. "Absolutely, sir. Anytime you want to come out with us, I'm sure HighBuy would appreciate seeing you."

"I'll take you up on that. But tell me how it looks for us to get back into their stores by Christmas."

Scott began rattling off a combination of war stories from meetings with the HighBuy representatives and numbers from T.E.'s competitive-analysis reports.

Rodgers nodded. "Seems like you're on track. Now, Seth—"

"One more thing, sir?" Scott asked. "If I might?"

"What is it, Zach?"

"I just wanted to make sure you saw, I put together a financial plan for how we can save—"

Rodgers chuffed and rocked back into his chair, arms crossed. "I saw. And I applaud the extra effort—there were some decent ideas in there. We should always be looking for ways to run leaner and meaner. But we are not—and let me make this abundantly clear— we are *not* positioning this company for acquisition. By *anyone*. As long as I'm CEO, *we* do the acquiring, not the other way around, understand?"

"Of course," Scott said.

While I was happy to see Rodgers rebuffing Scott even a little, the fact that Zach was doing extra work concerned me. I'd been so busy playing detective, I hadn't been putting any time into brainstorming what I'd do if I actually got the promotion. If Rodgers pressed me, I could make up something that sounded halfway intelligent—I mean, I'd been thinking about electronics-product strategy in one way or another since I was a teenager—but it was all pie-in-the-sky stuff. I hadn't put pen to paper the way Scott had.

Part of me wondered if that was a sign. About the likelihood of me getting the job or, even worse, whether I was prepared for it if I did.

I didn't have any time to chase that thought, though, as Rodgers turned to me next. "Do you want to say anything about Boost?"

I'd been wrestling with whether to raise the issue of Brooks and the exploit file since I'd learned about this meeting. I didn't feel comfortable doing so yet—not before I knew more about her mysterious partner. Until I'd resolved exactly what happened, the responsibility fell on me for not keeping the product secure. For not anticipating the risks.

Before I could start rattling off my prepared remarks, Rodgers spoke again.

"I have to say, Seth, I was really quite disturbed and disappointed by the stories I've heard. What happened to that young man on your team, Jonathan, was it?"

"Julian," I said, hoping my voice wouldn't crack. Rodgers's gaze was withering, and my eyes dropped to the tabletop.

"I'll be honest," Rodgers said. "At the start of this little competition, I considered you the favorite. But maiming employees in dangerous, unregulated testing is not exactly what puts you on the inside track."

I opened my mouth to speak, but none of the remarks I'd prepared seemed appropriate. All I could think about was Julian, still lying in his hospital bed. That's when the idea came to me.

"Don't you have anything to say?" Rodgers asked.

I looked up and stared him straight in the eye. I did my best not to glance at Brooks. "We're running another test next week. We'll be ready."

"I sure as hell hope so," he said.

"Then you should come," I said.

"Pardon me?"

"You should come watch the test, sir. You all can, if you'd like," I said, turning to the others. "Boost will be ready."

When the meeting was over, I tried to escape the boardroom as quickly as I could. Now that I'd set something in motion, I needed to make sure all the pieces would be in place. But before I'd gotten three steps outside, a voice called to me from behind.

I turned to see Scott hustling through the door to catch me.

"Hey, listen," he said, "I know you're busy. I just wanted to say—"

At that moment, the door opened again, and we both turned as Brooks stepped outside. She slipped a pair of Wayfarers over her eyes and strode past both of us, saying, "Boys," without any other form of recognition.

Scott watched her go and didn't speak again until after she'd climbed into her SUV.

"First off," he said, turning back to me, "I'm sorry about that guy on your team. I hope he's okay."

I nodded. "Thanks."

"The other thing is," he said, lowering his head for emphasis, "I think Brooks may be up to something."

"Oh yeah? Why's that?"

He glanced in both directions. "Ever since we had that first meeting with the boss, weird stuff's been happening in my department. Computer stuff, mostly. Files going missing, important numbers getting changed in our spreadsheets. A whole bunch of contact cards were irretrievably deleted yesterday."

"You think Brooks did it?"

"Honestly, I kind of assumed it was you at first. That's what I had in my head until I heard about your 'accident.' But if it wasn't you, and it wasn't me . . ." Scott cocked his head and raised his eyebrows.

"Did you tell IT?"

"No. I'm keeping this to myself—I don't want someone thinking I can't control my own department, you know?"

Since I'd come to the exact same conclusion, I certainly did.

"We both gotta keep our eyes open," he said. "That's all I'm doing for now. I just wanted you to know."

"Thanks."

He gave me a weak smile. "Good luck."

◆ ◆ ◆

"Wait just a second," Clarence said. "What exactly did you commit us to do?"

After the meeting, I'd headed straight to Clarence's office. Finding it empty, I tracked him down at home. Rachael had gotten sick overnight, throwing up all over the place—Shirley had managed to score an appointment with their pediatrician at the end of the day, so Clarence needed to stay home with Michael. I made a quick run out there, and now we were huddled at the dining-room table while Michael played with toy cars on the floor a few feet away.

"Another test run," I said.

He exhaled and nodded.

"Next week," I said.

"Next week?" Clarence's voice rose an octave on the final word.

"We only have two weeks left."

"I know. But we need every minute of those fourteen days."

"After what happened, I didn't have much of a choice," I said. "I had to prove we were on schedule. Announcing the next test was the best way to do it."

I expected Clarence's smile would return. That he'd laugh and make some joke about how we'd get through it. But he didn't. He simply stared at me, so I figured I'd better let him know the rest. "I invited Rodgers to come watch. And Brooks and Scott, too."

Clarence's eyelids fluttered, and he glanced to where Michael was playing. "You are really trying to kill us, aren't you."

"There's one more teensy-weensy thing."

He gave me a guarded look. "What? We have to build the car from scratch?"

Before I could answer, there was a loud clacking noise, and the front door of the house swung open.

"Mommy!" Michael bounced to his feet and immediately rushed to the door.

Shirley's face poked through. "Stay back, sweetie," she whispered, stopping Michael in his tracks. "Rachael's sleeping, and I don't want you catching her germs." Finally, she glanced over at us. "A little help?"

Clarence rose slowly from his chair, like doing so took some effort, but once he was up, he strode quickly to the door. He carried Rachael in her car-seat-carrier thing while Shirley went back outside and retrieved a bulky diaper bag and a bag of groceries.

"What'd the doctor say?" he asked. "Something serious?"

Shirley shook her head. "No, it's some kind of bug. Doctor said it might last a few days, though. We need to keep her hydrated."

Clarence took a labored breath. "I'll put her in the nursery?"

203

"Yes, please," Shirley said. "She can stay in the seat so you don't wake her up. I'm gonna go mix up some Pedialyte."

I moved to Clarence's office, pulled out my laptop, and went through some things while I waited. When he finally trudged into the room and joined me, his gaze was on the floor. "Sorry."

"Don't apologize. You okay?"

He looked up at me, and for a moment his eyelids seemed to quiver. His mouth was drawn into a tight line, and I worried he might start crying. But he swallowed hard and shook his head. "Just tired. You said there was something else? One more teensy thing?"

"Yeah," I said, "someone's trying to sabotage us."

"What?"

I laid out the whole history. How I'd found the exploit file, Brooks on the video. Even her assignation with the mystery man at the hotel, which turned Clarence's cheeks red.

When I finished, he said, "Wait a second." Behind the glasses, his eyes had grown even wider than normal. "They impersonated me?"

I nodded.

"Why me? Why use *my* ID to break in?"

I shrugged. "Probably because they know how much I trust you. They knew you were the last person I'd suspect, so it would mess with my head. Divide and conquer."

Clarence still looked panicked, his breathing a near pant. "If the company found out . . . if Rodgers—"

"Relax," I said. "No one's going to blame you. I've got proof it was Brooks."

His eyes locked on me. "You're sure? I'm safe? We're safe?"

I nodded slowly.

"You must've . . ." He shook his head. "When everything looked bad, did you think . . ."

Although I felt a pinch in my gut at lying, I tried not to hesitate in answering. "I mean, I had to check things out. But I never believed it."

He gave me a relieved smile, then looked down at the floor. After a moment of silence, he said, "So, we have to gear up for a new test, in front of the CEO and a bunch of other people, and someone might try to blow the whole thing up?"

"Oh, I absolutely think they're going to try and blow the whole thing up. In fact, I'm counting on it."

Over the next hour, I explained what I had in mind. When I was done, Clarence nodded. "I gotta admit," he said, "that's clever."

"What are you two scheming about in here?"

I looked up to find Shirley at the door, leaning against the frame.

"Seth's busy plotting to save our jobs." Clarence let out a nervous chuckle.

"Well, that's a good thing, I guess." Shirley's face said she wasn't sure how funny it was supposed to be. "I suspect Miss Rachael will be awake in a couple of hours, so if it's all right, I'm going to go lie down."

Clarence turned to me. "I don't suppose you're going to rest anytime soon."

I shook my head as I stood. "I need to go get started on what we just talked about. There's no telling when Brooks might make her move."

"Then I should come with you."

The way he was slumped in his chair, Clarence looked like he might fall asleep on the spot.

"That's okay," I said. "I got this."

He glanced up at me with a mix of hope and gratitude in his eyes. "You sure?"

I smiled. "Don't worry, there'll be plenty to do tomorrow. Help Shirley and Rachael tonight, and get some sleep."

He rose from the chair more easily than before. I was glad to see it and told myself I'd be better off working alone tonight anyway. It'd attract less attention.

I started out of the room, but before I could get through the door, Clarence grabbed my elbow. I turned to see what he wanted, and he wrapped me in a tight hug.

I patted him on the back a couple of times, expecting him to let go, but he clung there longer than I expected.

"Thank you," he said in a voice that was hoarse and hard to hear.

When he finally did pull away, I could see his cheeks were soaked. He kept his eyes down as he hurried out of the room.

# CHAPTER 27

*Thursday, February 23*

Thank God for Melissa Cooke.

I'd assumed she was still back in the Communications Center, so when she appeared a minute later on the tarmac, I did a double take.

"Let's go," she said, smiling proudly. "We're all prepped."

"Prepped for what?"

"To follow that plane."

"In what?" I asked.

"In this." She nodded back over her shoulder at a small jet rolling up. As it drew to a stop, its door opened, and a crew member lowered steps to the concrete.

The plane looked as nondescript as a private jet could. Painted flat white with no distinguishing markings other than the required ID number, it looked smaller and far less flashy than the one that had whisked El-Amin away. If you didn't know what to look for—the oval windows, for example, were a giveaway—you wouldn't have recognized it as a Gulfstream G650, one of the fastest private jets in the world.

"Where'd you get *that*?"

Cooke glanced over at Durham, who shrugged and gave another of his rueful smiles. "Just have it back by tomorrow. Now that he's in safely, VPOTUS has plenty to keep him busy until then. But I don't want to have to tell him his ride's missing when he's ready to go back to DC." Durham turned to me, and the smile disappeared. "End this, Walker. Whatever it is, whoever's behind it. Do whatever you need to—you have my full authority."

Now it was my turn to smile. "Yes, sir."

"Everything we need is already on board," Cooke said. "Let's go."

She made for the stairs, and I started to follow. After a couple of steps, I heard Cavin's voice call out from behind me. "Hey, Walker."

I glanced back to find her standing at the door to the fire truck. She'd pulled the oxygen mask away from her face to speak. "Be careful."

"Should be easy," I said. "You're not driving."

At first she cocked her head at me, then her mouth spread into a wicked grin.

◆　◆　◆

The cabin of this G650 reminded me vaguely of the Eastern lounge.

A handful of seats—far larger and roomier than even your typical first-class seat on a commercial jet—had been sprinkled around the interior to create two sitting areas, one for four, another for six. Between those sat a three-person couch across from a wooden credenza. Farther back, an additional cabin contained another couch.

On a different day, I'd have searched the plane to discover all its tech secrets. Today, though, I flopped into the first seat I came to, in the four-person area, and fastened my belt. The chair was easily the most comfortable, most supportive airplane seat I'd ever felt. With the chase over and the adrenaline ebbing, my muscles felt sore and my eyelids heavy. I scooped the audio player out of my pocket and put the earpiece back in my ear. The files Shen had sent me were all converted, so I swapped them in for the audiobook I'd been listening to earlier.

Cooke took a seat across from me, looking out one of the large oval windows that consumed the wall between us. Although I knew she hated to fly, her eyes were clear and calm, her face relaxed.

"You okay on a tiny little plane like this?"

She cracked a smile. "I figure you probably don't get much safer flying than on the vice president's secret plane."

"Fair enough."

I glanced out the window and saw we were already rolling across the tarmac. I sensed someone behind me and half assumed they'd offer me a drink. Or ask me to change clothes so I wouldn't sully the leather. When I turned around, though, the burly, suited man wasn't holding a tray, but rather a portable oxygen cylinder in one hand and one of the small plastic masks they'd given to Cavin in the other.

"Thanks, I'm okay," I said, waving him off.

"No," Cooke said, "you're not. All that coughing—"

"The smoke, yeah, I know. It's getting better."

"Oxygen's the only way to fix it." She looked up at the attendant. "Isn't that right?"

He nodded. "Plus, you've got burns on your scalp, and it looks like your chest is bleeding a little. You should get all that treated before it gets infected."

The attendant was six-something, built thick enough that he challenged the neck on his dress shirt. But while he might have intimidated some people, it was the weight of Cooke's stare that ultimately broke me. "Fine," I sighed.

The attendant sat on the edge of the seat next to mine and clasped the oxygen canister between his knees. With smooth, automatic motions that would have impressed a NASCAR pit crew, he mounted the regulator into place with one hand and spun the tightener closed with the other.

"You've done this before," I said.

"Once or twice." After affixing the plastic tubing to the nozzle, he stood, resting one knee on the seat as he draped the mask over my face and adjusted it.

The name tag on his jacket sat right at my eye level.

"Tennessee," I read aloud. "Is that where you're from?"

"Nope," he said. "My name's Tennessee Cumming, though most folks call me T."

T reached across me and pressed a spot in the wooden paneling next to my chair. It popped open to reveal a holder for the oxygen bottle.

"That's a neat trick," I said.

He smiled, his round cheeks gathering into dimples. "You'd be surprised. Plane's loaded with little touches like that."

As he secured the bottle, his blazer gaped open. I spotted a shoulder holster underneath.

"Wait, you're Secret Service?"

He held a finger to his lips. "Shh, it's a secret."

He disappeared behind us, and a moment later we were thundering down the runway for takeoff. The little plane's power was impressive, but the most noticeable thing was how smooth the ride was. No bounce or rumble, no herky-jerky motion side to side. Like an electric train, it was all silky motion and fluid power.

I let Cooke watch a bit of our climb before asking, "Where are they headed?"

"Probably Dallas. That's what their flight plan said."

"That doesn't actually mean anything, you know." While flight plans were required, pilots could alter them midair, and private jets got more leeway than commercial aviation when it came to changing plans and destinations.

"True," Cooke said. "But that plane is registered in Dallas. We know exactly which hangar stores it, and it's being tracked by civilian and military radar."

"Don't try and run from the government, huh?" I laughed out loud for the first time since putting the kids to bed in Fort Worth. Could that really have been less than twenty-four hours ago? It felt like an eternity.

Cooke smiled and nodded.

"Should I ping Jim Grayson?" A Dallas detective, he'd worked with Cooke and me on the Berkeley case and also helped me another time I was in a jam.

"I'd wait," she said. "They could still reroute."

"How does the timing look? If it's Dallas, can we beat them there?"

Her satisfied smile widened. "ATC knows to give them a bit of a runaround. Not so much they'll notice, but enough for us to get ahead, land first, and set up. But now comes the hard part—"

"Choosing between the cabernet or the sauvignon blanc?"

She chuckled. "Figuring out what the hell all this means. We've got about three hours to decipher it all."

We'd leveled off, and T reappeared with a medical bag. Although I tried to focus on Cooke, whatever he was pressing against my scalp felt cold and goopy.

"I've been struggling to put it all together," I said. "Too many weird pieces that don't make sense."

"It looks like you were right about El-Amin being innocent."

"Was he? Is he?"

"The way he was tied up and hooded?" Cooke asked. "They were clearly kidnapping him."

"That doesn't explain him planting the smoke grenade. Or the fire. Who assists in their own kidnapping?"

"I've been thinking about that. What if he was being coerced from the start? Blackmailed, maybe?"

"With what?" After wrapping some bandages around my head and tying them off, T seemed to have finished with me.

"The secret that he's gay?" she said. "That's pretty big. I think the larger question is, what's his value? If they wanted to kidnap El-Amin, it must be for a reason—so what is it?"

I wondered whether the files Shen had sent me might hold the answer, but I hadn't gotten far enough into them to know. "Do we know anything about the gunmen? Or the woman?"

"Almost nothing. Tranh was going to start running all that down. The first thing we need to do, though, is talk to one of El-Amin's sisters. San Diego PD had her lined up for an interview right before we took off. Hey, T," she called.

He reappeared from the galley.

"Is there a way to videoconference?"

T smiled. With three long strides he reached the wooden credenza, where with the flick of a switch, a flat-screen TV rose from a panel hidden at the back. "We've got Ka-band internet. You're all set."

Cooke and I moved to the couch. Lugging the oxygen bottle along was clumsy, but I had to admit that my head felt clearer since I'd been using the mask.

After T helped Cooke connect with SDPD, one of the two El-Amin sisters appeared on the screen. The one with the pixie cut and the wild blonde highlights. "I'm Sonia," she said. "Is there news on my brother? The police said he was dragged away?"

"The people who kidnapped him, they still have him," Cooke said.

"Oh my God." Her hand flew to her mouth, revealing long nails painted black.

"We don't know exactly *why* they took him, but we're in pursuit right now," Cooke continued. "As we try to get him back, it's even more important to figure out what these people want."

"Okay. I don't know if I know anything, but I'll try."

"Do you know what your brother was working on at Magnet?" I asked.

Sonia's face took on a pained expression. "I'm sorry, really—I have absolutely no idea. I was a history major. All his techno stuff always sounded like 'waah, waah, waah' to me." She made a talking motion with her hand.

"Not even big picture?"

She shook her head. "If I knew anything—anything at all—I would totally tell you."

"I got the sense when your parents were talking earlier," Cooke said, "that they might not really know what's going on with him."

"They're a little . . . old country."

"Has Anah told you about any problems the last few months?" Cooke asked. "Anyone threatening him?"

She shook her head slowly, as if trying to sort through whatever she recalled.

"I couldn't help but notice," Cooke said, "when the subject of your brother's sexuality came up, your parents reacted pretty strongly."

"Yeah, they have a hard time with that kind of stuff. Being gay isn't something they're used to thinking about."

"But I take it Anah has told you the truth?"

"Truth about what?"

"That he's . . ."

Sonia's eyebrows rose. After a moment, she snorted, then that became a full-throated chuckle. "Oh, you think *he's* . . . Oh no." She shook her head forcefully. "No, Anah is not gay. He's about the furthest thing from gay there is."

"Wait," Cooke said. "I saw you glance at your sister when I asked about that . . ."

Sonia winced, then hung her head for a moment. "All this has gotten kind of out of control. Anah was lying to my parents, but not about being gay. At least, not really."

Cooke smiled. "Now I'm totally confused."

I was glad it wasn't just me.

213

"Even though we moved to the United States, my family still believes in arranged marriages. It's kind of a big deal, especially here, where everyone's Iraqi American, and they all know each other. The parents get together and try to match us up when we're born. At least, mine did."

"Did they have a match picked out for Anah?"

Sonia nodded. "But he was *not* into it. Like, at all. He's always had . . . a type, if you know what I mean."

"What's that?" Cooke asked.

"Petite. Asian." Sonia smiled sheepishly.

Cooke and I exchanged glances.

"He dated a Korean girl, Kelly Quo, for three years in college. Kept it completely secret. He wanted to bring her home to meet my parents, but they were furious when they found out."

"What happened, exactly?"

"They lost their shit. Told him to end it. They said if he didn't, they'd never speak to him again. He didn't want to listen—he went out and bought a ring for her. But Kelly didn't want to be the thing that split our family up. So . . . she said no."

"When was this?" I asked. "Before Magnet?"

"Oh yeah," she said. "When he was a senior in college."

"But now your parents think he's gay," Cooke said. "Or bi, I guess, right? I mean, they're in denial, but it sure looks like, deep down, they've thought about it."

"For a long time after Kelly, he didn't date anybody. I think he'd kind of given up. Then, when he started working and got this great job, my parents saw it as an opening to raise the arranged-marriage thing again. When that happened, he was *so* pissed. He never claimed he was gay—he never lied. He just moved to the Castro, dropped some hints here and there, and let them fill in the rest."

"To tweak them?" Cooke asked. "Or to get them off his back?"

214

Sonia smiled. "Both. Definitely. He's always been a little bit of a joker, you know? I'd come home from a sleepover when we were kids, and he'd have covered my whole room in sticky notes. When his high school class wanted to play a senior prank, Anah was the one who dreamed it up—that kind of thing. Plus, he was . . . running interference."

"What does that mean?" I asked.

Sonia drew a deep breath and held it for a moment. "I'm gay. Anah's known for a while. Like, forever—since we were in high school. But my parents don't know. At all. They're pissed off enough about my hair. I think Anah figured that if he pretended to be gay, it'd take some of the heat off me."

"Okay," Cooke said, "that makes sense. But how does that square with his religious awakening?"

Sonia smiled and shook her head.

"What?"

"All that Islam stuff? That's all a bunch of bullshit."

# CHAPTER 28

"What did you say?" Cooke leaned forward on her seat.

"It's my fault, kind of," Sonia said. "Anah was working these crazy hours—he'd be at the office eighteen, twenty hours a day. So, one Saturday he calls me, from work, mind you, and we're joking around. He's so tired, he's punch-drunk and can't stop laughing. I tell him it's too bad he can't take off for some religious holiday, and I can tell he's playing with the idea. Anyway, a couple of weeks later, he tells me he made everyone believe he'd gone hard-core Muslim. He went to a thrift store in the Haight and bought a little rug, which he convinced everyone at work was a prayer rug. He said they started giving him breaks whenever he said he had to go pray. Plus, Mom and Dad were super happy about it. It was a win-win."

"He wasn't worried people might figure it out? Or trust him less?"

"That's not the way he thinks," Sonia said. "He looks at everything like a game, you know? He figures out what the rules are, and then how to win. When we were kids, I could never beat him at Risk 'cause he figured out the best countries to get at the start of the game. For the SAT, he got this book that explained how the questions were written— which answers they tempt you with. He's always been about outsmarting everyone else." She paused for a moment. "You don't think . . . I mean, the Muslim thing doesn't have anything to do with this, does it?"

Cooke kept her eyes locked on the screen. "We don't know yet. But thank you for being honest with us. We'll do our best not to share any of this with your parents."

"It's okay," she said. "We've been lying long enough. If my parents find out the truth . . . it's probably better that way."

Once the sister was disconnected, Cooke turned to me, shaking her head.

"All that. A big, fat lie—to his parents, to his boss, everyone. All to get some time off. Or at least to get one over on the system. Can you believe it?"

I didn't answer at first. The whole time Sonia had been talking, I'd been thinking about Shirley. Considering the secrets I'd kept from her about Clarence, I could hardly throw stones at El-Amin.

"Well," I said at last, "they weren't blackmailing him over his sexuality."

"Could have been the Islam thing. With all his bills, his mom's illness, El-Amin couldn't afford to lose his job. If they told Magnet he was faking . . ."

"Speaking of his job at Magnet, I have another video call I want to make. I may have an idea what's driving part of this"—I tapped my earpiece—"but I need to talk to someone about it."

"Okay," she said, "I'm going to follow up with Tony and some other people about evidence—you wanna go in the other room or something?"

While I didn't want to show it, Cooke's request was a relief. There were parts of this call I wasn't sure I wanted her hearing.

Before I could ask where to go, T spoke up. "I got you covered, boss. There's another setup in back."

He brought me to the jet's rear compartment. You could see it was designed as a private office/bedroom, separated from the rest of the cabin by a thick wood-paneled wall, which I figured would likely be soundproof, or close to it. The foldout couch set against one bulkhead faced a monitor.

I texted first, to let Shen know the call coming through in a minute would be from me. When he answered, I could see he was sitting at the computer in his home office, the silver Bose noise reducers I'd gotten him for Christmas clamped over his ears. Although he'd been out of the military for years, he kept the high-and-tight haircut, except for a small flop of hair he maintained on top.

"Hey, dude," he said. "Did you get my—whoa, what the hell happened?"

"I look that good?"

"Uh, no. I mean, I've seen you worse. But what's up with the mask and bandages?"

*Oops.* I'd forgotten about the mask. I pulled it off. "Smoke and burns. I had to help put out a fire at SFO."

Shen's eyebrows rose. "Wait, that was you? It's all over the news."

"What're they saying?"

"Multiple fires, gunshots, at least one terminal shut down." He chuckled. "I guess I should have known you were involved. Especially with you sending me research projects."

"Thanks for digging into those battery questions."

"And here I had my fingers crossed that you'd come up with a big new idea." Over the past few years, Shen had helped me file patents on the circuits and inventions that I doodled in my spare time. It had gone from a hobby to a lucrative business—the money I'd made from licensing them was what had allowed me to buy my Manhattan Beach house and help Shirley and the kids the way I did. "You get the patent applications I emailed you?"

"Yep, I've been listening to them. Pretty cool stuff."

Shen shrugged one shoulder. "Meh."

"Really? You're not impressed by the idea of charging your phone with ambient room light?"

"I mean, yeah, the idea's nice. But those applications I sent you, that's all they got in 'em: an idea."

For years now—decades, even—batteries had been a stumbling block for portable electronics. There were only so many chemical combinations to make electrons flow, and each one seemed to have some kind of inherent drawback. Ultimately, the industry had settled on lithium-ion batteries as the best option among all the trade-offs, but they were heavy, expensive, and, as accidents had demonstrated, flammable. Still, they'd been so widely adopted that instead of pouring resources into new battery solutions, companies simply developed better versions of the lithium-ion solution.

The patent applications Shen had pulled showed that Magnet—and particularly, El-Amin—had come up with a unique concept. Instead of building a different kind of battery, they'd essentially built a highly complex network of capacitors. A capacitor was a well-known circuit element—in traditional physical circuits, it was a component shaped like a sandwich, usually with two metal plates separated by nonconducting material in between. Over time, the world shifted to integrated circuits—computer chips—for most devices, but the same concepts applied to the patterns etched into the silicon. When voltage is introduced to a capacitor, an electric field develops between the separated plates—kind of like the pressure when you inflate a balloon. That "pressure" drives electrons, creating current through a circuit.

El-Amin's idea had been to use a computer-guided laser to carve out electrode patterns in special sheets of plastic. Each of those patterns acted as a capacitor; the precision laser enabled so many capacitors to be packed onto a single sheet that it could store more voltage than a battery of the same size. Even better, the electrical pathways charged faster than a traditional battery, and since there was no chemical reaction, the thing was super stable and not prone to overheating.

But El-Amin hadn't stopped there: he'd combined the new capacitor sheeting with a special kind of solar panel. Most solar panels are black because the dark pigment helps absorb the sun's rays. El-Amin had come up with a clear panel that could create electricity from the sun or even average indoor lighting. By combining that with the capacitor sheets, it meant never having to plug in your phone—or any other device—to charge again. You could simply hold it up outdoors or in a bright room and let the light charge it.

"Did you see the ages on those things?" Shen asked. "The apps I sent you were like two years old."

"You think they stopped the project?"

"Hell no. I'm guessing they're prototyping by now. And I'm sure they're filing a whole slew of applications full of really good shit, but keeping them confidential."

"Wait, what's that you just said?"

"Confidential," Shen said. "Patent applications publish eighteen months after their earliest priority date, but you can file papers asking the PTO to keep them confidential throughout prosecution."

"No, no," I said. "I mean, that's interesting—I'll want to remember that trick for my stuff. But I meant the other thing you said."

"What, prototyping? Yeah, they must have a working device by now, right? I mean, you were in the industry. Did you ever leave bet-the-company tech sitting around at the idea stage for two years?"

"Excellent point." So good, in fact, it gave me an idea of what might be at the center of all this.

"You know," Shen said, "now that we're talking, I bet they never even patent some of the tech in that thing. Like how best to pack all those little lines together—I bet they never share that with anybody."

"But if they don't get a patent, how would they keep people from ripping it off?"

"They could keep it as a trade secret—you know, like the Coke formula or the Colonel's secret recipe. That way it never expires. They can keep it from their competitors forever."

"What about getting the device itself, though?" I said. "If you buy it—or steal it—you could reverse engineer the thing."

"Maybe."

"What do you mean, maybe? We did that kind of stuff all the time at T.E. Everybody does."

"Yeah, but you know as well as anybody—some things you can't duplicate from the device itself. Like the perfect temperature for fabbing the thing, what color laser to use to cut the lines. Process stuff that your competitors will spend forever trying to figure out."

"No," I said. "They'll hire someone who knows. Throw a boatload of cash at some schlub who worked on it. Get the info that way."

"That, my friend, is called 'trade-secret misappropriation.' I'm guessing Magnet has their engineers sign NDAs out the yin-yang. You probably did at T.E., too."

"Yeah, sure." I think my hand still ached from all the signatures.

"You ever read one of those things?"

I shook my head. "No one did. It wasn't like you had a choice—you wanted the job, you signed everything they put in front of you."

"Exactly," Shen said, nodding. "But those contracts keep people from blabbing if they go somewhere else. 'Cause if they do, Magnet tracks them down and sues them for all they're worth. Along with who-ever hired them."

Now things were making even more sense. "So, you can't get the information voluntarily from someone who signed one of those contracts."

Shen shook his head. "Nope, not if they're smart. That's why I'm saying I'd use trade secrets to protect some of that shit. Although I'm sure Magnet has much smarter, more expensive lawyers than me on retainer."

"But none as good-looking. Or as good with a Glock."

"True, true." Shen nodded. "Say, where on earth are you calling me from?"

"A private jet streaking across the country."

Shen whistled through his teeth. "Look at you, moving up in the world. All you needed to do was burn your scalp off."

I grunted.

"Should I ask where you're going?"

"I'd have to kill you."

"You could try," he deadpanned. "When you back?"

"Hopefully a day or two. But I dunno for sure." If I was right about who might be involved, it might take longer than that.

"Okay," he said. "I think Brian wants to barbecue this weekend, so if you wanna come be our fire-safety officer . . ."

"Yeah, yeah," I said. "Go back to work."

"Never."

"And charge me for that work you did this morning."

"Sure."

I knew there was no way Shen would ever send me a bill for that time, but as he hung up, I wished he would. While I wasn't sure I liked where all the evidence was leading, his information might have broken the case wide open.

# CHAPTER 29

*Tuesday, August 21, Five Years Ago*

By the time I left Fort Worth, the evening rush hour was peaking. That gave me plenty of time in the Honda to think about what I'd be doing tonight, and what we had to accomplish over the next seven days.

Clarence's fragile emotional state had surprised me in the moment, but the more I thought about it, the more I understood. Between his demands at home and the way work was pushing us, he had to be seriously sleep deprived. A good night's rest would hopefully do wonders—I told myself to expect some kind of practical joke from him the next day.

That was, if I could keep *myself* awake. What I had planned promised to make tonight a long one.

My first stop was a Cabela's I'd seen in a strip mall not far from the T.E. campus. I was no hunter, but I had a feeling they might have what I needed, and sure enough they did. The three little boxes set me back a few hundred bucks, but if I was correct about what Brooks might do, it'd be money well spent.

Next, I headed for my office. A few quick internet searches turned up articles about Dallas's underground tunnels. I'd never heard about them, but apparently they were built back in the '70s and '80s to help beat the heat and reduce congestion. Since then, though, they'd fallen out of favor—some were now privately owned and locked; others were still used but only on weekdays. I downloaded those articles and ran them through software to convert them into audio for my earpiece.

While they played in the background, I unpacked what I'd bought at the hunting store and brought it all into the source-code room. As I'd hoped, the place was deserted, letting me work in peace. It took a while to figure out the right positioning for the little boxes and how to affix them sturdily, but soon I'd installed all three at various points around the space.

Finally, back upstairs, I had some other technical work to do. The Boost module we'd installed in Julian's car had been sitting in one corner of my office—I grabbed it now and hauled it over to my desk. Although the outer shell had taken a beating in the crash, on a quick inspection its internal components looked like they'd survived pretty much intact. That was good—it meant I wouldn't have to reinvent the wheel for what I had in mind.

After toying with that for another couple of hours to get it into shape, I looked up and saw the clock read 2:15 a.m. That left me time for a short catnap before my next errand. My office didn't have any furniture other than my desk and chair, but Clarence's had a couch.

I left the lights off when I ventured inside. Not only did I know the layout by heart, but I'd cracked the door so some light could leak in from the hallway.

Clarence's sofa was a two-seater, too short for my frame, but I'd learned how to contort myself to make it work. I set two alarms, five minutes apart, on my phone to ensure I'd wake up, then bent my legs and braced my neck against the side to squeeze myself in. Despite the position, I expected to fall right asleep.

Instead, a minute or two later, my eyes flicked back open. So many things were bouncing around in my head, I needed to calm my brain down. I ended up looking around the room, staring at the shadows, desperate to distract myself so the fatigue would kick in.

My eyes stopped at an object in a darkened corner.

The shotgun.

I'd seen it the day Clarence brought it in. A 20-gauge Remington Model 11 manufactured in the '30s with the original "Sportsman" engraving on the receiver and custom work on the stock.

Firearms were strictly forbidden at work. I guessed that, despite Texas's affinity for guns, someone in Legal had decided engineers weren't the most stable or trustworthy bunch. As lab manager, it fell to me to demand that Clarence get rid of the damned thing. But, since I knew why he'd brought it in and why he'd left it here, that was easier said than done.

The shotgun had belonged to Clarence's father, Jesse. I'd met the old guy once, a real character. One Memorial Day weekend, I'd gone to the Aikens' house for a backyard barbecue. While Clarence sweated over the grill and Shirley tended to side dishes in the kitchen, Jesse had held court in the backyard with their friends.

At least ten years removed from his thirty-six-year career in the marines, Jesse had kept the haircut and much of his original build. A Dallas Cowboys T-shirt with the sleeves cut off revealed meaty arms that looked like they could still pound out fifty push-ups without a problem. In a deep, raspy voice, he told slightly off-color jokes to the adults even as Michael tried to do chin-ups on his flexed bicep. Although I hated needles, I was fascinated by the tattoos that dotted his arms—Korea, Germany, Guam, the Philippines, outlined maps of each of the places he'd been stationed. He caught me staring and advised, "If it hurts, you didn't drink enough beforehand," then let out a huge belly laugh.

From my father's days in the navy, I'd met enough guys like Jesse that his loud, raucous personality didn't bother me at all. Clarence, you could tell, felt differently. He clearly loved his old man—when Jesse teased him about how well done a hamburger should be cooked, you could see the pain in Clarence's face. But you could also tell, from the way Clarence's eyes followed Jesse around, from the way Clarence called

Michael over a couple of times and quietly contradicted what Jesse had said, that their relationship was . . . complicated.

So, when Jesse died of esophageal cancer a few months back, I wasn't surprised that Clarence took it hard. He'd trudged into work the morning after the funeral looking physically ill, eyes puffy, skin pale. Although he'd worked at T.E. for fifteen years, he seemed . . . lost. He staggered into my office carrying the shotgun, but not menacingly. He had his hand wrapped around the end of the barrel, the stock down by his feet, like you'd carry a walking stick.

I stared at the gun, then glanced up at his face.

"He . . . left it to me," Clarence said in a halting voice. "I . . . I can't bring this home."

I understood immediately what he meant. Clarence didn't have a gun safe or anyplace to store a weapon. Michael was curious enough that he might find it, and Shirley would have been furious even at the idea of bringing it into the house.

"You . . . you take it," he said to me, holding out the gun. "I don't want it."

I shook my head. "I can't. You're gonna want that someday."

His expression said he disagreed, but he'd left my office and trudged to his own, propping the shotgun in the corner as if it were an umbrella that needed to dry.

It had sat there ever since.

Seeing it now as I lay on Clarence's couch, I was reminded that he'd taken some serious emotional hits lately. His dad. The Boost project. Never mind his parenting demands at home.

*We all just need to get through this,* I told myself. *A few more days and things will go back to normal.*

That thought finally closed my eyes.

One in three.

The maps of the Dallas tunnels showed that they connected three parking garages within the thirty-six city blocks they spanned downtown. Assuming Brooks's mysterious partner had driven to their hotel rendezvous—not a crazy assumption, given the size and sprawl of the metroplex—I had a one-in-three shot of guessing which garage he'd use and intercepting him on his way back to it.

That was, if my announcement of our next Boost test had caused Brooks to call another meeting with him. And assuming the man was her co-conspirator, not merely her lover.

When I weighed it all together, it was an awful lot of assuming.

I shook off any doubts. If Brooks were determined to sabotage Boost, she couldn't waste time: she had only two days to plant a new exploit if she wanted to be sure the security footage would be erased before our next test. That meant meeting her contact as soon as possible.

I timed my arrival downtown perfectly, parking the Honda in the garage closest to the Freemont at 6:30 a.m., just as the pedestrian tunnels were opening for the business day. Following the tunnel map from the garage to the Freemont on foot, I stopped at the switchbacks that led inside the hotel. Then I backtracked a few yards until I found a small alcove with a service door. Tucking myself inside, I sat on the floor and waited, not knowing how long it would take.

It turned out to be shorter than I thought.

The tunnel was silent until a few minutes before eight, when I heard soft footsteps approaching.

Although I clambered to my feet, I wasn't fast enough—a figure stalked past the alcove's entrance as I was rising. Stepping quietly into the hallway, I saw the figure's back several yards ahead. It was a man, roughly the same size as the one I'd seen the other night. Clad in jeans and a red tracksuit top with the hood pulled up, he was putting distance between himself and the Freemont quickly.

"Hey!" I called.

The man's head turned enough for me to see he was wearing sunglasses and a Texas Rangers cap in addition to the hood.

When he spotted me, he took off running.

I started after him, cursing the dress shoes I was stuck in after yesterday's meeting with Rodgers. This section of hallway had epoxy floors, and as I tried to accelerate, the slick soles slid like I was running on ice.

The mystery man's sneakers had no such problems. He doubled his lead on me, and the extra traction allowed him to lean into the corner we were approaching.

I did my best to round it as quickly as I could—thankfully, the flooring switched to a brick-like tile with a much better grip. A long straightaway stretched ahead, and the man had almost reached the end of it.

I put everything I had into catching him.

The straightaway ended at the junction room with the Dunkin' Donuts and the three passages radiating from it. I checked all three directions before spotting the man far down one tunnel with rounded walls like you'd see in a movie spaceship.

I dashed into that passage, already breathing heavily. My thighs were burning, and the air seemed to jab at the inside of my lungs. I couldn't remember the last time I'd gone for a run—I'd been too busy for any sort of exercise—and it was showing. Unfortunately, Brooks's hot-tub buddy was chiseled and showed no signs of slowing.

I sprinted down the hallway, following as it curved to the left. Although I desperately tried to keep the man in sight, he kept pulling ahead.

I pushed myself to reach the next junction, but the man had disappeared from sight. As I glanced down each of the two hallways leading out of this new room, I yanked out my earpiece and listened for any sound that might betray which path he'd taken.

All I heard was my own wheezy breathing.

I doubled over to try and catch my breath.

There had to be a way to catch the man in the tracksuit other than outrunning him. I closed my eyes as I sucked down air and thought about the map. Based on the turns we'd taken so far, only one of the three garages lay ahead. Once the man reached it, he'd need to get to his vehicle and drive out.

That might buy me some time.

This junction room featured a staircase leading upward. I forced myself over and onto it, climbing the risers over my quads' stern objections. Soon, my calves were screaming, too, and I looked up to find I was only two-thirds of the way up.

The stairs ended at glass doors that exited onto the sidewalk—I pushed my way through them and found I was on Patterson Street. The garage I needed was two blocks over.

I started in that direction. The next block was short, and with no traffic at this hour, I crossed the street diagonally. The boxy white garage sat straight ahead.

As I reached the final corner across the street from the garage, I spotted a wooden gate arm that marked a street exit. Sprinting to it, I heard tires screech inside the structure. But I still couldn't see anything.

I traced the garage wall to the right, peering inside, looking up and down the ramps for any hint of motion or a brake light. When I finally reached the far side of the structure, I glanced through the window hole cut into the concrete, and my stomach dropped. The way Federal Street sloped, the exit I'd reached sat on the second level. One floor down, at the opposite corner of the garage, something flashed and caught my eye—a small red convertible speeding away.

From this distance I had no hope of reading the plate. I couldn't even make out the model.

But while I couldn't be 100 percent certain, I now had a decent idea who Brooks's partner might be.

# CHAPTER 30

**Thursday, February 23**

When I emerged from the jet's private cabin, Cooke was working on her computer. She glanced up from the screen as I approached. "We're still headed for Dallas."

I nodded, not surprised. "I think I know what's going on. What the kidnappers were after, why they wanted El-Amin."

"Wow." Her eyes flashed, and she smiled. "I should send you to your room more often."

"We need to call Magnet back. That guy Singh likely has a lot more answers than he let on."

With T's go-ahead, we dialed Ajit Singh on the videoconference system where we'd earlier talked to Sonia. His assistant tried to give us the runaround, but Cooke flashing her badge and threatening to arrest him for obstruction of justice got things moving.

When Singh finally appeared on camera, he was all smiles. "Agent Cooke, Agent Walker. I am so sorry to keep you waiting. I was engaged on another call—"

"How big was the prototype?" I asked.

Singh squinted through his glasses. "I do not know what prototype you are talking about."

"The battery prototype. The one Anah El-Amin was carrying."

"Agent Walker, I see your head has been injured. Perhaps you—"

"Mr. Singh," Cooke cut in, "I should caution you here that lying to us is a violation of Title 18, Section 1001. Unless you'd like me to come to Magnet and arrest you for a felony, you need to tell us the truth."

Singh's face contorted into several different expressions, his mouth opening several times as if to speak before closing again. "I'm sorry, what was the question?"

"The battery," I said. "El-Amin was working on a new battery, right?"

"Yes."

"That's why he and his coworkers were talking about capacity and storage." I directed this at Cooke. "It wasn't about memory, though, was it? It was power. Polaris chews through power, so you needed something new and better to run your phones."

"Yes."

"And that's why El-Amin is named as a co-inventor on a whole series of patent applications Magnet's filed over the last few years."

Singh began shaking his head. "I don't see how legal rights that Magnet may or may not be pursuing are relevant here."

"They're relevant because El-Amin was carrying a finished proto-type of the battery. The TSA scanner showed a battery in his bag that I assumed was an ordinary backup charger. But that little box was the whole purpose of the trip to Israel, right? Let me guess: They were going to fab it for you?"

Singh didn't answer. His mouth drew into a narrow line as he squinted.

His silence caused my hands to curl up in fists. Without realizing it, I'd come halfway off my seat. "All that 'We love our employees' stuff you told us earlier, that was all empty talk. You wanted us to find the prototype, not El-Amin."

"Does it have to be one or the other?" Singh asked. "Why can it not be both?"

"Because one is a human being, and the other is a battery."

"That battery is worth *billions*."

A wave of anger hotter than the fire I'd fought washed over me. I bolted off the couch and leaned into the screen. "Right, and with that much money on the line, what's a little lying to get it back? And who cares about the kid who was carrying it?"

"You are putting words in my mouth. I—"

"No," I said, glaring and jabbing my finger at the screen. "I'm putting words to your actions."

"If we lose that technology, and the investment we made in it . . ." Singh shook a finger at me. "You of all people should understand, Mr. Walker. We answer to our shareholders."

"You also answer to the law, and—"

"Mr. Singh," Cooke said, shifting forward on the sofa, "arguments aside, it appears Anah El-Amin has been kidnapped. If getting their hands on this new technology of yours was the kidnappers' motive, can you at least tell us who would have wanted it?"

Singh sat back in his chair. "Anyone in the hardware sector. This battery will fundamentally change how we power handheld devices."

Cooke inhaled deeply, as if he were sorely testing her patience. "Can you be more specific than 'anyone,' sir?"

"I mean, if you'd like me to name off our competitors, I can do that," Singh said. "I don't know which of them would engage in openly criminal activity—"

"Forget it," I told Cooke. "I can list companies as easily as he can. And I won't lie about it."

"You know, Agent Walker," Singh said, "when you left T.E., it created quite a stir. Many people wondered what happened. And they were disappointed, because they'd looked forward to seeing what you might do in electronics. I, myself, always wondered what would have happened if I'd been able to lure you to Brilliance. It was a true regret of mine." He pursed his lips and shook his head. "Now, I see, maybe I was the lucky one. Maybe you were never cut out for this in the first place."

My teeth ground against each other. If shooting the television with my Sig would have helped, I might have done it.

"Thank you for your time, Mr. Singh," Cooke said. "I should reiterate that everything about our investigation—including our efforts to save your employee and now to retrieve your stolen property—all that would have been infinitely easier if you'd told us the truth in the first place."

Even as she was ending the call, I began pacing up and down the aisle of the plane. Stomping might have been a better description.

"He's gone now," she said, rising off the sofa. "It's okay."

I locked eyes with her. "No, it's not."

"You don't have to shout," she said, raising her hands. "Getting upset isn't going to help. I've never seen you like that—what's going on?"

Part of me wanted to explain, to tell her exactly how cruel a company could be. But the rest of me knew I couldn't—she knew too much already, thanks to Singh. "If we'd known about the prototype from the start . . ."

"It would have helped, sure," Cooke said, nodding. "But we still wouldn't have known the full story. The point is, where does all this information get us now?"

I took a deep, cleansing breath. The rage that had boiled up inside me started to cool, settling back into my chest. "Whoever took El-Amin did it to get the battery tech. Not only the box, but him, too. For his know-how."

"Okay. Now that we know El-Amin's straight, it looks like the Asian woman was a honeypot: someone figured out that she's his type and used her to lure him in. Between the lingerie and the condoms in his bag, he clearly thought today was some kind of romantic rendezvous.

But he's not holding another ticket, so . . . what? He comes in thinking they'll simply walk out of the airport together?"

"Maybe," I said. "Or that they'd buy tickets together. Or, maybe she promised him they were going somewhere and she welched—maybe that's why he jumped off his stool at the bar. But it still doesn't explain him planting the smoke grenade, or the fire, or his costume change."

"He planted the smoker first thing," Cooke said. "At that point, he's still all in, thinking she's waiting for him and whatever plan they have is in motion. We don't know exactly how the fire started. The costume change is after he stands up at the bar. Maybe that's when he learns what they're really after, or he gets bad news that the plan is different than what she told him originally. But he keeps going because he thinks he can't turn back. Maybe they do have something over him—some threat that keeps him going."

Before we could say anything else, Cooke's phone rang inside her jacket. She extracted it and said, "Looks like Tony." She put Tranh on speakerphone, and after a quick summary of the Singh interview, she asked what he'd found.

"We ID'd the guys Walker shot," Tranh said.

"And?"

"Gangbangers, all Chinese. Every one's got a rap sheet with SFPD. But a couple of interesting things. First, one of 'em was carrying another of the burner phones bought with El-Amin's and the woman's."

"The carrier told us there were four," Cooke said.

"Right."

"So, where's the fourth phone?" I asked.

"The carrier traced it to an address in Chinatown."

"I'm sensing a pattern," Cooke said.

"Oh, just wait," Tranh said. "The carrier also gave us call and GPS information for all the phones. We already knew the woman texted El-Amin from the bathroom. Turns out, that wasn't the only communication."

"What's the timeline?" Cooke asked.

"The woman enters the airport around 6:20 a.m. Her burner's on, while the one El-Amin ends up using is switched off. The gunman's burner is active out in the cell-phone lot. The Chinatown burner is on but stationary.

"At 6:57 a.m., the gunman's phone calls the woman's. Call lasts forty-five seconds."

I pictured the time stamps from the video of El-Amin. "That's not long before she was sitting at the counter."

"Right," Tranh said. "Less than a minute after the gunman hangs up with her, he dials the Chinatown burner. That call's forty-eight seconds. Thirty minutes go by. Then the mystery phone in Chinatown calls the gunman back for thirty seconds. Then the gunman calls the woman back for forty-two seconds."

Cooke squinted. "They're passing information back and forth . . . but this plan had to be in place for months. Seducing El-Amin over time. Buying burners in advance. So, something must've changed. They were adjusting in real time."

"Funny you should say that," Tranh said. "We looked back through all the day's duty logs to see if anything else might line up with the timing."

"What did you find?" Cooke asked.

"You saw the security we had going around the airport this morning for the VP's arrival. Checking cars so no one could pull an Oklahoma City. Well, twenty minutes before the gunman's first call to the woman, one of my officers spots a van parked outside Terminal 3 baggage claim. He asks the driver to move, but the driver gets belligerent, won't budge. My guy ends up impounding the van for an inspection to make sure there's nothing funny inside. Turns out, the van was clean. But the driver was—"

"Chinese?"

Joseph Reid

"Even better," Tranh said. "The driver's the brother of one of the guys Walker shot."

Cooke grunted.

"You said Terminal 3 baggage claim," I said. "Mission Bar & Grill is in Terminal 3."

"Right," Tranh said. "You walk down the pier from the bar, exit security, and the escalator to baggage claim's right there. Would have been a straight shot from the bar to the van."

"Okay," Cooke said, "so right before the woman meets El-Amin, they've got an empty van waiting outside. When that piece gets taken off the board, calls go up and down the chain. Next thing we know, they're executing this crazy escape off the balcony."

"All fits," Tranh said.

"And that's why El-Amin was wandering around," I said. "Burning time."

"Right," Cooke said. "Waiting for a text with the new plan."

"About the woman," Tranh said. "Her name is Shanshan Liu. Twenty-five, Chinese national, grad student in physics at Cal on an F-1 visa. Unmarried, been in the States for almost seven years since coming over for college. She was holding a one-way ticket for a plane to Seattle—that's how she cleared security."

"When did she buy the ticket?" I asked.

"Three weeks ago."

"If Liu was the bait and this was a honeytrap operation," Cooke said, "then she and El-Amin must have overlapped a lot. We're going to need to go back through, find all the places they went together—"

"Way ahead of you," Tranh said. "She's got no transit records—no BART, no Uber or Lyft—to places that intersect El-Amin. Looks like she knew that'd leave a trail. But Durham got us GPS from her primary cell phone. They overlap at several of those clubs in the Tenderloin."

"Meeting in places no one would see them," Cooke said.

"Or expect them," I added. "Anything tying Liu to the gunmen?"

"Not yet," he said.

"Still," Cooke said, "that's almost all of it. The big question now is who put Liu up to this. I doubt she sprang for a private jet on her PhD stipend."

I winced. Ever since Cooke had told me Dallas was the destination, there'd been a nagging feeling in my gut about which company had triggered all this. Now that we knew they'd used a woman to target El-Amin, things seemed even clearer. I had to ask, even if a part of me desperately didn't want to know. "Do you see any connection between Liu and Texas Electronics?"

Tranh took a minute to respond, and I imagined he was going back to whatever material they'd pulled on her. As the silence lingered, I tried not to acknowledge Cooke, who seemed to be staring at me. My muscles tensed, and I fought not to fidget. The dull ache from my scalp burns had receded, but a nervous energy crackled across my skin. The tattoo on my back shoulder, a math equation that was one of the first I'd had inked, started to hum.

"I'm looking now," he said.

I held my breath.

"Nothing I can see."

"Wait, what? Are you sure? No internships, no grants?"

"Nope," Tranh said. "Her résumé lists a scholarship, and who funds her research. She's listed on the web page of a UC professor, but he doesn't have any T.E. connections, either."

While I was sure Tranh had done his best, I knew there must be something. There had to be. He might have missed it, or it might've been too well hidden to decipher. But it was there.

Cooke let Tranh go shortly after that. When I glanced up, I found her staring at me again.

"You're thinking T.E. because the jet's heading to Dallas?" she asked.

Cooke asked questions so smoothly, she could lull you into forgetting interrogation was one of her specialties. Still, I'd worked with her enough, I could see purpose and resolve in the way her green eyes watched me.

"Yep," I said, trying my best not to make the answer seem too rushed. It was the truth, after all.

"What happened there, Seth?"

I shrugged. "How should I know? I haven't worked there in—"

"I don't mean *now*. Don't patronize me. I mean back when you were there. You've never told me the story."

*Exactly.*

"I . . . You heard it this morning."

"Your mentor committed suicide."

I nodded.

"How—"

"Do we really need to relive the worst moment of my life for the second time today?" I spat the words—all venom and indignation—in hopes that they'd prod her to move on.

They didn't.

"Yes," she said. "We do. Not because I'm trying to torture you, but because I need to know what I'm up against here. Whether you can handle this. Whether T.E.'s involved—"

"Oh, don't worry. I have no love for T.E."

"—or if they're not."

"What does that mean?"

"If you have some ax to grind, if you're looking for some kind of payback for what happened to your mentor, that could jeopardize our entire case. Hell, if they could even *accuse* you of that, it could blow us out of the water."

"So, this is all about the case, then?" I rolled my eyes.

Cooke leaned forward, her expression changing to a desperate, pleading smile. "I can't help if I don't even know what we're talking about."

For once, I stared back at her. Looked right into her green eyes, willing her to drop this whole discussion.

"If you can't tell me, you're off the case."

"You heard Durham," I said. "He ordered me—"

"You know he'll pull that order if he needs to."

"And you'd tell him to do that? Really?"

She sighed heavily. "If I need to, yes. For chrissake, Seth, I'm your friend. Just tell me what happened. It's over—it's in the past, it can't get any worse."

For the first time since takeoff, I glanced out the window. A layer of thin clouds lay below us, shielding the desert floor like a veil, the white wisps softening the terrain, obscuring its harsh edges, smoothing its jagged peaks.

Cooke really had no idea what she was digging at. As bad as things had been before, they could get a whole lot worse. If I told her everything, what assurances did I have that Shirley wouldn't find out?

A voice in the back of my head wondered if I should let Cooke pull me from the case. Refuse to cave to her demands, let her call Durham and bench me. She'd done that once before, in the Berkeley investigation. She'd do it again.

But no matter how much sense that option made, no matter how much safer it might be, I couldn't. If I ran away, if I missed this chance to set things right, I might never get another.

Of course, that meant getting past Cooke right now.

And I saw only one way to do that.

# CHAPTER 31

"My mentor's name was Clarence," I said, fighting to stop my voice from cracking. Still staring out the window, I didn't dare look Cooke in the eye. "Clarence Aiken."

"Okay."

"He hired me at T.E. straight out of school, based on nothing but his intuition that I might be a good engineer. I stepped into his lab, and from then on, I saw him literally every day. I'm talking long days, all-nighters when we were on deadline. We worked together, we traveled together. From the start, he treated me like a son. I spent almost all my spare time at his house. His wife, his kids, they were . . . they are like my own blood."

My voice gave way, and my eyes welled up.

"That's Shirley and your godkids you're talking about," she said softly. "The ones you visit in Fort Worth."

Blinking my eyes clear, I nodded, then looked at her sharply. "But I never told you their . . ."

Cooke cocked an eyebrow. "You think I haven't looked into this, even a little?"

"If you already know everything, then why are you forcing me—"

"I don't," she said quickly. "Not everything. I know what's in the police report." She splayed her fingers and started ticking facts off on her fingertips. "I know Clarence died from a self-inflicted shotgun wound. You found him and were distraught at the scene. I know about his family because they're listed in the report. I know you told the police that you were aware he had the weapon at the office, and that it violated company policy, but you didn't do anything about it."

Way more than I suspected she knew. I guess I should have known she'd do the research.

"Well. There you are."

"Knowing you," Cooke said, "I'm guessing you felt responsible."

I resisted any kind of reaction. This wasn't about my feelings—it was about facts.

"I figured guilt over Clarence is why you abandoned your dream job and moved to the West Coast," Cooke said. "But you go back to Texas every so often and support his widow and children. When Berkeley killed Sarah, I'm guessing that . . . dredged up all those old feelings. Which is why you've been torturing yourself, convincing your-self that her death was your fault."

"Sarah died because of *me*." The words tumbled out in a croak. "You were there. You know."

"You're right, I was there. And I do know. Which is why you need to listen to me right now. Berkeley killed seven people. She almost killed me, and Grayson, and she wanted to kill you, too. Absolutely none of that is your fault."

I shook my head. It all sounded so simple when she said it. So sterile and easy. "I provoked her. Berkeley killed Sarah to get to me. If I hadn't—"

"My God, Seth. Do you remember where Berkeley was when we caught up to her?"

I stared at her. We both knew the answer.

"Where was she?" Cooke demanded.

"DFW."

"Headed to do what?"

This was pointless. Dumb psychologist games designed to make me feel better.

"She was headed to kill more people," Cooke said. "If we didn't stop her—if *you* didn't do *your* job and stop her—"

"Don't," I said. "Just don't."

"Don't tell you the truth? Don't remind you about the good things you've done? The people you saved that night? Or the teenage singer who's alive because of you? All those people a couple of months ago? Christ, Seth, how many lives will be enough for you to forgive yourself? A hundred? Two hundred?"

I drew a long, slow breath through my nose.

"So, back to my original question: Why are you mad at T.E.? What did they do?"

"Everything," I said. "Nothing."

"Do you think they drove Clarence to suicide? Was he depressed because of work?"

Not knowing what to say, I simply shrugged.

"I'll take that as a yes."

"These companies . . ."

"These companies what? *What*, Seth?"

"You heard El-Amin's sister. They chew you up, they spit you out. Then it's on to the next thing."

"T.E. didn't care about Clarence?"

I laughed out loud. "Hardly."

"Are you going to be able to set that aside? I mean, it's likely to be different people involved in this."

"I'm not so sure you're right about that."

"T.E.'s a huge company," she said. "It's been years since you worked there. What are the odds—"

"The odds they're still there?" I shook my head. "Whether it's the same people or not, it's not like the place suddenly grew a heart or a soul."

Cooke's voice dropped to almost a whisper. "First of all, I'm not suggesting that. But second, what if they're *not* behind this?"

I did a double take. "They are. I mean, what about all the China connections? A Chinese conglomerate just bought T.E." I didn't tell Cooke, but I also knew exactly who at the company would have facilitated that takeover.

"If T.E.'s behind it," she said, "we'll nail them. Just like Durham ordered—I promise. But if they didn't . . ."

I took another long breath.

She stared at me hard. "I need to know this. If they didn't . . ."

Finally, I gave in. "Then we'll nail whoever did."

Cooke nodded. "All right. Then I need you to do one more thing."

I winced. "What—"

"Call Jim Grayson. We're going to want Dallas PD to meet us at the airport—we're not going to have much time to set up before Liu's jet arrives behind us."

# CHAPTER 32

*Tuesday, August 28, Five Years Ago*

The week leading up to the Boost test flew by, and before I knew it, I was standing beneath the large blue-and-white event tent we'd borrowed from Marketing and erected in the parking lot. A set of folding picnic tables supported the flat-screen monitors we'd moved outside along with enough computers to do a moon landing. Most of my engineers, including Clarence, sat in folding chairs around the tables while our three guests of honor stood lined up behind them, close enough to watch the action.

I stood to the side so I could address the team while also watching our observers' faces.

Randolph Rodgers, the CEO, was dressed in a sharp gray suit with a bolo tie, ostrich boots, and a black Stetson. He tilted the hat back a fraction and said, "I assume we're not out here to watch the Rangers play the Yankees. Wanna explain what we're going to be seeing today, Seth?"

"Sure. We've installed Boost in a Toyota Corolla. Here, you'll be able to see and hear everything as if you were the driver." I gestured toward one set of screens, where images from various angles inside and outside the car were being projected. Then I pointed at another set, arranged vertically, where lines of text were methodically scrolling upward. "This monitor shows you, in real time, lines of code running inside Boost."

His eyes narrowed. "I trust you've fixed what happened on the last go-round?"

I gave a curt nod.

"I hope you've got it locked down. Amara here beat both you boys by finishing her task first, so right now I'd say she's on the pole."

"That's an awfully . . . awkward way of phrasing it, Randolph." Brooks wore a mischievous grin with one eyebrow raised.

Rodgers looked confused a minute. Then his face lit up, and he laughed hard enough that his shoulders shook. "Whew, you got me there." He turned back to me. "Like I was saying, you got your work cut out, trying to keep up with her."

"Then we'd better get started," I said. "Ron Coslick will be our man in the car."

On the monitors, we could see a figure in a racing helmet climbing behind the wheel and waving at one of the little dashboard cameras.

"We can talk to Ron through this." I gestured toward a microphone on the table beneath the monitors. Holding down the "Talk" button, I said, "Ron, can you hear us?"

He gave a thumbs-up signal on camera. Speakers at either end of the tent boomed with his voice: "Loud and clear. I'm ready to go."

"Then take her out to the highway."

To fill time, I explained a little bit about Boost's voice control, as well as some of the user-interface touches we'd added to the new proto-type. Rodgers was listening, but I wasn't sure about Scott. Brooks took her phone out of her purse and began tending to it.

Once Ron guided the Corolla onto Route 75 and got it up to speed, I had him execute a few of the same moves we'd made during the first test. Finding music, changing volume.

All the while, I kept glancing back at Rodgers and the others to gauge their reactions.

Scott took a half step forward and pointed at the monitors showing the operations code. "What's going on there? It looks . . . different all of a sudden."

Everyone turned their attention to the monitors, where command lines were now appearing and scrolling by faster and faster. It gave the screens a frantic, helter-skelter feel.

"Those extra lines are from an external system," I said. "Someone is hacking into Boost through an exploit."

Rodgers turned to me, his face reddening. "I thought you said you fixed it."

"We did," I said, allowing myself a mild grin.

"I have no idea what you're smiling about," he said. "This isn't funny. It seems like—"

"Like everything's normal?" I moved toward the monitors showing Ron inside the Corolla, where Boost was faithfully following commands. Grabbing the microphone, I asked, "Ron, is everything okay with you?"

He gave the camera another thumbs-up. "All systems normal."

The CEO's eyes ticked back and forth, trying to square the divergent scenes on the two sets of monitors. "I don't understand . . ."

I stepped over to the command scroll. "This line"—I pointed to one near the top—"is where the outside system triggers the exploit. This one is where it causes the chip to start rewriting itself to give the intruder more privileges. And this one"—I pointed at a line about midway down the screen—"is where the intruder starts telling the system what to do."

"But if all that's going on," Rodgers said, "why aren't we seeing it happen in the car?"

"Because the code they're attacking isn't in the car."

In my peripheral vision, I saw Brooks glance up from her phone.

"When I announced this test last week, I had a feeling whoever sabotaged Boost the first time would try again. So, I had the team move our new code to a secure location only a few people knew about. That's the code running in the Corolla."

"The hacked code we're looking at there"—Rodgers nodded at the lines scrolling by on the monitor—"where's that?"

I nodded at Clarence. "Bring her out. If you can."

A high-pitched buzz cut through the air. Out on the blacktop, the scale-model race car I'd gotten as a present for Michael drove into sight. Strapped to its roof was the old Boost module I'd resurrected, its wires snaking down into the chassis. The remote-control toy started pulling toward us, but its motions were herky-jerky, as if someone were stomping alternately on its accelerator and brake.

"I figured it'd be a lot safer in there than out on the highway."

Rodgers chuffed, and some of the team giggled.

"We left the old code in our source-code room," I said, "so that we could catch whoever showed up to insert another exploit."

"Did you?" Rodgers asked. "Catch 'em?"

"See for yourself." I nodded to one of the engineers, who flipped the switch controlling the video input. "Here's the video our security cameras captured last night."

The monitors that had been showing camera views from inside the car abruptly changed to images of our source-code room taken by the same security cameras that had captured the hooded figure the last time.

After a few seconds of still video, the footage seemed to jump, and suddenly one camera was pointed at the ceiling. A few seconds later, the same thing happened to the other cameras.

Rodgers sighed. "They knew about the cameras and took them out."

"Only the official ones," I said.

He did a double take. Behind him, I could have sworn Brooks did, too.

"I set up extra cameras around the lab, just to be safe."

The trail cameras I'd bought at Cabela's now kicked in. They were motion triggered, designed to capture video of animals passing by it in the wild. In our case, they started filming when the lab door opened. I'd rigged the little boxes in places that were hard to see but that would get clear shots of an intruder.

The plan worked. The footage showed a well-dressed Amara Brooks stalking into the lab and sitting at the terminal. I'd even mounted one camera up in the ceiling tiles, pointing down at the keyboard. That one gave a nice close-up shot of her manicured nails dancing across the keys.

Rodgers, Scott—everyone—turned to Brooks, whose eyes had widened.

"I have a feeling if you check the phone she's been playing with for the past few minutes," I said, "you'll find some kind of controller for the exploit. She's been trying to crash our car this entire time, standing right next to you."

Brooks's expression turned defiant, even as her hand dropped to her side and slipped the phone into her pocket. "Randolph, you can't possibly believe this."

"I believe my own eyes."

Earlier this morning, I'd called ahead to Manny and warned him we'd need security to stop by our demonstration. Right on time, he and a couple of other uniformed guards arrived at the tent.

Rodgers took notice. "Manny, can y'all please escort Ms. Brooks to the police station?"

As the guards closed in around her, she twisted away from their outstretched hands, stepped toward Rodgers, and pointed a crimson-tipped finger at his nose. "You do not want to do this. The things I know about this company—"

"All of which you're obligated to keep secret under the NDA and nondisparagement clause that you had us add to everyone's employment contract," Rodgers said, standing his ground. "Now I see the value in all that."

She lowered her hand, but the scowl remained.

"Want to tell us who you're working with?" Rodgers asked. "If you didn't do this alone, you don't have to be the only one to suffer."

Brooks glanced around, made an odd face, and said, "I'm not saying a fucking word. Not without my lawyer."

Rodgers locked eyes on her. "That sounds like the kind of rock-solid advice you always dispense. Take her away, boys."

As the guards escorted Brooks out of the tent, I kept my eyes on Scott. If he was upset to see her go, though, he certainly didn't let it show. Since I lacked any evidence to prove he was her partner, I could only hope that she'd eventually turn on him.

When Brooks was gone, Scott sidled up to Rodgers. "Well, I didn't see *that* coming."

Rodgers grunted. "I think Amara had an awful lot of us fooled. Thankfully, not Seth here. That was some clever thinking you employed, son."

"Thank you."

"I know y'all need to finish your tests," Rodgers said, "but I think I've seen enough. Once you're done, why don't you come by my office so we can chat about things."

"Of course." I tried to keep a poker face, but fireworks started exploding inside my head. Talking with Rodgers? *In his office?* Did that mean I'd won the job?

Scott apparently seemed to think so. "Boss, I've got news, too," he said. "HighBuy is all lined up for us. With this new module to sell"—he nodded at me—"we'll way outpace our previous sales volume with them."

Rodgers beamed. "That's great news. I'm glad you mended those fences—you're gonna want to spend a lot of time with those folks over the next twelve months keeping them happy, making sure they don't stray again."

Scott's face cracked, but only for a moment, at the implication of what Randolph had said. A mix of surprise and anger that quickly gave way to another smarmy smile. "Of course," he said. "You know they're in good hands with me."

◆　◆　◆

Two hours later, it still seemed incredible that I was being shown into Randolph Rodgers's office.

Since it was on the top floor of the main building, I figured it would have a superb view. But as his secretary led me to one of the guest chairs arranged in front of Rodgers's desk, I saw that it was even more impressive than I'd imagined. The apex of the glass corner pointed directly toward the Dallas skyline, almost like a compass aiming at the magnetic north pole. With the sun still high in the sky, the glass peaks glittered in the distance.

Rodgers's secretary left me alone in the office, which was a unique mix of old and new—rustic wooden furniture and a twelve-point buck's head right alongside a series of flat screens and digital speakers.

I was trying to calculate how much Rodgers's desk—a slab of dark-stained wood approximately the size of my apartment kitchen—must weigh when his voice called out behind me.

"Seth!"

I turned to see Rodgers entering through a side door I hadn't noticed. His hat was gone, but he still wore the jacket and bolo, making me slightly self-conscious that I hadn't changed clothes to something fancier.

"C'mon over, let's be comfortable while we chat." He waved me toward a seating area adjacent to the door he'd used. As I was crossing the room, he presented me an open wooden box. "Cigar?"

"No, thank you, sir."

"Brandy, then?" His eyes flashed. "You ought to have a little something special to celebrate your accomplishments today."

"I'm . . . okay." I didn't want to mention my condition in case he wasn't aware of it. "But I don't mean to deprive you."

He let out a sharp "Ha!" before maneuvering himself onto one of the couches. "If you're staying all business, I guess I will, too."

I didn't know the exact etiquette of where to sit, so I took the end of the couch set perpendicular to Rodgers, suddenly hyperaware of my arms and legs and unsure how to position myself.

"How'd the rest of the testing go after I left?" Rodgers asked.

"Very well," I said. "I think Boost is ready."

"And, I'm guessing, so are you." His eyes twinkled.

"I wasn't sure if you'd made your decision about the promotion. Zach Scott is a solid candidate—"

Rodgers leaned back in his chair. "Zach has some good ideas. He's a little too focused on Asia for my taste—I think it blinds him to some other issues. But if you end up in the position, I think you ought to look at implementing some of the financial things Zach put together."

"So . . . you haven't actually made your decision, then?"

"I mean, there's obviously some things you and I need to talk through. Compensation, for one thing."

Truth was, I'd have taken the new position for my exact same pay. Although the back of my brain warned me against admitting that.

"But I'm guessing most of those will be formalities," Rodgers went on. "You're the leader in the clubhouse, no question. There's really just one more thing you need to do to cinch this thing up for good."

"Another test, sir?" I tried not to sound too disappointed.

Rogers's cheeks formed deep dimples as he smiled. "You could think of it that way. Although I have to admit, it was part of Zach's proposal. The piece that jumped out to us in management as making the most sense."

"Oh . . . what's that?" I had no idea what else they could possibly want to see from me.

"It's a little thing, really," Rodgers said. "A formality, almost. I hate to even ask it."

After all the craziness with Brooks and Clarence and Julian, I wanted the process to be over. I shrugged. "Name it."

Rodgers smiled. "Given the tough-mindedness you showed today, I'm sure it will be no problem at all."

# CHAPTER 33

*Thursday, February 23*

I hadn't been to Dallas's Love Field in months. Not since the last time I'd seen Detective Jim Grayson, in fact. That had been last summer, when I'd passed through town trying to figure out who was aiming to kill Emma, the teen pop star I'd been assigned to bodyguard.

While most people who fly tend to be familiar with DFW, the massive hub halfway between Dallas and Fort Worth, Dallas's second airport is smaller and quieter. Love Field sits within sight of the Dallas skyline, and as the freeways and suburbs have sprawled outward, they've surrounded the airport like concrete kudzu, boxing it in to the point where it couldn't expand even if it wanted to.

When we touched down, the G650 didn't make for Love's tiny T-shaped terminal. Instead, we taxied directly from the end of the runway to the string of commercial buildings that lined the eastern edge of the airfield. Although I hadn't realized it before, Gulfstream Aerospace has its own facility at one end, a small complex of offices and white triangular hangars, each with the company's logo on top. Our jet pulled to one of these pyramids, then maneuvered inside.

The sliding doors hadn't quite shut behind us when T lowered the steps and let us off the plane. Not knowing if I'd see him again, I shook his hand on my way out and thanked him for the first aid.

Cooke made immediately for a side door to the hangar, and I followed her outside. Although the tarmac felt like an oven, the Texas sun didn't pack quite the punch it did in the summer—despite shining brightly, it sat lower in the sky and allowed a breeze to tickle my forearms and work its way up my shirtsleeves. Runway noise was noticeable here, but not much louder than the hum of cars along the frontage road that bordered the field.

We'd emerged into a small parking lot wedged between the Gulfstream hangars. The lot was fed by a narrow tree-lined street cutting in from the frontage road toward the runways. The roofs of the next set of hangars were visible on the opposite side of the street, beyond the trees. Cooke started in that direction. When we rounded the corner of the Gulfstream hangar and got a full view of the street, though, we found a string of police cars parked and waiting.

"I thought you said you didn't get through to Grayson," Cooke said.

"I didn't. I left him a message—I guess he took it seriously."

We traced the line up to the lead car, an unmarked, nondescript Chevy. There, a dozen uniformed officers had gathered around a short man in a slightly rumpled gray suit. He was standing on the grassy shoulder, leaning against the car, talking and gesturing, his burnt-orange tie swinging this way and that as he pointed in various directions.

By the time we drew close enough to hear, he was saying in his thick twang, "—if we move too soon, the DA'll have my ass."

When he glanced over and saw us, he blinked twice. "You know, when I said we should bring extra backup, I figured y'all might call Plano, or Fort Worth. Not fucking Quantico." His weathered hounddog face cracked into a grin as he cut through the crowd toward us. He wrapped Cooke in a bear hug first, then did the same to me.

As he was pounding on my back, I realized he lacked the cane he'd used the last time I'd seen him. He still had the slightest trace of a limp—it gave his gait a kind of roll—but if that was all that remained from the multiple gunshot wounds Berkeley had inflicted, Grayson was a lucky man.

"What the heck brings you two to our fine city?" Grayson asked.

"Trouble," Cooke said. "What else? I'm glad you brought a big force. We might need them, depending how much firepower we're up against. I think we ought to—"

Grayson, who'd stared at her blankly, now interrupted. "Firepower? I don't know what you're talking about. Did dispatch tell you I was out here?"

"You mean you didn't get Seth's message?"

"What message?" Grayson looked from Cooke to me, then back again. "What are y'all even doing here?"

"We just flew in from San Francisco," she said. "We're chasing a plane, trying to arrest the people inside. It's going to land any second. We don't have time—"

Grayson's face contorted in a look of disbelief, his head shaking slightly. "We're here on a tip," he said. "Bad guys coming in from San Francisco, it just so happens."

"Tip?" Cooke asked. "What tip? What kind of plane?"

Grayson pointed to the far end of the street. Although the narrow lane dead-ended at a grassy circle out past some chain-link fencing, you could see directly onto the airfield. Out on the runway, a sleek silver jet was touching down.

"That plane," he said.

Cooke and I traded glances again. Then she said, "This is awfully weird, but we don't have time to sort it out right now. We need to get into place."

"Totally agree," Grayson said. "C'mon."

Grayson flashed hand signals to his officers. A trio jogged back to the end of the cruiser line and moved two cars into position to block the street. The remainder fell in behind us as we marched toward several squarish sky-blue hangars.

"We're headed for Hangar Two," he said.

We entered it through a side door. Inside, the layout closely resembled the Gulfstream hangar: essentially one big room with some small workspaces partitioned along one wall. Ultrabright white LEDs mounted on the ceiling created a broad rectangle of light on the polished cement floor, while leaving distinct patches of shadow around the periphery and in the corners. The vast center of the space stood empty, while pallets of crates and rolling toolboxes as tall as a grown man had been pushed out to the edges. This left plenty of places for Grayson's officers to conceal themselves. Cooke, Grayson, and I hid behind a row of steel drums that were centrally located. From there, Grayson could view and signal his officers on either side.

We had only a few seconds in our new positions before the large sliding door on the runway side of the building began to move with a loud hum. As it drew open, bright sunshine poured in, rendering the hangar interior darker and darker by contrast, until it seemed like our spot was shrouded in night, staring out at day.

Once the door retracted completely, the silver jet rolled in. I now saw that it was a Dassault Falcon 7X, one of the few jets that could give a Gulfstream a race. The biggest difference between them was the Falcon's third engine, mounted on the tail. But where our Gulfstream seemed to have been dulled down in appearance, this plane was exactly the opposite. It looked even slicker and sexier up close, its hull gleaming in the light from above. The plane pulled far enough into the building to clear the doorway, and its engines shut down. The heavy door began to slide closed behind it.

That wasn't all.

On the opposite side of the hangar, a matching slider began to yawn open. A black SUV pulled through and drew nose to nose with the plane. As the truck braked to a halt, the front hatch of the jet opened.

From our position behind the drums, Grayson signaled his officers to stand ready.

Cooke's gaze, I could see, was locked on the airplane staircase. In my peripheral vision, I detected two figures stepping down from the plane, but I didn't need to look at them—I knew who they'd be. The SUV was a different story. Its side windows were heavily tinted, yielding no clue as to who might be inside.

The license plate narrowed it down considerably: "TXELEX4."

As the moments ticked by, my pulse accelerated. I had that tunnel-vision feeling again, my vision gradually narrowing from the truck to the rear door, then from the door to its handle.

Finally, it swung open.

A man stepped out.

His black suit was impeccably tailored, his shoes buffed to a high shine. He didn't wear a tie—the collar of his shirt was unbuttoned and the most casual thing about him. He was built like an executive, no other way to say it: trim enough, he clearly exercised to control his weight, while the hint of a belly protruding over his pants confirmed he ate and drank richly. Once his soles rested firmly on the ground, the man buttoned his suit jacket and shot his cuffs. He didn't bother closing the vehicle's door. He simply circled around it with movements as crisp as the creases in his suit.

The man's face seemed both new and familiar all at once. High cheekbones and a cleft chin still framed a rugged triangle of a face. The hair, slightly thinner, had grayed only at the temples, while a thin gray goatee now adorned his chin. His skin was nearly the same bronze as Grayson's, but without the weathering—even from this distance, the man's hands and face looked supple enough, you figured he went through a bottle of moisturizer each week.

The giveaway, though, was the eyes. Blue, definitely, but so distinctively pale that if it weren't for the dark circles around the irises, they might almost have blended in with the whites.

Recognizing Zachary Scott spread an electric charge across my skin that raised every hair on my body. I tried to swallow but found my throat was nearly closed.

Scott circled around the front of the SUV. His arms were bent, almost folded across his chest, his hands up around the middle of his breastbone as if he were a surgeon guarding them from becoming unsterile. When he reached the bumper, he paused as his eyes darted to the side.

He was looking almost directly at our position.

My breathing froze, and my heart seemed to wriggle in my chest.

Finally, Scott's gaze turned frontward again, and he resumed walking.

I forced my muscles to relax, and my heart started pounding again, making up for lost time.

He walked straight up to Liu and Anah El-Amin, whose hands were no longer bound. The young man's shoulders seemed slumped, as if in defeat.

"Do you have it?" Scott asked.

To my right, Grayson raised his arm.

Liu turned and nodded at El-Amin, who produced a wallet-size metal cartridge. He held it out to Scott, his hand noticeably trembling.

In one smooth motion, Scott reached out, pinched it, and pulled it back to him.

That was when Grayson popped out from behind the drums yelling, "Dallas Police—everybody get your hands up!"

# CHAPTER 34

The police moved as a well-choreographed team. In a matter of seconds, Scott, El-Amin, and Liu were surrounded by uniforms who frisked them for weapons, while other officers gave the SUV driver and pilot the same treatment. A third group searched the vehicles.

Grayson remained behind the drums until he received the all-clear sign. Then he holstered his weapon and circled around to join his men. Cooke and I followed.

Scott was still facing El-Amin and Liu, although all three now had their hands on their heads. The uniform closest to Scott was holding the battery.

Grayson went straight to him and said, "Let me see that." He turned the small metallic device over his hands. He asked the cop closest to El-Amin and Liu, "Did you find anything else on them?"

"No, sir. They're clean, and the plane is, too."

Grayson turned to me. "Now that we got a minute, let's straighten some things out. Why exactly are you two here?"

"That box," I said. "It's a prototype of a cutting-edge new battery. He"—I pointed at El-Amin—"is the engineer who developed it. She"—I pointed at Liu—"seduced and kidnapped him to get it, shooting up SFO airport in the process. And finally, he"—I pointed at Scott, unable to resist a smile—"is the one who organized this whole thing, to steal this tech for Texas Electronics and its new Chinese owners."

Grayson rubbed his chin with his palm, his eyes shifting over to Cooke. She nodded.

"What he just said is completely and utterly false," Scott said. He kept his eyes forward, not looking at me as he spoke. "T.E. is the foremost electronics company in the world. We don't *steal* technology from anyone. We don't need to."

My chest swelled, and for the first time in hours, I felt new energy coursing through me. "And yet, there you are, standing with your hands on your head."

"Easy, Walker," Grayson said. "There's stuff going on here you don't know about—"

Scott turned when he heard my name. "Walker?"

His pale eyes squinted at me, and his mouth cracked into a smirk. "It *is* you. I didn't recognize you with the, uh . . . fashionable headgear."

"Don't worry about the bandages, Zach—I'll live. If you're sweating something, it ought to be innocent people dying from all the bullets your people fired at SFO. That's felony murder."

Scott shook his head dismissively. "You don't understand. Detective Grayson here is going to let me go. And if anyone's getting arrested today, it's him." Scott pointed with his chin at El-Amin. "For trafficking in stolen property."

"Whoa, whoa." El-Amin's mouth had spread into a nervous smile. "Let's all calm down here. I haven't—"

Cooke cut in. "Jim, you said you're here on a tip. What's that about?"

"Funny you should ask. I got a call early this morning. Mr. Scott here called to say that T.E. had been offered some stolen equipment. He volunteered to help us apprehend the thieves—he even offered to set this whole thing up with the company jet and all."

"You mean, like a sting?"

Grayson pressed his lips together and nodded slowly.

Scott had resumed staring straight ahead. In profile, the corner of his mouth had curled up into a noticeable grin.

"He's lying!" El-Amin's eyebrows rose, and his nostrils flared. His hands came off the top of his head as he shouted, "You can't believe him!"

In a flash, uniforms seized El-Amin by the arms. Those got twisted up behind his back with enough force that he ended up hopping on his feet like he was dancing. "Hey, hey!"

"Sir," Grayson said, "I'm gonna have to ask you not to make any sudden moves like that, 'kay?"

"Sorry, sorry!" El-Amin glanced all around him. "It's just that he—"

"If you're so innocent," Grayson said, "how do you know Mr. Scott's lying?"

"I . . ." As his voice trailed off, El-Amin looked at Cooke, then at me.

Grayson held up the battery. "You saying this belongs to you?"

El-Amin nodded emphatically. "Yes, that's my work. My ideas are in there." As he glanced from one of us to another, his face fell at the collective lack of response. Finally, he said, "I'm the victim here. They kidnapped me, threw a sheet over my head—"

"You liar!" This voice was higher pitched. I looked past El-Amin and saw Liu behind him, her face reddened with rage.

Grayson turned to face Cooke and me, his shoulders raised in disbelief.

"Don't you see what's going on?" I asked Grayson as I pointed at Scott. "He's in on it; he's giving you these two so he can walk off with the tech for himself."

"But I'm holding the battery, Walker." Grayson waved it in the air for effect. "Mr. Scott's the one who handed it to me. He's not getting anything out of this deal."

At that moment, Shen's comments about trade secrets echoed in my head. I turned back to El-Amin. "What did you do on that plane ride? What did you tell them?"

The young engineer's expression changed. The anger drained away from his face, and his eyes widened.

"You did it," I said, "didn't you? You gave them everything."

El-Amin looked too stunned to answer.

"Scott doesn't need the box anymore," I said, whirling around to Grayson. "He's got the know-how to manufacture it himself now—that's why he's happy to give it up. You've got to arrest him—he's behind this entire thing."

Over Grayson's shoulder, Scott grunted. "If you arrest me, after the way T.E. and I cooperated, so help me, my very first phone call isn't going to be to a lawyer, it's going to be to the governor. I'll have everyone in here charged with false imprisonment, wrongful arrest, malicious prosecution . . . you name it."

I locked eyes with Grayson, imploring him. "You can't let him get away with it, Jim. The tech in that battery is the next big thing. If Scott walks out of here with the information he's got, the Chinese will be pumping out copies in a month."

"Your badge, your gun," Scott said. "Your pension. I'll have it all."

Grayson retreated a step, glancing back and forth between us.

Cooke moved to his side and rested a hand on his shoulder. "Jim, let's talk over there a minute." She gestured to a spot ahead of us, between the SUV and airplane.

Slowly, he nodded. "Okay, sure."

I started to walk with them. But as I drew even with Scott, Cooke glared at me and stabbed a finger at the floor. "You, stay."

"I . . ."

"No." She spun on her heel and stalked away. Grayson followed. Several yards away, I couldn't hear anything they were saying. With their backs to us, there wasn't even the chance to read lips.

While I stared at them, my stomach churned. I was standing mere inches from Scott. Hands still perched on his head, he rocked back and forth from his toes to his heels and back.

Although I didn't want to make eye contact, I couldn't avoid it.

Scott was still grinning, even showing some teeth between his lips. "Watch," he said. "They're gonna come back and let me go."

I glanced back to Grayson and Cooke. Their heads were still bobbing.

"You seem awfully upset, Walker. You're taking this really personally. You still not over the old man offing himself?"

I inhaled deeply. Told myself not to listen.

"I guess not."

Grayson and Cooke looked like they'd almost finished. They'd turned to face each other now.

"Can't say I blame you," Scott said. "Real tragedy."

Cooke said something to Grayson. He nodded.

"Should've seen it coming, though. Management knew Clarence was weak for years."

My fists balled up, and I turned to face him. We were so close, I could feel his breath, see the red veins in the whites of his eyes. "Shut. Up."

"Take it easy," Scott said, "I'm complimenting you, Walker. Clarence's weakness is why you surpassed him. As soft as you are, you were still stronger than him."

My heart was pounding in my ears. In my peripheral vision, I could see Cooke and Grayson coming back. I needed to hold on for a few more seconds.

"Here they come," Scott said. "Get ready for bad news."

Grayson and Cooke stood shoulder to shoulder. I checked Cooke first, trying to catch her eye, but she stared past me. That wasn't good. I looked at Grayson as he started to speak.

"Mr. Scott, you're free to go for now."

"Wait, what?"

Grayson's lips kept moving, but I didn't hear all the words.

Scott lowered his arms and readjusted his shirt cuffs, grinning now, even as El-Amin wriggled in the cops' arms in protest. "I told you, Walker," Scott said, taking a step toward the SUV.

"Wait," Liu said. "You're leaving me with them?" She glared at Scott, enraged. "After everything I did for you—"

262

Scott shrugged and glanced around at the cops. "I have no idea who this woman is."

At that, Liu launched herself at him, landing a fist squarely in his gut, doubling him over and making him stagger. "Cannot believe I *slept* with you. *Nǐ shēng háizi méi pìyǎn.*"

She flailed at him with her fists, even as the cops stepped in to restrain her. They lifted her up to pull her away, but she lashed out with her feet, catching Scott on the shoulder.

"Go ahead and cuff her," Grayson said, looking annoyed. "Read her her rights."

Although one particularly burly officer had Liu squeezed in a bear hug from behind, she continued to thrash wildly. She continued cursing Scott in Mandarin and insulting El-Amin's looks and manhood.

I glanced over at El-Amin to see if he understood what she was saying. While he seemed oblivious to her words, he was clearly crestfallen. "You . . . you were . . . with *him*?" he said in disbelief.

Liu fired off more Mandarin insults aimed at everyone in the room.

Although his lower lip quivered, El-Amin got it under control. He puffed out his chest at Grayson and said, "They forced me into all this. They *kidnapped* me. I want to press charges—"

Grayson rolled his eyes. "Cuff him, too."

The officers quickly restrained El-Amin and dragged him over to join Liu on the periphery of the space.

Scott was recovering from Liu's blow, one arm pressed still against his midsection.

"You okay there, Mr. Scott?" Grayson asked. While his voice sounded concerned, he didn't budge from his spot several steps away.

Scott grunted. "Better now that you're doing your job, Detective. I don't suppose you're going to haul Walker here away for falsely accusing me."

"I said this before, sir," Grayson said. "Maybe you didn't hear me. You get to go *for now*. We'll see how all this shakes out."

"You're forgetting," I told Scott, "I'm with the good guys now."

"Big, brave lawman with a badge and a gun," Scott said, glancing down at his feet for a moment. "When you consider everything that happened"—he glanced up—"it's pretty impressive you can even look at a gun, let alone fire one."

The acid that had roiled my stomach now bubbled all the way up into my mouth. It scalded my tongue and deadened the feeling in my mouth as my cheeks and forehead burned hot.

"You know, Mr. Scott," Grayson said, "I'd be the slightest bit careful about pissing Seth Walker off, if I were you. I've seen him hit shots with that Sig of his that would make a SEAL sniper blush."

"Oh, really." Scott regained his sick smile, even as he waited a beat to speak again. "I guess Clarence helped you find your niche after all, Walker. Natural-born killer."

My hands balled into fists so tight, I could feel my fingernails digging into my palm. Although a part of my brain screamed at me to walk away, the image of Clarence's face filled my mind, followed by his body.

"I saw you that morning, you know," Scott said, leaning toward me, his voice barely a whisper. "Covered in his blood. Soaked—like you'd bathed in it."

I took a deep breath through my nose.

"Do you still feel the old man's blood on you sometimes? Like it won't wash off?"

Something in my head snapped. Like a screen going dark for a second. By the time I realized what was happening, my shoulder was already driving my fist forward.

I didn't pull back. Didn't stop.

Instead, I made sure every ounce of strength—every bit of leverage I could muster, every muscle fiber I could engage—was behind that punch.

The *crack* when my knuckles struck Scott's face was so loud that it echoed through the hangar.

# CHAPTER 35

On the plus side, Grayson kept me from having to spend the whole night in jail.

When I punched Scott, he dropped to the floor like I'd struck him with a hammer. Blood trickled out of his mouth onto the concrete, forming a puddle under his chin. But he didn't stay down for long: he pushed himself up to a sitting position.

And that was when he started laughing.

"You all saw that," he said. "Assault and battery." Eyes closed, he let his head fall back. The cheek where I'd struck him was noticeably dented. "Oh, fuck that hurts," Scott said, laughing again before pausing to spit out a mouthful of blood. "You broke my face, you splendidly stupid piece of shit. I cannot wait to sue you for every goddamn nickel you'll ever earn in that piece-of-shit, GS-whatever job. If you even keep it." His eyes flicked open, and he glanced around. "Well? Aren't you going to arrest him?"

The cops gathered around Scott. Helped him to his feet.

And then Grayson was at my shoulder.

"Do it, Grayson," Scott said. "I've got plenty of witnesses."

"I . . ." Grayson shook his head. "Amigo, I don't want to do this . . ."

The look on his face was what made me feel worst.

"I'm sorry, Jim. He—"

"Shut up, Walker. Don't talk, you've got the right to be silent, god-damn it. Use it."

He spun me around, not that I was fighting, and read me my rights while he clicked the cuffs shut.

Grayson walked me through every step of getting processed. It seemed to take forever, even longer than it took for an ambulance to arrive and cart Zachary Scott off to the hospital. By the time we climbed into Grayson's black pickup outside the dirt-brown correction center by the river, the dashboard clock said it was nearly seven.

He wasn't talking, so I didn't ask our destination as we traced city streets I didn't recognize. Eventually, we finally reached a building that I did: built mostly from unassuming red brick, it looked like a giant slab of white stone had dropped from the sky, slicing it in half. A silver five-pointed badge gleamed above the entrance.

I'd been to the Jack Evans Police Headquarters before and figured Grayson would lead us up to his cubicle inside the homicide unit on the fifth floor. Instead, we took the elevator to the third, winding through hallways to a set of paired interview rooms. Grayson strode right into one, and I followed.

This was the listening half of the paired rooms, with one-way glass you could see through and a suite of recording equipment. Cooke was seated at a table in the center, making notes on a yellow pad, clearly having already conducted a questioning session. When she looked up and saw us, she pursed her lips and gave Grayson a dirty look. "He shouldn't—"

"I know," Grayson said flatly. "I only came by to see if you'd made any progress. Then I'll bring Walker here to whatever hotel he's gonna spring for."

"You could have called," she said.

"If I'd called from the car, Walker could have eavesdropped."

"You could have called *after* you dropped him."

Grayson shook his head. "No way to be certain you'd still be here. And I don't have your cell."

Cooke smiled weakly, blowing air out her nose in a little sigh. "You know, you're pretty good at that."

"What twenty-six years on the force gets you." His expression never changed. "So, where are we?"

She sighed again, heavier this time. "El-Amin lawyered up right after we got here."

"Sounds like the smartest thing that guy's done this entire caper," Grayson said.

"Liu speaks English, but she's claiming she'll only talk in Mandarin. Not surprisingly, we don't have a translator at this time of night. So, she's going to have to sit and stew till morning."

"I'll do it," I said.

"Pardon my French," Grayson said, "but that's a fucking horrible idea."

"I agree," Cooke said. "We can't risk it."

"Do you know our extradition policy with China?" I asked.

"We don't have one," Cooke said.

"Exactly."

She shrugged. "Then they can't ask for her back."

"I'm not talking about her." I tapped my earpiece. "I've been listening to media stories about T.E. since we were on the Gulfstream. Zach Scott's moving to China."

"What?"

"With the recent acquisition, he's been tapped as the new head of global strategy. He's going to work out of their headquarters in Shenzhen."

"That means—" Cooke started.

"He'll be untouchable," I said.

"If you'd let me finish," she said, "it means we need to work fast."

"He's scheduled to start *next week*, Melissa. The company has its big annual black-tie banquet tomorrow night, where all the T.E. execs'll be drinking scotch and patting themselves on the back for jacking up the share price; then Scott flies out Sunday night."

Cooke's eyebrows rose. "Oh."

"So, if you're thinking you should keep me away from all this because I'll ruin your chance to prosecute his case, there's not gonna be one. It's now or never. And Liu's so pissed off at Scott, she's our best hope."

She closed her eyes a moment, then looked at Grayson. He cocked his head and raised one shoulder.

◆ ◆ ◆

When I entered the interview room, Liu looked asleep, her forehead resting on top of her arms on the table. Her hair was tied back in a long, loose braid.

She stirred when she heard the sound of the door. When she saw it was me, she made an unhappy face and muttered, *"Gwáilóu,"* under her breath. Literally, *ghostly man*, a common insult for Caucasian foreigners in China. Then she put her head back down, facing away from me.

"*Wǒ tīng dào nǐ shuō dí huà.*" *I know what you said.*

She turned back, startled.

"Yes," I said in Mandarin, "I speak Chinese. So, we can talk."

Liu furrowed her brow.

"You and I have something in common," I said. I shadowboxed a punch. "I think you hit him harder, though."

She smiled slightly at that. "You were smarter, to hit him in the face."

"I've known Scott for a long time. He uses women to do the things he does not want to be blamed for."

"I wish I'd known that." She looked away to a far corner of the room.

"Where are you from in China?"

"A rural village. You won't have heard of it."

"What is nearby?"

"It's approximately a hundred and fifty kilometers from Changsha."

I nodded. "Hunan province."

Her eyes grew. "You've been there?"

"Once. A friend took me to see the stone pillars at the Wulingyuan Scenic Area."

Liu smiled. "That's very famous. My village is in the opposite direction."

"What do your parents do?"

"They're farmers."

"Where did you go to college?"

"Peking University."

That was considered one of the two top schools in China, their version of MIT or Caltech, although the admissions rates were much lower. I'd seen statistics that only 0.05 percent were accepted to Peking University, and admissions were tilted in favor of those in urban areas. "You must have scored off the charts on the *gaokao*," I said, referring to the two-day national admissions exam all Chinese students took.

Her pale cheeks flushed pink. "When I was thirteen, my father wanted me to stop school. To help at home until I was older, then to get a factory job to make money. I begged him to let me continue with school. I needed to succeed to ensure his investment in me was rewarded."

"How did you end up meeting Scott?"

"He came to a conference where I was presenting. He found me afterward and gave me a card with his telephone number. I was hopeful he'd offer me a job."

"And you called him."

She nodded. "Several times he didn't answer. Then, after a few months, when I assumed there was no hope, he called me. He said he was in San Francisco for twelve hours only, but he'd make time to meet me if I could come to the city."

"What happened?"

"I put on my best suit and caught the next train. When I reached the city, he told me which hotel. And when I reached the hotel, he said he was making time before a dinner appointment, so I should come to his room to talk."

"There was no dinner?"

Liu's eyes dropped to the tabletop.

"If he forced you, that's a crime."

"It wasn't what you think. Not exactly. That first night, he didn't touch me. He was very flattering. He admitted he'd lied about the dinner appointment. But he said it was so we could talk privately, and that it was for my protection."

"How's that?"

"He said the American government didn't want T.E. to be acquired by a foreign company, particularly one from China. That it was a matter of national pride, and so the government was watching everyone. If I was seen with him, he said the government would conclude I was some kind of spy, sent here to trap Americans. They might revoke my visa. So, he said we shouldn't be seen together."

Although the China deal had closed several months ago, it had been publicly announced well before that. "So, this first meeting happened . . . what? Over a year ago?"

"Two years," she said. "It was St. Patrick's Day—I remember the parade and all the people dressed in green drinking that night."

"Then what?"

Liu sighed. "We continued meeting in secret each time he was in town. A few times, when we would be in the same location, he would arrange a rendezvous. For almost a year, it remained like that first night, the two of us talking. It wasn't physical, or even romantic. Much of it was about the company—his plans, how I could contribute. Until, one night, he claimed to have feelings for me."

"Did you have feelings, too?"

"I think so. Maybe? He was older and charming. I didn't have anyone else in my life. The relationship hadn't started out inappropriate, so whatever feelings there were seemed natural. He wasn't married, so it wasn't adulterous. He would just appear in San Francisco unexpectedly, or text and have me meet him somewhere. We met in Miami once. Chicago another time. It was . . . fun. Exciting."

"And it seemed like you had an inside track on a job."

She nodded. "Oh yes. We talked about what my position would be. My salary. The things I could do for my parents. With the acquisition of T.E., traveling home would be easier."

"How did Scott raise the issue of El-Amin?"

"It came up as an intellectual exercise. He gave me some papers to review, asked me what I thought about Anah's battery ideas."

"And?"

"I thought the approach was . . . clever. Not groundbreaking, nothing that upended the laws of physics. But a clever way to take advantage of things that had been known for a long time."

I found it funny that Liu's reaction was much the same as Shen's. "After that, how did Scott assign you to work with El-Amin?"

"That's the thing—he never really did. Scott commented how important the technology would be, how much of an advantage it would give Magnet over T.E. But he complained that he couldn't approach El-Amin, that if he so much as sent an email, he could be sued in court. The way he discussed it, the solution became obvious—I think I was the one who suggested that I approach El-Amin. I was thinking of T.E. as my company as much as Scott's."

Clever, the way Scott manipulated people. "Whose idea was it to seduce El-Amin?"

Liu looked up to the ceiling and smiled, almost in spite of herself. "Again, it almost seems like I suggested it. I remembered how Scott had approached me, how disarming it had been. So, I kind of did

271

the same thing. The secret meetings, convincing him he wanted to do this."

"Did he fall for you right away?"

She laughed. "Oh yes. Like a schoolboy. Plus, he was . . . angry at Magnet. The second he learned he could have me *and* hurt the company? It was a win-win."

"Why was he so angry?"

"He thought they asked too much of him. They made him work too hard."

"That's it?"

She nodded. "He's like many in this country—he wants to be rich, successful, but doesn't understand the wealth and opportunity he already has. A week of the work I did for my father as a twelve-year-old girl would kill him."

"Did you have feelings for El-Amin?"

Liu made a face like she'd bitten into week-old sushi. "Goodness, no."

"Then how did you . . ."

"I never let him touch me. The more I frustrated him, the harder he worked to get me."

"He thought you two would go off together at the end of this, right?"

She nodded. "He thinks of life like a little boy."

"Then what changed his mind? Why the pillowcase and the kidnapping?"

Again, Liu looked off to the far side of the room and smiled. "That was his big contribution. He didn't want Magnet to know he was cooperating with us. He has some . . . insurance policy, or something that will pay money to his family. It would be voided if he was a thief, but if he was a victim . . ."

"They'd still get the money." I remembered the look on his mother's face as she talked about her health struggles. "So, then, what? All the kidnapping stuff was an act?"

She nodded. "When the truck was impounded, Anah freaked out. He worried we'd be caught and he'd be exposed. Of course, he was so inept, he didn't even complete the one simple task we gave him."

"Which was?"

"He was supposed to place a box that would make smoke in the international terminal. Originally, we thought it would distract the police while we made our way out to the van. Once that wasn't possible, we still hoped to use the smoke as cover. But he never planted it. *Wōnangfèi.*" *Good-for-nothing coward.*

Liu obviously didn't know we'd intercepted the smoker, but there was no reason to share that with her. "Scott knew about the gunmen and the change in plan?"

"I assume."

"You didn't talk to him from the airport?"

"Not today, no. When we decided on the plan, he said he knew people in San Francisco who would help at the airport. The phones were left in my mailbox. There was a number to call, and I called it. But they were all Scott's people."

"Did you see them talk with Scott? Did any of them mention him?"

She closed her eyes and shook her head. "No time. I was just trying to escape. I didn't have a gun. I didn't want one."

"One last question. Will you testify? Against El-Amin? Against Scott?"

"Like in court? Like on TV?"

I nodded.

She gave a tiny shrug. "What will it get me? I can't stay in the US now, but if I go back to China, I have no job, and Scott and the company will tell everyone I'm a traitor."

"You have your degrees . . ."

"Meaningless. There are millions of people in China who can do physics. Who would want me?" She looked away. "I'm ruined."

# CHAPTER 36

"Poor girl," Grayson said.

I was in the listening room again. Grayson leaned back in his chair on two legs, jacket off, tie loosened. Cooke had her elbows on the table in front of her, hands clasped like she was praying.

"She rolled the dice and lost," Cooke said. "I don't feel the least bit sorry for her about that. I'll tell you who I feel for: El-Amin's family. They think he's this . . . upstanding guy, this caring brother and son, who sends money back to help them live better lives. And now, as he's going to federal prison, they're going to learn he's selfish and lazy. His mother, in particular, doesn't need this."

"I'm more concerned with what comes next," I said.

"Next?" Grayson asked. "Couple rounds of Shiner Bock is what comes next, far as I'm concerned."

I stared at Cooke, waiting for one of her usual plans to emerge.

She raised her arms, stretched them over her head, then flopped against the backrest. "For once, I'm with Grayson. We've ridden this train about as far as it goes."

"What about Scott?"

"What about him?" she said. "He's really smart. He's left himself a ton of reasonable doubt to hide behind. You saw her—if right now, at the absolute peak of her rage, she's going to admit that approaching El-Amin and stealing the battery was her idea, what's she going to say under a well-prepared cross-examination? Scott'll claim T.E. does things the reputable way. That he squealed on her the moment he realized what the misguided foreigner was trying to do for him."

"He must have left *some* loose ends."

Cooke nodded matter-of-factly. "I'm sure he did. And if you gave me twelve months to build a federal case against him, I'm pretty confident I'd find them. But I'm even more sure I'm *not* going to find them by Sunday."

I felt the rage rising again—the equation on the back of my shoulder burning like a brand. I'd taken bullet shrapnel that hurt less. I didn't want to be bitter toward Cooke, or at least I didn't want my bitterness to show, so I looked away.

"What?" she asked.

"He can't get away with this," I said. *Not again.*

"There's nothing more we can do."

"There's always something."

"Seth?" In the corner of my eye, I could see Cooke shift forward in her chair. "Seth, you need to let this one go . . ."

"No." I slammed my fist down on the tabletop.

"Don't be childish about this," she warned. "We did everything humanly possible to bring Scott in. But sometimes the bad guy gets away."

I stalked over to the one-way glass. I didn't want to look at Cooke, but I knew there was a kernel of truth to what she was saying.

"A little help here?" Cooke said behind me.

"Look," Grayson told me, "you ain't helping anybody right now. You're too upset, amigo. Let's get you someplace you can sleep this off. It'll look better come the morning."

I whipped around. "This isn't some bullshit hangover, Jim. We're talking about letting Scott go to China with breakthrough technology—"

Grayson shook his head. "Horseshit."

"Excuse me?"

"What you just said is nothing but a steaming pile, and you know it. You've got a hard-on for Scott because of whatever happened between you guys before. I get that. What you need to do is stop making this some kinda dick-measuring contest for just a goddamn second."

I sighed. "You don't understand."

"That's a pile of shit, too," Grayson said. "You think I never had a case go sideways? Some clever asshole outsmarts us or gets away from the DA? Of course, I have. We all have. Living with that's just part of the job. A shitty part, but there you go."

When I looked at the Dallas detective, his face was as sincere as I'd ever seen it.

"Jim's right, Seth. The best thing we can do now is work to put Liu and El-Amin away for as long as we possibly can. Maybe something tumbles out of that we can use against T.E. Maybe we find some silver bullet against Scott, and the next time he visits the States, you get to slap cuffs on him at the airport." She raised her eyebrows and smiled hopefully, but I couldn't let Scott go any more than I could forget Clarence or everything else that had happened.

"I'm free to go, right?"

Grayson closed his eyes and nodded.

When I walked out of the Jack Evans facility, it was just past nine. I needed someone to talk to, someone who'd listen without listing off all the reasons Scott was untouchable.

My first thought was Emma, the sweet but slightly sassy teen singer I'd helped last year. After a short stint in rehab, some solid therapy, and help from an emancipation lawyer Shen had recommended, Emma now had a small apartment to herself here in Dallas. Although I helped a little with the rent—the profits from her singing career were still tied up in litigation—at least she was out on her own, deciding for herself what came next in her life.

Then I remembered that Emma had traveled to Nashville this week. I'd checked her schedule when I'd planned my trip to see Shirley and the kids, only to learn that Emma had been invited to a songwriters' festival. It was a chance to meet agents and potential partners who could help relaunch her music career.

Nine here meant seven at home in California, so I texted Shen. Almost immediately, three dots showed he was typing a response.

**At dinner w/ gallery owner. Call u later?**

Shen's partner, Brian, was an artist—getting his work placed was a big deal.

**Sure, no prob.**

Lavorgna was a nonstarter—I'd have to explain the arrest to him soon enough, but I wasn't in any rush to do that. I thought briefly of calling Loretta again, but I knew she couldn't help. We never discussed the substantive parts of my job, only how I got from place to place; plus, there was a chance she'd say something to Lavorgna before I could explain the situation to him. I even tried a pilot I knew, Zonnie Begay, a Native American woman who'd started her own charter company. She texted from New Mexico that she'd be back to Dallas next week.

Maybe it was just as well. Pouring out all my anger and sadness onto someone else wasn't going to help anyone. I needed to plan, and I was better off doing that alone. Besides, it wasn't like anyone I still knew had had any ties to T.E.

Well. One person did, but I couldn't go there. Calling them was the last thing I wanted to do. Or *should* do.

I checked the clock on my phone. Out of habit, the back of my brain did the math on how many hours remained before Scott left forever.

Not much time.

I thumbed out a text and squeezed my eyes shut as I pressed "Send."

◆ ◆ ◆

Shirley seemed overjoyed at my text asking if I could come out to the house for the night. I spent the whole ride from Dallas to Fort Worth thinking about how to carry out the plan I'd come up with without getting either of us into trouble. While I knew Shirley didn't have time for much of a social life between her work and kids, I figured there had to be someone from T.E. she kept in touch with, whether it was via social media, the neighborhood, or through kids' sports.

T.E.'s annual banquet tomorrow night was the company's biggest party of the year, more elegant and better attended than the holiday party in December. Held each February, the black-tie banquet celebrated the founding of the company, so everyone, even retired executives and staff, was invited. To accommodate the crowd, T.E. rented out one of the posh hotels downtown. Dallas being Dallas, the black-tie affair had grown larger and more opulent each year, the men arranging to arrive in Lamborghinis and Ferraris, the women scoring the chicest designer gowns possible.

The banquet was always one of the hottest tickets of the Dallas social calendar, so it wouldn't be easy, but all I needed was to find one person who couldn't attend. A single invitation to get me inside.

When the car dropped me at the curb at nine fifty, Shirley was waiting outside the front door in her bathrobe and slippers. As I took my time getting up the flagstone walk with the duffel slung over my shoulder, she met me halfway with a warm hug.

"The kids are going to be so happy you snuck back," she said, smiling. "Is this for work?"

"Sort of," I said. "And I may need your help."

We made it to the rocking chairs out back before Shirley started peppering me with questions and plying me with iced tea.

"Because this is an ongoing investigation, there's a lot I can't say." I'd practiced that line in the car, hoping it would let me dodge any inquiries that got too inconvenient. "Do you remember Zachary Scott?"

"That preppy weasel you were up against for the promotion? Who could forget? I heard they actually gave him the job after you left."

"That's right."

Shirley's eyes narrowed. "Has he done something wrong?"

"I—I can't say. But I need to get in front of him before he moves to China on Sunday."

"China?"

I nodded and quickly explained about Scott's new role—and country of residence.

"Hmm . . ." She checked her phone for the date. "The banquet's tomorrow night . . . You remember it, right? *The* banquet? Everyone will be there."

I smiled. "That's exactly what I was thinking. I was wondering if you might know someone—"

"Ooh!" Her eyes widened, and she popped out of her chair. "I'll be right back."

She disappeared into the house for long enough, I wondered what she was doing. She returned with something clutched to her chest.

Shirley sat on the edge of her rocker, turned squarely toward me. When she lowered her arms, a greeting-card-size envelope was wedged between her fingers. "I get this every year," she said. "And I usually don't even open it, let alone think about going. But . . . ta-da!"

She pressed the envelope into my hands—it was heavier than you'd think, constructed from thick card stock. The address was printed in fancy cursive script, and when I turned it over, the T.E. logo was embossed across the seam like an old-fashioned wax seal.

"Open it," she said, her face aglow.

I slipped a finger underneath the flap and gently peeled it up. Inside was a shiny golden envelope inviting the recipient to the T.E. banquet at Hotel Crescent Court.

"This is great," I said. "I was going to ask you to hunt for a spare among your friends." I looked up from the invitation. "Thank you."

"I can't wait," she said, beaming. "I mean, I never get out of here. A night on the town, all dolled up? I won't know myself."

When I realized she was thinking of coming along, a knot formed in my stomach. "Shirley, I . . . uh . . . I don't know that you want to go to this one. If I get the chance to go after Scott . . ."

"You think I'd miss seeing that?" She let out a little chuckle. "Not a chance."

"I'm serious," I said. "I don't know how he'll react—it could be dangerous. And even if not, if you're with me, the company's going to blame you for giving me this."

"I don't care." She wore a broad, proud smile as she shook her head. "Not in the slightest. Like I said, I've never gone before; I doubt I'd ever go again. But to have a night out, to see you—man of action, in action—and to maybe rub it in to a few of those uptight jerks who never appreciated Clarence—all while you take down Scott? That sounds like just about the best night ever."

The knot in my gut cinched even tighter. If Shirley came along, the risk she'd hear or see something that might expose me was huge. But she was the only way I could get into the banquet to begin with, and now that I'd raised the idea, there was no way I could disinvite her.

As if to prove the point, she leaned forward again, wrapping her hands around mine and looking me in eye. "I know you're trying to protect me," she said. "And I'll do whatever you ask, but just . . . let this old girl have one big night on the town."

Shirley wasn't "old" by any stretch—if she was pushing forty-five, I would've been surprised. But I understood why she felt that way. While I tried to help out as often as I could, it was usually focused around the kids. Clarence's absence surely affected her as much as it did them, maybe more. Between working and taking care of her children, it left little room for herself. Seeing how desperately she wanted this, part of me yearned to give it to her.

Another part of my brain screamed against it. And the tattoo on the back of my shoulder seemed to sear my skin.

I couldn't take the intensity of her eye contact. Pressing me, pleading with me. I had to look away.

"Please?" she asked. Her voice dropped to a whisper. "I need this."

I wanted to swallow, but my mouth had dried up, and even if it hadn't, I didn't know that my throat would have allowed it.

"Okay, but promise you'll do whatever I say at the party. If I tell you to go hide in the ladies' room, you'll do it, right?"

She nodded without hesitation. "Absolutely."

I took a deep breath and sighed it out. "Okay."

# CHAPTER 37

*Friday, February 24*

The next day, I rented what might have been the last tuxedo in Dallas—I had to call three different shops before I found one that could help. Shirley let me borrow her car to retrieve it, and while I was out, I picked the kids up after school.

From his car seat in the back, ten-year-old Michael asked, "Hey, Uncle Seth, is my mom getting ready for tonight already?"

"I think so," I said. "She got her hair done this morning, and it sounded like she had some other things to do."

"Do you think she needs some time to finish up?"

"Maybe. Why?"

"There's a new ice-cream store all my friends have been talking about. If you wanted to waste some time, that would give us something to do."

I glanced up in the rearview mirror and saw the little man looking at me. He was trying hard not to seem eager, the effort obvious on his face.

I couldn't suppress a grin. "I don't know. I don't want to get in trouble."

"Mommy always says, when we're with you, you're in charge," Rachael said. "So, it's up to you, Uncle Seth."

How could I refuse?

We ended up at a place called Melt. Before we ordered, I forced Michael to answer twenty division problems and Rachael to spell *gorilla*, *purple*, and *rainbow*. Both passed with flying colors, and soon they were anxiously scooping spoonfuls from their respective paper cups.

Several bites into his Chocolate Chocolate, Michael brought up one of his new favorite topics. "When I get old enough, Mom said I can fly to California so we can hang out."

"That sounds like fun, little man. You gonna let me teach you to surf?"

"Oh yeah. Except, aren't there sharks in the ocean where you live?"

"I think there's sharks in the ocean everywhere," I said.

"Have you ever seen one?"

I nodded.

Rachael's eyes grew as wide as saucers. "And you survived?"

"Yes," I said, chuckling. "Sharks don't bother you. They just want to do shark things."

"Eating *is* a shark thing," she pointed out before loading a spoonful of Pecan Butterscotch Cake into her mouth.

"Does that mean you're not going to come visit me?" I stuck out my lower lip.

"I'll come visit," she said, swirling the spoonful around in her mouth as she talked. "I just won't go in the ocean."

"Where do you want to go?" I asked. "Disneyland? Something like that?"

"I saw a show on the Discovery Channel that said your Natural History Museum has a lot of *Tyrannosaurus rexes*. That's where I want to go."

"Fair enough," I said.

By the time we returned to the house, I needed to get cleaned up. Other than working around my injuries, the biggest problem getting dressed was the Sig: with my shirt tucked in and the jacket over it, my normal waistband holster wasn't going to work. Fortunately, I had a shoulder rig and twisted into that before pulling the jacket on.

It was nearly five by the time I came down the hall from the guest bedroom. Although the sitter had arrived, the kids were paying no attention, instead kneeling on the couch to play paparazzi to our red-carpet moment.

I received a couple of subdued "oohs," but when Shirley came out a moment later in a floor-length plum-colored dress, the kids went nuts. Michael was clapping; Rachael just knelt there silently, mouth agape.

"What do y'all think?" Shirley asked as she performed a little twirl.

"You look like a movie star," Michael said.

Rachael's mouth was still hanging open.

Shirley looked at me. "Well?"

"Fantastic." And I meant it—her short, chestnut hair was styled just so, and the gown's dark color contrasted beautifully with her green eyes. The gold pendant that hung from her necklace shimmered.

I recognized the outfit.

Years ago—back when Michael was still in preschool, before Rachael was even born—Clarence had taken Shirley out for their anniversary. Although he wasn't a fancy eater, he'd gotten them reservations at Fearing's, one of the hottest restaurants in the city. Shirley had worn this same dress. Clarence had surprised her with the pendant as a present; he'd had me buy it for him in Hong Kong while I was visiting one of our suppliers.

"You sure I look okay?" Shirley asked. "A bunch of women half my age have been planning their looks for this banquet for about three hundred and sixty-four days."

"Those debutantes have nothing on you," I said, giving the kids a wink. "We should head out, though. Otherwise we'll spend the whole night in the valet parking line."

The Hotel Crescent Court is one of Dallas's finest, set at the corner of Maple and Cedar Springs. Those two roads meet at a narrow, acute angle, creating a long, pointed protrusion in front of the hotel proper. The hotel made use of the awkward area by converting it into a cobblestoned plaza. That, along with the hotel's Renaissance architecture, made you feel like you'd come upon an old French chateau in downtown Dallas. For the banquet, the hotel had converted the cobblestone into a multiple-lane valet stand, where three cars could be dropped off at once.

Shirley's RAV4 stood out for being the only "normal" car in sight among the Benzes, Bentleys, and Beemers. The valet driver actually gave me a dirty look when he took the keys—pissed off, apparently, about missing the chance to drive the bright-orange Lamborghini Aventador that pulled in one lane over.

Once I reunited with Shirley underneath the awning, her head was on a swivel. Everywhere you turned, beautiful specimens of humanity wore jewelry that would have made Tiffany jealous.

"Maybe this was a bad idea," she said.

I certainly had my own worries along those same lines—who knew how many people might recognize me? But, wanting to reassure her, I gave her a smile and offered my bent arm. "They'll just have to get over you looking so good. C'mon."

While I recalled this event being "big," it had tripled in size from what I remembered. The procession indoors wrapped through the hotel lobby and around to several ballrooms. One was dedicated to dancing. Another contained an elaborate buffet spread. A third had been outfitted with tradeshow-like booths, showing off the company's latest and forthcoming products. The hallway linking the three ballrooms contained several open-bar stations and roving waiters carrying trays of appetizers and champagne.

When one strolled past us, I waved him off, but Shirley took a glass.

"My gosh," she said, giggling after a sip, "that tickles. Do you know how long it's been since I had a glass of champagne?"

I was only half listening as I scanned the bar lines for Scott.

"Where should we even start?" Shirley asked. "Do you have a plan?"

"I saw a program on a sign back where we came in. Management's supposed to deliver a keynote speech to kick things off. I'm guessing he'll show for that if nothing else. Otherwise, I just need to keep my eyes peeled. I'd prefer to catch him alone." I emphasized that last word, hoping it would stick. "If you want to, you know—"

"Oh my gosh, Helen? Is that you?"

Shirley had turned to our right, where a woman with curly red hair was moving between ballrooms. The two looked at each other with shocked expressions for a long moment, then hugged.

"What's it been, five years?" Helen asked.

"Longer than that, believe it or not," said Shirley.

I leaned close to Shirley's ear and said, "I'll leave you to it." When I got a wave in return, I strode off for the food room; I was a free agent for the moment.

◆ ◆ ◆

After an hour and a half, the good news was, I hadn't been spotted.

Nor had I seen any faces I recognized. I'd heard that T.E. had been suffering heavy turnover, especially since the acquisition. It was possible that no one I knew five years ago still worked there.

The bad news was, I hadn't had any luck finding Scott.

I'd started out watching the keynote. Delivered by the head of HR, it was a rah-rah speech about how the months to come were full of promise and excitement, thanks to the acquisition. Her comments about the company's record profits and share price elicited loud cheers from the crowd—from their wide eyes and broad smiles, they seemed to be eating it up as fast as the filet mignon at the end of the buffet line.

At every pause in the speech, people raised their glasses and clinked them with their silverware, nodding along like congregants at a revival.

If I'd still worked here, I'd have been worried. The expense of tonight's festivities, the feel-good messaging—all of it seemed designed to distract from whatever bad news was coming next. Downsizing, a reorganization . . . something.

Awash in champagne and chardonnay, with bellies full of brisket and broccolini, the crowd didn't seem to care.

With the buffet room a strikeout, I moved to the product show-room. I didn't expect Scott to spend any time in here—he didn't care about the products beyond their capacity to generate revenue—and, sure enough, it was another strikeout.

Finally, I checked the dance room. They were switching over from some kind of big-band act to a DJ. With the music momentarily paused, the parquet floor had cleared, and I got a good look at everyone standing around the periphery. No Scott.

So, I worked my way back out to the bars. The hallway was still crowded with people mingling and sampling the appetizers. I worked my way from one end to the other and back again, checking every face I could see. Although I kept spotting Shirley, she was engrossed in different conversations each time, allowing me to slip by unnoticed.

Finally, tired of pushing my way through the crowds. I set up against a wall adjacent to one of the bars. Across the way stood a set of doors the HR woman had used before and after the keynote. The more I watched that entrance—guarded by a uniformed member of the hotel staff—the more I suspected it was reserved for the highest-level executives.

I hadn't considered that there might be some other more exclusive gathering place in the hotel. If that was where the most important people were, that was where Scott would be.

I'd just started thinking about how to talk my way past the guard when Shirley sauntered up, carrying another glass of champagne.

She rested her free hand on my shoulder. "You doin' okay?"

"I'm fine," I said. "Are you?"

She gave me an exaggerated nod. "I've had more grown-up conversations in this last hour than I've probably had the whole rest of the year." She leaned closer and smiled. "Thank you."

I patted her hand. "You're welcome. But you may wanna slow down on that stuff before you set yourself up for too rough a morning tomorrow."

"I'm gonna go visit the little girls' room and get some water."

"Good idea," I said.

I crossed my arms, watching as she started away, the slightest wobble in her step. I'd been so preoccupied with finding Scott, I hadn't thought about the process of getting Shirley home. With me striking out on the former, the latter now seemed like a pressing challenge.

That was when a voice to my side said, "Jeez, Walker, the old man's widow? Maybe you've got less shame than I thought."

# CHAPTER 38

Scott had approached along the wall, staying out of my peripheral vision while I was talking to Shirley.

I spun, only to find him wearing one of those clear plastic face masks they give athletes when they've broken a nose. His voice sounded nasal and honky, like he was suffering from a bad head cold. But he was smiling wickedly, his eyes watching Shirley go.

"I mean, she always did have a certain Mrs. Robinson, MILF-y quality to her. Still, I never thought you'd go there."

My fists clenched, as did my teeth. "Leave her out of it."

"Easy, killer," Scott said. "You already got arrested once—are you really itching to go back to jail already? Although with all the tats, you'd fit right in."

"Why have you been hiding from me all night, Zach? You scared or something?"

"Hiding? Hardly. I've been watching you since you stepped out of that jalopy."

I stared at him blankly, unsure what he was getting at.

Scott chuckled. "We're a *tech* company, remember? This whole place is rigged with CCTV cameras and facial recognition—no one so much as pilfers a cheese puff without us noticing. I could have had you thrown out for trespassing anytime I wanted."

"So, why didn't you?"

Behind the mask, his eyes narrowed. "Because this is so much more fun."

"You always were a sick—"

"I'm not sick, just better than you. I've known people like you my whole life—smarter than me, more talented. But I always beat all of you because in the end, you just don't have what it takes to compete."

"Not this time," I said. "You had Liu do your dirty work, the same way you used Brooks before, and—"

"Really?" He cocked his head. "That's the best you've got? No wonder you're here alone—the police must have laughed you out of the building."

"I know you were sleeping with Brooks."

"If she'd had proof of that, she would have given it to the police."

"You were faster than me, running through those tunnels. I didn't catch you then, but I've got you now."

Scott stopped talking. That was how I knew I had his attention.

"This time you were sloppier," I said. "You paid for stuff and had Liu join you. You might have gotten her to cover her tracks, but people will remember. There'll be documents."

Scott scoffed. "The liar from China who's so desperate to stay she'll say anything at all? Good luck with that."

"Oh, we've talked to her. Not just me, the police. Her story's a lot more sympathetic than Brooks's ever was. No one believed Amara because she could be a ruthless bitch. Liu's not like that. And her testimony'll match really well with the phone records from San Francisco."

"I have no idea what you're talking about."

"When Liu's van got impounded, they panicked and called your intermediary in San Francisco. That's when you came up with the bright idea to give them the jet and hand them to Grayson. I mean, you were always planning to dump them; it was just a question of timing."

He glared at me, his silence telling.

"The burners were a nice idea, but once we found them, the cell records laid it all out. You getting that San Francisco call versus calling Grayson to tip him off—that timeline's clear as day."

His Adam's apple bobbed.

I was exaggerating how much the police had, but it was clearly working. I'd walked him up to the edge—now I needed to push him over. "Once the cops start looking, they'll find the data from El-Amin's battery, and then you're dead. T.E. won't protect you. You'll have nowhere to go."

"That's the way you think it works?" Scott grunted. "You think T.E.'s gonna to sell me out?"

"No American company—"

"T.E. *isn't* an American company, Walker. If anything, it's a Chinese company now, but even before the acquisition, we haven't been an 'American' company for years. We're a multinational corporation. *Multi*, meaning *many*. We belong everywhere," he said, waving his hand around. "We're way beyond nation-state border bullshit. That's an outdated anachronism, left to distract the rubes and keep government hacks like you busy."

His face spread back into a smile beneath the protective mask. "Honestly, though, I do have to thank you—your sudden departure opened up all kinds of opportunities for me. Rodgers would have fought me tooth and nail over opening up to China. But he backed the wrong horse when he picked you. Once you split, the board lost faith, and then it was just a matter of time till someone pulled the rip cord on his golden parachute."

Scott's expression suddenly morphed—he went from spitting his words to flashing an obsequious smile over my shoulder. Before I could deduce why, he said, "Mrs. Aiken, it's so good to see you again."

I whirled to find Shirley approaching a few feet behind me. She carried a glass of water, but her steps were still slightly uncertain. A jolt of fear hit me like an electric shock.

"Zachary," she said.

He pressed his palm to his heart, and his face grew solemn. "I'm so sorry, I shouldn't have assumed—is it still 'Mrs. Aiken'?"

"It always will be."

He nodded. "I should have expected. Can I ask you a personal question?"

"I think you just did," she said.

I winced. "Shirley, it's getting late—"

"Fair point," Scott cut in. "I just wonder, are you a Christian woman, Mrs. Aiken?"

I had no idea what Scott was playing at, but I needed to end this, now. "Shirley, we really need to go—"

"Yes," Shirley said, holding her chin high. "I am. But I don't—"

"See," Scott said, wagging his finger without pausing even a beat, "I knew it. I knew you had to be a Christian. I mean, you are easily the most forgiving woman I've ever met. I knew that had to come from somewhere."

"What on earth—"

Suddenly, I knew. "Shirley, the kids. We need to get you home." I wrapped my arm around her shoulders and started to steer her to the exit.

But Scott circled around us, stepping laterally to stay in Shirley's face.

"The kids?" he asked. "Oh, that's right, you and Clarence had two little bundles of joy, didn't you?"

I was sweeping Shirley along as fast as I could on her high heels.

"Let me guess," Scott continued, "they're as sweet and forgiving as you are."

"You're way out of bounds," I said. "Back off."

"I bet they even call him Uncle Seth."

"They do," she said indignantly. "As they should, considering what he does for them."

She smiled at me then. A proud, beaming smile—one she likely thought would show Scott who was boss and tell me how much she appreciated me.

It made my stomach turn.

I couldn't pick her up, but I needed to speed her along. Some way, any way, to get her out of there before Scott could do more damage.

"Don't you have to go pack for China?" I growled at him.

"You are quite correct," he said. "I'm headed to China, where they're not so big on organized religion. That's why I'm concerned about my eternal soul. Before I go, Walker, I just want to understand how Mrs. Aiken here can be so forgiving. So Christian."

"You keep saying that," Shirley said, "and I really don't know why. If you're mocking me . . ."

*No!* A voice in my head screamed. *No, no, no.*

It was one of those moments when time slowed down and tortured you with the inevitability of disaster. The car crash you couldn't avoid. The punch you didn't dodge.

"Not at all," Scott said. "I'm just in awe that a woman like you can be so kind to the man who killed her husband."

Shirley stopped dead in her tracks, and I nearly stumbled as her heels dug into the carpet.

"Don't you dare," she said, jabbing a finger in Scott's face, her expression a blaze of pure fury. "Don't you dare insult my husband, and don't you dare insult the man who helps me get by without him."

Scott must have put it together then. I don't know whether he always suspected and her reaction confirmed it, or whether he caught on in the moment. But the joy that spread across his face told me he knew exactly what happened. "Walker never told you, did he? Oh, you poor woman."

Shirley reared back and fired a slap across his face that knocked his head to the side and sent his face mask flying.

I heard a few gasps from people nearby. In a blink, we were surrounded by security. I held my breath a moment, hoping this would provide the exit I'd been looking for.

"C'mon, Shirley," I said loudly, placing my hands on her shoulders. "Let's get you home."

One of the guards piped up, addressing Scott. "Are you okay, sir? Shall we call the police or have them removed?" Gingerly, he handed Scott his face mask.

Eyes still clenched in pain, Scott put a hand to his injured cheek, shaking his head as if to clear the cobwebs. Finally, the corners of his mouth turned up, and he stared straight at me. "Leave them be," he told the guard. "I'm going to go; they're welcome to stay as long as they like. That'll give Walker time to explain how he fired her husband."

As he said it, a bomb detonated in my chest. I scarcely noticed Scott turn and stalk away—my brain was replaying the last moments I'd seen Clarence alive.

I'd come directly down from the meeting with Rodgers in his office. Clarence was still working, waiting to hear how it went.

I stepped in and closed the door behind me. My heart was fluttering, and my eyes were riveted to the ground. I kept telling myself that this was something I had to get through. Something I had to survive.

I didn't think at all about the shotgun in the corner of his office. Least of all that he might turn it on me. If I'd been smarter, or thinking more clearly, maybe I would have considered the possibility. Maybe pausing a second even for my own self-preservation would have given me time to think, to reconsider what I was about to do.

But I was too eager, too impatient.

Too fucking proud of myself.

I didn't want to do it, to fire Clarence Aiken. I'd resisted. But Rodgers had told me I had to, that it was Clarence or me.

And, in that moment, with the old man staring me down, I caved.

In my head, I did more twists than an Olympic gymnast to justify it. I replayed all the moments I'd ever been forced to defend Clarence, all the times senior colleagues had challenged me about him. I let myself recall every little time he'd disappointed me. If he wasn't fired now, I'd told myself, it'd be tomorrow, or next week, or next year. If I didn't do it, Rodgers would find someone else who would.

Clarence should have seen it coming, the voice in my head had said. All the signs were there—if he'd wanted to change course, he could have.

I was standing on the doorstep of everything I'd wanted. Everything I'd worked for and dreamed about.

If this was the last thing standing in my way, well . . .

I don't remember what I said to Clarence after I shut his office door. Some meandering word-salad that I'm sure made little sense, given that I'd never fired anyone. Least of all, someone I loved.

I do remember the look on Clarence's face.

The way his eyes, already small behind his glasses, grew even smaller. Rounder. The way they blinked once, twice. A third time.

The way his lips drew to a point as his chin started trembling.

He sniffled—one big, quick snort before he pinched his nose and touched the back of his hand against the corner of his eye to blunt the tear forming there. He looked confused and sad and overwhelmed, and the only thing I could think to do was to get the hell out of there before he started weeping and I did the same.

So, I turned and I walked out his door. And then I ran as fast as if a tiger had been chasing me.

I went straight home, telling myself the awkward feeling would melt away eventually. That, at some point, it would break like a nasty fever and I'd be cured.

I barely made it to the toilet in my apartment before I puked.

I fell to my knees, retching my guts out for what seemed like an hour. When there was nothing left to purge and my mouth was numb from the sour bile, I stood and stumbled to my bed. I remember flopping into it, thinking surely sleep would help.

Except sleep didn't come.

I tossed and turned that night—I never even got to sleep. That was the reason I'd headed in to the office so early the next morning. Not to get jump-started on the new day, or to demonstrate how eager I was. It was simply because it seemed like it might feel better than lying alone, miserable, in the dark.

I figured maybe if I went to the office, something would cheer me up. Something would remind me of the hellish stretch I'd gotten through, all the highs and the lows, and everything I'd accomplished.

And that was when I found Clarence's body in a congealing pool of his own blood.

Those memories rushed through me in a flash in the banquet hallway, holding me frozen.

Until I saw Shirley.

Tears were already streaming down her face, taking her makeup with them. Her mouth was open, but no sound came out.

She squinted, sending a rivulet of tears down her cheeks. "Did you . . . ? Did you . . . fire him?"

I had no words at all. My brain was still too confused to function.

Her head started rocking. Forward and back, just a millimeter or two. But then it picked up pace and the shakes became more forceful.

"You did," she said, looking away from me. "You did, of course you did."

I raised my hand toward her shoulder. "I . . ."

Shirley yanked her arm away. "No!" She retreated one step, then another. So fast, she almost tripped. "Don't . . . don't you ever . . ."

As her voice trailed off, her eyes dropped to the floor. She turned, grabbing the sides of her gown in her hands, and ran away as fast as she could.

# CHAPTER 39

I didn't go straight for a motel. Not at first.

My first stop was to try the house.

The Uber driver, already confused by the prospect of picking up someone like me wearing a tux, checked twice in the rearview mirror when I confirmed the address. He left me standing on the grassy shoulder, staring up the flagstone walk.

As long as I'd known her, Shirley had always left a light on. At the door, if nothing else. Home or away, even if she took the kids to see her parents in Oklahoma, she believed leaving a light on would keep away burglars, or anyone with malevolent intent. No security system, no remote internet camera I ever suggested was as powerful a home-defense mechanism in her mind as a simple sixty-watt bulb in the front-porch sconce.

I'd succeeded in getting her to switch to a long-life halogen, but that was the extent of my progress.

And that was why, when I saw the house completely blackened, no car in the driveway, I knew tonight was different.

Still, I trudged up the familiar stone walkway and rang the bell. Once, twice.

I banged on the door.

Useless gestures, but what choice did I have?

Part of me considered circling around the side. Reaching up over the wooden gate where the metal latch was hidden, squeezing past the trash cans in the breezeway, rounding to the back of the house to see . . . what?

I knew what I would find.

I also worried that one of the neighbors might call the cops about a tuxedoed stranger with a bandaged head sneaking around Shirley's house in the dark. Fifty-fifty my badge would get me through any questions, but those were long odds considering it would be my second arrest in two nights' time.

My things were presumably still locked up inside the house. All my clothes, my shaving kit, everything inside the duffel. Even my pad and mechanical pencil.

All of it replaceable, the least of my worries. But it meant I'd be trapped in this monkey suit until sometime tomorrow.

I trudged back down to the street. I called for another ride and had it deliver me to the nearest motel, a no-name place out by the freeway that still used metal keys on doors that faced onto the parking lot.

By the time I registered and reached the room, I'd already unclipped the bow tie. Inside the door, a single switch lit a circular fluorescent fixture mounted on the popcorn ceiling.

I immediately decided I didn't need more light than that. In fact, even it seemed like too much.

I shed the jacket first. Tossed it to the bed as I crossed the room. The shoulder rig followed.

I started to head for the sink, thinking I wanted to splash water on my face, but I'd no sooner reached it than I changed my mind. Spinning on my heel in the stupid, slippery patent-leather shoes, I began pacing back and forth past the foot of the bed instead.

I ripped open the front of the tuxedo shirt, plastic rental studs popping out and bouncing loudly off the particleboard furniture. The sleeves fought me like a straitjacket, but eventually I wrenched the shirt over my head and whipped it onto the bed.

All the motion tore at the road rash and bruising on my side, lighting the skin on fire, but I ignored it. My shoes flew across the room as I kicked them off. I kicked the pants, too, after dropping them to the floor.

I stripped all the way down, naked except for the earpiece and the slim little audio player that dangled from it. I held that in my hand, nearly oblivious to the air-conditioning nipping in places it normally didn't reach.

I'd started panting while shedding the clothes, and now my chest was heaving with every breath. The muscles under my collarbone constricted so tightly, I wondered if they were cramping. My ears became uncomfortable, and I wriggled my jaw, trying desperate to get them to pop, but fluid was sloshing around in my sinuses until eventually it found its way to my nose, and then my eyes.

I cried for a long time. Heavy, uncontrollable crying—wailing sobs that sounded like animal noises. Several times I thought I was done, but another wave of grief quickly overcame me. Although I couldn't see anything through the blur of the tears, I didn't dare close my eyes.

I was deathly afraid of what I might see.

I slid down, first to a squat, then to the floor, rough industrial carpet scraping against my bare ass, the metal bed frame cutting into my back, until I'd buried my face between my knees.

That whole time, my brain was cycling through questions. All the whys and what-ifs. I blamed and chided and reminded myself how the only one responsible for any of this was me.

I ached from the inside out.

Hands to my eyes, I tried, ham-fisted, to wipe away tears that wouldn't stop flowing.

Finally, my hands slid to my ears and pressed inward as I tried to shut out the sounds of my own voice reminding me of all my mistakes and how unworthy I was. Because the voices came from inside, my efforts naturally failed—there was no sound to keep out.

But as I covered my ears, I noticed something.

A touch—something hard, something solid.

My earpiece. Wedged in my right ear, as always.

For so many years it had served as my protection—a tiny piece of molded plastic that kept my odd neurological condition at bay, drowning out the cacophony that otherwise threatened to drive me mad. When I'm in the middle of one of those attacks, when my brain goes out of control, it's like I'm there but not—like a dream you can't wake up from, in which everything's happening to you, but you have no agency, no control. Whenever I've recovered from such an episode, the intervening time is lost. I don't remember what happened during my fit, what I was thinking about, or how it felt.

I rubbed the outside of the earpiece with the pad of my index finger. Its firmness felt comforting. Although I hadn't been actively listening, it had been pumping in a steady stream of narration from an audiobook about augmented reality. Material I'd been absorbing by osmosis, even as it helped maintain my tenuous grip on normalcy.

When my brain spirals out of control, there's physical pain that comes with it. Like a demolition derby in my head, all my thoughts start colliding—with each other, and with the inside of my skull—and I feel each of the impacts. The few times it's happened, inserting the earpiece is an immediate balm—it takes a little time for my thoughts to reorganize, but the pain vanishes almost instantly.

I wished I had an earpiece to tame this other pain. The hurt of losing Clarence, and Sarah, now Shirley and the kids. Something to keep it from growing out of control.

And that was when I realized that I could trade one pain for the other. I could let the cacophony take over, and it would wipe everything else away.

My thumb and forefinger came together where the wire met my earpiece. They closed around it and pinched it. It wouldn't take much pressure to pluck the plastic out. To open the floodgates and let madness wash over me until the pain was gone.

# CHAPTER 40

*Monday, February 27*

"It's gonna be okay."

Cooke said the words for what seemed like the thousandth time in the twenty minutes we'd been sitting in the car, making me wonder which of the two of us she was trying to convince.

Staring at the **"For Sale"** sign planted at the foot of the flagstone walk, I had a feeling whoever she was telling wasn't quite getting the truth.

When I pulled the earpiece Friday night, I expected to plummet off the edge and become a drooling mess—much as I deserved. But a funny thing happened instead: my own brain sabotaged me.

However far I'd sunk, as despondent as I'd felt, there must have been some small kernel of hope in there somewhere, because fear kicked in at the last minute.

I noticed it as soon as I had the earpiece out—my hand was shaking. That meant adrenaline, the one thing that could keep me from needing the earpiece in the first place.

As fear washed over me and my adrenaline surged, my thoughts fell in line like well-disciplined soldiers. I realized I needed to find someone, anyone, and not be alone. I stood, pulled on the wrecked tux, and texted Grayson and Cooke, the only two people I had left.

Cooke answered first.

She texted me the name of her hotel and her room number. When I showed up at her door, I was still trembling. Enough, in fact, that I barely registered this was the first time I'd ever seen her hair down.

Over the next hour—or two, or three, I honestly lost count—I spilled all my secrets. About Clarence and what I'd done to him. How I'd been dodging my parents ever since. My failure at the banquet, losing Shirley, and the depths I'd sunk to in my motel room.

Despite being someone who loved to talk, who always had a piercing question ready, Cooke simply sat on the bed cross-legged and listened. No psychologist tricks, no interrogation tactics.

At one point, she retrieved the box of tissues from the bathroom for me. At another, she let me rest my head on her shoulder to cry. She placed one hand on my neck and wrapped her other arm around my shoulders. I flinched at the contact—no one had touched me that way since . . . Sarah.

Cooke shushed me softly, and I relaxed, lowering my head again.

When she spoke next, it was to ask, "So, which one's for him?"

I looked up, unsure what she meant. "Which what?"

The freckles across her nose blurred together in a blush. "Which tattoo?"

"Oh." Twisting my torso around, I hooked my fingers inside the neck of my undershirt and pulled it aside. I tapped the back of my left shoulder. "Here."

She looked at the ink, then up at me and back again. "Math? I should've known."

"It's a DCT, a discrete cosine transform."

Cooke stared at me blankly.

"It's an algorithm—you use it in data compression."

"Oh. Of course."

I sighed. "When he was interviewing students for jobs, Clarence would ask a DCT question, to see if they could handle the equations."

"He liked your answer, I take it?"

"Yeah."

"Well," she said, "I only have one, and it's not math, but . . ."

"Wait, *what*? You have a tattoo?"

Her eyes flashed, fiery and defiant.

"I just . . . that's . . . I mean . . ."

Cooke's expression softened into a satisfied smile as she watched me stutter. "Not what you expected?"

I shook my head and raised my hands in surrender. "I'm not gonna touch that."

"Here." She swiveled completely around, gathered her hair, and twisted it into a tight ponytail. Pulling it up, she revealed a small image on her neck, directly below her hairline. A red oval surrounding a blue field with what looked like a sword drawn across the Washington Monument.

"What is that?"

"My father's army unit." She released her hair, and with a shake of her head, it fell back into place. "He died when I was five."

"Oh . . . I'm sorry."

Cooke turned back around, her gaze on the mattress. "Long time ago," she said. "One of those things that happens."

Facing me again, she took my right hand and drew it toward her, exposing my forearm. Then she trailed her index finger lightly over the heart tattoo. "People close to us die, but we have to keep on living."

When she glanced up, her green eyes locked onto mine. I'd received my share of hard looks from Cooke—angry, insistent, urgent. In a flash, my mind replayed them all. None had been like this.

As she drew up to kiss me, she kept her eyes open.

◆ ◆ ◆

The remainder of the weekend passed in a blur. I bought new clothes, returned the tux. We both wrote and filed our reports. We ate and laughed and talked and made love several times.

Now it was Monday, and real life had resumed. El-Amin and Liu had both been arraigned first thing, starting the long process of being put away, and Cooke had needed to attend. Liu's cooperation would likely earn her a little leniency, but with only El-Amin to prosecute, her testimony wouldn't buy much.

Grayson got me a moment alone with El-Amin, enough time for me to explain the rules on dedicating a patented invention to the public. I had no idea if the kid would follow through with the idea; exposing all the secrets of his battery might make Magnet even angrier and more litigious. But El-Amin was going to be sitting in prison for a long time—ripping the competitive advantage away from T.E. and sticking it to Zachary Scott from across the Pacific might salve the wound a little.

It was a triple bank shot for me, but the only one I had to play.

I'd already received several calls from Lavorgna that I hadn't answered, while Cooke had taken only a quick one with her FBI boss. Even as we were both being drawn back to our respective lives, though, I couldn't help dragging her out to the house to see if Shirley and the kids had returned.

I guess I wasn't surprised that they hadn't.

"She needs time," Cooke said.

"No," I said. "This is different. Bigger. She's taking the kids, and she's never coming back."

"Any idea where they'll go?"

"She has family in Oklahoma, but I don't know where."

"Is that your bag?" Cooke asked.

Focused on the **"For Sale"** sign and the empty driveway, I hadn't even glanced at the front door. Now I saw what she meant: my duffel was sitting where the welcome mat had been.

I collected it quickly, and we drove to DFW. With my badge, I was able to get Cooke through one of the airport's special security entrances, the private rooms the air crews use. When we emerged on the other side, she asked, "Is it always like that for you?"

I shrugged one shoulder. "Lots of times I go through the regular line to blend in. But it's there if I need it. Why, you thinking of changing careers?"

She looked up at me with an expression I hadn't seen before. A smile, but not a happy one. It seemed almost . . . wistful? I tried to read the emotions behind it, but before I could, she turned to look down the concourse.

Her flight to Dulles left first, so I walked her to her gate. As we strolled along, I tried not to think about Zachary Scott's trip through these same hallways the previous night. He likely hadn't landed in Shenzhen yet, but he would soon.

Half a world away and completely out of reach.

Cooke's plane was lining up to board when we arrived, still holding hands.

"I hate this part," she said. Her mouth drew into a taut line, and she sucked a long breath through her nose.

"The flying?"

She shot me a look. "Yeah, that."

I shifted my weight from one foot to the other and hung my head.

After a deep sigh, she said, "We are going to need to talk about this. What comes next."

I glanced up at her. "I know. First, I need to get back and see how much trouble I'm in."

She smiled weakly. "If they fire you, you could always move to DC."

Cooke took a step toward the jetbridge door. Our hands stayed clasped until the last possible moment.

Once she'd disappeared into the tunnel, I caught a Skylink train to my terminal. Thankfully, I didn't have to wait long before my flight was called. I shuffled down the jetbridge without even looking at my seat assignment. Once inside the jet, I checked and saw it was a middle.

When I reached my row, I stowed the duffel overhead, but before shimmying into the middle seat, I dug out my pad and mechanical pencil. I hadn't sent any electrical designs to Shen in a while, and it seemed as good a way as any to distract myself for the next three hours.

The window seat's occupant—a middle-aged businessman in an SMU golf shirt—was already settled, scrolling through spreadsheets on his laptop. I buckled in and leaned to my right, taking advantage of the aisle seat's emptiness while I still could. As I flipped open the pad to start on a fresh page, an envelope slid into my lap.

I recognized the handwriting immediately, but it took me a while to decide whether I wanted to open the envelope. Finally, I ripped the flap and pulled out two pages of stationery bearing the same distinctive cursive.

> Dear Seth:
> I hope you return to the house and find this note. I have some important things to tell you, and this is the only chance I'll have to say them.
>
> First, and this is *very* important, you need to stop blaming yourself for Clarence's death. He was a wonderful man whom I loved with all my heart. But he had problems. For a long time after he died, I assumed I was one of them. Maybe his biggest problem—after all, I was closest to him. I second-guessed everything I'd ever done, or not done, and wondered whether doing something different would have changed his decision.
>
> It was the kids who straightened me out, believe it or not. Michael asked me if Clarence's death was his fault. He still doesn't know how his father died, but Clarence being gone was enough to prompt the question. I told him no, of course. But as I thought about it, as I realized I was going to have to explain this event over and over to the kids and I didn't want them to blame themselves for a grown man's decision, that's when it hit me: I deserved the same peace of mind.

I know now how much you must have blamed yourself for Clarence's death. I can see it in everything you've done. From moving to LA, to helping that girl singer restart her life, to everything you've done for us. But you need to stop. It takes a special kind of selfishness to make someone else's death all about you.

While I can't say I'm happy you kept Clarence's firing from me, I do understand. Clarence's death made me do and think and feel all kinds of things I couldn't explain. If I had been in your shoes, facing a desperate widow and two heartbroken children, I can't say I wouldn't have done the same thing.

If there is some silver lining for me in what Clarence did, it is this: I do my best now to understand why things happen, why people do what they do. It doesn't always work, and I'm not perfect at it, but I try my hardest. It has also helped me realize that we *all*—you, me, the children—have been clinging to things to avoid letting Clarence go. I've kept us in the same house, kept the kids in the same school, and you come and go, all like nothing ever happened. But by pretending nothing has changed, we've kept ourselves from moving on. Being at that banquet, I remembered what it was like to be out at night. To have fun, to *live*. I deserve some nights like that. And you deserve to be free, to start a family of your own rather than being saddled with another man's wife and children. And Michael and Rachael deserve peace of mind, to grow up without questioning why their father did what he did.

That is why I've decided to give us all a clean start. I think it's the best thing for everyone.

I know you are incredibly smart, maybe the smartest person I've ever met (and I married Clarence, so that's saying something). You work for the government, so you have all kinds of resources. I'm not foolish enough to think I can "hide" from you. I won't even try. But I will ask that you stay away. For your own good, and for ours. The children love you—this will be hard on them, I'm sure—but as their mother and your friend, I think this is what we all need. Maybe not forever, but certainly for now.

I've told you many times that you are a good man. I know you never believed me when I said it, and now I know why. But that doesn't change the fundamental truth. Keep being good. And maybe we'll bump into you on an airplane sometime.

Until then,

Shirley

I stared at her signature for several minutes. Long enough, I didn't notice the aisle seat's occupant arrive and squeeze in next to me. I didn't feel us push back or taxi. I didn't hear the flight attendants run through the safety briefing or see them perform their final checks.

My eyes stayed riveted on the page.

Eventually, though, I folded up the note and slipped it back into the envelope. I slid it into the middle of the pad, up against the spine where it would be secure, and clipped my pencil over it to ensure it would stay. Then I tucked the whole mess into the seat pocket.

I looked up to find the airplane poised for takeoff. Before I could recall where we were or how we'd gotten there, the engines roared. A moment later, the seatback pressed against me, and we hurtled down the runway, lifting off and angling into the sapphire sky.

# ACKNOWLEDGMENTS

This is my third—and, in many ways, my most personal—novel to date, so acknowledging the how and the why of it feels particularly important. Ever since *Takeoff,* readers have asked for the reasons Seth Walker became an air marshal and what dark secret loomed in his past. While I always had this story in mind, and even alluded to some of it in the first two novels, now you all know the rest. I hope it was worth the wait.

Like my other books, this one is the product of significant research, but if I missed a particular detail here or there, I apologize. Any mistakes you see on the page are mine, and mine alone. That said, the technology presented in the book is all real-world stuff. If you're interested in learning more, details and resources will be posted on my website, http://josephreidbooks.com/.

More than ever, this book required the help and support of many other people. Tom Millikan endured my usual, seemingly endless string of electrical-engineering questions. A cadre of Bay Area insiders (including and especially Andy Alexander and Shelly Irvine) were equally helpful, and I'm thankful to the workers and staff of SFO Airport for their patience during my various tours through their terminals. Bing Ai and Mengke Xing provided information about China and helped with translation. A fleet of wonderful writers—Sara Bliss, Michele Cavin,

Ellison Cooper, Hilary Davidson, Danielle Girard, Bryan Gruley, Victor Methos, William Myers Jr., Alan Russell, and Chad Zunker—all provided support at necessary moments.

As always, I need to extend a huge and heartfelt thanks to Gracie Doyle, Sarah Shaw, and everyone else at Thomas & Mercer for all their efforts in shepherding *Departure* out into the world. I leaned more heavily on my editor, the incomparable Liz Pearsons, during the writing of this book than ever before, and I'm eternally grateful for both her input on this story specifically and her unwavering support of me and the Seth Walker series more generally. My agent, Cynthia Manson, works tirelessly on my behalf—I could not ask for a better champion. Ed Stackler remains the reason I've maintained my sanity, or whatever passes for it.

I wrote a significant portion of this book while on tour supporting *False Horizon*. For that reason, I'd be remiss if I didn't thank the many fans and friends who attended events, emailed or called, and otherwise supported the tour however they could. Knowing people are reading your work and enjoying it is one of the biggest motivations to press through on those occasions when the words aren't necessarily flowing or when the plot seems to have hit a wall.

Finally, I simply couldn't do this without my wife and daughters. Writing requires time above all else, and all three have been incredibly understanding about the hours I spend on these novels. I hope the result makes them proud.

# ABOUT THE AUTHOR

*Photo © 2017 Makela Reid*

The son of a navy helicopter pilot, Joseph Reid chased great white sharks as a marine biologist before becoming a patent lawyer who litigates multimillion-dollar cases for high-tech companies. He has flown millions of miles on commercial aircraft and has spent countless hours in airports around the world. Published in both of his academic disciplines, he is also the author of *Takeoff* and *False Horizon* in the Amazon Charts bestselling Seth Walker series. A graduate of Duke University and the University of Notre Dame, he lives in San Diego with his wife and children. For more information, visit www.josephreidbooks.com.